Acclaim for Merry Shannon's Fiction

"...a terrific adventure, coming of age story, a romance, and tale of courtly intrigue, attempted assassination, and gender confusion as the young princess learns, grows, and comes into her own. This is a rollicking fun book and a must-read for those who enjoy courtly light fantasy in a medieval-seeming time. Merry Shannon is a bright new voice in lesbian fantasy fiction, and this one's highly recommended."
— *Midwest Book Review*

"First time author Shannon keeps the tension riding high like a pro... Shannon balances personal development, love story and political drama with confidence and a swift, lively style." — *Curve* Magazine

"Shannon creates a believable, fascinating world...Shannon's skill as a romance writer shines most especially in one of the best choreographed love scenes in a lesbian fiction story." — Sandra Barret, author of *Lavender Secrets*

By the Author

Sword of the Guardian: A Legend of Ithyria

BRANDED ANN

by

Merry Shannon

2008

ISBN 10: 1-60282-003-1
ISBN 13: 978-1-60282-003-6

THIS TRADE PAPERBACK ORIGINAL IS PUBLISHED BY
BOLD STROKES BOOKS, INC.,
NEW YORK, USA

FIRST EDITION: JANUARY 2008

CREDITS
EDITORS: CINDY CRESAP AND STACIA SEAMAN
PRODUCTION DESIGN: STACIA SEAMAN
COVER DESIGN BY SHERI (GRAPHICARTIST2020@HOTMAIL.COM)

Acknowledgments

This book was written during a period of great change for me, through some of the most difficult and also most triumphant times I have experienced thus far. I wish to first thank my beloved friend Layne, to whom this book is dedicated, for being there for me unwaveringly through the darkest as well as the most wonderful parts of my life. She always seems to "get" me, even when I am beyond words. In addition, I want to thank my amazing friend Logan, for giving me a place to call home when I felt completely lost and displaced. I love you both and am so very proud to call you friends.

I would not have found the motivation to finish this book were it not for the encouragement and enthusiasm of all my beta readers and friends on LiveJournal—what a treasure trove of knowledge you are, and this book is so much richer for all the little details you provided as it was being written. Special thanks to Cecile Piret for helping with the French translations!

I also want to acknowledge the support and love of my mom, who is in the middle of a great transitional time of her own at the moment. Mom, I appreciate so much the way you are willing to accept me for who I am. I wish you great joy and happiness no matter what the future holds.

To Radclyffe, who has made this dream of mine come true now for a second time—I will never be able to thank you enough for your inspiration, your encouragement, and your support. I am so fortunate to work with you! And to Cindy Cresap, my editor, I also owe great thanks for your insight and assistance in shaping this story into its final form. Also thanks to Jennifer Knight, whose input on my first novel has carried over into this one and made the editing process so much smoother. Big hugs to Sheri for her beautiful work on the cover. (And she gets extra points for using so much yellow, which is my favorite color!)

Finally, I would like to thank my wonderful girlfriend Shasta, for making my life a million times brighter than it's ever been before. I love you.

Dedication

To Layne,
whose friendship is one of my life's greatest treasures.

"will rule over it all as mistress while I am away in the city on business. It's going to be a new life for both of us."

Violet squeezed his hand, and Isaac knew she'd understood the gentle implication of his words. A chance to start over in a new world, where no one knew her past, where no one could judge them. This move to the West Indies was an expensive venture, and he had undertaken it almost entirely for her benefit. But the happiness on those pretty features was well worth every single shining crown he'd spent.

"It's like a dream," Violet breathed, clasping her hands. "Oh, Lord of Heaven, how I thank thee for thy generous blessings and divine provision."

Isaac was accustomed to his young wife's spontaneous bouts of prayer, though he was not a particularly religious man himself. Violet was the kind of woman most men could only dream of marrying— young, pretty, graceful, devout—and only he knew how hard she had worked to become so for his sake. However, he feigned cheerful indignation and chucked her beneath the chin with a finger. "Hey, now, what about *my* blessings and provision, eh? Or don't I deserve any of that gratitude of yours?"

Dismay spread over her face. "Oh, Isaac, you know I hold nothing but the deepest gratitude for you and everything you've done for me. You've saved my life in so many ways, I can't even—"

He pressed a finger to her mouth, and she flushed when she realized he'd been teasing her. She kissed the finger against her lips earnestly. "I'm so unworthy of your generosity."

"Nonsense," he replied firmly. "That a pretty young thing like you would marry an old goat like me is a miracle in and of itself." Isaac saw her eyes widen, and he could guess what her next argument was going to be. He shook his head. "Let's just agree that we rescued each other from our respective unhappy situations, shall we?" Violet's lips curved into a slight smile, and he could not resist bending to capture them with his own.

"Shall I rescue you again?" she mumbled provocatively into his kisses, and he pulled back with no small measure of regret.

"Not now, I'm afraid. I've already been away from my duties too long. The captain's apt to toss me overboard for shirking my work."

"That might be difficult, seeing as you own this vessel he's sailing," Violet pointed out wryly, then straightened the shoulders of his jacket. "Tonight, then," she promised in a much quieter tone, and gave a little wink before pushing him gently toward the deck steps.

❖

As she watched her husband descend to the lower deck, Violet marveled for the hundredth time at her incredible fortune. Though Isaac Watts was nearly three times her age, she would have married him all over again in an instant. Isaac was her savior, her benefactor, and her dearest friend. True, she might not be passionately in love, but she was certainly very fond of her doting husband, and after all Isaac had done for her, she was determined he should never want for anything in a wife so long as she breathed. Violet turned to look over the back end of the ship again…the *stern*, Isaac called it. She stared down into the water, mesmerized by the white foam-tipped waves that danced in their wake.

It was a strange experience, being on a ship. Isaac had given her the full tour before they'd left port, spouting off so many nautical terms that they made Violet's head swim. Still, she found that the more time she spent on board, the more she became familiar with words like "forecastle" and "mizzenmast." No one was more surprised than Violet herself to find that she possessed a blessedly strong stomach. They'd been at sea for nearly a month now, and she had only endured the misery of seasickness for the first two days before her body became accustomed to the feeling of the rocking decks. The captain had been less than thrilled with the idea of bringing a woman on board his ship, but since Isaac Watts was his employer and intended to relocate permanently to his West Indies office, the captain could hardly refuse.

Her husband's business, the British Indies Security & Trade Company, was one of the most successful merchant trade industries in all of Europe. Violet didn't know much about commerce, but from what she did understand, Isaac succeeded where many others failed in transporting a wealth of goods between the lush West Indies and the lucrative seaport of London.

Piracy was the biggest culprit for most. The sea was full of thieves who set upon any ship carrying valuable cargo, and the closer one got to the West Indies, the more dangerous the waters became. She wasn't sure of the details, but she knew that her husband somehow managed to run a trade line that avoided encounters with such undesirables. How he did it was not a complete mystery. Violet had known Isaac Watts almost all her life, and she remembered a time when he'd been close in arms with those very same undesirable men…as had she, though she preferred to think of that as little as possible.

Trailing her hand along the rail, Violet crossed the stern to the right side…*or rather, the starboard side*, she corrected herself. She paused at the edge of the deck and leaned over the rail again, marveling at the sheer vastness of the water surrounding them. It was beautiful, this ocean that seemed to change moods as often as a person, shifting color and texture from one minute to the next. There was something very desolate and lonely, yet deeply spiritual about this place, adrift on an elaborate contraption of wood and canvas in the center of a barren sea. *Oh, Father, what miracles thy hand doth work*, she mused, tilting her face upward, heedless of the danger the afternoon sun posed to her complexion. Isaac found her freckles charming, and how could anyone hide from such glorious sunlight?

Violet suddenly straightened a bit and shaded her eyes as something on the horizon caught her eye. At first she thought it was only the white crest of a wave, but it was far too defined for that. She turned and called to one of the men scurrying around on the main deck. "Sailor, there's something out there."

He shrugged without bothering to follow the line of her pointed finger. "Probably a gull, Missus Watts, the sky's full of them today."

"It's too far away to be a seagull," she insisted.

He gave an impatient sigh and trudged up the deck steps to join her. "Where?"

She pointed again, and this time he did actually take more than a cursory glance at the starboard horizon. A frown creased his brow then, as he, too, spotted the little white object. "Wait here, missus." He found a small brass spyglass in a nearby chest and pressed it to his eye, twisting the metal tube until the object came into focus. His frown deepened and he gave a grunt.

"Well?" Violet asked, and he scratched his head.

"Looks like a ship," he replied, "but I ain't never seen one all white like that before. I'll get the captain. He probably ought to see this."

Violet watched the little white spot on the horizon for several minutes before the sailor returned with the captain in tow, followed closely by her husband. "I think it's getting bigger," she said, pointing it out once more, and the captain took the eyeglass from the sailor and looked through it himself.

A hiss of air escaped his teeth. "It can't be." Turning quickly, he bellowed at another of the sailors. "You there, Marks, take this glass up the mainmast. Look out there and tell me what you see."

Obediently the man took the instrument from his captain and hopped down to the lower deck, where he climbed the narrow rungs set into the thick mast. When he'd topped the mainsail and had a clearer line of sight, he put the glass to his eye. "It's a ship, Captain. Headed this way, moving fast."

"I know that, you bilge-eating vermin." The captain spat on the deck before suddenly remembering there was a woman present and blushing abashedly. "Your pardon, Mistress Watts."

She gave him a dignified nod, resisting the urge to laugh. Such language was hardly foreign to her ears, but these men believed her to be a proper lady, and she didn't want them thinking otherwise. The captain cleared his throat awkwardly and returned his attention to the man on the mast.

"Sailor, tell me, what color is yon vessel?"

"She's white, Captain. Never seen anything like it, white from the tip of the mast down to her hold."

The captain's face blanched. "What colors does she fly?" he shouted up, and waited for the sailor to refocus on the ship in question.

"Her flag is red, sir. Hard to tell from here, but looks like there's a skull on it, and…" The eyeglass suddenly fell from the man's hand, striking the deck with such force that the glass inside cracked audibly. Violet frowned in confusion. The sailor was shaking so badly she feared he might fall right off the mast.

"And what, man? Speak up!" Isaac demanded, and the sailor looked down at them with a face white as death.

"The skull and burning cross," he managed to croak out, and simultaneously Isaac and the captain cursed violently.

"The *Ice Queen*," the captain breathed. "God preserve us, it's Branded Ann. And she's flying scarlet." He suddenly spun to stare coldly at Isaac. "What are we carrying on board this ship, Master Watts?" Isaac shook his head, and the captain's glare only darkened. "Branded Ann does not waste her time with mere textile cargo, and you know it. She wouldn't be chasing us if there wasn't something she wanted on this ship. Now what is it?"

Violet laid a hand protectively on her husband's arm. The captain's tone was dangerously angry, and Isaac shook his head again. "God's honest truth, Captain Gates, I don't know. She must have us mistaken for another ship. All we have in this cargo are silks and linens bound for the Indies." He bit his lip. "I specifically chose this ship for my wife's safe passage. As you said, textiles don't generally make for a very interesting prize."

Violet's gaze moved between the two of them quickly. "I don't understand," she said with confusion. "What's happening? Who's Branded Ann?"

"Only the bloodthirstiest bitch ever to sail the Caribbean," the captain shot back before again realizing his lack of decorum in the presence of a lady. He flushed. "Pardon, Mistress, but ever since she got her hands on a ship of her own, Branded Ann's become the most dangerous pirate on the sea these days, in spite of how she's a woman. Her kind don't have much respect for the fairer sex, but even they don't dare lay a hand on her. It's said she's mistress to the Devil himself." He turned and began barking out orders.

"Look sharp, men, we've got the *Ice Queen* coming up on our starboard side and she's flying scarlet! Man the guns! Hoist every sail we've got and see to your arms!" He strode down to the main deck as sailors scattered in all directions to follow his instructions, and Violet turned anxiously to her husband.

"Is it really that bad?" she asked, and he nodded, his lips pressed tightly together.

"When pirates fly a red flag, it means they're offering no quarter, no mercy. They're out for blood. It doesn't make any sense. We don't have anything she'd want." He turned to watch as the sailors pulled bales of cargo from the hold and dumped it overboard, and Violet saw him wince. She guessed that less weight meant they could sail faster, though it had to be a terrible financial loss for her husband's company. Maybe they'd get very lucky and Branded Ann would be happy with the floating goods? But from the gravity of Isaac's expression, she doubted he was holding any such hope.

And then another more disturbing thought occurred to her. "She's not... Isaac, you don't think she's after you?"

Isaac shook his head. "I doubt it, my love. I retired as a privateer years before Branded Ann was old enough to set foot on a ship." He pulled a pistol from his belt and checked the powder, stuffing the barrel with shot from a pouch at his waist. "Take this."

The weapon was strangely bulky in her hand, but she made no comment, tucking it into the waist of her skirts. Uneasily she followed him into the captain's quarters beneath the poop deck. Whenever Isaac sailed, the large cabin was divided to allow him, as owner of the ship, a comfortable berth alongside the captain himself. Violet watched her husband dart about the room, searching through chests of their belongings and pulling out various weapons and papers. He strapped a cutlass to his waist and rummaged through a pile of clothing looking for anything else he might need. Violet reached up to the shelf above their little bed and pulled down her thick leather-bound Bible, clutching it to her chest. The solid feel of it in her arms was comforting. *Yea, though I walk through the valley of the shadow of death, I will fear no evil, for thou art with me.* The Psalm blossomed into her memory, steadying her nerves.

Isaac gave a sudden sharp intake of breath as he pulled a piece of paper from the bottom of a heavy wooden chest. Violet couldn't see what it was, but her husband's hand shook suddenly. "It couldn't be," she heard him mutter.

"What is it?" she asked.

"An old regret," he replied evasively, his attention drawn to the Bible in her arms. He reached for it and she handed it to him obediently, watching as he folded the paper carefully and tucked it into the book's leather cover. He returned the Bible to Violet with a steady gaze. "Hold on to this." Isaac stood and gathered up the armload of guns and knives he'd piled on their narrow mattress. "Violet, I want you to get below, into the hold. No matter what happens, no matter what you hear, don't come back abovedecks until I come for you, you understand? If anyone comes within arm's reach of you, shoot him between the eyes. Shoot to kill, Violet."

She shuddered, but nodded her understanding and allowed him to lead her back onto the main deck, where the men were scurrying frantically to load their guns and arm themselves. Small groups clustered around each of the starboard cannons, stacking heavy iron balls of shot and barrels of powder where they would be in easy reach. The white ship had drawn closer; Violet could see it clearly now, delineated starkly against the dark water. A strange, rhythmic pounding filled the air, and she was startled to realize that it seemed to be coming from the pirate vessel. She turned a questioning gaze on her husband and he gave a humorless laugh.

"It's called 'vaporing.' They're trying to frighten us. We can't outrun them, Violet, even if we throw every bit of cargo and half the crew overboard. There's no use surrendering, either. That red flag means they intend to kill everyone on board, God knows why. We're going to have to stand and fight." He brought her to the hatch and opened it. "Get below now, and remember, don't come back up until I come for you." Isaac pressed a kiss to her forehead, but Violet took hold of his collar and pulled him in for a real kiss on the lips.

"Be careful," she said, and he nodded.

"I love you, sweet Violet." And then he was pushing her gently toward the hatch, and she descended the ladder carefully, her heart pounding in her throat and the Bible hugged tightly to her chest with one arm.

❖

"We're almost upon them, Captain," the quartermaster grunted as he approached the tall pale-haired woman at the gunwale. A cold smile spread across her face as she turned to look at him, bloodlust sparking in her ice blue eyes.

His gaze twitched uncontrollably to the scar marring the left side of her face, the sun-lined skin there puckering into the distinct shape of a crucifix. It began right beneath her left eye, only a fraction of an inch from her lower eyelid, and trailed all the way down to her jaw. She'd never explained where the brand came from, though there were rumors amounting to legend as to its possible cause. The most popular theory was that she'd violated a nun and God himself had marked her as one of the damned.

The quartermaster found that unlikely; in spite of her infamous appetite for pretty girls, any man who sailed with Branded Ann became quickly and intimately familiar with her opinion of those who forced themselves on women. He'd heard the suggestion that she'd made some sort of pact with the Devil, or that she was the blood sister of Satan himself. However it had come about, that cross brand on her cheek was Ann's most recognizable feature and added a touch of fearsomeness to what would otherwise be considered too pretty a face for violent intent.

"Is the crew ready, Barclay?" Her voice, crystalline and frosty, sent a little shiver down his spine no matter how many times he heard it. He nodded.

"All ship-shape 'n Bristol fashion," he replied briskly, then dared to broach the subject they'd all been wondering about for the past hour. "Captain Ann, this ship we're after is a textile transport."

"So?" A glint entered her eye, and he swallowed but pressed ahead quickly.

"Well, the crew's a mite perturbed, Captain." Ann lifted one silvery eyebrow as he continued. "The men don't understand why we're chasing it down, or why you gave the order for no quarter. A cargo like that hardly seems worth blinking at."

"You're saying they don't trust me?"

Barclay shook his head. "It's not that, Captain, the boys'd follow you into the mouth of Hell itself on your orders, you know that. They're just a bit…curious."

She turned her attention back to the ship on the horizon. "Do you know who owns that ship?"

"I heard it was the British Indies Securities."

"Precisely. And do you know why most privateers stay clear of the B.I.S.?"

He scratched his neck. "They're better armed and better manned than other merchant vessels. Dangerous to confront."

"The B.I.S. employs pirates, Barclay. Every last one of their ships is swarming with them. And why is that? Because the owner and founder of British Indies Securities is none other than Ironsides Isaac Watts. And I have it on good authority that he happens to be on that very ship."

"The old turncoat himself, eh? You got something against him?"

Her smile was predatory. "You could say that." She rested a slender hand on his shoulder. "Never fear, Barclay, I assure you I wouldn't take the *Ice Queen* into battle on a personal grudge alone. This is the first step toward taking the finest prize any of you sea rats have ever laid eyes on." She turned and strode from the bow to the helm, and shouted down at the crew below.

"Look alive, boys, we're coming up fast. Vapor her loud and strong, and when we're in range, spray her decks with everything you've got so we can grapple her. Barclay!" He sprang to her side. "Lead the boarding party. Do whatever you like with the rest, but I want Isaac Watts brought to me alive."

"Aye, Captain." The hungry look in her eyes almost made him feel pity for the unfortunate Master Watts. He marched down to the main deck to see to any last-minute preparations, and the pirates set up a heavy thumping rhythm on the ship's rails with a chant of "Death, death, death!" that was deliciously ominous.

❖

Ann smiled to herself as she returned her gaze to the ship they were pursuing. They had tossed their cargo overboard, large bales of canvas-wrapped fabrics bobbing here and there on the ocean's surface, sinking slowly as they absorbed the seawater. Watts was no fool, willing to sacrifice his merchandise for more speed, though he had to know it was hopeless to think the *Ice Queen* could be outrun. This would be a nasty battle, if past encounters with the B.I.S. were any indication, but well worth it. Ann patted the twin flintlocks tucked into her sash and checked to be sure her cutlass, dirk, and boot daggers were all safely in place. She'd dressed for the occasion, in a pair of snug black breeches and a loose white shirt open at the collar. A wide scarlet sash girded her hips and a festive calico kerchief held her unruly hair out of her eyes. One golden hoop glinted from her right earlobe. She'd chosen her garments with care, for this day would be a momentous one. Today, she would finally be putting some of her demons to rest. Picking up her musket, Ann tapped the helmsman's shoulder.

"Bring us along their starboard side!" she shouted above the din of the chanting men, and Barclay nodded his understanding. Until they pulled alongside, they had a greater advantage: less exposed hull for their intended victims to shoot at, while their own chase guns mounted at the bow could fire off the initial volley. The trick was to give the firing order at exactly the right moment, when they were close enough that the shot would hit its target, but still far enough that there would be maneuvering room to swing alongside as they approached. Ann waited, judging the distance repeatedly, and finally gave a sharp nod.

"Chase guns, fire!" she bellowed, and the order was followed by an immediate lighting of the forward cannons, a quick hissing noise as the fuses burned, and then several deafening booms in succession. She shaded her eyes to judge the impact and grinned at the large holes that had formed in the rigging. That ought to slow their prey down, and they'd have time for another round. "Again! Bundle shot across her decks!"

The pirates scrambled to reload, stuffing the powder down the muzzles followed by the packs of short metal bars known as "bundle shot." The ammunition was designed specifically to clear the decks of a ship to be boarded, and it usually did its job with impressive efficiency. They were closer now thanks to the slowing effect of the first volley, and Ann didn't even wait for the smoke to clear before ordering the helmsman to swing them alongside. She put her musket to her shoulder.

"Have at her, boys!" There were booming sounds from the merchant ship as their cannons fired at the pirates. Ann took careful aim down the musket barrel, targeting one of the cannon crew and pulling the trigger. The man reeled back, clutching at his chest, and she grinned, pausing to reload. The air quickly filled with the irregular music of battle, musket and cannon fire punctuated by the shouts and cries of men from both sides. Adrenaline surged hotly through her limbs and she took aim again, picking off the cannon crew methodically. The decks began to clear as the pirate's barrage of shot did its work. She called for the boarding hooks to let fly.

And let fly they did, the wicked iron hooks singing through the air to lodge in the opposite gunwale. Several pirates heaved at each line, lashing the cables to draw the ships together for boarding. Ann continued to lay cover fire as Barclay led the boarding party swarming over the side of the pirate vessel and onto the merchant ship. The gunfire became more sporadic while the clash of swords and screaming grew louder. Cutlasses were far more effective than guns at close range.

Satisfied that the majority of her crew had boarded, Ann tossed the musket aside and climbed onto the gunwale, leaping a space almost two meters wide, landing with a solid thud on the other ship's deck. She drew the flintlocks from her sash, firing them both and taking out the first two men who came at her, then dropping the empty pistols to pull her cutlass. She'd been right. These were not just any merchant sailors. Several of them bore battle scars and the grizzled, unkempt appearance of sea bandits. Still, Ann was not daunted by any man, be he soldier or scoundrel. The blade danced in her hand as she pulled a dirk from her belt with the other.

The deck beneath their feet was already slick with blood. Ann cleared the remaining sailors from the forecastle, then leapt onto the main deck to join the fighting there. A shadow passed suddenly to her right, and without turning her head she slashed toward it. The scream that followed caught her attention, however, with its unusually high pitch. She couldn't help cursing when she saw her adversary. He was no more than a boy, judging by the sparse blond hair just beginning to shadow his upper lip; a thin but well-dressed kid, likely the son of some wealthy merchant who sent his heir off to sea for a little worldly experience before taking over the family business. He was grasping in futility at his stomach, which had been opened in one clean slice. The blood soaking his hands and shirt was dark, almost black, and Ann realized he had been gutted.

She had no choice. Either the boy would die slowly, and in agony, or she could end it quickly now. Gritting her teeth, she swung again, and there was a grisly thump as the boy's head fell from his shoulders to the deck. Ann looked up as someone nearby gave a cheer. Diego, one of her men, was grinning at her, and she forced a grimace in reply. Ann turned her back to the lifeless body and hacked her way across the deck in the opposite direction, trying not to think about how many other such youths might be on board. In battle there was no time for such concerns. She did what she had to do to get what she needed. The only good thing about killing—if one could call it good—was the way it contributed to her bloodthirsty reputation. A fearsome reputation was often the only thing that kept a pirate alive, and in her case, that was especially true.

The battle was decided in a matter of minutes. She had ordered no quarter, and so her crew surged over the decks, entering the cabins of captain and crew, pouring into the hold and killing everything in their path without reservation. She noted out of the corner of her eye that Barclay had isolated an older man on the poop deck, the only one who was not being unceremoniously butchered. From the finery of his clothes and his relative age she knew he had to be her target, Old Ironsides himself. A surge of excitement flooded her limbs. She was so close.

The noise died down as the last of the merchant crew were disposed of. One of the pirates stuck his head out of the hatch. "Captain, this vessel's taking on water! We must have punctured her with one of the cannon shots."

"Damn your eyes, Maclairen," she cursed under her breath, though she knew it probably wasn't their Scottish gunner's fault. The cannons could be notoriously inaccurate, especially from chase distance. Still, the general intent was to capture a ship, not sink her. Her attention was diverted by raucous cursing as two of her men, Dipper and Roberts, dragged something out of the hold. Their eager exclamations told her that they'd found an unexpected treasure, and when she caught sight of the young woman they were hauling along the deck she understood why.

"I said no quarter, boys," she hissed impatiently.

"She shot Truman, Captain. Took his face right off, the little wench, with this." Roberts held out a small single-barrel pistol. "So we thought we'd bring her up, and…"

Ann rolled her eyes. She stuffed her cutlass back into the scabbard at her belt and stalked over to them, ignoring their disappointed protests. "And nothing, my hearties. You know the Articles." Ann lifted her dirk to cut the prisoner's throat, but before she could apply pressure to the blade the woman lifted her head and looked the pirate captain straight in the eye.

Ann faltered.

The young woman's eyes were unlike anything she'd ever seen before, enormous and richly hued like gemstones. Her fair, delicate countenance was strikingly beautiful, in spite of the blood spattering her features. For a moment Ann experienced the strangest sensation of being swallowed into a midnight sky. Those huge eyes scanned her curiously, pausing with interest on the brand marring her left cheek.

"Alas, oh Lord God, for I have seen an angel of the Lord face-to-

face." The captive's voice was husky and unexpectedly sultry, and Ann felt goosebumps rise on her arms.

"Violet!"

Ann looked up at this cry, coming from their only other prisoner. The old goat was gazing with near desperation at the girl on the point of her knife. Ann looked back at her captive, noting the finery of her expensive gray silk skirts, the elegant mother-of-pearl buttons that marched modestly down the front of her bodice, and the dainty French lace detailing on the sleeves. This was no galley maid. Ann's attention dropped to the small hands clutching what looked like a big book, and landed on the gold band encircling the woman's left ring finger. She put this information together quickly and pursed her lips with a delighted grin. "Well, well, Mistress Watts." She stuck the dirk back in her sash and said to her men, "On second thought, boys, we may have use for her after all." The way their faces lit caused her to snort. "Don't look so excited, the Articles still stand."

The deck beneath her feet swayed dangerously. "All hands back on board the *Queen*!" she barked. "This ship's going down!" She watched Isaac Watts sharply as Barclay yanked him down to the main deck and over the boarding plank. He never looked back, didn't eye any part of the ship with regret or anxiety save his pretty little wife. *He has it on him*, she decided, not quite sure how she was so certain, but her instincts were uncanny at times and she chose to trust them. "Bring her," she ordered without looking back.

Ann leapt lightly onto the boarding plank and took position along the center of the *Ice Queen*'s foredeck as she waited for the rest of her crew to reboard. She could hear the grumbling already. It had been a costly battle. Barclay hauled Watts to the foredeck behind her, and she turned to address the quartermaster in low tones. "Report."

"We lost seven men, Captain, and have twelve more pretty bad carved up. Two prisoners. No booty to speak of, a few gold crowns from the captain's quarters and whatever they could rifle from the crew's bodies as they lay." Ann nodded, and Barclay's brow contracted. "The boys ain't happy, Captain Ann. That was a lot of blood and brawl for nothing."

Ann patted him on the shoulder. "Not worth divvying the loot this time, Barclay, so tell the crew they can keep whatever they snagged. I'm after a much bigger prize." She gestured to the two men who'd brought the girl—Violet, was it?—on board, and they shoved her up the deck stairs to join her husband behind the captain.

Waiting until the last of the surviving crew had assembled on the lower deck, Ann could hear the grumbling grow louder as the pirates realized just how very little they'd gained from this venture. She put two fingers in her mouth and gave a sharp whistle. "Pipe down!" she demanded, and after some rebellious muttering she was obeyed.

Ann arched a brow and glared. "All right, my hearties, you're wondering why we just went to all that trouble to take a ship with no real profits." This was answered by a chorus of affirmative and rather hostile grunts. Ann stepped back and seized the lapel of Watts's jacket, hauling him forward and licking her lips with anticipation. "This here is Master Ironsides Isaac Watts, owner of the British Indies Security and Trade. You may have heard of him. He turned against his fellow gentlemen of fortune," she gave a wry smile at the epithet pirates liked to use to describe themselves, "so the bloody Crown would line his pockets." Someone from the lower deck threw a rotted cabbage, probably looted from the merchant ship's galley, and it struck the prisoner on the shoulder with a gooey, smelly thud. Ann chuckled. "Easy now, boys, we're getting there. Master Watts, you want to tell them the real treasure we've just liberated from your ship?"

There was no doubt the man was a former buccaneer. Ann could see the defiance in his eyes and felt her own blood heat. When he spoke, the words were tightly controlled. "I don't know what you're talking about, woman."

She drew her lips back in a snarl and lifted one hand, turning the ruby ring on her middle finger until the large jewel lay against her palm. Then she slapped him, drawing the sharp facets of the stone against his cheek and drawing blood. "Your tone lacks proper respect, I'd say." When he glared sullenly without reply, Ann held up her hand again, and in one smooth movement she seized his groin in an iron grip. This time Watts yelped as she deliberately ground the ruby into the sensitive flesh. The crewmen below hooted with laughter.

"That's why they call her the Ice Queen, boys!" she heard Dipper cackle, and gave her men a grin before turning back to her prey. She could tell that he was not going to be easy to break, which meant this was likely going to be a very unpleasant afternoon.

"Indeed. Did you know, Master Watts, that when my former captain gave me this ship he christened her with one of my nicknames? I have so many I can scarcely keep them all straight. Most of them shouldn't be spoken in the presence of a lady," she cast a roguish wink in Violet's direction, "but Ice Queen's always been one of my favorites. Has a nice regal sound to it, don't you think?" She dropped the conversational tone then. "Since your memory seems to be troubling you, Master Watts, let's see if I can't sharpen it." She tightened her fist even more and he shuddered.

"Eighteen years ago you served as quartermaster on board an English privateering vessel. Does the name Daniel Goddard mean anything to you?" Understanding dawned on his face, and she knew he was aware of her intent now. "I see your memory hasn't completely failed you, Master Watts. Enough games. I want the map."

"I don't have it," came the reply, followed quickly by a near whimper as Ann squeezed him again, this time adding a slight twisting motion.

"I have very little patience for liars, Master Watts. And if I have to, I will cut you into pieces an inch at a time, until you give me what I want." She let go of his crotch and made a show of wiping her hand on her trousers in disgust before waving at Barclay. The quartermaster wheeled up with a small iron cart. "I don't know if you've heard of my branding station, Master Watts. It's a rather ingenious trinket of mine that's proven quite useful in conversations such as these." Barclay lifted the cover of the cart to reveal a deep concave depression in the iron surface; this depression was filled with burning coals. A grill above them prevented spills, and several long pokers had ends buried among the coals. Barclay drew one out. It had a broad, flattened end that was glowing red.

"The idea's a simple one, really. We cut something off, and then cauterize the wound so you don't bleed to death and we can keep playing. A particularly nasty way to die. It can last for days. Lots of fun for us, not so much for you, savvy? So I'll say it again: I want the map."

"If you know about the map, then you must know it's useless," he argued.

"To you, perhaps. But you see," and she leaned forward until her lips were nearly touching his ear, "I have the other."

He pulled back to stare at her, disbelief written all over his face. "The…the other? That's impossible." Ann only grinned and he shook his head. His gaze flickered nervously to his wife and then back again. "I tell you, I don't have it."

Ann caught the brief shift in his attention and decided to take a risk in the interest of shortening this interrogation. If she was very lucky, perhaps things wouldn't have to get messy after all. Of course, if she wasn't, she'd have no choice but to make good on some extremely distasteful threats. Hoping her instincts were right, Ann gave a theatrical sigh. "Really, man, you said yourself the map's useless. Is it worth dying for?" She took Violet's elbow and drew her closer, running a hand appreciatively over the silky dark hair and trailing fingers down the side of her neck. It was more for Watts's benefit than his wife's, but Ann felt a shudder run through the other woman's body and her brow twitched as her own irrepressible libido responded with instant, reliable enthusiasm. She took a deep breath and shoved those feelings away. What came next was pivotal, and for the girl's sake she had to be as terrifying as possible. It would be best if Watts could comprehend immediately that Ann was not bluffing. Pulling one of Violet's hands by the wrist, she held it up before the old man. The dirk came up in her other hand, and she tapped it playfully against the pads of the young woman's fingertips.

"Perhaps, Master Watts, you would be more cooperative if I were to start with these pretty fingers, rather than those gnarled stubs of yours. One at a time, of course, we wouldn't want to be cruel." She stroked the satiny pale skin of the woman's wrist with her thumb.

"Violet…" His mouth fell open as he looked from one woman to the other.

Violet appeared astonishingly calm, holding the Bible to her chest with one hand even as the other was threatened with amputation. Isaac was regarding his wife almost frantically, and Ann was startled to hear that breathy voice again. *"Though I speak, my grief is not assuaged: and though I forbear, what am I eased?"*

"Job 16," Barclay interjected with an amused snort, then met Ann's questioning gaze. "She's quoting the Good Book, there." He indicated the Bible.

"Well, what do you know? Seems we have a real lady of God

amongst us, boys." Ann's declaration carried over to the men on the lower deck, who broke into laughter. "Well then, Sister Violet, care to share what all that flowery talk means?"

Violet looked up at her evenly. "It means you're going to kill us both anyway, whether he tells you what you want to know or not."

"Smart girl," Ann murmured, then tore her gaze away before those luminous violet eyes could prove any more hypnotic. "She makes a good point, Watts. It's not a question of whether you die, but of how you die. We could alternate between the two of you, I suppose. A piece of her, then a piece of you, until there's nothing left. Or you could give me the map now, and you have my word I'll make it quick." He still appeared undecided, and Ann knew she'd have to press her point. "Have it your way." She pressed a mocking kiss to the tip of Violet's first finger, and then laid her thumb on one side with the blade on the other as though she were about to slice up a carrot. She was mildly impressed that the young woman did not so much as whimper. Ann paused for as long as she dared. *Come on, come on...*

"Wait," Isaac Watts finally croaked, and Ann felt a jolt of triumph when she looked into his face. She'd broken him. Careful to keep her own expression neutral, she pressed her lips together expectantly.

"Yes?"

He heaved a sigh and nodded toward the Bible under his wife's arm. "It's in there."

Ann released Violet's wrist and took the heavy book from her, fanning the pages. "In the cover," Watts directed, and she slid one finger beneath the leather cover, drawing out a folded paper. She opened it and scanned its contents, and let out a breath of genuine delight, dropping the Bible, forgotten, to the deck.

"At last."

"Just tell me one thing," Watts said in a defeated tone, and she looked up. "Who are you?"

Ann curled her lip. "When you see old Dan Goddard in Hell," she snarled, "you tell him his daughter Annie is keeping her promise." She returned her attention to the map, so overwhelmed with excitement that her fingers trembled. Greedily she took in every line, every shape, every scrawled calculation. She'd waited so long for this.

Barclay asked, "All done here, then, Captain?"

"Aye," Ann replied absently without looking up.

Something warm suddenly spattered her face, and she cursed when several drops of red liquid stained the paper in her hand. Barclay had slit the prisoner's throat.

CHAPTER TWO

Violet felt like the wind had been knocked from her lungs as the body of her husband fell lifeless to the deck. She closed her eyes tightly, but not before the sight of the pulsing scarlet flood erupting from his neck had been forever ingrained in her memory. She swayed a little, but somehow remained standing.

"Feed him to the fish," she heard the quartermaster say, and opened her eyes in time to see several swarthy men heave her husband's body unceremoniously over the gunwale and into the water below. She wanted to cry, but no tears came, and she didn't know if it was from grief or shock. It didn't matter anyway. She'd be joining him soon. Vaguely she wondered if perhaps the captain would just let her throw herself overboard and save them all the trouble.

Branded Ann waved the paper she'd taken from Violet's Bible and spoke to the crew. "This, my hearties, is what we were after all along. This is the map to Black Dog's secret hiding place."

Astonishment swept through the amassed sea bandits. "That treasure's a myth, ain't it?" someone shouted up.

"Not at all," the pirate captain replied evenly. "Black Dog's treasure is very real, and now that we have the map it's going to be ours. You're going to be rich, boys, beyond anything you've ever dreamed."

"I heard it's supposed to be haunted, Captain!" A chorus of agreement followed. "They say Black Dog put a curse on the gold before he died. Them what hid it couldn't even find it again. How're we supposed to fare better?"

"There are no curses, Maclairen. 'Them what hid it' had only this map, which shows the route to Black Dog's island, when they went to retrieve their gold. But without a second map, one that marks the treasure's location on the island itself, it's still impossible to find. And boys…I have that second map."

Violet's brow furrowed. She knew Isaac used to sail as a privateer in the same way these pirates did. But how had he managed to get such a thing, a map to pirate treasure so legendary it had cost him his life? *Oh, husband, what have you done?*

The pirates had begun a more excited murmuring now, and Branded Ann lifted a hand. "The terms of our Articles are nearly fulfilled, my hearties. We're returning to Tortuga to careen and stock up before we set out on the greatest adventure any of you sea rats have ever seen. If any man among you wants to stay ashore, I'll not fault him…though I'll pity his foolishness."

"Speaking of the Articles, Captain Ann…"

Violet felt a shove at her back as the man called Barclay pushed her toward the pirate captain, and she lost her balance, stumbling right into Ann. She was suddenly encompassed in powerful arms, her body pressed up against Ann's lean frame. The pirate smelled of rum and sea salt, a harsh, exotic scent that tingled in her nostrils. Righting herself quickly and pulling away, Violet rather wished she'd been permitted to fall on her face. She wrapped her arms around her midsection with a shiver.

She looked up to see Branded Ann watching her with a peculiar fire in her eyes; it was a look that Violet was well acquainted with, and it made her blood boil with indignation. "Just kill me and get it over with," Violet snapped, and the pirate woman's lips twitched.

"You're that anxious to die?"

Belligerently Violet refused to answer. This seemed to pique Ann's ire, because she swept an arm in the direction of the men on the lower deck. "Well, *Sister* Violet," she said, emphasizing the mocking honorific, "the crew has been at sea a long time without the comforts of a woman. What say you, my hearties? Shall she be rogered at the rail before we send her to Davy Jones?"

The pirates set up a bawdy cheer, and Violet felt a heavy weight settle in her stomach. She wasn't really surprised, nor was she frightened, but she was struck with a deep sense of hopelessness. Everything that she'd worked for in the past two years meant nothing after all. No matter how she'd tried to leave her past behind, she had just ended up right back where she started. Isaac was dead, and now she was as good as dead herself.

Something in her snapped at that moment, something she hadn't felt in years, and she met Branded Ann's self-satisfied gaze with a calm she didn't quite feel. "You think I don't know what that means, but you're wrong." She bit the inside of her lip so hard that she tasted blood. *"As a dog returneth to its vomit, so a fool returneth to his folly. So be it."*

Violet turned her back on the pirate captain and gripped her collar, ripping the buttoned front of her bodice open to reveal the stays and shift underneath. She held the torn fabric out and leaned over the rail to ensure that the men below got a good look at her soft, pale cleavage. "Is this what you want, gentlemen?"

They were astounded into momentary silence. Certainly it was unexpected that a Scripture-spouting merchant's wife would suddenly expose herself so brazenly to a pack of rogues and criminals. It didn't take long, though, for the silence to be broken by a few hoots of approval.

"Then come and get it. Who wants to be first?" One of the younger men quickly stepped forward, yanking on his belt, and Violet's smile turned cruel. "You? Really? But you cry when you come. Are you sure you want your mates to see that?" His face suddenly took on a look of consternation, and the scarlet flood that abruptly rose to his cheeks told Violet she'd made an accurate evaluation. Even after a couple years, she hadn't lost her intuition. Her attention shifted to the shorter pirate at the young man's elbow, the one with a gold tooth and lazy eye. "And you, sir, like a little pain with your pleasure. I'll be happy to oblige. And you," she focused on the taller man behind them, his shoulders as wide as three men, and his beefy arms coated with vulgar tattoos, "I'm not really what you want at all, am I? But I understand. You can take me from behind if you prefer, and pretend I'm one of the peach-fuzz boys you like so much." It was almost amusing to watch their expressions, mingled anger and humiliation that suggested her assertions were correct. Violet licked her lips delicately.

"Gentlemen, there isn't anything you can do to me that hasn't been done by a hundred before you. One at a time could take a while. Why don't we do this in groups of, say, three or four? Get it over with so you can get on with the killing and feeding to the fishes and so on."

The more she spoke, the more nervous the men became. She heard a couple of them muttering, and gave a mirthless grin. "What's the matter, boys? Changed your mind?"

❖

Ann watched this scene with astonishment at first, then irritation. Where the hell had the girl learned to talk like that? Damned fool wench had called her bluff, and now she was going to get herself brutalized. The Articles would protect a woman who was unwilling; every man had to agree to Ann's terms when they signed aboard her ship, and it was a provision she was careful to include on every voyage. But Violet had just essentially begged the men to take her. Ann ground her teeth, telling herself it wasn't her fault. She was only trying to instill proper fear in the girl before they sent her to join her husband. By all rights she ought to toss the little idiot to the wolves and let them have their way with her, but the thought was unappetizing. Ann saw only one way to get the girl out of this now, and gave a sigh of annoyance.

"Hold it, boys." Ann held out a hand and stepped closer to the rail, stopping some of the men in their tracks as they were preparing to ascend to the foredeck. She made a show of raking her gaze appreciatively over the captive woman. "I've changed my mind. I'm going to invoke captain's privilege."

The men shouted protests and disappointed jeers, but she just shrugged. "You know the rules, my hearties. If any of you wish to challenge my claim, get up here now and do it with the point of your blade." She laid a hand lightly on the hilt of her cutlass.

"A woman on board's bad luck, Captain!" one of them shouted.

"In case you've forgotten, Master Porter, I happen to be of female persuasion myself. Have I in any way brought harm to your fortunes?"

Subdued murmurs followed her question. The truth was, Ann could rightfully claim credit for the success of their recent raids. At that very moment the *Ice Queen*'s hold was full of loot they'd managed to take from Spanish galleons and English trade ships throughout the West Indies. They'd be returning to Tortuga with more gold to each man than most could earn in one or two years, and they knew it was thanks to their captain's fearsome reputation. Ann smiled coolly. "Anyone have a real objection, one they'd like to back up with their sword?"

Not one of the crew moved to accept the challenge. She'd known they wouldn't. They might be unhappy, even angered and superstitious, but she could take any one of them in a fight and knew they were none too anxious to lose their heads or other valued body parts for the sake of one little wench.

Satisfied, Ann pushed Violet back a few steps and snapped her fingers at Barclay, who lifted the cover of the branding station again. Ann reached among the pokers until she found the one she was looking for and pulled it out. The end of this one was shaped like a cross, a perfect mirror of the brand on her own face, and it was glowing red-orange. She turned to face their captive, twirling the iron casually between her fingers and sweeping it out so Violet could see it.

"You belong to me, now, my lovely. And from now on you're going to wear my mark so everyone else knows it as well."

To Violet's credit she did not break down, fall into a swoon, or cry for mercy like Ann would have expected from a dainty English lady. Instead her lips tightened, and she stared defiantly back at Ann. "You can mark my body any way you like. I belong only to the Lord God of Heaven."

Ann brought the end of the branding iron inches from Violet's left cheek. "We'll see." She turned to Barclay. "Hold her."

The quartermaster complied, pinning Violet's arms and bracing her against his own body. Ann drew the iron closer, until the heated metal cast a dull orange light on Violet's cheek. She could see Violet's lips moving, and it took her a moment to realize that the girl was either praying or quoting Scripture again, she couldn't quite tell. But as Ann prepared to press the design into the pale skin, she hesitated. Frustrated, she reminded herself this was a far gentler option than repeated raping by the pirate crew. A visual representation of her claim on the girl would be the greatest protection she could offer, and she had inflicted similar marks on more than one man for disciplinary reasons. Yet Violet was such a small, delicate creature, quite innocent in all of this, and as Ann stared down at the glowing cross she could remember all too well what the agony of branding had felt like. The screams that haunted her nightmares echoed in her memory, and the branding iron trembled in her hand. Slowly, she withdrew it.

"On second thought," she said, raising her voice to ensure that the men could hear and tracing her captive's satiny cheek with one finger, "It seems a shame to mar such a pretty face, doesn't it, boys?"

The men jeered and laughed. Violet's complexion had gone nearly white, and her pupils constricted. *"This is my comfort in my affliction: for thy word hath quickened me…"* Her eyes suddenly rolled back in her head, and she lost consciousness in Barclay's arms.

Ann spoke quietly so that only the quartermaster would hear. "Take the girl to my cabin for now, and have O'Hare bring me a bit of hard tack from the galley." Barclay nodded and swung Violet's limp form into his arms, carrying her off in the direction of Ann's quarters.

Ann turned back to her men and addressed them in her most sinister tone. "Let's be sure we have an understanding, my hearties. You all witnessed my claim go unchallenged. Captain's privilege says the girl is mine. Any man who lays a hand on her without my permission is going to lose it, as well as any other bodily appendages I feel like removing at the time. Savvy?" Several of them shifted their weight nervously, and Ann was certain she'd made her point. The crew knew very well the things she was capable of. "Now, all of you get back to your stations. Take the injured to the galley where O'Hare can tend them." She saw Barclay emerge from her cabin, and nodded in the quartermaster's direction. "They're all yours, Barclay."

"Step lively, hearties, let's get this tub a-moving back to old Tortuga!" The quartermaster smacked his hands together. "Edwards, take the wheel and turn us about. Mason, Saunders, Jenkins, you three get up the rigging and tighten the sails. Porter, you dog, get your scrawny hide below and start patching the holes them merchant guns put in our lady…"

Ann didn't bother to listen to the rest. She buried the end of the cross-shaped iron back among the still-smoldering coals, then dumped a bucket of water over them and tied the branding station back into place by the gunwale so it wouldn't go sliding about the deck. She was about to descend to the main deck when her gaze fell on Violet's large Bible, lying face-down on the planks by her feet. She bent and picked it up, tucking it under one arm before heading down the steps.

Barclay was still shouting orders, and she wound between the men who were scurrying to obey them. Barclay was a good ship master, the best she'd ever sailed with. On a pirate ship the quartermaster was the one who really ran the show; the captain's authority came in battle, but the quartermaster had the final word on everything else. She patted him on the shoulder as she passed. "I'm going to see to the prisoner, and then you can put me to work, old man."

"Just you make sure she don't tire you out," Barclay grunted. She replied with a glare that was only partly in jest before ducking into her cabin.

The captain's cabin on a sailing ship was sometimes almost the size of the entire crew's quarters. She'd had the *Ice Queen* modified when they first took her, reducing the area of the aft cabin by almost half. She had no need of such extravagant accommodations. Up until she'd taken command of this, her first ship, she'd slept in the bunks of the crew's quarters just like any other man. But she was finding she enjoyed the luxury of a private cabin. It was her own space, a place she could retreat to at the end of a long day or when she needed quiet time to plan raids and sailing routes.

Ann dropped the Bible onto the heavy table as she entered, and went to the looking glass bolted to one wall. Blood spattered her complexion, and she swept the kerchief from her hair to scrub it away. Her hand lingered for a moment, as it always did, over the brand on the left side of her face. Her gaze moved to the prostrate form of the young woman who'd been laid out on her bed, and she cursed mildly.

This last raid had gone well: few casualties considering the experience of their enemy, a complete obliteration of the target, and most importantly, she'd obtained the precious map. That elusive piece of paper had haunted her for years since her father's death, and at long last, it was in her hands. Ann went to a nearby cabinet and withdrew a little chest. Carrying it to the table, she unlocked it with a key from the pouch at her belt and tugged from her sash the map she'd just acquired from Watts. Then she reached into the chest and pulled out a matching folded paper. Ann held both maps up and stared at them, allowing the triumph of the moment to wash over her.

"I did it, Father," she muttered under her breath. "It won't be long now, I promise." After another pause, she tucked the papers together and returned them both to the box. When they reached Tortuga she'd find a sailing master to go over the new map with her, to determine their route, but for now, it would have a place of honor among her most precious treasures. She locked the chest again and put it back in the cabinet. Aye, it had been a perfect raid, save for one thing.

Ann dragged a chair over to the bunk and straddled it backward, studying the young woman now occupying her mattress. From the looks of her Ann would have guessed her age at about fourteen, but she knew Violet had to be older than that. Pirates were superstitious to the point of paranoia, but there was good reason for the belief that a woman on board brought bad luck, especially one pretty as this. It wouldn't do to have the men fighting amongst themselves over the wench's attentions. Fortunately their fear of Branded Ann kept their lustier drives in check, and she would just have to make certain it stayed that way. A knock on her door caused her to jump up. It was O'Hare with two dry, hard biscuits from the ship's food stores wrapped in a handkerchief.

"I brought what you wanted," he said, his speech slurred from an old injury to the back of the head that had rendered him a bit slow ever since. O'Hare was an Irishman, a pirate before Ann had even been born, and he lived for the sea, though he could no longer master it as he once did. Ann kept him on board as their cook and surgeon. He had no culinary skill to speak of, but he did have battle experience and rudimentary medical knowledge.

"Thank you, O'Hare." Ann took the food from him. "How are our wounded boys?"

"They'll live, methinks, Lady Captain. One of 'em's got to lose a hand, though."

Ann pressed her lips together. "Which one?"

"The left one."

She did her best to suppress a smile. "No, O'Hare, I meant which man?"

"Oh. Turtle, Lady Captain."

Ann inhaled heavily. Turtle was their youngest crew member, about fifteen if he was telling the truth about his age, which Ann doubted. He was just the ship's boy and shouldn't have been in the battle at all. Unwelcome images of the boy she'd killed on Watts's ship suddenly rose to mind. "I've warned him again and again that he's too reckless and headstrong for his own good," she spouted angrily, and O'Hare nodded.

"Aye."

"Well, do what you must, and tell Turtle that I'll hold to the Articles for him, even if he is a blithering idiot. Five hundred pieces of eight for the loss of the left hand."

"Aye, Lady Captain." O'Hare left the cabin then, and Ann rubbed her forehead wearily. Not quite a perfect raid after all. She should have guessed Turtle would sneak into the boarding party, and berated herself for not anticipating his foolishness and having him chained in the hold for his own protection. The generous compensation for loss of limb was another provision written into the Articles that governed the ship, and would be a small fortune for the boy, but it was laughable to think that any amount of money could actually be a consolation for such a terrible injury.

Realizing she was still holding the biscuits in her hand, Ann returned to the bedside and debated whether she should try to wake the girl up and feed her. She wasn't quite sure why she was even bothering to keep the girl alive to begin with. Violet was unlikely to have much ransom potential now that her husband was dead, and she was useless on board a pirate vessel. The most prudent thing to do would be to cut the girl's throat and pitch her overboard like her husband.

There was something bizarre about this pretty little woman who spouted Bible verses and carried herself like a London debutante, yet dangled herself in front of a crew of unkempt men with the vocabulary of a street whore. And stranger still, Violet didn't seem cowed by Ann at all. Not when her husband had been killed in front of her eyes, not when Ann had threatened to let the crew gang-rape her, not even when she'd nearly pressed a glowing iron brand into the girl's skin. Many emotions had crossed her face, from shock and disgust to fear, even hate and anger, but never resignation or surrender. Ann found that infuriating.

It was hard not to notice the pretty swell of the girl's breasts, exposed beneath the torn blouse and rising and falling lightly as she slept. A wicked smile curved Ann's lips as she admired the valley of creamy softness tucked firmly into the stays. It was no wonder she fainted, Ann thought with a disparaging look at the constricting undergarment. It was a miracle Violet could catch a breath at all with a cage of whalebone strapped around her lungs. What a torturous contraption. Ann was suddenly struck by the amusing mental image of incorporating corsets into future prisoner interrogations. She could just picture stuffing some overweight, oversexed merchant captain into a set of stays and lacing them until his face turned purple. The thought made her snicker.

At the sound Violet moaned, and her dark lashes fluttered open. Ann watched as the young woman's eyes flashed with recognition, followed very quickly by an intense and burning hatred. She brought a hand up to her cheek and seemed relieved when her fingertips found no damage.

"No worries, my lovely, I've decided to leave that pretty skin unmarked. For the time being, at any rate." She held out a biscuit. "Eat."

Violet pointedly ignored the food. "So it's to be you, then. I'd rather the Devil himself, but at least you're not the first."

"First what?" Ann asked with a hint of amusement, taking a bite of the rejected biscuit herself. It was not an easy feat; hard tack had earned its name for a reason.

"The first woman to 'roger' me, as you vile pirates like to say." Violet struggled to sit up, but only succeeded in lifting her head an inch or so above the pillow before Ann pushed her back down. The handkerchief and both biscuits fell to the floor with solid thumps.

"Let me make something very clear, Sister Violet." Her tone held the same chill that it did when she was anticipating a battle. "I am every bit the monster you've heard. I am the dark-hearted demon who haunts your every nightmare. I steal, I kill, I inflict pain on anyone who gets in my way. But there is one thing that I have never done." She lowered her face so that her lips were nearly brushing Violet's ear. "I have *never* forced a woman into my bed."

"Well, good for you."

The reply was so laced with sarcasm that Ann had to laugh. She sat back and eyed her captive with skepticism. "Do you have a death wish, my pet?"

"I don't have much else left to wish for, now do I?"

Silence followed, until finally Ann demanded, "How old are you?"

"Nineteen." Older than Ann had expected, certainly older than she looked, but still very young to have been married to a man of Isaac Watts's advanced years.

"And where did a nice God-fearing girl like yourself pick up such filthy language?"

"Either ravish me or kill me or toss me off this ship, but please do something other than bore me to death with your questions, Captain. We both know I have only one use to you." Violet's defiance was becoming less startling every time she spoke. Ann found herself coming to expect the heated rebukes.

"I'll decide what your use is to me, and when and if you are to be disposed of. However, as it turns out, we have just lost the assistance of our ship's boy for the time being, and the decks are filthy after a battle. All that blood starts to reek after a day or two. I assume you can handle a pail and brush. You'll report to Barclay, the quartermaster, and he'll put you to work. If you do a good job and don't eat too much, I might not kill you tomorrow."

Violet did sit up then, swinging her legs over the edge of the bed. "And if I refuse?"

"Do you really want to find out?"

Ann could read the thoughts flitting across Violet's face as if they were written in legible print across her forehead. Hate, anger, rebellion, but they were all eventually overpowered by grim determination. "You're not afraid of me, are you?"

Violet gave a perceptive twist of the lips. "That's why you can't just kill me, isn't it?" She rose to her feet and took a few steps until she was nearly nose to nose with Ann. "Perhaps you're the one who's frightened by me, Captain. I think you fear anyone who isn't petrified of *you*."

Ann whipped the dirk from her sash and brought it to Violet's throat. She read the challenge in Violet's eyes, as if daring her to go through with it, and clenched her teeth. "Make no mistake, my lovely, you hold no such power over me. However, I will kill you at my own will, and not because you've goaded me into it." She lowered the blade, picked up the Bible from the table, and shoved it at Violet. "Get this rag out of my quarters and report on deck. I wouldn't backtalk to Barclay if I were you, either. He's got a cat-o'-nine-tails with a wicked bite."

Ann flung the door open and pushed Violet through it, calling for the quartermaster. He appeared from behind the mainmast. "Captain Ann?"

"Sister Violet here is going to be our new swabbie while Turtle's out of commission. Show her the ropes, would you?"

Barclay's forehead was pushed into a mass of wrinkles by his rising eyebrows. "Aye, Captain, if that's your wish."

She didn't have to tell him not to grant the girl any special consideration. Every person on board pulled their own weight or paid for their laziness with blood. Barclay would ensure that their newest recruit gave them her best work. Ann was watching so intently as he led the girl away that she didn't notice Maclairen come up to her elbow until he spoke.

"What's the matter, Captain, did yon Missus Watts turn you down? You did just pitch her hubby over the rail, now." His thick Scottish brogue was lilting and full of mischief, and Ann turned to face the good-tempered gunner with irritation. He was one of the only men on board who dared to openly tease her. "Don't worry, Captain, no lassie can keep her sweet treasure from the likes of you for long."

She glared. "Watch it, Maclairen. One of these days you're going to push me too far."

"Not today, Captain, not today!" he replied cheerfully and shuffled toward the hatch that led down to the gun deck.

Ann sighed with irritation and grabbed a coil of rope from a pile by her feet, then seized a section of the rigging and started to climb. A little time above the sails, with the salt breeze blowing on her face, was exactly what she needed to clear her head. After a few hours of mending netting and restringing sails, she'd manage to put all thoughts of their pretty captive out of her mind.

CHAPTER THREE

Violet was no stranger to hard work. She'd scrubbed many a floor in her day, and a ship's deck was not much different, though the bloodstains saturating the wood were a little more than what she was used to. Progress was slow. It was difficult to remove the stains and dirt ground into the waterlogged planks. But as Violet worked she quoted Bible verses under her breath about turning the other cheek and doing all for the sake of the Lord. She decided she would scrub the decks as if God Himself had asked it of her, rather than the brutal, soulless heathen who had brought about the murder of her husband.

Truthfully, Violet was confused as to why she was still alive at all. The pirates had obtained what they wanted from Isaac, and the only use they could possibly have for Violet herself was physical pleasure. One look at the pirate captain told her that Branded Ann was certainly not uninterested, and the crew had seemed more than eager to use her in such a way. Yet no one had yet laid a hand on her. Violet was utterly convinced that somehow God was protecting her, though for what purpose she couldn't guess. Still, she was determined to show her gratitude. If the Lord saw fit to spare her life and virtue, she would work her hardest at whatever task He set before her…including scrubbing the filthy and rather smelly deck of a pirate ship.

She found herself grudgingly growing to respect Barclay. He was a strict taskmaster, demanding complete dedication to duty, but he was fair. Nobody received preferential treatment from the quartermaster. He tolerated disrespect and laziness from no one, and treated Violet exactly the same way he did the ship's carpenter, gunner, captain, and crew.

It was strangely satisfying, in fact, to hear him speak to the infamous Branded Ann with the same terse, militarian barks that he used to direct Violet's work. More than once Violet found herself smirking as she overheard Barclay giving the pirate captain various orders, even rebuking her when he felt she hadn't done something correctly.

Scrubbing the decks took hours, and Violet was exhausted before she was even halfway through. Barclay had her clean the fore and aft decks first, as they bore less traffic. As the sun began to go down, splashing orange and pink across the sky and turning the ocean blood-red where it touched the horizon, Violet had nearly finished the last few square meters of the poop deck.

❖

Watching their young prisoner from beneath the mainmast, Ann turned to Barclay. "Well, what do you think of our new crew member?" she asked with deliberate sarcasm.

Barclay rubbed his chin. "She's a good worker. Takes instruction better than Turtle, even. I don't think our foredeck's ever been that clean. Could practically see my face in it."

Ann gave him an incredulous stare. "And she hasn't given you any trouble?"

"Not a peep, Captain Ann. Hasn't so much as asked for a cup of water all afternoon. Maybe it's just you she doesn't like."

She shot him a suspicious look, but his face remained completely deadpan. "Well, when she's finished, take her to the hold and let her find a place to sleep."

"Aye, Captain."

She could see curiosity flicker across his face, and she knew he was probably wondering why she didn't want the attractive prisoner to share her cabin. Ann couldn't explain it herself, other than that something about the girl made her uncomfortable. She felt somewhat off balance, and that was not a notion she enjoyed.

"Make sure she finishes the entire deck. Tonight."

"Tonight?" Barclay's brows drew together. "Captain, she's been working like that for hours. Little thing that she is, she's probably about dead from exhaustion. I was going to have her do the main deck tomorrow."

Chapter One

From the aft rail of the merchant ship, the glittering blue expanse of the Pacific rippled toward the horizon in an endlessly shifting landscape. Sunlight gilded the tips of the waves as if teasing the shadows below, and a salty breeze tossed stray wisps of dark hair into Violet's eyes as she leaned over the ship's rail. She looked up at her husband with excitement dancing across her face. "Tell me again about this place we're going."

"You've heard it a hundred times already," Isaac Watts replied with amusement.

"Please?"

He could not refuse her when she turned those huge jeweled eyes on him. Violet had the most unusual eyes he'd ever seen: an intense dark blue, so luminous he could swear they were as purple as the flower for which she was named. As if that weren't enough, her small, delicate features made her appear even younger than her nineteen years and effected an unintentional air of innocence, ironic and perversely charming considering her coarse upbringing. Isaac sighed and gave in without argument.

"Well, as you know, the Crown has granted us two hundred acres of sugar plantation in the West Indies, on the southern coast of Jamaica." He grinned as Violet's expression turned dreamy. "It's beautiful country, covered in royal palms and coconut trees, hibiscus, orchids, poinsettias—brilliant color everywhere you look, and the air perfumed with exotic flowers and the salt of the ocean. Our land is just a few miles from the coast, and less than a half day's travel from my office in Port Royal. You, my dear," he planted a kiss on her temple,

"Tonight. And no food or water till it's done."

"Captain." Barclay's tone held a note of reproach, but she flashed him a glare that said she was not in the mood to argue.

"Give her half rations. She won't eat much anyway. Not a bite till the entire deck shines like the ocean becalmed, savvy?"

She could tell from his expression that Barclay disapproved, but she knew he wouldn't say so. Violet belonged to her, per the privilege she had invoked. She could do anything she wanted to the young woman, including working her to death or withholding food and water. That wasn't her intention, but Ann knew she'd have to emphasize her claim on the girl at every possible opportunity, in order to keep the men mindful of it. And it was especially important at the beginning, to keep anyone from getting any bright ideas. So she remained firm, and after a pause Barclay shrugged.

"Aye."

Ann cast one more glance at the young woman who was steadily scrubbing away by the stern. Violet's bodice remained open in the front, the dainty mother-of-pearl buttons torn off in her melodramatic display of bravado earlier. The sleeves were rolled up above her elbows, and her breasts were so tightly constrained by the stays that they did not even bounce with her movements. The hair pinned into a knot at the base of her neck was beginning to look disheveled, and Ann could see sweat stains marking the collar and underarms of the gray silk. Violet really did look tired, and Ann forced herself to remain focused on the bigger picture. If the men forgot her authority, the girl's fate would be far more terrible. But anger seemed to give Violet strength, and Ann knew the young woman would need all she could get to make it through the night. She turned to Barclay. "Make sure she knows I'm the one responsible for her misery."

❖

He lifted an eyebrow as the captain crossed the deck and disappeared through the door of her cabin beneath the poop deck. He wasn't sure what the girl had done to incur Ann's wrath, but whatever it was he certainly didn't envy her position. Barclay gave a soft snort. The poor kid was really in for it.

He ascended the deck steps and waited for Violet to drop her brush into the pail and look up at him. He felt a strange twinge of sympathy at the weariness in her eyes. Sympathy was not an emotion he was accustomed to feeling, but somehow Violet managed to arouse protective instincts he didn't even know he had.

"You must be tired," he said gruffly, and she nodded, rising to her feet stiffly. She winced as her knees straightened, but didn't offer so much as a word of complaint. Barclay sighed inwardly, but kept his expression stern. "You still have the main decks to swab tonight." He tried to ignore it as her face fell a little. "No food, water, or sleep till they're done. Captain's orders."

Violet's lips parted slightly, but she didn't protest. In fact, Barclay noted that at his last words her expression hardened. *No wonder the captain's peeved*, Barclay thought with some amusement. *This little wench is as stubborn as she is.* He eyed the poop deck. "You done here, then?" Indeed, he couldn't find a single area that wasn't perfectly spotless. Impressive, considering that the *Ice Queen*'s decks had borne heavy stains from her years as a merchant transport before the pirates had ever even gotten their hands on her. He should have pushed young Turtle harder. In one day this dimunitive woman had cleaned the decks more thoroughly than their ship's boy ever had.

Violet nodded. "Done, Master Barclay."

He picked up the pail, which was full of water so dirty it was nearly black. "Refill this, and get started on the main deck. Most of the crew will be heading off to their bunks, so you shouldn't have much trouble with them walking all over your handiwork."

Violet gave another nod and took the bucket.

Violet dumped the dirty water over the gunwale and went to the reserve water barrels. She filled the pail, and bit her lip to keep back tears. Her hands were burning as if they were on fire. Though the skin remained unbroken, her knuckles were bright red and blisters had formed on her palms. Her back and shoulders ached to the point of numbness, and her knees felt like they'd been bruised right through to the bone from hours of kneeling. *Oh Father, I need your strength.* She turned to face the main deck and felt those same dangerous tears well up again as it seemed to stretch out endlessly between the two upper decks. The main deck was easily bigger than the other two put together.

Telling herself that the sooner she got started, the sooner she would be done, Violet carried the pail to the far starboard corner. She knelt, pulling the brush from the pail and beginning to scrub again. Her arms moved mechanically in heavy, brisk circles. To keep herself focused she started reciting, under her breath, every Bible passage she could remember. She'd found memorization to be a relaxing pastime in the evenings while Isaac was going over various business ledgers and reports. Now she found that the rhythmic words and their religious significance gave her something comforting to concentrate on. Well, that and her seething, growing dislike of the woman holding her captive. The captain seemed hell-bent on punishing her for something, though she had no idea what it could be, and Violet would be damned if she'd let Ann break her.

The night wore on as she slowly crisscrossed the main deck from right to left, occasionally rising to empty and refill the bucket. By the time she finally reached the last bit of deck by the reserve barrels, her recitation had subsided into an unintelligible mumble. Violet herself wasn't sure what she was saying, or even if it was still biblical. The words had degraded over the past few hours into a string of not-so-pious curses called down on the head of the pirate captain.

The sky was beginning to lighten on the eastern horizon as she stood to empty the bucket for the last time and return it to its place by the water barrels. Barclay appeared at her elbow with a lantern in hand, and she wondered vaguely if the man ever slept.

"Finished?"

Violet nodded, though she could hardly believe it was true. The task had seemed never-ending.

"Drink this." He held out a dipper of water, and she took it obediently. Lukewarm and musty, it nevertheless tasted honey sweet to her parched tongue. "Easy now," Barclay warned as the liquid dribbled down her chin. "You don't want to get sick all over this what you just cleaned, do you?"

Violet heeded the warning and drank more slowly, but it was still scarcely enough to take the edge off her thirst. She handed the empty dipper back to him and met his eyes almost shyly. "May I…" Her voice was hoarse. "May I have more?"

One of Barclay's eyebrows shot up, but he refilled the dipper wordlessly. She drained it a second, and then a third time, thankful for his unexpected generosity.

When she was finished drinking he returned the dipper to the barrel. "Hungry? We can get some grub in the galley…"

Violet shook her head weakly. "I'm too tired to eat."

"All right, then. Follow me and we'll find you a spot to sleep."

Violet retrieved her Bible from beneath one of the portside cannons and followed Barclay through the hatch and down a ladder to the ship's gun deck, then through another hatch that led to the hold. He guided her among the stacks of boxes lining the ship's underbelly. The pale yellow light of the lantern cast strange shadows on the cargo.

Barclay nodded toward a pile of gray wool sheets stacked on top of a crate. "There's blankets, and you can set up anywhere down here that you like."

Violet looked around with trepidation. The floor beneath her feet was damp with puddles of seawater, and there did not seem to be much of anything that promised to serve as a comfortable mattress. She turned to the quartermaster. "Master Barclay, can you tell me where"—she flushed, trying to find a delicate way to phrase the question—"where a person would go to, um, relieve themselves?"

"Oh." Barclay scratched the back of his neck. "That'd be the head, missy."

"The head?"

He pointed in the direction of the bow. "On this level, up at the head of the ship. I'm afraid a vessel like this one ain't really designed for womenfolk, though, and you'll find it a mite crude. I'll talk to Captain Ann—"

"That won't be necessary," Violet interrupted quickly. "I'm sure the, uh, *head* will be just fine."

Barclay appeared doubtful, but he shrugged. "Well, ain't much privacy, so you're best off making use of it while the crew's asleep." He turned to go, then jiggled the lantern in his hand thoughtfully before turning back. "There's hard rules about open flame on a sailing ship." He held the lantern out. "I'll give you this if I have your promise you'll blow it out before you sleep. Captain Ann'll have my hide if you burn a hole in her ship, but it seems wrong to leave a lady alone in the dark down here."

Violet took the lantern gratefully, amazed by the gruff quartermaster's kindness. "I promise," she agreed earnestly, and gave him a little smile of appreciation. "Thank you."

He reddened slightly and shuffled his feet. "Yeah, well, get some sleep. More work to be done tomorrow." With that he turned and ascended the ladder out of the hold.

Violet was left standing in the small circle of light cast by the lantern, not quite sure what she should do next. Her entire body was crying out for rest, but the screaming of her bladder was far more demanding. She followed the direction Barclay had indicated, her Bible clutched to her chest with one arm while the other held the light out in front of her.

The head, she discovered, was really not much more than a small square hole cut in the deck at the bow of the ship, hanging out over the water below. There were no walls, no privacy screen, nothing to afford even a hint of modesty, and Violet shuddered. Barclay had been right. It certainly was not designed with a woman in mind, and she would have to be careful to use it only when the majority of the crew were asleep. Looking around quickly to be sure she was alone, Violet set her Bible and the lantern down. She lifted her skirts and lowered her under-drawers, squatting over the hole and gritting her teeth. The relief was so welcome it was almost worth the humiliation.

When she was done, Violet stumbled back to the pile of blankets that Barclay had pointed out earlier. Now she faced another quandary. She was loath to lay herself down on the damp wood floor, even with a blanket between her body and the puddles. Eventually she climbed rather awkwardly on top of a large crate, wrapping the blankets around herself and curling into a little ball. At least the crate was elevated off the floor, and dry.

Remembering her promise, Violet blew out the lantern and was immediately swallowed in chilly darkness. She drew the scratchy wool tightly around herself, suddenly grateful for the exhaustion that blocked out the cold, the pain, and nearly all her discomfort. She was too tired to feel anymore and sank into a heavy, deathlike sleep.

❖

Ann gave a low whistle when she emerged from her cabin. It almost looked like someone had gifted her with an entirely new ship overnight. The decks were gleaming in the morning sun. Her little prisoner might be cocky as hell, but she sure knew how to use a scrub brush. Ann gave a luxurious, catlike stretch in the morning sun, surprised to realize she was in a remarkably good mood. She ascended to the foredeck where Barclay was bent over the rail, scribbling some calculations and measurements onto a piece of paper while periodically shading his eyes to gauge the exact position of the sun.

He turned and handed her a mug of coffee before she even said a word. Ann's ill temper in the morning was notorious, and no one dared speak to her until she was well on her second cup.

"Good morning, Barclay." Ann took a sip from the mug and made a face. O'Hare couldn't make a decent cup of coffee to save his life. But even bad coffee couldn't put a damper on her high spirits this morning.

The quartermaster seemed startled, as much by the unexpected greeting as by the brightness in her tone. "Uh, good morning, Captain. Sleep well?"

"Aye." She cast another appreciative glance over the deck. "You did a good job with our new swabbie last night." He gave a small grunt in reply, and she scanned the rigging and decks as the crew went about their morning duties. "Where is the wench, anyway?"

"She's sleepin', Captain Ann."

"Sleeping? At this time of morning?"

Barclay nodded. "She only just finished the decks little over an hour ago."

This gave Ann pause, and then she declared, "No one on this ship sleeps the day away, Barclay. Wake her at once."

The quartermaster straightened indignantly. "No." She gave him a warning glare, but he stood his ground. "The kid worked her hands to the bone last night, Captain, gave us better work in one night than half the men on this crew do in a week. I'll slit her throat on your command, but I won't be responsible for working her to death."

He could not be allowed to defy her once she'd given an order. "Wake her, Barclay."

"I won't. She's your prize, Captain Ann. You can bloody well wake her yourself." The defiant words would have been more impressive had they not been punctuated by a nervous licking of the lips. "I'm master of this ship," he reminded her quickly, probably in the hopes of defusing some of her anger. "I follow you in battle, Captain, but when it comes to sailing you answer to me, and I've better things to do than help you play games with your little toys."

"You pulling rank on me, Barclay?" But one corner of her mouth tugged into a half-smile. "Lucky for you, I'm in a good mood this morning. Fine. I'll get the girl myself."

She left the foredeck, tossing open the hatch and dropping down one level, and then another, without bothering to use the ladder. It was dark in the hold, and Ann scuffed her way through the rows of cargo looking for Violet. She stopped short when she finally caught sight of her, curled up beneath a wad of gray wool blankets atop one of the bigger wooden crates.

For a few seconds Ann stared. How like a child the young woman looked, her thick lashes resting in perfect crescents on pale cheeks, one hand tucked beneath her face as a pillow while the other rested on top of her thick Bible. She was very small, and Ann felt a twinge of guilt. Noticing an unlit lantern on the floor by the crate, Ann lifted an eyebrow. Barclay was not known for his thoughtfulness, and Ann wondered if somehow he, too, had been softened by their pretty little captive. She snorted uneasily.

"Get up," she ordered, discomfort sharpening her voice. When the girl didn't stir, she reached out and tapped her under the blanket. "Up."

Violet gave a moan and shrank away from the captain's touch. She blinked heavy-lidded through a haze of exhaustion and pain, and Ann avoided her gaze, instead yanking the blanket back. She bit her tongue and exhaled. The girl's hands had been rubbed raw, the knuckles cracked and bleeding, and Ann could count at least four blisters on each palm.

"Come with me." Ann didn't wait for a reply, pulling Violet from atop the crate and half dragging her in the direction of the hatch.

The *Ice Queen*'s galley was on the gun deck by the stern. The galley was generally used as the ship's kitchen, but it doubled as a first aid station and a hospice after battle. Ann led Violet by the arm between several low cots that had been set up against the bulkheads.

She couldn't suppress a wince as they passed Turtle lying in a feverish daze near the galley entrance. The boy's left arm was wrapped tightly in strips of cloth, ending unnaturally halfway between the elbow and the wrist. Ann gritted her teeth and looked away.

"O'Hare! O'Hare, you old seadog, you down here?"

"Lady Captain." A delighted smile crossed the Irishman's face as he popped out from behind the copper pit that served as a cookstove. "You come for more coffee already?"

"Not quite." She pulled Violet up beside her so the cook could get a good look at the girl's hands. "Anything you can do about this?"

He clucked his tongue, then leered appreciatively into the prisoner's face. "Quite a bonny lass you have here, Lady Captain."

"O'Hare—"

"Aye, aye." He shuffled over to a cabinet against the wall. Inside, each little shelf had a low rail built across the front to prevent its contents from tumbling out every time the door was opened. He poked through the vials until he found the one he was looking for, a brown glass bottle that he uncorked and sniffed. "Here we are. Sit her over there and we'll get it taken care of."

Ann guided her to the stool O'Hare indicated. Violet hadn't said a word yet, and Ann couldn't help observing the pallor of her face, the dark circles beneath her eyes that were so vivid they looked like bruises. As the cook applied the foul-smelling ointment to one palm, Ann lifted the other up to examine it, and grunted. "I bet these hurt like hell."

Violet pulled her hand away with a ferocity that belied her weakened state. "They're fine, thank you." She flinched a little as O'Hare rubbed the ointment into her knuckles, but her expression was defiant. Ann was struck suddenly with how very like a broken doll the small woman looked, with the shadows beneath her eyes standing in stark relief against porcelain skin, silken tendrils of hair wisping about her pale throat, and the tattered silk clothes that exposed her bosom to the point of indecency. Yet even in such a state Violet's tenacity was not diminished. Ann probably should have found that aggravating, but all she felt was admiration—and a nagging sense of guilt.

She let out a puff of air. "I don't have time for this. Barclay needs me abovedecks. O'Hare, I want you to put her to work down here for the time being."

The old cook looked confused. "Pardon, Lady Captain?"

"See if she has any hand with the stove, or have her help you tend the wounded. I don't really care. Just keep her out of my way and make sure that infection doesn't spread." Ann turned and swept from the galley.

❖

Violet could relax slightly once Ann was out of sight, but she felt the tension returning at O'Hare's lecherous, gap-toothed grin as he tended her hands. Gradually his fingers moved upward, stroking the soft skin of her forearm appreciatively. "Bonny indeed," he murmured, and Violet drew her arm away. His grin widened, his missing front teeth providing a window to the flickering tongue behind them. "You know, if you ever wanted something a little extra from the galley, I'd be willing to make you a fine deal on it. Lady Captain wouldn't need to know." He wriggled his tongue in a manner that Violet was fairly certain was intended to be sensual, but instead made him look idiotically senile.

She gazed at him thoughtfully. He was repulsive, to be sure, but it was best to keep her options open. O'Hare might be a little off in the head, but he did have the run of the ship's galley, and that meant food. She let her attention drift around the cupboards and barrels, finally resting on a few dry biscuits sitting on a low table behind them. They were just like the ones Ann had offered, and her stomach gave an audible rumble. "I *am* hungry," she admitted quietly, then fluttered her lashes at the old Irishman.

"Are you, now?" He followed her gaze to the biscuits, and picked one up. "Maybe you'll be wanting a bit of hard tack and salt pork, then?"

She licked her lips as her mouth began to water. Having refused Ann's offer of food, she hadn't eaten since breakfast the previous day. Violet gave O'Hare her most charming smile. "That would be lovely, if you had some to spare."

He leaned forward then. "Hows about you spare me a kiss, and I spare you the grub?"

Violet didn't have the chance to reply, because they were interrupted. "O'Hare, you dumb brute, lay off the girl or the captain'll be wearing your insides for a hat."

Violet was startled to see a young boy's face pop into sight, and O'Hare grunted, handing Violet the biscuit and going to the boy's cot. "Mind your own affairs, Turtle lad," he retorted good-naturedly, and disappeared around the corner. Violet took the opportunity to stuff the biscuit into the pocket of her skirts and snatch another from the table before following.

"She's spoken for, O'Hare, you know the rules," the one called Turtle replied insistently, and Violet eyed him with curiosity as the cook firmly pushed him back onto the thin mattress and felt his pale forehead. She was both fascinated and horrified when O'Hare pulled the boy's arm up to change his bandages, and she realized that the entire hand was missing. Violet nearly choked on a mouthful of biscuit, but Turtle didn't seem disturbed. In fact, his eyes shone almost gleefully in spite of the pain tightening his face. He winked at Violet as the cook unwrapped his wounded arm.

"Pay no mind to O'Hare, miss. He's daft in the head at times."

Violet swallowed the food in her mouth. "What do you mean?"

"Well, Captain Ann owns you. Everyone around here heard her say so." Violet stiffened indignantly, but before she could reply the boy snickered. "Hey now, no need to get huffy. You're lucky."

"Lucky?" Violet repeated incredulously. "My husband's dead because of that bitch!"

"Shut your mouth." O'Hare sprang to his feet with a quickness that was impressive considering his age, and he struck her across the face. "Don't you ever talk like that about the Lady Captain."

Violet's hand flew to her cheek and she stared at the enraged Irishman in shock. He pulled his hand back as if to hit her again, but then seemed to think better of it and went shuffling back into the galley, muttering under his breath. Turtle was inspecting the clean bandages on his amputated arm, and he snickered. "Hey, do O'Hare a favor and don't tell Captain Ann he walloped you, eh? He means well, just doesn't like no one speaking bad of the captain."

Violet's cheek was still stinging. "I don't understand."

Turtle used his good hand to pat the deck beside him, indicating that she should sit down. Violet complied, sinking to the floor next to the cot and carefully avoiding the puddles scattered here and there over the wood. "You belong to Captain Ann. Ain't no one who can lay a hand on you without her say-so. Like I said, you're lucky."

"I really don't see how that makes me lucky. Everyone acts like I'm her slave."

Turtle raised an eyebrow. "Well, you are. The captain claimed you, she can do anything she wants to you, and ain't none of us'd stop her. But she's the only one. Everyone else has to keep their hands off or answer to her blade." He eyed her critically then. "And with you being so pretty, that's a real blessing."

"Blessing?"

"Sure. You must have noticed you're not among the most gentle-like of fellows, now. Let's just say there's a lot of men on board that wish you weren't under her protection."

Violet sucked in a breath. She wasn't so sure she wouldn't prefer being the crew's pleasure slave to being...whatever it was she'd become to their captain. Ann was by far the worst of all of them. "I can't say that makes me feel much better, knowing that"— she cast a glance toward the galley before reconsidering her words—"*woman* has exclusive rights to me."

Turtle chuckled. "Aw, I know she's scary when she wants to be, but the captain ain't that bad, really. And she likes you."

Violet shuddered. "I sincerely hope not."

"You wouldn't be alive if she didn't like you." The boy suddenly winced as pain shot through his arm, and Violet leaned forward instinctively to help him. He grimaced and waved with his remaining hand. "It's all right," he managed, slowly relaxing as the spasm faded. His eyes were still very bright, and Violet realized Turtle was feverish.

"I should let you rest," she began, but he caught her elbow.

"Please stay," he implored quietly. "I don't think about the hurt as much when I have someone to talk with."

Violet drew her brows together. "But...what do you want to talk about?"

"It don't matter, anything."

She considered this. "I could read to you, I suppose."

"You got somethin' for reading?"

"Aye, something very good for reading. I'll be right back." Violet stood and went back to the crate where she had slept, picking up her Bible and returning with it.

Turtle made a face. "Aw, missus, not that."

"And why not?"

The boy wrinkled his nose. "Ma used to make us go to meetings every Sunday. Nothing exciting ever happens in there, just a lot of old fellows preaching."

"Well, maybe you just never got to the exciting parts." He gave her a doubtful look, and she smiled. "Give it a try, at least. I promise, if you find it boring I'll stop."

Turtle was still skeptical, but the pain in his amputated arm apparently convinced him to give it a try. "All right."

Violet opened the book. "So tell me, Turtle, what do you find interesting, exactly? Battles? Politics?" She gave him the tiniest of knowing smiles, and leaned forward to whisper in his ear. "*Sex?*" His look of astonishment almost made her laugh aloud.

"There's...that...in there?"

"Sure." Violet winked mischievously. "But those are the passages you won't hear at a Sunday meeting with your mother." Turtle flushed very red. This time Violet did laugh as she flipped through the book's gilded pages. "Hmm...I think we should start with Samson and Delilah."

CHAPTER FOUR

C ome now, Captain Ann, be reasonable."
Ann smashed her fist on the table emphatically and Barclay jumped, but he did not back down. "Morale's kind of low after our last raid, and we're less than two weeks away from Tortuga. What could it hurt?"

"You know perfectly well what it could hurt, Barclay. I want to get the *Ice Queen* back to Tortuga in one piece. Every battle we engage in is one more risk that we might not come out of alive. I've spent my entire life searching for Black Dog's map, and now that I have it—"

"You want to get back to Tortuga as fast as possible so you can set off for the treasure. I know, Captain, I know. But this is easy pickings. A merchant galleon, nigh within hailing distance and riding low in the water with her belly full of Spanish gold. We've taken such ships a hundred times. What's one more?"

Ann leaned back in her chair with a frustrated sigh, propping one booted foot up on the table. He was right, and she knew it. Their enterprise so far had been a profitable one, but every additional ship they took meant another small fortune to each of the men on her crew. And as much as she despised the idea of a delay, it would be better for everyone if they were to ride into Tortuga fresh out of battle with victory still singing in their veins.

Barclay pressed his point a little more emphatically. "The boys have been a mite melancholy-like since we went after that textile ship, Captain. One more raid won't take but a day off our schedule."

Ann sighed again. "Very well. How long till we'd be in gunning distance?"

A wide grin spread across the quartermaster's face. "An hour, tops, Captain. Most of the men are already itching to go, so shouldn't take long to get them battle-ready."

"Tell the helmsman to change our course, then. I'll start the preparations."

He ducked out of her cabin with a bounce in his step, and Ann had to grin. The man certainly loved battle. And she had to admit, one more fight before sailing into port would do her good. She took her flintlock pistols from a trunk by the bed, loaded them, and stuffed them into her sash. Guns were not carried on board unless in preparation for a battle. The danger of accidental discharge was too great. Her cutlass, however, was nearly always at her waist, and various smaller blades arranged on her person. She emerged from her cabin to find many of the men already loading the cannons and checking weapons in anticipation of the coming battle.

"All hands on deck!" Ann bellowed, stamping her foot on the main deck to alert those below. She crossed the deck and threw open the door to the crew's quarters. "All hands on deck!" she repeated, startling out of their sleep those who had worked the night shift. Ann went to the hatch, tossing it up and calling down the ladder. "All hands on deck!"

When she turned she was nearly run over by Violet, who was carrying a pail of dirty water to the rail to be emptied. Ann sidestepped neatly, putting out a hand to keep the heavy bucket from spilling on her pistols. Wet gunpowder was useless.

The movement threw Violet off balance. She fell backward, spilling thick black water from the pail all over herself and the deck she'd been scrubbing. This brought a chorus of guffaws, and Ann couldn't help laughing herself. Much of the dirty liquid struck the young woman's throat, trickling down into the cleavage above her exposed stays and leaving a dark line of dirt that emphasized that alluring valley.

"Oops," Ann chuckled, bending and holding out a hand. "You should be more careful where your feet are leading you, Sister Violet."

Violet slapped her hand away. "Don't trouble yourself, Captain." This inspired more hoots and snickers. Ann laughed again, withdrawing her offer of help and watching the sodden young woman try to right herself on her own. Violet's heavy, wet skirts and the slippery deck beneath her feet made it hard to regain her balance. After several awkward seconds of flopping on the deck like a fish she finally managed to obtain her footing, but a sudden lurch of the ship cast her right into Ann again.

Ann caught the girl with her own body, stepping out to maintain her own balance and bringing her hands to Violet's waist. Ann looked down and her breath hitched. Fury had a way of making Violet impossibly beautiful. Her dainty features contracted with rage that was at once incongruous and incredibly sensual. Ann felt her body responding instantly, drawn into that starry midnight sky that seemed to be self-contained in the young woman's eyes. Forgetting all about keeping her flintlocks dry, and ignoring the fact that her thoughts were uncharacteristically waxing poetic, Ann drew Violet against her until she could feel the dampness of her captive's clothes seeping into her own.

Violet's attention focused on Ann's scar with the inevitable curiosity of anyone who got close enough to her to get a good look at it. Ann realized with a jolt that her lips were scant centimeters from Violet's. Quickly she drew her senses about herself and pushed the girl away.

"I must be winning you over, my lovely," she quipped, running a hand through her hair. "Any excuse to get into my arms, eh?"

"I'd rather the arms of the Devil himself," Violet spat back. Stiffly she picked up the empty pail, and Ann led the crew in another round of laughter.

Violet moved to push past her toward the water barrels, but Ann reached out and caught her arm. "Never mind the decks now," she said, speaking loudly that the assembled men would hear. "We're going into battle!"

The pirates cheered. Violet wrenched herself from Ann's grasp, and Ann ignored her as she addressed her crew. "In less than an hour's time we'll be coming alongside a lovely Spanish lady who's ripe for our attentions. So see to your equipment, my hearties, because we wouldn't want to disappoint her." She was answered with several bawdy shouts, and Ann hooked her thumbs into her sash with a feral grin. "Let's run up the Jolly Roger and let the lady know we're coming a-courting, shall we?"

The men scattered with enthusiasm. Several went to send up the *Ice Queen*'s black flag, the one that would announce their arrival and hopefully terrify the merchant sailors into panic. If they were very lucky, they might even get their victims to surrender without a fight. Branded Ann's reputation was certainly fearsome enough to warrant such a response.

❖

Violet stood uncertainly by the portside water barrel, watching as Ann strode about the deck barking orders. During those brief seconds in the captain's arms she'd seen something perplexing in her expression, something she didn't quite recognize. Violet knew desire when she saw it, but not desire like this, a strange possessive admiration as if Ann wanted something from her that went beyond carnal lust. Isaac used to look at her with a similar expression, though his was almost worshipful like a little boy, shy and full of awe and self-consciousness. This was different. Ann was stronger and more commanding, but her steely greed was tempered with a hint of vulnerability that Violet hadn't thought the pirate capable of.

Dropping the bucket in its place by the barrel, Violet moved to the gunwale and peered out over the expanse of glittering ocean. She could see, near the horizon, the speck that had caught everyone's attention. Violet felt deep sympathy for the unfortunate Spanish merchants. Still, this might be an invaluable opportunity, and Violet eyed the ship in the distance thoughtfully.

The pirates were so busy running around the deck making preparations for the raid that no one seemed to notice her, and that suited Violet just fine. She wedged herself between the portside barrel and the ship's gunwale, hidden by the deck stairs, and watched as they drew closer and closer to the Spanish galleon. It was a massive ship, she realized as they neared, much bigger than the pirates' modified brigantine, and she wondered how Branded Ann could possibly hope to conquer it. From Violet's perspective the *Ice Queen* seemed like a puppy trying to goad a fully grown mastiff into a fight.

She had to plug her ears as the pirate guns thundered the first volley. Her only previous experience with sea battle had been mostly from the hold of her husband's ship, where the sounds of the cannons had been muffled. Abovedecks they were deafening. The gunwale less than a meter from her hiding place splintered with the merchants' return fire, and she gave a shriek. Quickly deciding she might be safer on the other side of the water barrel, she ducked behind it just as another shot from the galleon sent tiny pieces of metal spraying across the decks. Grape shot, the pirates called it—little balls of metal that could pulverize a ship's deck and anyone standing on it. The scent of gunpowder hung heavy in the air.

For a crew of ruffians and cutthroats, Branded Ann's men were remarkably organized and professional when it came to fighting. Isaac had once explained that most pirates were former naval officers turned criminal, and watching them methodically discharge their cannons and guns, laying down cover fire for one another, calmly moving the injured into the hold and out of danger, she was impressed to see such teamwork among such otherwise uncivilized men.

The *Ice Queen* pulled alongside the merchant vessel and grappling hooks flew gracefully through the air, one after another. Violet realized that although the galleon was a bigger ship, she carried a smaller crew, and the Spanish merchants would be no match for the bloodthirsty pirates preparing to suck them dry. The two ships were lashed together, just like the attack on her husband's boat. The pirates had obviously done this hundreds of times before, and as Violet watched she came to understand that for most of these men it was not bloodlust that drove them, but greed. They weren't interested in killing, though they had no qualms about doing so to get the gold they wanted. In fact, the pirates' demeanor was oddly businesslike as they boarded and began looting. Only those who resisted were cut down. The rest, for the most part, were largely ignored so long as they didn't get in the way.

Violet noticed Branded Ann balancing confidently on the *Ice Queen*'s gunwale, her long, wild hair tangling in the breeze. She was calling out orders and occasionally firing a musket from her hip at any of the merchant sailors who seemed to be getting too seditious. Only when most of the crew had boarded did Ann drop her gun and grab a hanging rope, swinging to the deck of the other ship to direct the looting party. Violet crept from her hiding place by the barrel and climbed the steps to the foredeck, trying to stay out of sight. When she reached the rail, she scanned the other ship anxiously.

There had to be a way for her to get off the pirate ship and onto the merchant vessel. The two ships were so close to one another, and God only knew when she'd have another opportunity like this. But she certainly couldn't jump the distance, nor could she just saunter across the boarding planks joining the main decks. *Oh, Lord of Heaven, hear thy daughter and come to her aid.* She racked her brain for an idea.

"You need help, *señorita*?"

The words were heavily accented, and Violet looked up in surprise. One of the merchant sailors was standing on the galleon's aft deck nearly a meter above her, bending over the rail and looking down at her curiously. He was starkly handsome, with sharp features and dark eyes. "You in some trouble?"

Violet's heart leapt. "Oh, please, help me, please, the pirates have taken me prisoner."

"No fear, Diego will help you now." He disappeared for a moment, returning with a rope in his hands which he tossed down to her. "Take this, *señorita*, and hold on tight. Diego will pull you up."

Violet took the rope, wrapping it around her waist securely and climbing onto the gunwale. She cast a glance down at the main decks where the pirates were busy swinging back and forth between the two ships with chests of Spanish gold. None of them were paying any attention to the foredeck, at least not for now. "Oh, please hurry."

He gave a tug on the rope, and Violet could not suppress the lurch of fear in her stomach as her feet were lifted from the rail. For several breathless moments she was dangling over the water, gripping the rope for dear life as it tightened around her ribs. It probably would have crushed her lungs were it not for the unforgiving whalebone stays protecting her torso. After several hard jerks she felt strong hands lifting her over the galleon's rail, and she looked gratefully into the face of her rescuer.

Diego eyed her torn bodice, with the stays brazenly exposed beneath. "Filthy pirate *puta*," he muttered, casting a dark look at Branded Ann, who was strutting around the galleon's lower deck. "Quickly, we will hide you in the captain's cabin until they have gone." He whipped the jacket from his own shoulders and wrapped it around her; it smelled of sweat and stale pipe tobacco, but Violet didn't care. She snuggled into it quickly and let him plop a wide-brimmed hat, several sizes too large for her, over her hair.

"Move slowly, *señorita*," he instructed. "Don't want to catch their attention. No fear, you are safe now." Obediently Violet followed him down the deck stairs. The galleon was a much finer ship than the pirates', with iron-wrought steps leading to the upper decks. She hunched behind the merchant's broad shoulders, only moving when he did, and he casually edged sideways to the captain's quarters beneath the aft deck. Violet was impressed to note that the door was inlaid with elegant panels of frosted glass.

Diego spoke over his shoulder. "Go on in, *señorita*, the pirates have already taken everything they wanted from this cabin and won't be back to search it again. When it's clear I'll bring the captain to meet you."

"Thank you," Violet replied earnestly before opening the door and slipping inside.

Ann's crew had been there, all right—papers and fragments of broken china littered the floor, trunks had been thrown open and the clothes within tossed carelessly about the carpet. Violet tsked and pulled off the borrowed hat and jacket, laying them neatly across the back of a chair. Then she set about refolding the rumpled clothing and straightening the room. The Spanish merchants were her God-sent saviors, and she would do whatever she could to show her gratitude.

After stacking the scattered papers neatly on a low table beneath a porthole, Violet peered at the *Ice Queen* through the round glass window. Most of the pirates had reboarded. She spied Ann's unmistakable silver hair and watched as the captain returned to her own ship. Violet held her breath and prayed. If only the pirates would forget about her and sail away without noticing she was gone. One by one the boarding planks were withdrawn and the final ropes untied. Through the window glass Violet could hear the pirates laughing, taunting the merchants with their victory. And then, ever so slowly, the whitewashed hull of the pirate vessel began to draw away.

Violet sank into a chair at the table and let out a breath. She'd done it! She'd escaped the notorious Branded Ann. "Praise thy name, great and merciful Lord. Thank you. Oh, thank you."

She had no idea what she was going to do next. She'd probably ask the merchants to drop her off at the next civilized port they came to. Perhaps she would join the church. It was a thought that never would have occurred to her a few years ago, but now seemed quite appealing considering her status as a widow. Violet could picture herself leading a life of devotion, serving in an abbey or perhaps a chapel, even a school. She felt a twinge of sorrow as she realized that she had left her Bible behind on the pirate ship, but it didn't really matter now.

She had won. Violet Watts had outsmarted the most feared pirate on the Spanish Main, and she was filled with an almost petty sense of satisfaction.

She stood quickly as the door opened, smoothing the front of her skirts and suddenly feeling self-conscious. What a fright she must look, with her clothing torn and stained and her hands calloused and red from scrubbing the pirate's decks for days. Her eyes were probably ringed with dark circles, too. The man who entered, however, did not seem to be bothered by her disheveled appearance. In fact, as soon as she met his gaze Violet gulped. She knew that look, the smoldering greedy fire that spread across his face at the sight of her, the way his gaze lingered on her exposed throat and bosom. Violet suddenly wondered if her situation was really that much improved on the merchant vessel.

"Captain Hector Santiago, at your service, *señorita*." He swept the plumed hat from his head. "I regret our first meeting must be under such unpleasant circumstances, but it is a privilege to liberate such a lovely treasure from those Godless pirate savages."

Violet did her best to stifle her paranoia. Not all men who desired her were scoundrels, she reminded herself firmly, and the captain spoke like a God-fearing gentleman. "Mistress Isaac Watts," she replied with a polite curtsy, deliberately emphasizing her married title. "It is an honor, Captain. I am indebted to you and your crew for your assistance. You have truly been the answer to my prayers."

His gaze went to her wedding band, and he bowed again. "My apologies, *Señora* Watts. Your husband, was he also on board the pirate's vessel?"

Violet was suddenly tempted to lie, and it took a great deal of effort to shake her head. *Thou shalt not bear false witness...* "No, he was...they murdered him." She might have avoided breaking one of the Commandments, but the crafty look that entered the captain's eyes rather made her wish she'd gone ahead with the sin.

"I see." He stepped farther into the room. "You have my most sincere condolences, *señora*." He waved at the table. "Please, have a seat. May I offer you some tea?" Santiago didn't wait for an answer, striking a match and bending to light the coals resting in his little pot-bellied stove.

Violet was impressed. "You have a stove in your quarters?"

"España builds the finest ships in the world, with every modern convenience." He set a copper teakettle on top of the stove with a clank, and then strode over with a plate of small cookies in one hand. "You must be hungry. I hear pirates are not the most generous of captors."

Violet's mouth watered. The truth was, the half-rations that the pirates had been feeding her were scarcely enough to take the edge off her hunger, and it had been days since she'd felt the comfort of a full belly. But as she reached out for the plate Santiago pulled it back slightly, instead holding one of the cookies to her lips. She looked up at him uncertainly, not liking the implication of that gesture, but her appetite got the better of her. Gingerly she took a bite of the cookie in his fingers before reaching up to take it from him. She swallowed and thanked him politely.

Santiago smiled and set the plate on the table in front of her, and though Violet did her best to remember her manners, she was so hungry that she finished the cookie in her hand and two more before looking up to realize that the Spanish captain was watching her with a very different sort of hunger. She felt a flush creeping into her cheeks as he looked over her attire once more, this time clucking his tongue with disgust though he looked anything but disgusted.

"Foul creatures, the lot of them, keeping a lady in such a state of undress." He crossed the thick carpet to a stack of trunks against the wall, and rummaged through the top one. "If the vermin haven't spoiled it…ah, here we are." Santiago turned around with an armful of ivory silk, which he shook out so Violet could see it was actually a gown, one of the finest she'd ever seen. "I bought this as a gift for a lady of my acquaintance, and," he looked Violet up and down, "I think you're in more need of it than she. Here, try it on."

Violet stood, brushing crumbs from her lap, and Santiago laid the gown across the bed. For several moments he stood looking at her expectantly, then tilted his head. "You do not like the dress?"

"It's lovely, Captain, but I was wondering if you might excuse me while I change?"

"No need to be shy." He smiled.

Rather like a cat playing with a mouse, Violet thought, and she closed her bodice at her neck in a gesture that was more defensive than demure. "Captain, surely you do not mean to deny a lady her privacy?"

As he stepped forward she could see plainly that he did. "Come, *mi belleza*, you have nothing to fear. We have been at sea a long time and miss the comforts of home. I will not touch, only look."

Violet took a step back. "That is entirely out of the question." She did not add that she knew his type. Her intuition said he would not be able to stop himself at just looking. *Are you punishing me, Father? You must be, for I cannot seem to escape the pit into which I have fallen.*

Santiago's face darkened and he moved forward again. "My crew and I are plundered by pirates in order to pluck you from the sea and you would refuse this small request?" He reached out and took her arm none too gently. She struggled to free herself from his grasp, looking around frantically for something she might use as a weapon. Fortunately she was saved by a sudden pounding on the cabin doors.

"*Capitán! Venga rápidamente! Capitán Santiago!*"

He dropped her arm, apparently regaining some measure of common sense at the interruption, and backed away with pink tingeing his cheeks. "My apologies, *señora*. I do not know what came over me. Please, accept the gown as a gift and put it on in my absence. I will return in a moment." He went to answer the incessant pounding, and was gone.

Violet stared from the frosted glass doors to the dress on the bed. She probably wouldn't have much time; better to change out of her torn clothes now than have Santiago come back thinking he would help her out of them. Rubbing her arm where his grip had left slight bruises, she went to the bed and unbuttoned the waist of her skirts.

❖

"Report."

"No deaths, seven wounded, but O'Hare says nothing serious, Captain. All in all, five thousand pieces of eight 'n a couple of chests of bar silver. Some pieces of jewelry, too, off some of them Spanish dandies."

Barclay was obviously pleased, and Ann gave a low whistle. "Nice haul for one raid," she admitted, cracking her knuckles with satisfaction. "Tortuga will be glad to see us coming with the kind of money our boys will have to spend."

The quartermaster grunted his agreement. Ann strode to the rail of the poop deck, watching the crew milling excitedly around the mainmast, livened considerably by their triumph. Pirates were a boisterous lot when they were celebrating. Ann could already hear Maclairen's bagpipes trilling across the foredeck and several of the men stomping their feet in rhythm. "Our little swabbie will have her hands full tomorrow," she commented dryly. Barclay cleared his throat nervously, and she looked over at him suspiciously. "What?"

"Well, Captain Ann, I was waiting for a good time to tell you…"

"Tell me what?" Her voice cooled several degrees.

"The girl. We…we can't find her."

"Can't find her?"

"No one's seen her since the battle started."

Ann cursed and marched to the stern to glare out at the merchant ship that was now scarcely a speck in the distance. Barclay came up beside her. "Maybe she jumped overboard, Captain. She was looking pretty upset before."

"She's on that ship." Ann's gaze was pinned to the horizon. "Turn us around, Barclay, we're going back."

The quartermaster bristled. "You're in charge of battling, Captain, but I'm in command of sailing. We don't have time. Little mite's probably better off on that ship anyway, 'n it's not like she was doing us that much good here. We stay our course."

❖

He knew the minute she turned eyes on him that his answer had been the wrong one. Ann's fist smashed into his abdomen, bringing him to one knee as he gasped for breath, and in one smooth motion she positioned herself behind him, one hand gripping his thinning hair as the other pressed a blade to his throat.

"So help me, Barclay, I will paint the deck with your entrails if you do not turn this ship around right now."

Maclairen's bagpipes silenced, and Barclay flushed as several of the crew were drawn to watch the commotion. He didn't have much choice. "Helm," he croaked carefully, trying not to disturb the knife digging into his Adam's apple, "Come about."

"You heard him, Johnson," Ann barked at the helmsman. "Turn us around. Now!" The last word was a guttural snarl, and the frightened man leapt to obey, yanking on the wheel. Several of his mates moved to help, and Ann lowered the dirk from Barclay's throat. "That's better. No one escapes my ship, Barclay. No one. We're taking her back."

Barclay nodded, rising to his feet and mopping at the blood that trickled from his nose. He never knew if he'd pushed her too far until it was too late, and it always ended unpleasantly. At least this time he hadn't lost any teeth. Straightening himself as best he could, Barclay descended quickly to the main deck to continue their change of course.

❖

Ann heard the quartermaster calling for some of the sails to be brought in to allow the ship to turn, and indeed the *Ice Queen* was making a slow but definite arc through the water. Glowering at the merchant ship in the distance, Ann bit her lip until she tasted blood. *Merchant sailors are no better than pirates when it comes to a pretty piece of woman-flesh. If even one of them lays a hand on her...* Ann ground her teeth.

It took almost twenty minutes to return to the galleon, which was sailing in the opposite direction, and Ann spent the entire time pacing the foredeck. When they pulled alongside, the Spanish sailors and their captain had assembled on the galleon's deck, staring nervously at the pirate ship and clutching at their weapons. Ann leapt onto the gunwale, holding a section of rigging for support, her cutlass bared in the other hand.

"Branded Ann," the captain acknowledged nervously, "is there... something else...we can do for you?"

Ann didn't bother returning the greeting. "You have something that belongs to me. I want her back."

"Her?" Santiago seemed genuinely surprised, and Ann could practically see his mind working. He was probably trying to figure out if the girl had some enormous ransom significance he wasn't aware of. Not much else could have caused the pirates to go to the trouble of returning for an escaped captive. The gold they'd taken seemed worth a hundred such prisoners.

Ann sneered. "You have exactly one minute before I give the order for my boys to burn your ship."

Sweat broke out on the man's forehead, but before he had the chance to reply the door to his cabin opened and Violet stepped onto the deck. Silence fell as everyone, including Ann herself, gaped at the apparition gliding toward them.

Ivory silk clung to Violet's soft curves, draping across her hips and shoulders in lush folds like a Grecian statue. The cut of the bodice was low, and Violet's hair fell over her shoulders to frame her pale throat and bosom. Ann could not tear her eyes away, and her stomach gave a strange, dizzying lurch. It was a good thing she'd forced Barclay to chase the Spanish ship down again. Looking like that, Violet would not have been able to stay out of the hands of these lecherous merchants for long.

Ann took hold of a rope hanging from the yardarm and flew to the galleon's deck, landing solidly in front of the merchant captain. "You will return her to me. Now."

Santiago turned to look at Violet with regret. "I am sorry, *señora*, but it seems I have little choice."

Violet shook her head numbly. "It's not your fault, Captain." She did not move as Ann put an arm around her waist, nor did she make any effort to hold on as they both swung back onto the *Ice Queen*.

When they reached the deck of the pirate ship, Ann shoved Violet into Barclay's waiting arms. Every man on deck still seemed to be staring greedily at Violet, and Ann stomped a foot to get their attention. "Well, hearties, what are you waiting for? Resume course!" She threw a cocky salute in the direction of the Spanish merchants as they began to pull away, and then stalked over to glower down at Violet.

"That was terribly foolish, my lovely. I am not so easily outmaneuvered." When the young woman didn't come back with a snippy retort, Ann took hold of her chin and made Violet look into her eyes. She saw none of the defiance she expected in that innocent face. In fact, there was nothing, no emotion at all, and somehow that was far more disturbing. Had Violet at last given up? Ann was surprised to realize that she actually felt disappointed at the thought. But the men were watching, and after such a blatant breach of her authority she would have to inflict consequences. Ann released Violet's chin and stepped backward. "Throw her in the brig."

❖

The brig was on the lowest level of the ship, near the head. A small area by the bow sectioned off with steel bars and a gate, it was meant to detain unruly sailors who'd had a bit too much to drink, or in more severe cases to imprison mutinous crewmates. Another small, square hole was cut into the deck in the far corner, its purpose obvious. Violet offered no protest as Barclay ushered her behind the bars and locked the gate with a chain and padlock. He attempted to ask her something, but Violet couldn't hear much beyond a faint ringing in her ears.

God was taunting her, or torturing her, or punishing her for something…it had to be, for how else could He be so cruel as to tantalize her with the hope of escape, even the illusion of triumph, only to snatch it all away and return her to the pirates' hands? *Even God Himself has turned His back on me.* Finally Barclay gave up and left, and Violet put a hand on one of the steel bars.

"My God, my God, why hast thou forsaken me?"

CHAPTER FIVE

No Bible reading today, Sister Violet?" Turtle eyed her with concern. "You don't look so well. You sick?"

In truth, Violet was fairly certain she'd been running a low fever most of the day. Barclay had let her out of the brig that morning, but the long night spent shivering in a dark cell without so much as a blanket had taken its toll. The light silk gown given to her by the Spanish merchants did little to protect against the piercing cold, and though she was far from freezing to death, it was still enough to set her ill. Her body felt heavy and dull, and so did her spirit. She'd never felt so alone in all her life.

Violet shook her head wordlessly and waited for him to finish eating. One of her duties was to tend to the boy as he healed. Ann had expressly forbidden Turtle to leave the galley or his cot until O'Hare pronounced him fully recovered. Usually Violet spent the morning meal reading to him, but she just didn't feel like it today.

She'd had a long time to think during the night, as the miserable cold rendered her unable to sleep. At first she'd paced the small cell to keep her blood flowing, but finally she was too exhausted for even that. She chose the driest corner she could find and sat down, tugging her knees to her chest for warmth. The more she thought about it, the more painfully obvious it became—her faith was a cruel joke. How arrogant she'd been, to assume that God had the slightest interest in what happened to her, that she could somehow impress Him with her piety, that she could make up for the grievous sins of her past with prayers and Scripture quotations.

Turtle seemed to sense that Violet didn't feel like talking, and he did not press any further. After she'd carried away the dishes and ensured that he was comfortably settled back on his cot, Violet climbed to the upper decks to fetch the pail and scrub brush. They had become like extensions of her own body in the past few weeks. Every afternoon she scrubbed the ship decks for hours, and by morning they were filthy again.

The silk gown was entirely inappropriate for manual labor. The long underskirt had something of a train in the back that trailed beneath her feet. It was already badly stained from the night spent in the brig, but she had no other clothes to wear. With a heavy sigh she sat and struggled with the tiny buttons of her boots. Going barefoot on the ship would be far more practical than wearing heels, which provided very little tread against the slick wooden decks. She even considered tossing the shoes overboard, but could not bring herself to be so wasteful. Instead she deposited them inside a coil of heavy rope and set to work.

Hot, salty tears rolled down her cheeks as she scrubbed, and Violet made no effort to hold them back. She wasn't sure why she was crying; inside she felt completely numb. But as the afternoon wore on, her hands reddening from the incessant scrubbing and her muscles tiring with the strenuous exercise, she found herself slipping into a deep sense of hopelessness. *Why am I letting them do this to me?* She wasn't afraid of pain. Really, what could the pirates do to her if she refused to suffer their orders any longer? They could kill her, of course, or torture her, but ultimately they couldn't force her to scrub a deck or stir a pot if she outright refused to do it.

The sky was getting dark as she finished the poop deck. As she stood and emptied her bucket over the rail for the last time that night, she found herself staring down for several long moments into the churning water beneath the rudder.

How easy it would be, to put an end to this. And who would miss her? Isaac was dead. God Himself would probably fail to notice she was gone. She was sick, she was hungry, she was exhausted, she was alone, and none of it mattered to anyone, not even Violet herself. She was beyond caring.

Possessed with a sudden wild impulse, Violet took hold of the rigging overhead and used it to climb up onto the gunwale. There she steadied herself, gripping the smooth, damp wood with bare feet. When she'd gained her footing, Violet let go ever so slowly and held her arms out, balancing on the rail as she'd seen Ann do on multiple occasions. She peered into the dark water below. It was the first real emotion she'd felt all day, a strange pounding in her head and tightness in her limbs as she stood quite literally on the edge of death. Tipping her face back, she let the cool salt breeze bathe her skin, her arms spread in a wide embrace. It would take so little, a slight shift in her weight and she'd go tumbling off the stern. It would be like flying, if only for one glorious instant.

❖

Ann scarcely noticed when Barclay joined her at the helm for his evening report. She was preoccupied by the sight of the young woman perched precariously on the rail of the poop deck a few feet away. Barclay grunted and took a step forward, but Ann put out a hand and caught his shoulder. The quartermaster looked back at her incredulously. "Ain't you gonna stop her, Captain Ann?"

"No."

"But, Captain, if she pitches herself overboard—"

"Then I've won," Ann interrupted quietly.

"What?"

Ann couldn't explain, not without it sounding as petty as she knew it was. If Violet gave up and took her own life, then Ann would win their unspoken battle of wills. An uncomfortable ache in her chest had been growing steadily all day as she'd watched Violet move mechanically about the ship, those once-vibrant eyes vacant and dark. Now that ache was pulsing with each beat of her heart and her mouth was dry. She would not move to help Violet, and was angry with herself for wanting to. The girl was an idiot, she reminded herself, and essentially worthless. Ann had no real need of her, nor would the ship suffer from her loss.

Then why did you threaten Barclay within an inch of his life to get her back? a rebellious little voice in her mind questioned pointedly.

It's the principle of the matter. She'll have to take her own life, because I'm not going to give her the satisfaction. Ann had killed hundreds of men in her lifetime—women, too, for that matter. It would not be the first time a person had committed suicide to escape her, but it was the first time she found herself strongly tempted to save someone from such a fate. Violet's melodramatic displays were utter foolishness, yet they gave Ann the inexplicable longing to somehow save the girl from herself.

The ship hit a swell, and Ann's heart leapt into her throat as Violet teetered on the rail, hands suddenly flailing to maintain her balance. Before Ann realized it she'd moved forward to catch her, but Violet did not fall. She managed to get hold of the rigging nearby just as she slipped. For a few seconds she hung suspended above the water until she planted her feet on the gunwale and steadied herself once more, and Ann let out a breath.

Violet panted with relief and clung a little more tightly to the ropes. She hadn't understood until that instant that she didn't really want to fall, and a wave of embarrassment swept over her. In those seconds of dizzying peril, when she could have easily fallen to her death, Violet experienced a revelation.

God hadn't done this to her. She had been brought to this by her own pride, and He was simply allowing her to suffer the consequences. Since the moment she'd set foot on the pirate ship, Violet had been determined to despise everyone and everything on board, as if the blood that flowed in her veins was truly any bluer than theirs. The pirates were wicked men, to be sure, but she'd been cut from the same cloth as they. She didn't need a change in circumstances, she needed a change of heart. *God helps those who help themselves.*

She'd never thought of herself as a silly girl, prone to the tantrums that seemed to be the mark of good breeding. In fact, Violet prided herself on being stronger than any woman she knew. As cruel as life had been, she still loved the day-to-day adventure of survival. She had allowed the pirates to make her forget that, to make her feel victimized, a mindset she had never tolerated from herself or anyone else. She was standing on the rail of their ship, ready to toss herself into the sea in a theatrical show of self-pity, having willingly handed over her dignity and even her faith. Those were things no one could take from her by force. Violet was thoroughly ashamed. *I will not let them take my God from me.*

Violet held on to the rigging and lowered herself to the deck. When she turned, she paused with surprise. There it was again, that hint of humanity in the pirate's face.

Ann inhaled as Violet's luminous eyes pinned her once again, and a peculiar flutter of joy winged through her stomach as she realized that the star had reappeared in that private sky. Something was changed in her captive's face, in her entire demeanor. The defiance Ann had grown accustomed to had been replaced with an unexpected calm.

Violet gave a small, but genuine smile. "Good night, Captain Ann." She picked up the bucket and brush, and padded to the deck stairs.

Ann watched her go, awash with unfamiliar emotions. There had been no challenge in the girl's tone, and still no fear, but she'd perceived a touch of respect that had not been there before. Suddenly Violet had given Ann no fuel for her temper. What she was left with was that *other* feeling, the one that always accompanied the irritation but was somewhat overwhelmed by it—a lingering fascination that was tinged with desire. She was relieved, and annoyed at feeling relieved. She was also confused. Was it over? Who had won?

Ann spoke distractedly to the quartermaster. "Helm's yours for the night, Barclay." She strode off toward her cabin without waiting for a reply.

Violet had made up her mind that if she couldn't change her situation, she would change her attitude. Over the next few days she worked as efficiently and obediently as ever, but now she made a deliberate effort to be cheerful, to keep a friendly tone when answering to orders. Her duties on the pirate ship weren't so bad, really. The work was hard and usually thankless, but it was honest and she could take pride in it. And the rest of the pirates seemed to be taking notice.

Rough and dangerous as they were, she found herself coming to know and even like many members of the crew. Turtle, for instance, whose bravado was far bigger than the rest of him. Even the loss of a hand hadn't seemed to throw a damper on the boy's spirits, and he spoke to Violet like a favorite elder sister. O'Hare, the ship's cook and sometime medic, was a lecherous half-lunatic who loved the ocean like a drunkard loves his ale. Caught in the right mood, the batty Irishman could be coerced into telling some of the most fantastical tales Violet had ever heard, stories of sea monsters and mermaidens and cursed treasures, all of which he swore were the complete and utter truth. Then there was Mason, a giant of a man with skin so black it shone like polished ebony when he sweat in the sun. Rumor had it that Mason had originally been captured from Africa by pirate slave ships, and the captain had been so impressed—or perhaps intimidated—by the enormous man that he'd recruited him.

The *Ice Queen* was a mosaic of languages and cultures, from Europe to China, Africa to the Americas. Nearly every major European country was represented somewhere among the crew. There were even a few that Violet had difficulty placing, from parts of the world so exotic she'd never heard of them. She was fairly certain that both the ship's captain and quartermaster hailed from the American Colonies; they shared the same cocky, broad accent. Ann in particular was obviously more educated than the lot of them, and had a fascinating way of speaking, with a soft rounding to her *R*s that was almost elegant, and a colorful vocabulary of British navy slang. While every man on board had a story that somehow made him seem just a little more human, the only other woman on board became an even greater mystery the more Violet learned of her.

No one seemed to know exactly where Branded Ann came from, what her past was like, if she had parents or siblings, if she had ever been anything other than a pirate. No one could explain how she'd come by the vivid cross-shaped brand on her cheek, or why she engaged in piracy. Violet was able to glean only a few tidbits of truth from the rumors and tall tales surrounding the infamous pirate captain.

The stories agreed that Branded Ann had served as quartermaster for several years under a pirate captain known as Mad Jack Raider. Together they had captured and pillaged hundreds of ships in and around the West Indies, mostly Spanish and French merchant vessels. As a woman, Ann faced more opposition than most, both from the merchants and slavers who underestimated her abilities, and from the men on her own crew. Her skill with a sword became legendary as she survived repeated challenges and plots against her life, even taking on entire groups of men at once. She gained a reputation as an unforgiving disciplinarian who demanded absolute and immediate obedience; the punishments inflicted on those who failed were swift and terrible. After capturing a large brigantine from English slavers, Raider gave the ship to Ann as a gift. This generosity was possibly out of fear for his own life, as Ann had made it increasingly clear that obtaining a ship of her own was her primary goal. Assembling her own crew aboard the newly renamed *Ice Queen,* she had spent the last several months furthering her reign of terror across the Spanish main. She liked strong coffee and busty women, and she wasn't a morning person. But otherwise, Branded Ann was a complete enigma even to her own crew.

Despite Violet's newfound determination to get along with the pirates, she struggled with feelings of hate for the woman who'd murdered her husband. She prayed, every night, for the Lord to grant her His divine forgiveness. After all, if He could forgive her own past misdeeds, how could she not do the same for someone else? But it felt like Ann enjoyed antagonizing her at every turn. She could feel the pirate woman's gaze on her, scrutinizing her daily work, waiting for her to do something that would invite criticism. It was as if Ann took every possible opportunity to assert her authority over Violet, especially when any member of the crew was nearby, and Violet felt certain the pirate woman found amusement in humiliating her. Just a glimpse of the cross-marked face was enough to make Violet forget all her good intentions.

One morning as Violet was helping O'Hare ready the afternoon mess, Ann appeared in the galley, coffee mug in hand. Violet recoiled toward the stove while O'Hare beamed happily at the unexpected visit.

"More coffee, Lady Captain?" But his nose wrinkled in confusion as he looked down into her mug. "You're not even half done yet."

Ann glared suspiciously. "O'Hare, did you do something different to the coffee this morning?"

He gulped and shot a glance at Violet. "Actually, 'twas our Sister Violet here what made it today. I had my hands full with Turtle's dressings, and…"

Ann fastened a stare on Violet. "What did you do?"

Violet was genuinely baffled, and cringed beneath the pirate's gaze. "I…well, I did wash the cheesecloth, it was filthy." She was not a coffee drinker herself. The drink was a strange habit, especially for a sailor, as it required a ration of precious fresh water in order to be made. O'Hare said that the *Ice Queen* was the only ship on which coffee was a necessity rather than a luxury. Ann's addiction to the stuff was legendary. Violet wondered if perhaps the cloth used to filter the ground beans wasn't supposed to be cleaned. She should have asked.

"I'm sorry, Lady Captain," O'Hare said quickly. "'It weren't her fault, she didn't know. I'll make a fresh cup—" He reached to take the captain's mug, but she pulled it back.

"O'Hare, from now on you will see to it that she makes the coffee every morning. Understand?" She took the pot from the stove and topped off her mug before striding away.

Violet's mouth dropped open slightly as the pirate woman left, and she exchanged astonished glances with O'Hare. He scratched his head. "Guess I should've washed the cloth sooner," he said apologetically.

"I don't mind, really. That's about the nicest she's ever been to me."

He gave her a gap-toothed grin. "If you be wanting someone to treat you nicely, now…" He reached out to tweak her pale cleavage, an action that any other self-respecting woman would have found shocking. But Violet swatted his hand away playfully, knowing the Irishman's flirting was harmless. *Well, mostly harmless, anyway.*

"Come now, Master O'Hare, we don't have time for that. If mess is late, the men might just decide to cook us up for dinner instead."

He chuckled and returned to stirring the pot on the stove. "Aye, lassie, that they might."

❖

Ann stood at the wheel on the aft deck, periodically sipping from the mug in one hand as she watched O'Hare, Violet, and one of the other deckhands, Porter, moving about the main deck serving mess. Her eyes followed her little captive as she darted between the pirates, dishing scoopfuls of some sort of stew into wooden bowls and distributing mugs of carefully rationed drinking water. Edwards, the ship's carpenter, reached out with one hand to pinch the silk-covered buttocks as Violet passed him. She dodged artfully out of the way and turned to deliver some comment that Ann couldn't quite hear, but that elicited howls of laughter from the men nearby. One of them tapped Edwards's shoulder and pointed toward Ann, probably as a reminder that the captain was watching, and she gave him her best intimidating glare when he met her eye. Maintaining constant reminders of her claim on Violet was sometimes almost exhausting, but the boys could not be allowed to forget that Violet was under her protection.

Violet seemed to be managing herself quite well. The girl was smart, Ann had to give her that. She'd learned quickly which of the men it was safe to tease and which to avoid. Most of the crew seemed to like her, or at least tolerate her presence with cool disinterest. And the kid could make a damned good cup of coffee.

Ann suspected that O'Hare was allowing Violet more than the half-rations she'd ordered because her captive was looking healthier and more energized. She still wore the ivory silk dress that the Spanish merchants had given her, though it was now ruined with stains, the train torn off completely and the hem tattered nearly to her knees in places. But they were almost to Tortuga anyway, and Violet could take care of the matter herself once they arrived. Ann had decided to leave her captive in Tortuga before they set sail again. It was an uncharacteristically generous decision, but Ann didn't relish the idea of slitting the young woman's throat. Once left to her own devices in Tortuga, Violet would no longer be Ann's concern.

She was startled by Barclay's voice in her ear and turned to see the burly quartermaster standing at her elbow, looking at her expectantly. "What was that?"

"I said mess is over, Captain," he repeated patiently. "O'Hare wants me to tell you that dinner's waiting in your cabin."

Ann nodded and handed the wheel over to him. "Thank you, Barclay." O'Hare insisted on the tradition of a formal captain's dinner, which meant that most afternoons he prepared an entirely different and much more varied menu for Ann to enjoy in the privacy of her cabin. It was a frivolous custom that Ann didn't think much of, but since someone had to man the wheel during mess she indulged him.

As she descended the deck stairs she passed Violet, who was stacking bowls for washing. She looked up with a breathtaking smile that dimpled her cheeks. "Enjoy your meal, Captain."

Ann paused, then gave a brief nod. As she entered her cabin she sighed. *Christ, and I thought she was trouble before. With a smile like that she's apt to sink my ship before we even reach port. Bad luck, indeed.*

❖

Violet rinsed the brush in the pail for the last time and stood, surveying her handiwork. "Two down, one to go." She preferred saving the main deck for last, as it was usually busiest during the day and the pirates had little patience when she got underfoot. The sun was just beginning to slide below the horizon, eerie twilight giving everything a dreamy, otherworldly look. She refilled the wash bucket leisurely, looking forward to climbing into her little hammock in the hold when she was done with the day's chores.

After spending several uncomfortable nights trying to sleep on top of crates and boxes, Turtle had suggested that she string one of the extra sails from storage between two of the bulkheads. The idea was brilliant, as the makeshift hammock was not only dry, but cradled her against the rocking of the ship. Violet's sleep had improved drastically ever since.

She began with the starboard corner in front of the forecastle, where she could methodically crisscross back and forth to be sure she didn't miss any spots. The only other people abovedecks were Lamont, the scrawny Frenchman with a lazy eye who was taking a turn at the helm, and Maclairen, the ship's gunner, blowing absently into a set of bagpipes from his perch on a portside barrel. The sea was quiet and the breeze steady, so the sails didn't need much tending. The rest of the men were probably lazing about their bunks in the crew's quarters or the galley, playing games of cards and drinking.

The moon had already appeared, brightening as the cerulean sky gradually deepened to gray, and Violet hummed along with the bagpipes as she scrubbed. Maclairen soon switched from improvisational melodies to Scottish folk tunes, some of which Violet was familiar with. She had nearly reached the mainmast when he began to play a song that Violet knew very well, one she'd heard many times as a child.

A-rovin', a-rovin, since rovin's been me ru-i-n
I'll go no more a-rovin' with you, fair maid.

She didn't realize she'd been singing along until she looked up to see Maclairen watching her, his cheeks puffed comically around the mouthpiece of the pipes. He winked, encouraging her to go on. Violet flushed slightly, but couldn't help a grin, and after a slight hesitation she continued.

In Amsterdam there lived a maid
Mark ye well what I say!
In Amsterdam there lived a maid
And she was mistress of her trade
I'll go no more a-rovin' with you, fair maid.

Maclairen tapped his foot and increased the tempo when they reached the chorus again, and Violet was surprised to hear a masculine voice suddenly join her, such a deep bass that the deck vibrated beneath her feet. She turned to meet Mason's eye as he finished the chorus, then stopped uncertainly as if he didn't know the rest. Giving the shy giant a smile, she sang the next verse.

Her dainty arms were white as milk
Mark ye well what I say!
Her dainty arms were white as milk
Her flaxen hair was soft as silk
I'll go no more a-rovin' with you, fair maid.

Several of the other crew members heard the music and emerged from the forecastle, gathering along the gunwale and deck stairs to listen. A few knew the verses, and nearly all of them knew the chorus. O'Hare appeared and took Violet by the hand, tugging her up from her knees and gleefully acting out the lyrics, much to the amusement of the other men. Violet played along, laughing so hard she could barely get the words out.

The song had more than ten additional verses that grew progressively more bawdy, and Violet knew them all. The pirates clapped and stomped, drawing the notes of the chorus out until they ran out of breath, and when it was finally over they clamored for more. Maclairen obediently launched into another popular sea shanty familiar to most of the crew, who now filled all three decks. The sky was black now, but the moon shone bright enough to light their revelry. Violet gave up the idea of finishing her deck cleaning. The pirates wouldn't hear of it, begging her to sing for them, delighted with her seemingly endless repertoire.

Someone started passing around mugs of rum and whiskey, and the songs turned into drinking games in which Violet proved the champion. The amount of strong liquor she could down without apparent difficulty gave the pirates no end of entertainment, and she drank until she was quite tipsy. Several of the men demanded she dance with them, and finding that the tattered silk of her long petticoat was in the way, Violet tore it off completely. The overskirt attached to the bodice still draped halfway down her thighs in front and to the knees in back, but her legs were left encased only by long white underdrawers. The crew hooted with approval and Violet was swept into the dancing.

❖

The noise interrupted Ann's concentration as she bent over the maps spread on the table in her cabin. There were feet pounding directly overhead, and with irritation she threw open the cabin door to demand some quiet in which to work. But when she glimpsed the source of the commotion, the reprimand died on her lips.

Violet was singing, her unusually deep tones a sweet music all on their own, supported by Maclairen's bagpipes and a few wooden flutes. She stood on a barrel planted at the base of the mainmast, surrounded by the crew, who were stamping and cheering as she led them in some lascivious drinking song Ann didn't know very well. Unobtrusively Ann moved past the men reclining along the deck stairs and picked her way along the gunwale until she found a spot where she could watch without being noticed.

The men had been drinking, and from the looks of things Violet had as well. Two brilliant points of color had risen in the girl's cheeks, her eyes shining a little too brightly. She'd apparently discarded the silk petticoat of her gown, and in the middle of a particularly vulgar verse Violet climbed into the nearest pirate's lap with a shocking whoop that was answered enthusiastically from all sides.

Ann chewed on her bottom lip, vacillating between amusement and annoyance. The crew was enjoying themselves, and she didn't begrudge them that. They worked hard, and their vocation was a dangerous one, with entertainments few and far between. She didn't even mind the blatant disregard for their rum rations. They were nearly at port, and it was unlikely they'd run out of spirits before they arrived. But the alcohol was already beginning to strip away common sense. Many of the men were already leering rashly at Violet, and by the end of the night most would be too far gone to remember Ann's claim on her.

When the song ended Ann stood and held up her hands, catching Maclairen's eye before he could begin playing again. "Well, my hearties, I hate to break up such a fine party, but we all have work tomorrow, and you know Barclay won't be cutting slack to any man foolish enough to drink himself sick during the night. I'm sure our dear Sister Violet doesn't want to scrub your filthy retching from the decks in the morning." Some of them booed good-naturedly. Ann took Violet's arm. "And just to keep anyone from getting any bright ideas, the lady will be spending the night with me. Savvy?" She ignored the responses, most of which were obscene, as she escorted Violet through the knot of men and into her cabin and closed the door firmly behind them.

She turned to face Violet with an uplifted eyebrow. "You just had to go and get them all riled up, eh? Where does a good Christian girl learn such dirty songs?"

"I'm not staying here," Violet insisted unsteadily, trying to reach past Ann to the door. Ann caught her by the wrists and chuckled.

"Oh yes, you are. You're in no shape to be out there alone with them."

Violet wrenched herself free from Ann's grip and straightened. "I'm not as drunk as you think I am, Captain."

"It's not *your* drinking that concerns me." Ann went to the table and folded the maps she'd been working with. "Some of the boys get a little careless with their bellies full of rum. They might just forget you're in my custody and do something we'll all regret later. Best to keep you out of their way altogether until they've slept it off." She looked up to see Violet glaring at her.

"You don't own me, Captain Ann."

"Where the men are concerned, I do, and that's what matters. After all, you left me little choice, didn't you?" When her captive furrowed her brow Ann sighed. She went to the wall and pointed at a piece of paper hanging behind a glass frame. "These are the ship's

Articles. Every man must sign this agreement before he's allowed to set foot on board, and anyone who breaks one of these rules suffers the consequences of his disobedience. Read it."

Violet stepped forward and squinted at the paper, slurring a little over the words. "Every man shall obey civil command. The Captain shall have one full share and a half in all prizes. The Master…"

"Yes, yes, skip down to here by my finger." Ann jabbed at a spot about halfway down.

"If at any time you meet with a prudent woman, that man that offers to meddle with her without her consent shall suffer present death." Violet furrowed her brow. "So that means…"

"It means that if you'd just kept your mouth shut and your," her gaze flickered to Violet's exposed bosom, "*goods* covered, the Articles would have protected you." Ann swiped the handkerchief from her hair, wavy strands immediately springing into her face. "But you just had to go dangle yourself out there like a tavern strumpet. Now I'm the only thing standing between those men out there and your virtue, Sister Violet." Deliberately Ann ignored the internal voice reminding her that she was the one who had goaded the poor girl into desperation. Eyeing her again, Ann pursed her lips and moved to a chest against the starboard wall. She dug through it and pulled out one of her own shirts, tossing it in Violet's direction. "Put that on. You can't walk around the ship dressed like that. You might as well wave a juicy cut of beef in front of a pack of sharks."

Violet bent slowly and picked up the shirt, turning it in her hands as if she wasn't sure what to do with it. Ann rolled her eyes. "Come on, then, let's get you changed." Violet took a step backward as Ann approached.

"I can do it myself."

"Bloody fine by me," Ann said testily. But Violet made no move to undress, and Ann cocked an eyebrow. "Well?"

"Will you…will you leave me for a minute?"

Ann snorted. Violet's expression turned pleading, causing a twinge in the pit of her stomach, and she did something she had never in her life done for a prisoner. She gave in. "I'll turn my back. You have one minute." She felt silly even as the words came out of her mouth. She didn't owe Violet any favors, and was mildly perturbed at the strange power her little captive seemed to hold over her, undoing her confidence with the merest bat of an eyelash. But Ann kept her word and turned around, tapping her toe impatiently as fabric rustled behind her back.

"Done."

Ann turned back around. The shirt was far too big for Violet, falling far below her hands and almost to her knees. Ann picked up the tattered ivory silk from the floor. "At least it covers you better than this thing." Tossing it on the table, she dropped into a chair to remove her boots and jerked her head in the direction of her bunk. It was wide, probably designed so the brigantine's original captain could enjoy a bedfellow if he desired, and there would be plenty of room for both women. "Go on, lie down. I'll be there in a moment." Violet didn't move, and Ann took off the other boot before looking up with exasperation. "What now?"

"I don't want to."

"You don't want to what?" She watched Violet's gaze move uncertainly from the bed back to her. "Oh, bloody hell. I already told you, I never force myself on a woman. Especially not a servant of the almighty Lord." She pretended to cross herself with an exaggerated flourish.

"Is it true, then?"

"Is what true?"

"Your scar." Violet reached out to touch the brand on Ann's face. "They say God punished you, for…"

Ann caught Violet's wrist. "I've heard the stories. And I don't like repeating myself. Savvy?" Violet winced, and Ann realized she was gripping her so hard her own hand shook. She shoved Violet away and stood, yanking sharply at the knot in her sash to take the edge off her rising temper. She knew which rumor Violet was referring to, and it was the only one that truly irked her. While she didn't mind the numerous other barbaric acts attributed to her name, the very idea that she would rape anyone, nun or otherwise, made her sick. She gave a little growl as the knot finally came free.

"I'm sorry," Violet said softly. Ann looked up, surprised by the genuine contrition in her words. She was even more surprised at how effectively it defused her anger. "People have said some nasty things about me, too. I should know better than to believe everything I hear."

Ann grunted and unwound the scarlet sash from her waist, unsettled by how accurately Violet had interpreted her change of mood. She tossed the sash on the table with Violet's ruined dress, then held her hands up in a gesture of mock surrender. "Look, you have my word as a gentleman, I will keep my hands to myself."

Those words brought a faint smile to Violet's lips, and Ann couldn't resist a bit of teasing. She fingered the top button of her trousers with a wicked grin. "Usually I sleep naked," she said mischievously. It was only partly a lie. Of course she never slept nude during a voyage; there was far too great a risk that she might be called upon at any hour of the night. However, it was a luxury she occasionally allowed herself when on land. Ann grinned as she caught the alarm in Violet's expression, and pretended to seriously contemplate before saying, "But if it makes you feel better, I'll keep the trousers and shirt tonight."

Ann laughed at Violet's emphatic nod, and held out her hands in invitation. Violet did not take them, but she did turn and climb willingly onto the bunk, scooting as far to the opposite side of the wide mattress as she could get. Ann followed, reaching up to extinguish the oil lamp hanging from a hook over their heads. "Sweet dreams, Sister Violet."

CHAPTER SIX

The port at Tortuga was just as Ann remembered it, an exciting, chaotic scramble of money and liquor and sex. Unlike the rest of her crew, Ann did not look forward to these periodic stops on dry land, necessary though they were. Even the promise of a few nights' pleasure in the arms of some busty tavern girl was scarcely enough to make it worthwhile. She felt strangely heavy when she was on land, a sensation almost amounting to claustrophobia. Beneath her feet the solid ground felt uncomfortably still, and she much preferred the gentle, unpredictable sway of a ship's deck.

The *Ice Queen* would need to be careened while they were in port, which meant an extended stay while the ship was dry-docked so the barnacles could be scraped from her hull. In the meantime Ann had business of her own to attend to. She had to report to Governor D'Ogeron to fulfill the terms of their privateering license. Then there would be the matter of finding a sailing master to read Black Dog's map and reassembling the crew for a new voyage. She had plenty to keep her busy, but the delay grated on her nerves.

Several enthusiastic hoots from the main deck brought a smile to her lips. The crew was in high spirits, as well they should be. Their expedition had been a highly profitable one. Every man would receive a small fortune as his share of the prizes. Ann knew from experience that their newfound wealth would be short-lived. Most of them would probably manage to spend or gamble away every last piece of eight before they even reboarded. The indulgence that ran rampant through the privateering trade never ceased to astound her.

"Your coffee, Captain Ann."

Ann turned to see Violet holding out a mug of the steaming dark liquid. She took the mug and lifted it to her lips. As Violet turned to go, Ann sighed. She had been avoiding this moment for over a week, but now it seemed best to just get it over with. "Sister Violet, a word."

"Captain?"

Ann sipped at her coffee. "I suppose now is as good a time as any to tell you. Today is your lucky day, my pet. I have decided to set you free." At Violet's look of surprise, Ann deliberately hardened her voice. "On one condition. I don't want it going around that Branded Ann is getting soft. Bad for business. So you're not going to tell anyone you were ever on this ship, understand?"

Violet was quiet, and Ann found herself mildly annoyed. She had been expecting a bit more gratitude, or at the very least relief. Violet couldn't possibly understand what a risk she was taking by simply letting her go. If word got out, it could do great damage to Ann's most important piece of armor—her reputation.

At last Violet replied, "I understand, Captain. I…" She bit back whatever it was on her tongue and instead said simply, "Thank you."

Ann watched Violet's gaze flicker to the dock, where rough seamen strode the wooden planks hauling cargo between ships and catcalled to the scantily clad women draped along the rails between unused buoys and storage barrels. Somewhere in the distance men were shouting, followed by several pistol shots. She recognized apprehension in the other woman's face. No doubt Violet was afraid for her safety in Tortuga, and she had good reason to be.

Ann felt a pinch of guilt that she stubbornly decided to ignore. What did it matter to her what happened to Violet once she was off her ship? Ann had already been more lenient with Violet than with any other prisoner that she could remember. She'd even gone so far as to share her bunk with her captive every night since the drunken deck party. *For the girl's own protection*, she reminded herself firmly, though she couldn't explain why she was so interested in protecting Violet in the first place. Ann blamed it on her overactive sex drive. It was just another reason to get Violet off her ship, and soon. As a rule she did not mix business with pleasure, and she couldn't afford such frivolous distractions.

"They're setting up the gangplank now," Ann said gruffly, "and the men will be disembarking as soon as Barclay finishes distributing the shares. I'd suggest you leave before they do if you don't want to be trampled in their mad dash for town."

"Aye, Captain."

Ann supposed she ought to say some sort of good-bye, but it was not as if they were friends parting after a pleasant afternoon tea. She was held breathlessly for several moments by the liquid heaven of the other woman's gaze, until heat began to simmer in her thighs and stomach and she found herself wishing she could change her mind and forbid Violet to leave after all. But that was foolishness. She cleared her throat and looked away. "Don't forget to take that book of yours with you. And you can keep the clothes."

Violet looked down at the borrowed shirt and trousers she was wearing, both from Ann's wardrobe, and nodded. "Thank you." After more awkward silence, she gave Ann another little nod and descended the deck stairs. Ann turned her back so she wouldn't see her walk away.

"Good riddance," she muttered, and strode to the bow where Barclay sat hunched over a barrel, crates and bags stacked neatly around him. He was scribbling something in one of the ship's ledgers, and when her shadow fell across the page he looked up.

"Almost done, Captain. The boys'll be mighty pleased. Each man's getting near six hundred pieces of eight in pay." He picked up a sack of coins by his feet and held it out to her. "This is for you."

Ann lifted an eyebrow. "Barclay, you know perfectly well that's not mine."

"Aw, Captain, don't be like that," Barclay protested. "After a haul like this there's not a man aboard that'd begrudge you your share."

Ann bit the inside of her lip to keep herself from smiling. He knew the Articles as well as she did, and while she appreciated the gesture, she wouldn't break her own rules. "I claimed captain's privilege," she reminded him sternly. "I gave up my share in the prizes."

"But..." His eyes traveled to the gangplank, and Ann looked to see Violet step carefully onto the Tortuga dock. Violet looked nervously from side to side as people bustled around her, and she clutched the Bible in her arms tightly. Barclay grunted. "She weren't much of a claim, Captain. We did so well, the boys won't care if—"

"No, Barclay." Ann pushed the sack of money away. "Take that back and distribute it among the men. They earned it." She didn't want to turn back around, didn't want to watch Violet walking away, and so she bent and pretended to inspect his ledger for several moments. "You will see to it that the *Ice Queen* is careened and stocked for our next voyage?"

"Aye, Captain, just like I always do."

She straightened and ran a hand through her hair. "Divvy up the goods and get these men off my ship before they wear holes in the deck with their excitement. I'll meet you in two weeks at the Virgin to draw up new Articles. And take good care of my ship, Barclay. This is going to be her greatest adventure yet."

Barclay nodded. "Aye, Captain."

Ann returned to her cabin, resisting the temptation to glance back at the dock. She closed the cabin door behind her and went to the cabinet against the wall, retrieving her little box and unlocking it. "I don't care about the money. This is the real treasure," she whispered, pulling the two folded maps from the box and spreading them on the table. She traced the lines on the yellowed parchment with her fingertips, and felt a lump rising in her throat. "I'm close, Papa. After all these years, I'm finally so close..."

She reached into the box and pulled out a thick gold ring. It was formed into the shape of a grinning skull, with two small rubies set in the eye sockets. Her father had always worn it on his little finger, but it was big enough to fit on her middle one, and she slid it on with reverence, watching the blood-colored rubies reflecting the lamplight. He'd given it to her as they were leading him away for the last time— along with the map that had become her sole reason for breathing in the grief-stricken months and years that followed. Slowly she brought her fist to her lips. *I'll find it, Papa. I promise.* She smiled when an excited whooping and stamping began overhead. Barclay was passing out the loot.

Ann returned the ring and maps to the box and relocked it. Her father's legacy had waited for eighteen years; it could wait just a little longer. She went to the Articles hanging on the wall, and opened the glass to remove the sheet of paper that bore the signature of every member of the crew. Behind it was the *Ice Queen*'s Letter of Marque, the license issued by the French government of Tortuga that allowed her ship to carry out acts of piracy against any Spanish ship in the Caribbean. Now that their expedition was complete, she would return the letter to Governor D'Ogeron with the government's agreed share in their prizes. Ann would not be accepting another such license. The coming venture would be an independent one, and the profits shared only among her crew.

She tucked the Letter of Marque into her sash and opened a drawer beneath the cabinet. There she laid the Articles on top of a stack of those from previous voyages. Ann drew up a fresh set with each new venture, to ensure that every man fully understood the way her ship would be run before they even stepped aboard. She stood and picked up the box from the table, carrying it to her bunk. It would be several more minutes before the men had finished collecting their shares and dispersed. Ann was always the last one to disembark. She wanted to avoid setting foot on land for as long as possible. Lying back against the pillow of her bunk, she stretched one leg out along the mattress and tucked an arm behind her head.

Her nose twitched at the warm, heady scent that permeated the quilt beneath her. Violet. How ironic that devoutly pious Violet was the first woman to ever share Ann's bed for more than one or two nights in a row. True to her word, Ann had kept her hands to herself, though Violet proved more of a temptation than Ann had anticipated. More than once Ann had awakened in the middle of the night, startled by a warm weight pressed up against her back and soft breathing in her ear. Evidently, in sleep Violet would sometimes mistake Ann for her husband, cuddling along the length of Ann's body and in the process managing to ignite a dangerous desire in her blood. Ann quickly learned that if she did not immediately change their positions and nudge Violet to the other side of the bed, she would find herself engaged in a long, uncomfortable battle with her own libido. Ann gave a soft snort. *It's just as well she's gone.* But the memory of Violet in her bed, lush curves just scarcely covered by one of Ann's shirts, little heart-shaped lips relaxed in sleep, was enough to renew the familiar pulsing low in her abdomen. Ann grinned. *Maybe spending some time in port isn't such a bad idea after all.*

❖

Violet had heard stories of Tortuga, the Caribbean paradise of pirates. Isaac used to regale her with tales of the island's exotic allure, a place where thieves and scoundrels could carouse and carry on their wickedness in broad daylight with little fear of sanction. The local French government openly supported piracy of Spanish and occasionally English merchant ships, and any buccaneer who accepted a commission from Tortuga's governor could count on finding a safe harbor on the island between raids.

But what was she to do, alone in such a place, without money or a proper escort? The only thing she could think of was to try to locate a chapel or mission and beg for refuge. Surely there had to be at least one house of God, even in such a depraved place. Violet didn't dare ask for directions. The port was teeming with pirates like the ones on Branded Ann's ship, only these men did not answer to Ann. She kept her head down as she wound her way from the dock to the streets of the town—if it could even be properly called a town.

Tortuga reminded her of the back streets of London, wild and filthy and humming with sin, but punctuated strangely by the occasional palm tree and the scent of hibiscus. Men stumbled about in drunken stupors in spite of the fact that it was scarcely midmorning, and on one street alone she watched at least three fistfights break out, all of which ended with an inevitable pistol shot or cutlass swipe that dropped one of the combatants in the dirt. The only other women Violet could find were gap-toothed, frizzy-haired whores, their skirts tucked rakishly into their waistbands and their breasts dangling freely beneath loose chemises. Every gambling house and tavern seemed to have an array of women who hung from the balconies and called to the men below. Violet's heart sank forebodingly at the sight of them.

After wandering the twisted streets into the late afternoon, Violet knew she would never find the chapel, if there even was one, without help. She decided it would be far safer to ask one of the street whores than risk drawing the attention of a pirate. One woman, straddling a barrel in front of a bordello, caught Violet's eye. She had a bottle of liquor in one hand and seemed far more interested in drinking than in the men who were passing in and out of the brothel. Violet gathered up her courage and approached.

"Excuse me, miss?"

The prostitute turned bleary eyes on Violet. When they fell on the Bible in Violet's arms, she gave a croaking laugh. "I already tell you pious bitches," she said in a heavy French accent, "I have no care for your books and prayers. Leave me alone."

Hope sprang in Violet's heart and she reached out to take the other woman's sleeve. "Then there is a chapel here in Tortuga after all. Please, can you tell me how I can get there?"

The woman wrenched her arm from Violet's grasp and took another swig from the bottle in her hand. She regarded Violet curiously, for the first time taking in her odd attire, the borrowed trousers and loose linen shirt several sizes too large for her slight frame. "You is a strange one, no?"

"Please, miss." Violet could not keep the desperation from her voice. "Please, I must find the chapel as soon as possible. Before it gets dark."

With a hearty laugh the prostitute hiked her skirt up around one thigh and scratched at an itch. "With a pretty face like that you *should* be afraid of the dark. You won't even last the night." She lowered her skirt and leaned forward, peering closely at Violet's face. The whiskey on her breath assailed Violet's nostrils, and Violet did her best not to wrinkle her nose in disgust. "Can you sing? Dance, maybe? Monsieur Girard, he always looking for new girls." She jerked her thumb in the direction of the brothel's entrance. "Is much safer than working the street on your own."

Violet shuddered. "Thank you, but no." She hugged her Bible even closer to her chest. "I must find—"

"The chapel, yes, I know where it is. It will be of no use to you. Men are all the same, *chérie*. All the same." But when Violet remained insistent, she sighed and waved the whiskey bottle in the direction of the street. "Very well. Down this street, turn left at the Blue Fish on the corner, go three streets up, right at the changing house, and the chapel is after the graveyard."

Violet beamed at her. "Thank you, oh thank you so very much." *Thank you, Father.*

The woman looked at her with an expression that could almost be described as pity. "If you do not find what you are looking for," she said drunkenly, "you come back, no? Ask for Colette."

Violet nodded. "Thank you," she repeated, and then headed off in the direction the Frenchwoman had indicated. She kept to the side of the road, near the buildings, and tried to remain inconspicuous as she followed Colette's instructions, turning at the Blue Fish tavern and then again at the money-changing hut. It felt as though she were sneaking along the dirt streets rather than walking. She sought out the busiest carts to follow, tried to disappear on the fringes of a knot of sailors. Years of experience had taught her how to avoid unwanted attention, and she carefully kept her attention on the ground and her pace steady. Most passersby were too wrapped up in their own business to pay her much mind, but still it felt as though her heart was beating its way out of her chest. It would only take the notice of one man, a split second that someone took interest in her, and Violet knew she would not be shown the same miraculous mercy she had received on the *Ice Queen*. As she passed the cemetery and finally glimpsed the chapel, she drew a breath of relief. The sky was beginning to darken already, and she hurried eagerly toward the small whitewashed building.

The door was open, and she stepped inside to find a small sanctuary filled with a few rough-hewn benches arranged in front of a small altar. A crucifix, complete with a gaunt, nearly nude carving of Jesus Christ, hung on the back wall above the altar. The chapel appeared to be empty, but Violet did not care. She sank to her knees as tears spilled down her cheeks. She had survived the sea, the pirates, the infamous Branded Ann, the streets of Tortuga. It was over, and she was safe. Here in the arms of her Lord no one could hurt her. "Oh, Heavenly Father, I praise thy name. I praise thy mercy and compassion, thy very great love. Thou hast delivered me from the hands of mine enemies…"

She didn't know how long she knelt there murmuring prayers of gratitude, but when she heard voices approaching she quickly stood and turned. Her heart leapt when she saw a priest making his way toward the chapel door, his long black frock coat with its distinctive white collar an unmistakable and most welcome sight. Everything was going to be all right now.

❖

Ann leaned back against the tavern wall, her expression a careful mask of nonchalance. "Well?" Her tone betrayed none of the excitement that gripped her as she watched the wizened man bent over the map on the table. Just one map, of course. The other was safely tucked into an inner pocket of her vest, pressed closely against her heart. Her companion rubbed his chin and shook his head for what must have been the hundredth time, then looked up at her wide-eyed.

"You must be a damned fool."

Ann gave a harsh laugh. "Watch your tongue, Yestin, or I may just relieve you of it."

The little sailing master did look properly intimidated, but even so he dared a incredulous grunt. "This ain't no pleasure cruise you're looking at, Captain. Can't you see this here route takes you right smack-dab to the heart of the Devil's Triangle? You'd have to be mad to take your ship in there. Most what sail the Devil's seas never return to tell of it. They say there's storms to rouse the dead to life, and places of such calm that the sea's like glass and the sun bakes a man's brain right in his skull. There's rocks and islands what appear out of nowhere and vanish again. Entire ships disappear out there, just," he gestured with his hands, opening the fingers suddenly and making a puffing noise with his lips, "stop being there altogether."

Ann took a sip of rum and grinned. "Sounds like fun."

"It's a bleeding death trap." He pushed the map back across the table toward her. "Sorry, Captain Ann, but no man in his right mind would take on such a patch of sea as that."

"Yestin." Ann laid a hand on the map and leaned forward. "We're not talking about a few measly merchant galleons. This is Black Dog's treasure. The greatest fortune ever amassed at sea, twenty years of booty collected by the most daring pirate who ever sailed the Spanish Main. Just one man's share of such a treasure would serve up more coin than the mother-swiving King of bloody England has in all his coffers."

Yestin licked his lips. "But, Captain, that treasure's only a myth."

"It's not a myth!" Ann snapped, then lowered her voice again when a few from neighboring tables cast curious glances in their direction. "Black Dog's treasure exists, and so does his island. This map is going to take us there, but I need a good sailing master to get us through. Damn your eyes, Yestin, you're the best I know."

"I won't do it, Captain Ann. If you're wrong and it ain't real, we'd be taking on the Devil's Seas for nothing. And if you're right—" He cleared his throat nervously. "I've heard the stories, same as every other man. They say that gold's protected by the powers of hell, and any man what goes looking for it has to answer to some mighty angry spirits. And I'd rather let you gut 'n skin me than take me chances in the hands of the Devil himself." Ann toyed with the hilt of the knife in her belt, as if tempted to take the man up on his declaration. He watched her fingers and gulped. "But I might know a man who could help," he offered quickly. "He's the only man I hear who's sailed in and out of the Triangle in one piece more than once."

Ann stilled her hand on the knife hilt. "I'm listening."

"Name's Carter. Ashford Carter. Craziest god-forsaken whoreson I've ever met, and in this trade that's saying something. But he's a fine hand at sailing. Better than me, even. He likes his adventure, he does, and the more so when it's a likely death. I'm betting just a mention of the haunted treasure, and he'll be begging to go along."

Ann knew Yestin for a coward, but he was admittedly a good judge of seamen. "Where can I find him?"

"Port Royal. He's taken up with a trollop there. Though…I hear he swore off the sweet trade after his last time out."

"Well, I'll just have to change his mind." She observed Yestin draw a breath of relief and reached out to refold the map, tucking it back into her vest pocket. "I don't suppose I have to tell you what will happen if I hear you've been running your mouth about this venture of mine." She drew the dirk from her belt and used the tip to clean beneath her fingernails.

Yestin's nod was so quick Ann half expected him to shake his head from his neck. "God's truth, Captain Ann, I swear I won't be telling no one."

"Let's hope you don't." Ann stood, sheathing the dirk smoothly, and finished the mug of rum on the table in two swallows. She grimaced. Business must be slow for the tavern. The rum was watered down almost as much as what she rationed to her men at sea. She gripped Yestin's shoulder lightly, a gesture meant as a friendly warning. "We've seen a lot of water and blood together, Master Yestin. I'd hate to have to put a sorry end to such a long-standing friendship, savvy?"

She waited for him to nod again before turning, the hem of her dark cloak billowing around her legs. As she strode to the tavern's exit, a commotion at a nearby table caught her eye. It was nothing particularly unusual, several drunken ruffians gathered around mugs of liquor, but one of them leapt onto the tabletop with a large book in his hand, and Ann paused.

The man opened the book and raised one finger in the air. It was doubtful that he could read the contents; most pirates were completely illiterate. But he lifted his voice comically, obviously imitating a woman, and pretended to quote words from the page. Ann didn't pay any attention to what he was saying. All her focus was on the book in his hands.

In three steps she had crossed the tavern floor and snatched the book away, amid protests from his friends. She looked at each one in turn until they had all received a clear glimpse of the brand marring her cheek, and their protests died away, replaced with furtive whispers of her name. Ann inspected the heavy, leather-bound volume, and recognized it easily as Violet's Bible. She glowered at the man standing on the table.

"Where did you get this?" she demanded quietly.

"Ain't none of your business," he retorted, his bravado obviously heightened by the drink in his belly. "I ain't feared of you, branded bitch."

Faster than a pistol shot, Ann yanked the man from the table by his belt, then pulled the knife from her sash. In his intoxicated state, he hit the straw-covered floor hard, unable to maintain his balance. A well-placed kick rolled him onto his back, and Ann's booted foot was suddenly crushing against his larynx. His mates rose to help him, and with quick, expert strokes she slit the throat of one and cut an ear off another. Blood spattered the faces of the remaining two, who quickly stepped back a respectful distance. The one whose ear she'd removed crumpled to the ground beside his dead friend with a scream, holding his hand to the side of his head.

Ann glared around the tavern to see if anyone else would decide to challenge her. She was one-handed, the book held in one arm and the blood-covered blade in the other, but even so she was confident she could handle any of the half-drunk patrons. Her reputation, however, was again her greatest weapon. Once most of them had gotten a good look at the cross imprinted on her cheek, mutters spread like a wildfire through the room. Tension buzzed thick in the air, taut as a violinist's bow, as the younger and more headstrong debated the wisdom of taking on the legendary Branded Ann in a bar fight. To defeat someone of her reputation would be a great coup, but only if one could actually survive the encounter. After several long seconds it seemed that none were inclined to take the risk, and so she turned her attention to the man beneath her boot.

"I didn't ask if you were afraid of me, you scurvy grog-sucking son of a swineherd." She held up the book. "I asked where you got this."

He made a frantic choking sound, and she eased the pressure of her foot just enough to allow him to speak. "Fou...found it," he managed to gasp, and Ann frowned.

"Where?"

"The graveyard," came the wheezing reply.

"You lie." Violet would never leave her precious holy book lying about. Someone would have had to pry it out of Violet's dead fingers, and the thought made her blood run cold. She dropped to one knee beside the inebriated man, and deliberately let her knife point trail over the crotch of his trousers. "I have no patience for liars."

The man whimpered. "I swear on me sweet mother's life I did. Found it under a tree by a headstone. I'll show ya, if ya want..." He was shaking now, his voice hoarse from the abuse to his vocal cords.

What the hell are you doing, Ann? her common sense questioned, permeating the rage flooding her vision. *You're bloody well ready to geld the man, and for what? The wench isn't your concern any longer.* Ann drew a shaky breath and stood, the Bible disappearing beneath the folds of her cloak. "If I find your word false, you can expect to see me again." The relief in the air was nearly palpable as she turned and made her way purposefully to the door.

Stepping out into the street, Ann wiped the blade of her knife on her trouser leg and jammed it back into her sash. She was bothered by how quickly the sight of Violet's book had aroused her fury. She was even more bothered by the thought that some harm had come to the pretty widow. *What did you expect? You turned her loose into the center of Sin City itself. Surely you didn't think such a fine little prize would go unnoticed.*

She pulled the Bible from beneath her cloak, looking it over in the moonlight. There were dark stains on the lower corner that had seeped through several pages. *Blood.* And it wasn't fresh, so it couldn't have belonged to the men in the tavern. Somewhere in Tortuga, Violet was hurt. Or worse. Suddenly Ann's legs trembled with the urge to charge off to the cemetery and see for herself. That impulse frightened her more than anything else. Since when did a bit of woman-flesh hold such power over her?

Ann clenched her jaw so tight that her teeth hurt. The best thing to do would be to just drop the Bible right there in the dirt and walk away, to put the whole thing from her mind and never think on it again. But try as she might, she couldn't bring herself to let go of the book. She pulled it close to her chest again, beneath the wool of her cloak, and forced her feet in the opposite direction, toward the shabby inn where she'd secured a room for the stay in port. Perhaps she would seek out a companion for her bed for the night, someone to warm the sudden chill that had settled in her bones.

❖

It took every ounce of Violet's remaining energy to slap her palm against the dilapidated kitchen door. She was afraid no one would answer. They were coming for her, she could hear their boots pounding the earth, their gleeful taunting whoops. "Please, oh please," Violet sobbed under her breath, thumping the door with all the strength her spent muscles had left.

They were getting closer. In a moment they would be on her again, and she knew she wouldn't be able to fight them off this time. She pressed her forehead against the door as salty tears stung the cuts on her cheeks. *"Not my will, but thine be done. Not my will, but thine be done. Not my will…"*

The door opened so abruptly that she was pitched headfirst into waiting arms. She looked up into garishly painted features, scarlet lips and brilliantly rouged cheeks, shocked gray eyes lined in thick black pencil. "Colette," Violet managed to croak. "She said I could…"

The woman's attention moved to the open door as shouts echoed through the back street. Violet was pulled inside, the door closing quickly behind her. Footsteps approached, combined with irritated yelling, and Violet held her breath. There was a scuffling noise, and then her pursuers continued down the street.

"Oh, thank God." Violet's body had long since reached its limit and could no longer support her weight. She collapsed into the arms of her rescuer, who cursed in French and called out for some assistance. Someone helped her into a chair, and she looked up to see a familiar face, also brightly painted, staring with horrified sympathy.

"Ah, *ma chérie*, what has become of you?" A cold, wet rag touched her cheek, gentle against the bruised flesh as it wiped away tears and blood. "Easy, *chérie*. Easy. Colette will take care of you."

"The priest," Violet choked. "He's no man of God. He…"

"Ah, I try to tell you, no? Men all the same. But hush now, *chérie*. We clean you up, then you meet Monsieur Girard. He will like you for sure. Give you a good job here."

Violet could not keep the sobs from racking her shoulders as the prostitute continued her well-meaning attentions, clucking her tongue comfortingly and murmuring on in French. But Colette didn't understand. Violet wasn't crying from the pain of her brutalized body or terror at so narrowly avoiding death. She wasn't even crying at the priest's unexpected depravity. Violet cried because she'd come so far. She'd struggled so hard to escape her past, but in the end it didn't matter. Her life had finally come full circle, and she cried because she didn't have the courage to choose death over the alternative. The prodigal whore had returned home.

"Good to see you, Barclay." Ann slid onto the bench next to the burly quartermaster and waved at one of the serving girls. She took two mugs from the girl's tray, then produced a gold coin from her sleeve and tucked it between the ample breasts that hovered conveniently at eye level. "*Merci*, pretty Louisa." The girl giggled, exposing a mouth with several missing teeth, and winked before she sauntered off.

Ann plunked one of the mugs in front of her first mate and took a long draught from the other. Barclay watched her with a grin. "Enjoying your stay on land, Captain?"

Ann snorted and wiped her lips with the back of her hand. "I suppose. But no matter how fine the comforts," she eyed the wench's retreating backside, "I'll be glad to get back on my ship with the waves beneath me and the horizon a distant memory."

He chuckled and lifted his mug. "I'll drink to that."

Ann matched his toast and took several more swallows. The liquor was a pleasant burn down her throat, even if it was a little coarse. "So how is our fair *Queen*?"

"More lovely than ever," Barclay said. "After two weeks of pampering she's squeaky clean bottom to top, with a fresh coat of paint, and ready for another tumble in the sea whenever we are."

Ann nodded. "She won't have to wait much longer."

"You've found us a sailing master, then?"

"In a manner of speaking. The first man I had in mind refused to sign aboard."

"Yestin? Let me guess. He turned yellow on us and started blabbering nonsense about spirits and curses and the powers of darkness."

Ann snorted. "He always was a damned superstitious fool. But he did point me in the direction of another man he says is better for the job. Ashford Carter." At Barclay's grunt of approval, she asked, "You've heard of him?"

"Sailed with him once. Yestin's right, Carter's a far better navigator than he is, and we won't have to worry about any absurd ghost stories scaring him off."

"We'll have to make a stop at Port Royal to bring him aboard, but I think the extra trip will be worth it." Ann looked up as a man stepped into the center of an elevated stage and clapped his hands for silence. With an elbow she nudged Barclay. "See, now this is why the Gilded Virgin's my favorite meeting spot on this godforsaken island. Always a good show."

As quiet fell over the room the man onstage lifted his arms. "The Virgin is happy to present something to please the eyes and warm the blood," he announced in a thick accent, and there were cheers from all sides. "Do not forget, if you see something you like, you just let us know, yes?" He gestured to a musician in the corner, who immediately struck up a lively tune on his fiddle. A line of whores tittered their way onto the stage. Their faces were heavily rouged and powdered, skirts hiked nearly to their waists exposing stockings and garter belts. With a chorus of high-pitched exclamations, they kicked their legs into the air.

It was a crude performance, obviously more intended to drum up business for the brothel than to provide quality entertainment, but their audience was so oversexed and drunk that it didn't matter. Ann sipped slowly at the spirits in front of her and watched appreciatively as the dancers jiggled to the fiddle's cheery melody, their breasts bouncing scandalously beneath chemises that were barely there.

Barclay passed a hand in front of her face. "Captain, we've got business to tend to," he reminded her. "You can sate your other appetites later."

She smirked at him, but moved her mug aside so he could lay a piece of paper out in front of them. "Let's get to it, then."

Ann had taught Barclay the rudiments of reading and writing, enough so he could keep the ship's logs and ledgers if it ever became necessary. Together they bent over the paper, and Ann wrote out a new set of Articles for the upcoming voyage. Most of the provisions were standard and she'd written them so many times she could probably recite them in her sleep, though Barclay would occasionally toss in a suggestion unique to the particular venture they were about to undertake. Ann scribbled his additions in wherever they seemed appropriate.

If at any time you meet with a prudent woman... Ann's fingers stilled against the paper as thoughts of Violet consumed her. She'd managed, fairly successfully, to keep the girl from her mind for the past week. Though it was almost certain that Violet was dead, Ann would not visit the graveyard to find out, determined that she must no longer be involved. Yet at the same time, she could not bring herself to throw the Bible away. For now, the heavy book was safely stored away out of sight at the bottom of her trunk, and she'd had a steady stream of bedmates to distract her from it. But with each passing night those indigo eyes haunted her dreams, and even now she could still hear that low, musical voice singing in her memory. "Captain. Captain Ann, look." Barclay smacked her arm lightly with the back of his hand to get her attention, then pointed at the stage. "Ain't that—?"

Ann's heart skipped a beat as she realized that the sound she was hearing was not just in her imagination. A new group of girls had taken the stage, dressed in ridiculous feathered masks and underbust corsets, leading the audience in a rowdy drinking song. One voice carried above the others, pure and deep, and Ann's attention fastened uncontrollably on the source of that sound.

"Violet."

CHAPTER SEVEN

Ann could scarcely believe her eyes. Even with her face half-obscured by an enormous, faded mask of multicolored turkey feathers, Violet's delicate features and distinctive heart-shaped lips were unmistakable. She was dancing third from the left in a line of about nine girls, matching their brazen flashes of thigh and buttocks. Her hair was stringy and limp, most of it pulled into a loose bun. A waist cincher gave definition to the sweet curves of her breasts and hips. Amid the other gap-toothed, pox-marked whores, Violet's natural beauty stood out like a shore beacon on a moonless night.

Louisa, one of Ann's favorite Gilded Virgin girls, was serving a table nearby. Ann lifted a hand to catch the wench's attention, and Louisa bustled over to her.

"What I can do for you, Captain Ann?" she asked coquettishly, and leaned forward so Ann could whisper in her ear. Louisa straightened and grinned. "Ah, the new girl, I knew she'd catch your eye. Only the best for you, Captain. I bring her to you." She moved off, and Ann returned her attention to the stage, a thousand questions buzzing through her mind.

Violet was still alive! But even the relief that accompanied that realization was overpowered by astonishment at what she was seeing. Violet's hips pulsed in sensual bursts as she ran her hands lightly along her own thighs and throat. Unlike the bright, empty smiles plastered on the faces of the other girls, Violet's lips were slightly parted, her face tilted back as though she were lost in the arms of some imaginary lover. She knew the motions too well, seemed far too comfortable at being paraded around like a trussed-up Christmas goose for men to salivate over and devour. With shock Ann concluded this could not be Violet's first time on such a stage. The delicious ache throbbing low in her belly suddenly spread like brandy through her blood, warming her insides and tingling between her thighs.

The girls onstage gave a final whooping cheer and several of them turned, flipping their skirts up to treat the audience to a view of their naked behinds. Violet was not one of them, and Ann was glad for that. She watched Louisa pull Violet to the side, speaking in her ear while she motioned toward Ann's table. Violet gave a visible start as she recognized the pirate captain. Ann met her stare evenly, with a calm that belied her heated blood, and lifted her mug in a cocky salute.

Violet approached the table without removing her feathered mask. She lifted herself onto the tabletop and crossed one leg over the other, then leaned forward on one hand so her breast was pressed upward by her upper arm. The calculated sexuality of the pose was not lost on Ann. But when Violet spoke, her tone was flat. "What's your pleasure, Captain?"

Nearby, Barclay coughed. "If you don't mind, Captain, I think I'd like to seek out some company for myself for the evening."

Ann flicked her hand dismissively, and there was a scuffle as he folded up the unfinished Articles and rose from the bench. For a long moment Ann and Violet stared at one another. "So you're a whore," Ann finally said, keeping her tone casual.

"Oh, I'm something much worse than that, Captain." Behind the feathered mask, Violet's eyes were nearly black. "I'm the daughter of a whore. Born and raised in the brothels of East London, sold to my first customer as soon as I was old enough to bleed."

Of course. Ann found herself replaying the memory of Violet's first few moments on her ship, the way she'd ripped her blouse open to dangle herself defiantly before the pirate crew. *I should have known.* But all she said was, "I suppose that explains why you're able to drink most of my men under the table."

Violet's lips twisted into a bitter smile. "I suppose it does."

"Funny, you don't talk like a London street harlot."

"My husband went to great expense to train me as a proper lady. I had tutors for everything—etiquette, reading and writing, needlepoint. It took me two years to rid myself of my childhood accent. Not that it matters now, of course."

Ann took a swallow from her mug. "Take off that mask. You look ridiculous." When Violet hesitated, she arched an eyebrow. "Are you in the habit of refusing your customers, woman? I said take it off."

Violet's jaw set. "As you wish," she said tightly, and reached up to untie the mask's strings. She removed it slowly, and as it came down Ann's heart clenched.

Without thinking she leapt to her feet. "My God, who did this?" Livid bruises colored the entire right side of Violet's face, slashed with long, jagged scabs above the brow and over the cheekbone. Her cheek was swollen, though the bruises were more brown and green than purple, which meant they'd been healing for a while. Someone had beaten her, and quite viciously. Ann felt a flood of rage as she remembered the bloodstains on Violet's Bible. *That simpering dog in the tavern. I knew I should have killed him where he lay.*

Violet shrugged. "Does it matter?"

It didn't. Or at least it shouldn't have, though Ann was so infuriated she was starting to see spots. Violet slid from the table, and as she moved the hem of her skirt hiked up, exposing her thigh nearly to the hip. Ann caught a glimpse of more bruises mottling the creamy flesh there and knew that Violet had been ravaged as well as beaten. She ground her teeth so hard her jaw ached.

"If you'll excuse me, Captain, I need to get back to work." Violet moved to return to the stage as the fiddler struck up another popular tune.

Ann's hand snapped out and grabbed hold of Violet's wrist. "You're not going back up there."

"Let go of me, Captain." When Ann refused to relax her grip, Violet wrenched her arm away. "Let go!"

The exclamation was loud enough to catch the attention of Girard, the bordello's owner, who signaled the two burly men at the door. All three of them came over, and Girard held his hands out between the two women. "Is there a problem, ladies?" he asked over the music. The bordello's hired musclemen moved to flank Ann on either side.

"*Ça n'a rien à voir avec toi,*" she said in terse French, warning him to stay out of it. She wasn't looking for a fight. Not yet, anyway. Her focus remained on Violet. "You can't stay here. Look what they've done to you."

Violet glared, incredulity written all over her battered features.

"Spare me your pity, Branded Ann. You're the reason I'm here." Ann was taken aback by the venom in her words. "I had a good husband who loved me. Loved me, Captain, despite what I was, do you understand that? I had a home waiting in Jamaica. I was going to have a new life, a chance to start over where no one knew what I'd been." Seemingly emboldened by the presence of the two heavyset guards, she stepped forward as well, till she was almost nose to nose with Ann. "And then you and your crew came along and butchered my husband like a bloody farm-pig, and didn't even have the decency to send me after him."

Ann blinked, startled as much by the sheer hatred that swept over the pretty face as she was by Violet's sudden lapse into a broad Cockney accent.

"Instead you dumped me on this God-forsaken island to be raped half to death by a bunch of black-hearted God-be-damned bastard pox-rats. So don't you *dare* pretend you give a bleeding dog's arse what happens to me now!" The profanity was delivered with shocking ease. "But at least here," she nodded in Girard's direction, "I'm paid a wage of me own when I spread me legs, and I'll save till I've the money to be free once and for all. I escaped this life once before, and I'll do it again if I have to sell me tits and arse to every last mother-diddling pirate on the Spanish Main!"

Ann actually took a step back, Violet's fury searing into her until it hurt to breathe. A feral smile curled Violet's lip. "But I'm a woman of business, and much as I hate you, Branded Ann, I'll still fuck you senseless for a handful of gold. So if you're not like to hand over the coin, leave me be for the paying customers. I got work to do."

Breathless silence fell through the room as the fiddler ceased his playing. Everyone, from the whores onstage to the customers at the tables, watched for Ann's reaction. Ann was stunned speechless—but only for a few seconds. Then her infamous temper snaked around all the other conflicting emotions and wrapped them tightly back under control. With a shaking hand Ann reached inside her cloak and pulled a money pouch out of the inner pocket.

"If it's gold you want, woman, then take it." She flung the pouch at Violet, hard, and heard Violet's grunt as it hit her stomach. Violet caught it in her hands, and Ann could see the surprise on her face as she realized just how heavy the purse was. "Now, if you don't mind, this *paying customer* cordially requests that you sit that lovely ass down, shut your trap," she seized a tumbler of rum from a passing serving wench's tray and held it out with an incongruously civilized bow, "and have a drink with me."

Girard wrung his hands and gave Violet an urgent, almost pleading look. Ann smirked. She knew she was far from the Frenchman's favorite customer. Her last few visits to the Virgin had erupted in chaotic, destructive fistfights that invariably culminated in several dead patrons and countless smashed tables, bottles, and chairs. Her response to Violet had been tame as a newborn kitten in comparison. Ann was actually rather proud of her own restraint.

Violet looked from the bag of money to Girard, then at the tumbler in Ann's hand. Finally she nodded to the two guards, and they stepped back. She tucked the money pouch between her breasts and accepted the offered drink. A collective sigh rippled through the bordello as Ann returned to her seat. With a last nod to Girard, Violet joined her on the bench, and the fiddler began to play again.

Neither woman spoke for several long minutes. Ann emptied her mug and summoned a girl to refill it, then sent her away. After downing nearly half the liquor in a few swallows, she set the mug down and rolled it between her palms. Out of the corner of her eye she watched Violet, who was sipping at the rum only halfheartedly. Ann couldn't explain why the sight of those pretty features, discolored with bruises, caused such a heavy ache in her chest. She'd inflicted far worse injuries herself on many a victim.

An idea was forming in her mind, an idea that her logical side recognized as pure folly. Yet she could not let it go, and spoke quickly before she could talk herself out of it. "So you're a woman of business, are you?" Violet looked up, and Ann could read the question on her face. "No, I do not mock you, my lovely. As one woman of business to another, I have a proposition for you."

"A proposition?" Violet repeated. "If you're about to invite me back on board your ship, Captain, you can save your breath. I may be a trollop and a whore, but I won't be anyone's personal pleasure slave, not even for a mountain of gold." The crude accent had vanished, and Violet was again speaking as daintily as a well-bred English lady in a tea parlor, though the words leaving her lips were still absurdly colorful.

"This life," Ann waved toward the stage, "will be the death of you, long before you'd save the kind of money you need to free yourself from it."

Violet gave a humorless laugh. "I'll survive. It's what I do."

Ann smiled back only slightly. "Even if you do, it would take twenty, maybe thirty years of whoring yourself to these lice-ridden sons of apes before you'd manage it." Did she imagine the faint shudder that ran through the other woman's body?

"Are you now to steal my hope as well as my dignity, Captain?" Violet stared down into the tumbler of rum.

"Far from it." Ann was surprised at the gentleness in her own voice, and could hardly believe what she was about to suggest. "I'm not asking you to enslave yourself to me or anyone else. What I'm proposing is a change of vocation. A place on my ship, among my crew. Your name on the Articles just like all the others. Duties to fulfill, and a share in the profits if you complete them." There, the offer had been made. She leaned forward. "Violet, the treasure we're after will make you wealthier than you could ever imagine. Never again would there be need for you to sell yourself like this."

"This treasure. It's the reason you pirates killed Isaac, isn't it?"

"Aye." Ann fought the urge to say more as memories of her father surfaced in her thoughts. She felt no regret over the man's death. In fact, if Barclay hadn't killed Watts she certainly would have done it herself; what the man had cost her was far too much to go unanswered. But what Ann did regret was the terrible loss Violet had suffered in the process. She'd already been made a widow, and that was enough. Ann had no desire to tarnish Violet's memories of her husband, and so she remained silent.

Violet's lips parted, and Ann watched the pale breasts rise and fall briskly. She was considering it, at least. Ann turned to scan the room for Barclay, and located him in a far corner with a tavern girl on his lap and another draped over his shoulder. She lifted a hand and caught his eye. The quartermaster rose from his seat and returned to her table.

"The Articles," Ann said, holding out a hand, and Barclay tugged them from a fold in his wide sash. Ann took the sheet of paper and unfolded it, then spread it on the table. They weren't quite finished yet, but it was still enough to bind Violet to her ship for the upcoming voyage. She picked up the quill lying nearby and held it out. "Take the offer," she said softly.

Violet read the lines under her breath, then looked up. "What makes you think I won't just use this as an opportunity to slit your throat the first chance I get?"

Ann laughed. "If you want to try, go ahead."

Slowly, Violet reached out and took the quill from Ann's fingers. Ann pushed the inkpot within her reach, and Violet dipped the quill tip into it. After a brief hesitation she signed her name beneath the Articles—*Mrs. Violet Watts*.

Ann drew the paper away. The curling signature at the bottom was oddly thrilling. "Welcome aboard, Sister Violet."

❖

The lower decks of the *Ice Queen* were a cacophony of noise, with chickens squabbling and hogs grunting, the bleat of a goat or two and the unpleasant smell of animal excrement permeating it all. Violet made a face as another crate of hens was brought into the galley to be stacked atop the others.

"I don't remember there being such creatures here when I first came aboard," she said to the galley master. O'Hare grinned.

"Aye, lassie, that's on account of how we'd been at sea for nigh on two months and eaten them all before you arrived."

"Eaten?" Violet looked at the pens and cages. She hadn't thought of it before, but it made sense to bring live animals aboard in preparation for a long journey. Meat spoiled too quickly when it was not fresh. "I see." She wrinkled her nose. "Does it always smell like this?"

"The first week's the worst. Once we start thinning the herds, the smell gets better."

Violet made a mental note to add scrubbing the animal pens to her list of daily chores. She didn't know if she could endure preparing food in a galley that smelled so foul. She caught a glimpse of a familiar face among the men rolling barrels in their direction. "Turtle!" she exclaimed, genuinely delighted to see him. He was one of the few crew members that she'd grown quite fond of.

The boy looked up. "Sister Violet! I heard a rumor you was coming back aboard." He pushed a barrel into the corner of the galley and O'Hare moved to help him set it upright. His eyebrows went up when he noticed her bruised face. "What happened to ya, then?"

"Tortuga," Violet replied evasively. Ann had made it very clear that she was not to disclose her previous profession to the crew, and had even sworn Barclay to silence, on pain of death. If the pirates knew she was a whore, it could mean unpleasantness for everyone, even with her name on the Articles. Turtle didn't seem put off by her tone, however, and he nodded.

"Ah. Lucky the captain has such a soft spot for us sorry souls, eh?" He waved his left arm, where a wooden claw had been affixed to the stump. "I can still fight with the other, though I won't be much good for swabbing no more. Captain Ann agreed to take me back on, even with this bum hand. Them what says there's no honor among thieves ain't never met our Captain. She's good people."

Violet was inclined to disagree, but she didn't want to start an argument, so she just offered a slight nod.

"All right, enough yammering, there's work to be done." O'Hare shoved an armful of buckets and brushes at Violet. "Take these here abovedecks and put them someplace out of the way."

Violet took them. "Aye." With another smile at Turtle she left the galley. She had some difficulty with the ladder thanks to her unwieldy burden, but finally managed to climb from the hatch and find a corner to stash the cleaning supplies.

That done, she straightened herself and turned to observe the flurry of activity on the main deck as men hauled trunks and barrels and boxes of supplies up the gangplank, lowering the heaviest through the hatch on a system of pulleys. Here and there along the masts and rigging she could see members of the crew clinging to the rope nets, threading rope and tightening knots for the sails.

Branded Ann's cloud of hair caught her eye. The pirate captain was up on the foredeck with Barclay, directing the loading of supplies and last-minute preparations. They would be setting sail very soon. Violet took a deep breath and clutched at the pouch in the pocket of her borrowed trousers. Her conscience had been pricking at her unmercifully, and she knew it would not give her peace until she complied with its demands.

She crossed the main deck carefully, trying to keep out of the crew's way, then climbed the deck stairs and approached the captain and quartermaster. She pulled the pouch from her pocket, the heavy gold coins inside jingling slightly. "Captain?"

"Aye, what is it?" Ann said absently without turning around, then shouted angrily at one of the men below. "Look alive, you ape-wit, that barrel's full of gunpowder! You want to blow us all to Davy Jones before we even leave port? Get that down to the gun deck where it belongs!" She gave an irritated mutter under her breath as the crewman scurried to obey.

Violet very nearly changed her mind. Perhaps it would be better to return later when things were not quite so hectic. But Ann noticed the money pouch in her hand and turned. "What's this?" she queried coolly.

"I..." Violet bit her lip and held the pouch out. "I wanted to apologize, Captain. For losing my temper the other night. I suppose you must think me a complete heretic by now."

Ann's eyebrows nearly disappeared into her hairline, and Violet cleared her throat uncomfortably. "I have every right to despise you, Captain," she added defensively. "But God commands we love our enemies and do good to those who hate us."

A peculiar expression crossed the scarred features. "I don't hate you, Violet."

"Well, I hate *you*," Violet replied bitterly, and the captain's eyes narrowed slightly. "Only I don't want it on my conscience any longer. I don't know that I'll ever be able to love you as the good Lord says, but I am going to try to forgive you. And...well...just take the money back, won't you?" She reached out and took Ann's hand, pressing the heavy pouch into her palm.

Ann looked at it silently, then tucked it into her sash. "I have something for you. Come with me." She turned to Barclay. "Sound the whistle when we're ready to set sail."

"Aye, Captain," the quartermaster said with a salute.

Violet couldn't imagine what Ann had in mind, but the pirate obviously expected her to follow. She let Ann lead her to the captain's cabin and stepped inside as Ann closed the door. Ann went to the tall cabinet against the wall and retrieved something wrapped in oilcloth from a drawer.

"I believe this belongs to you," she said, and pulled the oilcloth back.

Violet gasped. She reached out and took her Bible from the protective cloth, running her fingers over the leather cover. "I thought

I'd lost it," she breathed. "How did you—?" Ann averted her gaze, and Violet shook her head. "I don't think I want to know." Tears filled her eyes as she opened the cover and traced the inscription with her fingertips. *For my beloved wife, 1667.* "Isaac gave this to me as a present for our first wedding anniversary," she whispered. "He never put much faith in God himself, but he loved it that I did."

Looking somewhat uncomfortable, Ann took the Bible from her arms. She settled it back in the oilcloth. "You should leave it here. There's no safer place for it on the ship than in my cabin."

"Oh, but I do so like to read from it a bit each night before I sleep—"

"No reason why you can't. You'll be bunking with me." Violet's mouth dropped open, but before she could protest Ann cut her off. "You may be a member of the crew now, Violet, but you're still a female on board a ship of coarse men."

"So are you," Violet pointed out rather petulantly.

"And you can't imagine the things I had to do to make it this far." Ann's expression turned so grave that Violet shuddered. "The men don't touch me because they don't dare, and the only reason they won't touch you is their fear of me. But fear is a fickle ally, and I'd prefer to test it as little as possible."

Violet still wanted to argue. Sharing a bed with Ann for the next few months was a disagreeable thought, and she would have preferred her little hammock in the hold. But when she considered the possibility of certain members of the crew attempting to join her there, she could see Ann's point. She sighed unhappily.

A shrill whistle sounded above them. "Sounds like we're ready to set off," Ann declared, and Violet could hear the eagerness in her voice. "So how about it, Sister Violet, you want to come abovedecks and watch the horizon slip away?"

"If it's all the same to you, Captain, I've seen enough of that place to last a hundred lifetimes."

"Suit yourself." Ann moved to the cabin door, then paused. "Before I forget," she pointed at a chest in the corner by the bunk box, "that trunk is for you. If you're going to be a member of my crew, you'll need some properly fitting clothes. Mine are too big for you. And from now on," she eyed Violet's long, unbraided hair as it cascaded over one shoulder, "either you keep that mane of yours tied back or I'll cut it off, savvy? Loose hair and clothes can be a death sentence on a sailing ship, especially for one as green as you."

Violet's hands flew to her hair and she eyed the dirk in Ann's sash. She had no intention of allowing that blade anywhere near her head. Ann gave a small nod. "Go ahead and get yourself settled in here. We'll have plenty of work for you come afternoon."

"Aye."

After Ann left the cabin, Violet surveyed the room in a slow, dazed circle. Here she was again, back on board the ship she'd once thought to take her own life to escape, a Cockney whore turned merchant's wife turned...pirate? Violet didn't think of herself as a pirate, though she supposed that with her name on the Articles that was exactly what she had become. *Lord, surely thou dost work in very, very mysterious ways.*

She went to the trunk on the floor that Ann had indicated, and opened it. Inside she found two white cambric shirts and a pair of dark gray trousers, both sized for a young boy rather than the men's sizes that Ann wore. Beneath were a pair of sturdy leather boots, a belt, and several pairs of woolen socks. She pulled these out in wonder and held the sole of one boot up to the bottom of her foot. With the thick socks, it would be a perfect fit.

She peeked back into the trunk and heat rose in her cheeks when she realized what the next items were: three sets of linen undergarments and a stack of neatly folded, soft cloth rags. *She thought of everything*, Violet realized gratefully, knowing that her monthly bleeding would begin in the next few days. She didn't know why she was so surprised. After all, Ann had been a sailor for years and must have been through countless cycles of her own while at sea. Still, Violet had not anticipated such thoughtfulness.

Something dark and rigid was rolled up alongside the undergarments, and Violet pulled it out curiously. It was a pair of bodices, stiffened with buckram and laced with leather thongs. Violet recognized them as the kind worn by farm women and tavern girls, not meant for tight lacing but rather for support and mobility. The fabric was fine enough to be worn outside the loose white shirt rather than beneath it, which would afford her a hint of femininity in her otherwise masculine wardrobe. Violet felt herself blushing again. She'd never seen Branded Ann herself wearing such a garment. The pirate was lean, almost too slender, and had very little in the way of curves; her normal attire consisted of a shirt and sash, and occasionally a vest or frock coat. But Violet was much more full-figured, and Ann must have guessed she would be uncomfortable without some measure of support.

A flash of metal caught her eye, and Violet reached back into the trunk to withdraw the last item. At first she was confused. In her hands was a small silver box. It was a dainty thing, much finer than anything Violet would have expected the pirate to own, with little scrolled legs and a top engraved with flowers. She opened it slowly. Inside, it was divided into two velvet-lined compartments: the smaller held an assortment of delicate silver hairpins, and in the other was a silver-backed hairbrush.

Violet lifted the brush from the box with astonishment. "It's beautiful," she whispered, turning it in her hand. Like the box, it was engraved with a pattern of teardrop-petaled flowers that she suddenly recognized as violets. She ran a fingertip over the bristles, stiff enough to work out even a difficult tangle, but still soft to the touch. Violet carried the brush to the looking glass bolted to the wall above the washstand. She pulled her long brown hair over one shoulder and ran the brush through it experimentally.

In a matter of minutes she had transformed her limp, snarled tresses into two sleek, shining braids, one over each shoulder. She picked up the silver box and pinned the braids, crownlike, around her head. She counted the pins as she went. There were thirty of them, and Violet made up her mind to be very careful not to lose even one. As she put the brush back into the box, she was suddenly struck with a disturbing thought.

Does Branded Ann mean to seduce me? Violet could think of no other reason why the pirate would have given her such an expensive and unnecessary gift. A few whalebone pins and a boar-bristle brush would have been sufficient, and these fine silver things were far too elegant, too carefully thoughtful, to be just tools for her day-to-day survival. Violet knew Ann preferred female bedfellows, and a lifetime of experience allowed her to recognize the desire that often lingered on the cross-marked face when the pirate gazed at her. She was also certain Ann would never force herself on her. But she might not be above outright seduction.

She has to know I would never...I wouldn't, would I? For a split second Violet found herself wondering what it would be like if she gave in to the lust in those ice blue eyes. She'd been with women before, knew the scent and the texture of their bodies. She could please a woman far better than most men, for she understood their needs in a way that men never would. What would it be like, to have the indomitable Branded Ann completely at her mercy, trembling for her touch? A wicked grin curved her lips, but then she quickly pushed those thoughts away. *For shame, Violet Watts. The woman stole from your husband, and her crew murdered him right before your eyes. She's probably hoping this will keep you from cutting her throat as she sleeps.*

Violet snapped the box shut and carried it to the trunk, setting it back into place carefully so she could change out of her borrowed clothes. As she tugged one of the new shirts over her head, her gaze drifted back to the shiny little box in the trunk. *I did say I'd try to forgive her. But if she thinks I'm going to dive between her legs over a pretty trinket, she'll be sorely disappointed.*

With that thought stubbornly resounding through her mind, Violet sat in a nearby chair and began to pull on her boots.

CHAPTER EIGHT

A nn awoke as a heavy arm crept over her waist and small fingers came to rest lightly against her chest. She barely managed to contain a groan. Once again Violet was cuddling against her in her sleep, and Ann could feel with excruciating sensitivity the soft breasts pressed into her back and warm hips fitted snugly to her own. Ann didn't like to be touched as she slept. She didn't even allow the girls whose company she paid for to share her bed more than a few minutes after their business had been concluded. She found it jarring to be awakened nearly every night by Violet's unconscious embraces. She was beginning to remember why she'd been so relieved to get Violet off her ship in the first place.

Even so, Ann was strongly tempted to leave Violet's arm where it was. The little hand had drifted dangerously close to one nipple, which Ann could feel hardening traitorously in anticipation of even accidental contact. She wanted to roll over and press her face into the unbound hair and let it run through her fingers like threads of fine silk. Perhaps she would cup one of those perfect breasts in her palm and taste the creamy flesh at the junction of neck and shoulder, the velvet spot of the throat where blood pulsed just beneath the skin, until Violet's throaty voice moaned breathlessly in her ear... These thoughts brought an immediate, insistent thrumming to her very core, and Ann cursed silently. Quickly she squeezed her eyes shut and fought to control her breathing by flooding her mind with the most unappetizing things she could think of. After successfully conjuring up the image of the *Ice Queen*'s most unattractive crew members dancing buck naked on her cabin carpet, she managed to slow her pounding heart enough that she was able to slide from beneath Violet's arm and leave the bunk.

Violet did not seem disturbed by the movement. Moonlight streamed from the round porthole above the bunk box to play across her pretty features. The swelling was gone now, the bruises reduced to faint yellow stains across her cheek and forehead. *Such a deceptively innocent face.* Ann reached out and pulled the quilts over one naked thigh that had escaped from the covers, finding it much less of a temptation when it was out of sight. She would have to find a way to ask Violet to wear trousers to bed in the future.

She'd always thought of whores as nothing more than puppets with stringy hair and lurid makeup. Most prostituted themselves because they were desperate and hungry, or greedy and ambitious, and too homely to find men willing to marry them. But Violet was different. Born in the brothels of London, Violet had managed to retain her extraordinary beauty, an asset that must surely have cost her dearly in the whoring trade. It was a miraculous achievement.

Even more remarkable was how she had captured the heart of a man whose wealth could have won him any number of highborn, attractive girls. Isaac Watts had doted on Violet enough not only to marry her away from a life of harlotry, but to engage private tutors to transform her into a lady of propriety and whisk her away to a new life on the other side of the world, where no one would know Violet as anything other than a respectable businessman's wife. Like some rags-to-riches princess in a fairy tale, Violet had secured wealth, stability, and love—things that even the most well-bred women could only hope for.

Ann had robbed her of that.

Silently Ann took her small knife from the table and stuffed it into her sash, then left the cabin. She needed some fresh air. Porter was working the night shift at the helm, and he cast her a curious glance as she emerged. Ann ignored him. She moved to the mainmast and took hold of the narrow wooden handholds nailed to the thick shaft. With a deep breath, she began to climb.

The crow's nest was Ann's favorite thinking spot, high above the decks and water, where even the slightest toss of the sea was exaggerated. Most of the men abhorred it, as it was easily one of the most dangerous positions on the ship. To Ann, however, the little circular platform with its flimsy railing represented freedom, in both its fragility and its tenacity. She reached the nest and threw one leg, then the other, over the rail. With her back against the mast she settled herself cross-legged on the platform and stared out over the shimmering expanse of ocean to the south. It was too dark to make out the rugged landmass of Jamaica on the southwestern horizon, though Ann knew it was there. They would be arriving sometime the next afternoon, if the winds held.

Branded Ann never apologized. She was a pirate, cold-blooded and merciless, and as one of the only known female privateers in the Caribbean she could not afford to be otherwise. On many an occasion she'd slit a man's throat or keelhauled a member of the crew for even small infractions of the rules. The men had to believe in her hair-trigger temper as much as her legendary skill with a cutlass. Even the menacing scar that crossed half her face was an important part of the carefully fabricated reputation that had kept her alive these years at sea. Yet she could feel it all coming undone every time she looked at Violet. Ann found herself feeling things she'd forgotten: regret, compassion, guilt, even self-consciousness, emotions that creaked rustily to the surface of her thoughts and jarred her otherwise perfect sense of control. She'd killed men for less.

What was it about Violet that did this to her? Her attraction to Violet was as magnetic as a compass. She was fascinated by Violet's strength, a very different sort from her own. Violet didn't fight her circumstances; she simply refused to let them rule her. It didn't matter if she was a wayside harlot or a society matron, Violet Watts belonged only to herself and would not be broken by any outside force. Ann had entertained some brief fantasies of seducing the pretty widow, foolish though it might be during a voyage like this. But for the first time in her life, she could admit she'd found a woman who was too good for her.

Ann looked up at the glittering mass of stars overhead. Immediately her sea-trained eyes picked out several key constellations, each in its proper place for the time of year and the *Ice Queen*'s position. Such a comfort, to look into the sky and know exactly where one was. Ann sighed. *If only life were as easy to navigate as the ocean.*

❖

"Your coffee, Captain Ann." Violet was startled when she saw the shadows ringing Ann's eyes. "Didn't you sleep well, Captain?" she asked self-consciously. Violet had been meaning to bring up the subject anyway. The crew was convinced that she was only on board for the captain's entertainment, and their current sleeping arrangements did nothing to dissuade this impression. And she was beginning to think perhaps Ann had overestimated the dangers the crew posed to her; so far the men had left her almost entirely alone. "Perhaps it would be better if—"

"We'll be landing at Port Royal in another hour or so," Ann interrupted distractedly, indicating the approaching Jamaican shore. "It was to be your destination, with your husband, wasn't it?"

Violet winced. "Aye."

Ann's expression was unreadable as she sipped at her coffee and turned back to the horizon. "Port Royal's a real town, not like that miserable den of sin we just left. The new governor just passed anti-piracy laws last year, and though some areas are still rough, there's plenty of opportunity for honest folks to make a living. There's a shortage of women there, and with a pretty face like yours you'd have no trouble securing a good husband." Without looking at Violet she continued, "If you want to stay, I'll release you from the Articles."

Violet's mouth fell open. She was growing very tired of Ann's power games—the pirate had seemed so anxious to be rid of her on Tortuga, only to practically bribe Violet to return to the ship. Now, just when Violet was beginning to look forward to Ann's promises of treasure and a new life, it seemed that Ann wanted to get rid of her again. "Oh, no, you won't. I signed your precious Articles just like every other crewman," Violet snapped. "I've a right to sail on this ship and collect my part of the treasure when we find it, and you're not taking that away from me."

"Then forget I offered," Ann replied sharply, her tone clearly implying that she'd been doing Violet a favor. Violet shook her head.

"You're not going to push me around at whim like everyone else, Captain. Whether I'm dependent on just one man or hundreds of them, it's all the same, isn't it? I don't want another husband, I want my own fortune. I want—"

"Freedom," Ann finished for her, and Violet paused midway

through her indignant speech. A melancholic smile flitted across the pirate's face. "I understand."

Violet wasn't sure how to respond to this, and before she could think of anything else to say one of the crew called to Ann from the main deck. A strand of Ann's wavy hair had escaped its ponytail and Ann tucked it behind her ear. "Stay or go, Sister Violet, it's up to you." She walked off, leaving Violet to stare tongue-tied after her.

❖

The Port Royal dock was a much more orderly affair than the one in Tortuga. Though the British government seemed willing to overlook most criminal activity for the sake of the Jamaican economy, blatant disregard for the law was punished with imprisonment and even hanging. With the recent illegalization of piracy, it was best to keep a low profile when doing business here.

This was especially true for Ann, whose face and ship were so easily recognizable. A bounty had been issued for her arrest in Port Royal, due to her occasional assaults on English trade ships. The risk was great, but Ann had been seeking Black Dog's treasure her entire life and she wasn't about to give it up now. She ordered the *Ice Queen* to fly British colors as they approached port. Though she didn't expect it would fool anyone, it would be one less way to draw attention to themselves.

Barclay disembarked immediately upon landing to sniff out their target. When he returned, he had the information they needed: Ashford Carter had adopted the alias Andrew Cartwright, for like Ann, there was a price on his head. He lived in the west end of the city, above a small shop he ran with his young wife where he sold compasses, maps, books, and navigational tools to fellow seafarers.

Though Ann could have easily found the place on her own, she agreed to let Barclay accompany her in case of trouble. She pulled a wide-brimmed hat low over her face to conceal her distinctive hair and scar, and donned a cloak that fell to her ankles. Ann was taller than most women, but about average height for a man, and with her lilting sea-legged walk it would be easy to pass for a simple merchant sailor in port on business—as long as she kept her head down.

As soon as she set foot on the dock Ann felt uneasy. While the British authorities weren't likely to arrest her unless she made trouble, anyone who recognized her might attempt to turn her in for the reward. That would mean a nasty fight, and the possibility of a hangman's noose if she lost. Ann shivered and put a hand on her cutlass hilt. "I hate land," she muttered under her breath.

"Captain, look." Barclay pointed at a young boy standing on a stack of crates nearby. He was gaping open-mouthed at their whitewashed ship. "You there, what do you think you're doing?" he called out gruffly. "Get away now, go on. Get out of here."

The child turned, and Ann was startled to realize it was a little girl, not a boy like she'd assumed from the close-cropped sandy hair. She was about seven or eight years old, with the spindly arms and legs of an energetic youngster. Instead of appearing frightened by Barclay's harsh reprimand, the girl looked them both over curiously. When her eyes fell on Ann they grew to the size of doubloons. Ann quickly tugged her hat down, but it was too late.

"I knew it! I knew this here was the *Ice Queen*!" the child crowed, and leapt from the crates to land, catlike, in front of them. "I know all about you, Branded Ann, my papa's told me all sorts of stories. You're the greatest pirate to sail the sea in nigh a hundred years!"

Ann slid a dirk from her sleeve into her hand. Praying that none of the dock workers were paying much attention, she whipped her cloak around the child. She spun them both around so that their backs were to the wharf, and pressed the blade against the girl's neck. "What's your name, kid?" she demanded quietly.

"Charlotte Price," she replied, not seeming disturbed in the slightest by the knife beneath her chin. "But Papa calls me Charlie."

"Tell me, Charlie, if I am who you say I am, what makes you think I won't slit your throat ear to ear for announcing me to the entire bloody port?"

The child actually giggled. "You won't kill me," she said confidently.

Not sure whether to be annoyed or amused, Ann bit her lip. "What makes you so sure?"

"'Cause when I grow up I'm going to be a pirate, just like you." Though this was not terribly logical, Ann hesitated as voices from long ago suddenly played through her memory.

"I want to be a pirate like you when I grow up, Papa."
"Annie, my darling, women can't be pirates."
"Then I'll grow up to be a boy."

She could still hear her father's laugh. How young she'd been then. How little she'd known. Ann felt her temper ebbing and became acutely aware of her own foolishness. Not more than five steps onto the dock and she was threatening the life of a mere child in broad daylight with innumerable witnesses milling about. The girl wasn't that great a threat. Most people probably wouldn't pay much attention to a child obsessed with pirate tales who ran about the docks insisting she'd seen the infamous Branded Ann. Ann slipped the dirk back into her sleeve and shoved Charlie away. "Go home, kid," she growled, then emphatically turned her back on the girl and held a hand out to Barclay. "Give me your scarf."

The quartermaster reached into his pocket and produced a thick wool scarf, which he wore during storms at sea to keep the rain out of his nose and mouth. The day was blistering hot, but nonetheless Ann wound the scarf around her neck and face until only her eyes were visible above it. Better to endure the sweltering heat than risk being identified again. *Blast this infernal scar.* Ann adjusted her collar around her ears and face, then nodded at Barclay.

"Let's go."

❖

Malcolm Newbury, officer of His Majesty's royal navy, watched the cloaked figure as she strode away. He'd gotten a glimpse of Ann's cross-scarred face just before she'd wrapped it up. *What do you know? The kid was right. It really is Branded Ann, bitch of the Spanish Main. The bounty for that woman is nearly a year's wages.* He had almost apprehended the pirate woman there on the dock when the girl pointed her out. He rather wished Ann hadn't let the brat go. If he'd caught her red-handed at the murder of a child, it would have been very easy to take her into custody then and there, and any number of witnesses would have helped him bring her in.

From a safe distance Newbury pursued the woman and her burly companion across the docks. Familiar with her deadly reputation, he didn't dare accost her when he was outnumbered. But he didn't want to go back to the barracks to enlist aid; that would mean splitting the reward, and the glory, among his fellow officers. He would trail them until the perfect opportunity arose, and then... *The bitch will hang, and I'll have money to burn.* And when his superiors heard of how he'd single-handedly brought down one of the most wanted pirates on the Spanish Main, he was sure to be promoted. Newbury snickered.

He followed his prey through the busy Port Royal streets. They moved at a leisurely pace, but neither paused to examine the contents of the store windows or street carts they passed, so they had to have a particular destination in mind. Newbury trailed the pair all the way to the western side of the city, straight to a small mapmaker's shop nestled between a cooper and a tavern. He assumed a casual position against the tavern wall and watched from the corner of his eye as Ann and her companion entered the shop.

Through the open window Newbury saw Ann approach the merchant's counter, not even bothering to feign interest in the shop's wares. He strained to catch her words.

"I'm looking for Ashford Carter."

Newbury frowned. Carter? The infamous daredevil? Newbury had never met the man, himself, but like every other sailor in the Caribbean he'd heard his share of stories. Carter was said to be a foolhardy navigator, known both for the crazy risks he took and his miraculous ability to survive them. And if Newbury wasn't mistaken, there was a reward out for Carter's arrest as well. What could Branded Ann want with such a man? This promised to be interesting, and Newbury pricked his ears even more keenly toward the conversation.

"You must be in the wrong place," the man behind the counter answered slowly, looking the two pirates up and down. "The name's Cartwright. Ain't never heard of no Carter."

"Well, that's a shame." Newbury saw Ann produce some sort of scroll from her sleeve. "Because I have something I think he'd be very interested in." She held the rolled paper out, and after a brief hesitation the mapmaker took it from her.

He unfurled it, then whistled through his teeth. "This what I think it is?"

"That depends. Are you Carter or not?"

The man grunted uncomfortably and then nodded.

Well, what do you know? Two wanted pirates in the same place. It must be my lucky day, Newbury exulted silently. *With the kind of money they'll bring in, I could buy my own ship!*

Carter waved the paper at Ann. "Where'd you get this?"

"That doesn't matter. Are you interested?"

"Of course," he replied, "but I don't think I can afford to pay what it's worth."

Ann reached out and took the paper away from him. "The map isn't for sale."

Newbury could just make out Carter's puzzled frown. "Then what…?"

Spreading the map on the counter, Ann jabbed at it with her finger. "I want you to guide us here." Newbury wished he could see what she was pointing at, because Carter suddenly guffawed.

"You're talking to the wrong man, me hearties. I'm retired. Much as I'd like to take on the Devil's seas again, I've promised the wife that I'd give up sailing."

"And much as I'm loath to ask a man to break his word to a lady, I can't take no for an answer." Ann pulled the scarf from her face, and Carter took a step backward.

"Branded Ann…"

"I've been chasing Black Dog's legacy my entire life, Master Carter. Now I have all the missing pieces. Everything I need, except you."

Newbury's mouth went dry, and he wondered if he'd heard her correctly. Had Branded Ann really discovered a map to Black Dog's secret island? That island was rumored to hide a fortune greater than all the gold and jewels in England's royal treasury. Yet no one had found it in the eighteen years since Black Dog's death at the hands of his own crew. Such a treasure could make a man rich beyond his wildest dreams.

Longing appeared on the man's face. "What you're offering is the opportunity of a lifetime, I know that. Cursed gold hidden on a secret island in the Devil's Triangle? Believe me, if you'd asked a year ago I'd have jumped at the chance! But…I can't." He leaned across the counter. "It's me wife, you see? She's fixing to have our first babe, and I can't leave her to go gallivanting off on some mad treasure hunt." Carter's regret certainly sounded genuine.

"I'm willing to offer you two full shares in the prize, if you'll sign aboard with us. Think of the life you could provide for your wife and child with such wealth."

Carter wrung his hands. "I'm sorry, I truly am. But I gave me word."

Ann sighed. She rolled the map up again. "I hope you'll at least give me the chance to change your mind. This really isn't the place for such negotiations. Take some time to think about it, and meet me tonight at the Grinning Whale."

Newbury looked over to see that the tavern next door had a hanging sign depicting a fat gray whale with a ridiculous smile. He turned back just in time to catch Ann's shrug. "I promise I'll make it worth your time. At the very least you'll get a free drink out of the deal."

"I'll be there," Carter said finally, though he still sounded uncertain.

Newbury snapped back into position against the wall as Ann and her companion left the mapmaker's shop, but he didn't bother to follow them as they headed back down the street the way they had come. His mind was reeling. Black Dog's legendary treasure had driven all rational thought from his head. He put no stock in such things as ghosts and curses, but gold... Now, that he believed in. Even the reward for two captured pirates was a mere pittance in comparison. But perhaps, if he played his cards right...

Newbury peered back through the shop window as a woman, belly swollen with child, made her way down the stairs behind the counter. Carter moved to help her, and a slow smile spread across Newbury's face. Yes, if he handled things just right, he might be able to get his hands on both the treasure *and* the pirate bitch. When he was certain Ann was too far down the street to notice any commotion, Newbury drew his pistol from its shoulder holster. He shoved the shop door open and leveled the gun at the mapmaker.

"Ashford Carter. In the name of His Majesty King Charles II, I am placing you under arrest for crimes committed against the English crown." He heard Carter's wife gasp and eyed her contemptuously. "And I'm afraid, Mistress Carter, that you are also under arrest, for harboring a known pirate and villain beneath your roof."

Carter's brows lowered, and he leapt over the counter with an agility that was surprising for his age. "I won't let you take her," he snarled.

Newbury backed up a step, but recovered quickly and pointed the pistol at the woman instead. "Stop right there, Master Carter, or I'll be forced to put a bullet between your wife's lovely eyes." The mapmaker froze, and Newbury nodded with satisfaction. "That's better. Now, it is my duty to take you into custody to stand trial. Mistress Carter's belly plea will likely grant her a few extra months of life before she's hanged, but I'm afraid you, sir, will face the gallows in a matter of weeks." He paused to let the effect of those words sink in.

Carter exchanged glances with his wife, and held his hands up. "Please, your officership, sir, I'll go with you without a fight. Just let me wife and babe go. I swear they didn't do nothing to deserve the hangman, sir." He took a tentative step forward. "I have some money, sir, I'll give you whatever you want, please."

Newbury pursed his lips and pretended to frown. "Are you trying to bribe an officer of the royal navy?"

Carter shook his head quickly. "No, no sir, I just—"

"Because I have a better idea."

It took Carter a moment to register this. "A better idea, sir?" he asked hopefully.

Newbury grinned. "Perhaps you could do a favor for me. And in exchange, I might just forget entirely about you and your little wife over there."

"What kind of favor?" Carter asked.

Newbury's smile widened.

Ann frowned at the short, brown-haired man at Carter's side as they took seats at the table across from her and Barclay. Though he wore a patch over one eye, his hands were too smooth and his skin too pale for a seaman. He was young, scarcely thirty if her guess was right, with a sharp, triangular nose that reminded her of a shark. And there was a glint in the man's one visible eye that Ann did not like. "Who's this?" she grunted, and Carter gave a chuckle that sounded nervous.

"He's the reason I'm gonna agree to your offer."

Ann straightened. "You've changed your mind?" She'd expected a long night of arguments, a significant amount of rum, and possibly a few death threats before the man would concede. She had even prepared Barclay for the possibility that they might have to abduct Carter against his will. This seemed far too easy, and now she stared at Carter's companion even more intently.

"Aye, on one condition. This here is me apprentice. I'm training him to handle the shop for a while after the baby is born. I told you me wife is expecting?" Ann nodded. "Well, as you can probably tell, he ain't got much experience on the sea. First time out poor lad lost an eye, and ain't been on a ship's deck since. But there's some things that can't be taught without doing, you know? So the wife and I, we talked it over. It'll be a risk, but we figure with the kind of money you're offering and the exposure it'll give me boy here," he reached out to ruffle the young man's hair vigorously, "this venture of yours is worth trying. Sorta my last affair with the sea, you understand, before I leave it forever."

Ann waved a tavern girl over to deliver another round of drinks, and sat back to eye this newcomer critically. She hadn't missed the anxiety in Carter's tone or the young man's malevolent glare as he smoothed his disheveled hair. "And does this apprentice of yours have a name?"

The two exchanged glances, and finally the one-eyed man spoke. "You can just call me Patch."

Ann knew when she was being lied to, and she didn't like it. But whoever this "Patch" really was, once he was on board her ship he would be a fool to try to make trouble. The most important thing was that Carter had agreed to join their crew. So long as he led them to Black Dog's island, Ann didn't care if he wanted to bring an entire entourage of suspicious "apprentices."

"Well then, Patch, you're sure you understand the mission of this voyage?"

Patch licked his lips. "We're seeking Black Dog's gold, ma'am."

Ann hated being called "ma'am." She grunted her displeasure, but continued, "That's right. Most likely it will be a very dangerous venture. You think you have the stomach for it?"

"I don't believe in all the stories, Captain, but if that treasure really exists I can't pass up the chance to lay eyes on it myself."

Ann nodded, and lifted her mug. "It's agreed, then. We meet tomorrow morning on the *Ice Queen* and you'll both be signed aboard." The men lifted their drinks as well, and the glazed clay mugs made a dull clatter as they met across the table.

CHAPTER NINE

Violet shaded her eyes from the sun as she watched three strange figures board the *Ice Queen*'s main deck. It took her a while to recognize Ann, who was wearing a cloak and had her face swathed in a woolen scarf. When the captain saw her, she pushed back her hood and pulled the scarf down so she could speak.

"You're still here? I gave the crew three days' leave in town." Ann threw off her heavy outer garments and left them in a pile on the deck. Violet could see sweat staining the collar and underarms of her shirt.

Violet pretended not to notice the blatant leer that passed over the younger man's face as the two strangers stared at her curiously. "I know, Captain, but I still have work to do here."

"What work would that be?"

"I—" Violet faltered under Ann's penetrating gaze. The truth was, Turtle and O'Hare had both tried to entice her into accompanying them into Port Royal and had been sorely disappointed when she refused. Violet couldn't bring herself to set foot in the place that had, at one time, been the dream she was to share with her husband. Ann's eyes narrowed as though she could read the thoughts flitting across Violet's face. Finally the pirate shrugged.

"Well, if you want to spend your leave on board scrubbing pots and cleaning feed pens, I won't stop you." She indicated the graying, lanky man next to her. "Master Carter, this is Sister Violet—ship's swabbie, galley hand," Ann flashed Violet a wicked grin before adding, "and my little bunk warmer, hmm?"

Violet bristled. It was bad enough that the crew believed she was on board solely for the captain's pleasure. It certainly didn't help that

Ann seemed delighted to perpetuate that misconception. She opened her mouth to retort indignantly, but was interrupted by Carter's chuckle as he took her hand. "Well ain't that just a blunderbuss to the ballocks, Captain! It ain't enough that you're planning to tangle with some of the most devilish waters known to man, you have to tempt fate even further by bringing a fine piece like this on board." Carter pressed Violet's hand to his lips in an unexpectedly civilized manner. "'Tis a right pleasure to make your acquaintance, Mistress Violet. I hope you ain't been taken in by this jackanape's silver tongue—I seen her playing with the tavern girls last night and she can charm the shell off a bloody sea turtle." He winked, and Violet caught Ann's scowl out of the corner of her eye. Not many men had the nerve to tease Branded Ann so recklessly. Violet could tell she was going to like Ashford Carter. She could not resist returning his greeting with her most innocent smile.

"Thank you, Master Carter, but please don't worry yourself. I can assure you I remain quite unaffected by the charms of Branded Ann's tongue." Violet wasn't sure which was more rewarding, Carter's hearty guffaw or the rare expression of consternation that crossed Ann's face. She cast the pirate a brief smirk before turning back to Carter with feigned confusion. "Did I say something funny?" she inquired, fluttering her lashes. He laughed even harder, and Violet noted with glee that for once the swaggering pirate captain actually seemed at a loss for words.

But then Ann stepped forward with a strange expression and took Violet in her arms. Violet's first instinct was to wriggle away, but the intensity darkening Ann's eyes held her with fascination and she found she did not want to move. Their faces were so close that Violet could see the sprinkling of freckles that peppered the pirate's nose and cheeks, the sun lines at the corners of her mouth. The heat of Ann's body pressed against her hips, her stomach, her ribs, her breasts, and Violet suddenly realized she was leaning into that solid presence rather than away from it.

The tongue previously in question appeared as Ann moistened her lower lip. Violet's pulse quickened, all her attention focused on the pirate's mouth. Was Ann going to kiss her? Her skin tingled as apprehension and excitement mingled in her veins and made her light-headed. She had to grip Ann's forearms so as not to lose her balance.

Ever so slowly Ann lowered her head, and Violet surprised herself by tilting her face up expectantly.

But when Ann's lips were just close enough to brush Violet's, she stopped, her body trembling. "Unaffected, are you?" she murmured, mischief crinkling the corners of her mouth.

Violet had to pant to catch her breath as Ann pulled back. Embarrassment and confusion flooded over her as she realized that, for an instant, she'd actually wanted the pirate to kiss her. Violet couldn't ever remember wanting a kiss before. Certainly no one had ever made her feel so dizzy, and weak, and…and *hot*. Her whole body felt like it was radiating. Violet could recognize desire in others but had never felt it herself, and it was a very disconcerting experience.

Ann grinned at her, which only made her stomach churn. She raised a hand to strike the pirate in the face, but Ann caught it easily in midair.

"Ah-ah."

Violet wrenched her arm free and backed away a few steps, shaking with frustration. A fit of temper would only add to Ann's victory, but Violet was too bewildered to think of anything clever to retaliate. With as much dignity as she could muster, she stalked away.

❖

Ann's smile faded as she watched Violet leave. Usually, such a powerful response to her seductive skills gave Ann a great sense of triumph. And she had felt the anticipation shimmering from Violet as if it were tangible; there was no doubt that Violet would have allowed the kiss, that she probably would have even encouraged it. Ann supposed she ought to be pleased with herself, but instead all she felt was fear. That was the closest she had ever come to losing control. For a few seconds, desire had nearly overwhelmed her, and her muscles were still quivering with the effort it had taken to hold herself back. What she had intended as a mischievous bit of flirting had turned into something quite different, and she cursed her own foolishness. But she hadn't expected the intensity of Violet's reaction, and it had taken her off guard.

Ann took a moment to regain her composure before turning to

Carter. He and his apprentice were snickering, and Ann rolled her eyes.

"Enough. We have business to attend to. Follow me."

When both men had placed their signatures with the others on the *Ice Queen*'s Articles, Ann replaced the document in its glass frame and led them back to the gangplank. Violet was nowhere in sight.

"We don't set sail until tomorrow, boys, so I recommend you enjoy your last night on land. May be a while before you see it again." She observed the apprentice's one visible eye flickering eagerly over the decks of her ship. He'd scanned her cabin in much the same way, as though he were taking mental inventory of everything he saw. Ann pursed her lips. "Patch, was it?"

He jumped and nodded, and she bared her teeth in a smile that was anything but friendly. "Perhaps you would join me for a drink this evening."

Patch shook his head quickly. "No, no thank you, Branded Ann…I mean, Miss Ann…Miss Captain Ann…"

"'Captain' will be just fine," she interjected dryly.

"Oh, of course. Captain. No, I want to start this voyage with a clear head."

"Suit yourself." She turned to Carter. "What about you?"

He scratched his head. "Afraid not, Captain, I have a wife waiting for me at home."

Ann shrugged and slapped Carter on the back good-naturedly. "And I'm sure she wouldn't appreciate it if I kept her man out drinking on your last night together. Get on back to her, then, before she comes looking for you." Both men shuffled off down the plank to the dock, and Ann looked almost wistfully at the open hatch leading to the lower decks. Violet was probably in the galley, and briefly Ann considered going to look for her.

Why? You want to apologize? The thought brought a scowl to her face, Branded Ann never apologized, and besides, she hadn't really done anything wrong. Violet had responded to her of her own free will, even if she hadn't meant to. Ann picked up her cloak and scarf and covered herself again. Time to go find a few women who would appreciate her company—or at the very least, appreciate her money enough to pretend they did.

❖

Many hours later, Ann stepped unsteadily into her cabin, her stomach and limbs burning pleasantly. The rum she'd liberally downed for the past few hours was finally beginning to do its work, and now she struggled to remember why she had left. Her body was taut with arousal, and she could have had her pick of girls in the place. She vaguely remembered a few in particular who had come to sit on her lap as they poured her drinks, grinding their hips into hers suggestively. But even as desire throbbed through her abdomen, centering wetly between her thighs, she didn't find the thought of any one of them attractive, no matter how satisfying the release. She wanted…what exactly did she want, anyway? Ann peeled out of her heavy, hot outer garments and managed to light the oil lamp on the table. Her head swam in a pleasant, glowing haze of warmth as she moved to the bed and lay down, noting with tipsy amusement that the familiar rocking motion of the ship was, from a certain point of view, powerfully sensual.

Closing her eyes, Ann lay still for several moments feeling her pulse beat rapidly and lightly in her throat and lower legs, her rum-soaked muscles tingling with hypersensation. She imagined that she could feel every thread of her clothing, the loose white shirt brushing faintly against her breasts as she inhaled, the rough-spun trousers encasing her legs. A maddening, firm pressure rubbed against her aching center, courtesy of two bulky pant seams that met at just the right spot. Drinking always made her randy, and she cursed herself for leaving the brothel. These trips to dry land, where the pleasures of a woman were in no short supply, were uncomfortably few and far between in the privateering trade.

Still, it was for that very reason that she had become adept at alleviating such situations herself. Fumbling with the buttons of her trousers, she tugged them open and slid a hand down through the coarse curls that lay beneath. She gave a shuddering sigh as her fingertips reached their goal and began a quick, insistent stroking that she knew would be effective in a matter of minutes.

❖

Violet rinsed the pot for the last time, finally satisfied that she'd removed the last of the scum that had been baked into the iron. She dried the inside and outside vigorously with a rag, knowing that if she left the metal damp it would likely rust before the night was through. Hanging the pot on a hook by the galley door, she wiped the sweat from her brow and stretched.

She'd scrubbed every inch of the galley, taking her frustration out on the pots and pans, the floor, the big table, and every utensil, mug, and plate she could find. By the time she was done, the galley nearly gleamed in the lantern light and the physical exertion had succeeded, for the most part, in calming her boiling blood, though it had not quite been able to quiet her chattering mind.

Violet was an expert at thwarting unwanted advances. The second Ann took hold of her she could have easily brushed her aside with some witty but decidedly off-putting remark, and that would have been the end of it. So why had she just stood there, holding her breath, letting the pirate's lips get closer and closer...and why in God's name had she actually found herself *disappointed* when the kiss didn't happen? She hated Ann, didn't she? The woman was supposed to make her skin crawl, not set her heart racing.

After extinguishing the stove that had heated her wash water, Violet took the lantern and ascended the aft ladder through the hatch. Perhaps she'd climb the mainmast while everyone was gone. She had always wondered what the view was like from the crow's nest, and she certainly wasn't ready to return to the captain's cabin yet.

A warm Jamaican breeze caressed her cheeks pleasantly as she emerged, and Violet inhaled deeply of the exotic perfume lingering in the air. Tropical flowers, spices, and the salt of the ocean, it was a glorious scent that promised adventure and freedom. Violet snickered. She was beginning to think like a pirate already.

Illumination caught her eye as she turned starboard, and Violet frowned as she realized that there was a seam of golden light beneath the captain's cabin door. Ann was always so careful about onboard fire. Had she really been so distracted by the prospect of drinking and whoring that she'd neglected to put out her lamp? The woman was as bad as any man. Violet decided to check. It wouldn't do to have the *Ice Queen* go up in flames before they could even leave port.

She opened the cabin door and stopped short in confusion. There was indeed a burning lamp on the table, but beyond it Violet could make out an unmistakable cloud of hair resting in the bunk, framing a cross-marred face. Long legs stretched out atop the coverlet, feet still booted. Ann's eyes were closed, and Violet supposed she was asleep. Why had she come back? Violet had a hard time imagining what could possibly draw the pirate away from a night of drinking, gambling, and busty, willing tavern wenches.

Then Violet glimpsed movement, a small quick pulsing at the crotch of the captain's trousers, and in a split second she realized that Ann was not asleep at all. She followed the tense line of Ann's forearm, her wrist disappearing into unbuttoned pants. Violet sucked in a breath, mesmerized.

Ann suddenly gasped and jerked upright. Violet gave a start herself. She knew the other woman hadn't reached the peak of her self-pleasure quite yet. Ice blue eyes, dilated with desire, stared into her own with such hunger that Violet could have sworn she was actually the object of that lust. Then the glassy look cleared, and Violet could read the change in expression as Ann realized she was not alone in her cabin—confusion, then alarm. Violet had never seen Ann appear more vulnerable, and she found it strangely exhilarating.

Violet moved forward slowly, holding Ann's gaze, not quite sure why she hadn't already turned and left the captain to her privacy. Her heart quickened in her throat as she approached, almost afraid Ann might bolt. She recognized in the other woman a need that she knew exactly how to fill, if Ann would let her, and she was possessed by the overwhelming desire to show the arrogant pirate captain that she wasn't the only one who knew a thing or two about seduction.

❖

Ann was not ashamed at being caught in a private moment. As a rule she made no apologies for having a healthy libido. However, her rum-fogged brain wondered frantically if somehow Violet had read her mind, knew that it was her face that had appeared in Ann's imagination. She half expected Violet to run disgusted from the cabin. But Violet's face showed no indication of disgust, or even embarrassment. Instead she seemed intent on approaching the bunk, a strange shine in her starry eyes. Ann's initial anxiety faded and she lay back against the pillows, watching Violet curiously.

"Let me help." The unexpected whisper sent a delicious shiver down Ann's entire length. Violet reached out and tugged Ann's hand from her trousers, bringing the fingers to her lips. Her warm mouth closed over Ann's fingertips, sucking lightly at the moisture that still clung to them, and Ann's entire body responded with immediate delight. Astonished and very aroused, she withdrew her hand slowly. Violet must have been even more affected by their encounter that afternoon than Ann had realized. She could practically feel the other woman's body thrumming with excitement. She had promised herself not to make a move on the girl, but she certainly would not reject what was being freely offered. Ann moved to unlace the front of Violet's bodice, but Violet firmly stopped her hand.

"No. This is about you."

Ann blinked fuzzily. Violet held her wrist with one hand and daintily trailed the other across Ann's collarbone to the sensitive hollow at the base of her throat, then downward. Ann's shirt opened almost magically beneath deft fingers that barely even paused to twist each button loose. This was different. Ann was accustomed to being the aggressor in bed, as in all other things. Yet she was too foggy with drink to protest.

"I envy you, Captain," Violet murmured, snaking her hand beneath the shirt to trace the erect nipple beneath. Ann exhaled. "It's so easy for you, isn't it?" Violet's touch was expert, delicate and firm in just the right places, and Ann arched into it luxuriously. This was it, this was what she'd been longing for all evening and couldn't put a name to. And she might be dreaming—this could easily be nothing more than one of her more tangible erotic dreams, brought on by too much drink and the memory of Violet's sensual dance at the Tortuga bordello. But if it wasn't real, Ann hoped she wouldn't awaken anytime soon.

❖

Such a magnificent body, Violet thought, far more beautiful than most she'd seen. Ann was long limbed, tightly muscled, her skin tanned by the Caribbean sun and unexpectedly smooth. *Iron under silk.*

Even the small breasts with their hard little points spoke of strength and power. Only now that powerful frame was trembling beneath her fingers, guided entirely by the smallest movements of her hands, practically purring at her touch. Violet couldn't help a wistful smile.

"For me, this has always been a duty, you know." A slight quiver in Ann's muscles each time Violet spoke told her that Ann was aroused by her voice. Violet was used to it. Many found her throaty, breathless tones to be exceptionally provocative, and what she said wouldn't matter so long as she kept up an erotic murmur in Ann's ear. With one last teasing caress Violet let her hand drift from the pirate's breast across her stomach, gliding purposefully downward beneath the open trousers.

"I don't think I ever learned to enjoy my body. So many other people were using it for their own needs." Ann gave a soft moan as Violet parted her with one finger and swirled firmly through the soaked folds. Violet watched Ann's face carefully as she made several experimental strokes that would tell her exactly how the other woman needed to be touched, how much pressure to use, which spots were most sensitive. "Even my husband, dear that he was, never excited me. But I liked to please him, for he was so very good to me in every other way."

She dipped slightly into the heated opening, felt the eager muscles clamp around her finger, and withdrew gently. That was too much. "But you, Captain, even though you trust no one, care for no one, you still indulge your senses whenever you can. And even then you're always in perfect control, aren't you?" In a few seconds she had learned all she needed to know. She adjusted the position of her fingertip, flicking it lightly and steadily against the delicate nerves. Ann grunted and lifted her hips, but Violet laid her other hand flat against the pirate's belly.

"Shh. You may be used to giving the orders, but this time you're just going to have to trust me." Violet was amused to catch the slightest hint of desperation in Ann's expression. "Trust me," she repeated.

❖

Violet's touch was maddening, fragile and insistent like the flutter of a butterfly wing. Ann fought the urge to press against it again, and held Violet's eyes defiantly. She craved much more intense contact, but

Violet's smile kept her from saying so. *She's enjoying this*, Ann realized with annoyance, but her rebellious body would not allow her to throw off the other woman's attentions now. Ann got the feeling that Violet wanted her to beg. She wouldn't.

A pleasant, warm sensation simmered deep in her pelvis, as though a fuse had been lit in the marrow of her bones. The heat built steadily, increasing exponentially with every tiny brush of Violet's finger. It melted her thigh muscles and glowed through her buttocks and lower stomach. Violet's voice was in her ear, a low, unintelligible rumble. The yearning became unbearable then, and Ann bit her lip in an attempt to keep from crying out the word on the tip of her tongue. *Please.* She couldn't stop her hips from tilting up, but somehow Violet kept the tip of her finger just out of reach, never slowing its faint, rhythmic tease.

Without warning, the fire building beneath her suddenly blazed outward, streaking into her legs, burning her lungs, lifting her off the bunk until Ann wouldn't have been surprised had she found herself suspended in midair. And then Violet pressed down once, firmly, with the pad of her finger, against that aching spot. Once was all it took.

Ann gave a strangled cry as explosions burst through her abdomen, her hips, her thighs, her chest, in rapid-fire succession. Her head felt light, blood ringing in her ears as shock waves of pleasure racked her limbs. For several long minutes she lay panting for breath, so completely bereft of strength that she wasn't even sure she could convince her hand to make a fist.

She'd never come like this before, never felt liquefied by the force of it. *And she barely touched me.* Ann couldn't imagine what the release would have been like if Violet had gone deeper, like Ann had wanted. *I might not have survived it. My heart probably would have stopped beating altogether.* She chuckled breathlessly. *I wonder if she's ever actually killed anyone this way?*

"Something funny?"

Ann looked up to see Violet watching her. "I was just thinking that you'd make a good assassin."

"You mean, go around fucking people to death?" Violet asked, her eyes twinkling. Ann didn't know if she'd ever become accustomed to hearing dirty words coming out of the same mouth that spouted Scripture on a daily basis. "I'll take that as a compliment."

"You should." Ann grinned and reached out for her. "Come here. I happen to have a few lethal skills of my own to show you."

Violet quickly withdrew from Ann's reach. "I don't think that's a good idea." Ann was perplexed by the shadow that suddenly crossed her face. "I've been meaning to find a bunk in the crew's quarters, anyway. Now that I'm a full-fledged crew member, I ought to be sharing berth with the rest of the men."

"Don't be ridiculous." With considerable effort Ann managed to force her shaking muscles into a sitting position, and she stared at her incredulously. "Violet, you don't want to bunk with the crew."

"It's not right for me to stay here, Captain. You promised, when you let me sign the Articles, that I'd get equal treatment. No more, no less. But so long as I'm sharing your cabin they'll never really think of me as an equal."

"The Articles be damned, Violet, you're not safe with the men." *And you want me. I know you do. What are you so afraid of?*

Sadness flitted across the pretty features. "I think it's safer than staying here." Violet turned to go.

Ann's temper flared and she stood. She caught Violet around the waist and held her firmly, deliberately pressing her heated body along the other woman's back. "I've already told you," she growled, "I don't waste my energy on the unwilling. I seem to remember that you're the one who started this. You want to end it, fine, but don't be a fool. I'm not one of your bloody tavern patrons, Violet."

Violet twisted away and spun to face her. "You certainly smell like one," she retorted coolly.

She must mean the rum. Ann was mildly taken aback. She'd nearly forgotten her earlier tipsiness. Now she felt completely sober and inexplicably angry. She took a threatening step forward, determined to tie Violet to the bunk if that was what it would take to keep her from carrying through with this ludicrous idea. But Violet held up a hand.

"I don't know what you think just happened here, so let me make it simple for you. I'm a whore." Her eyes had darkened into twilight, leaving the secret star within them white-hot.

"So you want me to pay you?" Ann snapped, and regretted the words almost immediately as Violet flinched.

"Why don't we just consider tonight a gift? A little thank-you for bringing me back on board. We'll leave it at that."

"Violet—"

"Leave it, Captain Ann. I'm not staying here, unless you want to break that cherished rule of yours and force me," Violet said with a sneer. "Maybe you should be asking yourself why it's so important to you that I stay."

Ann ground her teeth and turned her back. "You want to go, then go, but don't come crying to me when you get yourself rogered by half the crew in the middle of the night."

"I can take care of myself."

Ann heard footsteps and then the slam of the cabin door, and managed to return to the edge of her bunk before her knees gave way. Cursing, she pulled herself onto the wide mattress. A sick weight had settled in her stomach, growing heavier as her initial burst of anger drained away. Why did she care, anyway, what happened to the little wench? Violet had been trouble since the day they'd brought her on board. She should have left the Scripture-spouting tart at the whorehouse where she'd found her.

Obviously it's her calling, Ann thought bitterly, remembering how easily Violet had learned her body, read its needs in a matter of seconds, effortlessly taken her higher than anyone ever had. The memory alone was enough to make her groan, a liquid rush renewing between her legs. She wanted it again. Her limbs still felt like jelly from the first encounter and she was craving a second—a proper tumble this time, with Violet writhing beneath her, that beautiful face tipped back in throes of pleasure, the creamy skin of her throat turned golden in the lamplight. But Violet had been careful not to let Ann touch her. Ann suddenly recalled that Violet had never really allowed her touch for more than a few seconds, even casually, except in sleep.

Abruptly she sat up in the bunk. What was it Violet had said about duty? It made sense. Violet's body had never really been her own. She had no reason to welcome the touch of another person. Bitterly Ann recalled the victorious smile curving Violet's lips as she'd sent her over the edge. For Violet it had been a game, hadn't it? A chance to exercise the only kind of power she could over someone bigger and stronger than herself. Though Ann had sensed no hate or anger in Violet's touch, she certainly recognized the triumph in her eyes.

She ought to be angry, or at the very least frustrated with herself for letting Violet get the better of her. But all she experienced was an unfamiliar surge of compassion. *She doesn't understand.* Ann was suddenly willing to bet a thousand silver doubloons that in all her years as a prostitute, and even as a wife, Violet had never crested that wave of pleasure herself. She probably didn't even know she was capable of it. And Ann discovered with consternation that she wanted to be the one to show Violet that sex wasn't just an exchange of power, that it wasn't always a one-sided affair.

Isn't it? the little mocking voice in the back of her mind asked. *You've always preferred it rather one-sided yourself.*

That was true, but not so much anymore.

Not with her, you mean. Admit it, Ann, she's gotten to you.

Ann shook her head in protest, though there was no one to see it. *That's ridiculous, she's just some tavern strumpet—*

Who makes your heart skip like a bloody spring lamb every time she looks at you.

Shut up. Ann lay back down again. *She's a good kid who's had some tough breaks. I'm just trying to help her out.*

Really? By bringing her on board a ship full of pirates and cutthroats? You know she's not a sailor. You know what the boys will do to her if they can. When they find out she's a harlot all hell is going to break loose.

For all her earlier flippancy, the thought of Violet in the hands of her men turned her stomach. But Violet would be safe enough for the night. The crew wouldn't be returning until tomorrow morning.

And then? What about tomorrow night? The night after that? How long do you suppose the men will be content to sleep chastely beside such a fine little prize?

I'll kill anyone who lays a hand on her. She was stunned by the vehemence of the thought.

The voice laughed. *You really think you can take on your entire crew?*

"If I have to," she gritted under her breath.

You're not that good, no matter what the stories say. She's not worth it. Ann wanted to argue, but the words repeated themselves stubbornly. *She's not worth it.*

And Violet wasn't worth it, not by any logical line of reasoning.

Ann had never let anyone get in the way of her mission before and she'd be damned if she was going to allow it now. She'd been waiting her entire life for the hunt they were about to begin. *Then let the wench bilge on her own anchor, I don't care.* She rolled over and punched her pillow into a more comfortable position, but it was a long time before she fell into an uneasy sleep.

CHAPTER TEN

From the feed pens at the head of the gun deck Violet heard the scuffle, a terrible screeching and banging of pans coming from the galley. She dropped the bucket of grain in her hands to dash back toward the stern.

"O'Hare, what in the world—" Violet stopped short as she surveyed the ship's kitchen in utter disarray. Chicken feathers and flour floated in the air. Pots and pans lay scattered topsy-turvy on the chopping table, and a bag of the captain's precious coffee beans had spilled out across the deck. She gaped at O'Hare, who appeared to be struggling with a wriggling, shrieking bundle of rags that was nearly half his size. The Irishman grunted.

"Get over here, then, and help me hold the little bugger!"

The thing in his arms screeched again. Violet glimpsed little pale hands, then a face beneath a mop of stringy hair. She gasped. "Why, it's a child!"

O'Hare grunted again, and managed to lift his captive's feet from the floor. He slung the screaming youngster over his shoulder like a sack of meal and headed for the hatch. Violet didn't like the grim set of the galley master's jaw. "O'Hare, wait. What are you going to do?"

She followed him abovedecks, where the crew gathered to watch as he dumped his burden none too gently by the mainmast. The urchin jumped up, shaggy head twisting nervously from side to side. Suddenly Violet realized that, in spite of the ragged trousers and shorn hair, this was a little girl. She couldn't be more than seven or eight years old. How she had managed to steal aboard, Violet couldn't guess, but looking around at the leering faces of the crew Violet had the sinking feeling that the child's fate would not be pleasant.

"Avast! Cease that noise!"

The captain's order rang out over the jeering crew, and they parted to allow her through. A cold knot formed in Violet's stomach at the sight of Ann making her way to their midst.

Ann's gaze swept the assembled men and settled briefly on Violet. Violet watched a shadow pass across the pirate's face and quickly looked away. The uncomfortable tension that had sprung up between them over the past few weeks was so palpable that at times Violet could feel it crawling along her skin.

Neither of them had exchanged so much as a word since their strange, intense encounter the night before the *Ice Queen* had set sail. Violet continued to sleep in the crew's quarters, her Bible safely tucked beneath the thin straw pallet that served as a mattress. Barclay insisted she take the bunk directly above his, and he glared menacingly at any crew member who took more than a passing interest in her presence among them. She suspected that Ann had ordered the quartermaster to keep an eye on her, perhaps even protect her from the other men.

But Ann herself had said nothing. She even began sending Turtle to collect her first cup of coffee from the galley in the mornings, avoiding contact as much as possible. Violet became increasingly certain that she had made a grave mistake. She had hoped to gain just a sliver of advantage over the arrogant pirate, and to her surprise, it seemed to have worked. Raw hunger tensed every line of the captain's lean frame when Violet was nearby, kept in check only by Ann's fierce pride. Ordinarily Violet would have found this knowledge immensely satisfying, but somehow, the haunted look in Ann's eyes only pricked at her most uncomfortably.

The ship was far too small for them to avoid one another completely, and Ann grew more peevish with each passing day. Even the rest of the crew had noticed their captain's foul mood. Violet felt somewhat responsible for the fate of the child who was facing judgment at the hands of such a dangerously ill-tempered woman.

❖

Ann could not stop her eyes from greedily traveling the length of Violet's body, the close-fitting trousers and bodice that hugged those delectable curves like a second skin, the linen blouse open at the collar to expose a generous expanse of throat. Today Violet wore her dark hair in two girlish braids, one over each shoulder, and a smudge of flour lingered impishly on the tip of her nose. Ann felt her blood tingle lecherously in her veins. This was torment. She couldn't get the memory of Violet's touch out of her mind. Every day the desire to experience it again grew stronger, but Violet made it very clear she had no interest in an encore performance.

Ann had never felt such helplessness before. Surely this was how a person went mad, yearning for something they could not have. She was furious with this absurd weakness that she could not seem to contain. Since when had she ever let another human being, beautiful or otherwise, affect her so?

But most of all, Ann was disturbed by the sinister awareness that she did not have to suffer this discontent if she didn't choose to. Branded Ann, bloodthirsty queen of the Caribbean, could have whatever she wanted. All she had to do was take it.

Never in her life had Ann been so afraid of her own darkness.

And Violet had to feel it, had to have sensed it that night when Ann reached for her. No wonder she insisted on sleeping with the men. Now she wouldn't even meet Ann's eyes for more than a few seconds at a time. Could she somehow see, written on Ann's face, the horrific things Ann did to her in her dreams every night?

As if on cue, Violet dropped her gaze, suddenly appearing very interested in the planks of wood beneath their feet. Through sheer force of will Ann quelled the miserable churning of her stomach. She was still master of this ship, if nothing else. Coldly she turned her attention to the galley master.

"What is the meaning of this ruckus, O'Hare?" she snapped, the words coming harsher than she'd intended.

"Seems we got a stowaway, Lady Captain."

Ann followed the line of his pointed finger to the ragged urchin standing beneath the mainmast. She arched an eyebrow. "So I see."

The kid brushed stringy hair out of her face. "I ain't no stowaway!" she protested indignantly. The pirates burst out laughing at her absurd defiance, but Ann bent forward to get a better look at the girl's face.

"We have met before. Charlie, wasn't it?" The girl nodded. Ann tapped her fingers against the hilt of the cutlass thrust through her sash. "I distinctly remember telling you to go home. You should have listened."

"We have penalties for stowaways, don't we, Captain?" one of the crew shouted gleefully.

Charlie glared. "I said I ain't no bleeding stowaway!" she insisted. When the pirates continued to laugh, she made an obscene gesture in their general direction. "Oh, piss off!"

Barclay abruptly struck the girl across the face and knocked her to the deck. Charlie sprang back up. A thin trickle of blood seeped from her nose as she pulled a rusty dagger from her sleeve. "You filthy bung-farting pirate devil, don't touch me!"

Ann reached out and caught Charlie's wrist as the girl awkwardly swiped at Barclay with the weapon. She dug her thumb into the tendons and wrested the blade from the small fingers. "No one," she said with careful calm, "comes aboard my ship without my say-so."

"But you wouldn't have let me come if I'd asked," Charlie replied staunchly, "and I gotta be part of your crew, Branded Ann! You're the greatest pi—"

Losing what little patience she had left, Ann pushed the girl down until she was sitting on the deck, her back against the mast. "Shut up." The wounded look in Charlie's eyes only served to fuel Ann's temper.

"Get this through your thick skull, kid. This isn't one of your daddy's wide-eyed adventure tales. I'm no hero. I'm a thief. A murderer. A monster." She spat on the deck to emphasize her words, and Barclay stepped forward.

"I say we get this useless weight off our ship," the quartermaster grunted, and several members of the crew cheered their agreement.

Ann clenched her jaw. She knew he was right, they really had no other choice. The child would be better off drowned in the sea than left in the hands of these men. But before she could give the order, Violet cried out in protest.

"No!" Violet stepped between Barclay and Charlie and held her arms out to shield the girl behind her own body. "I won't let you do this," she said defiantly, glaring at Ann.

It was the first time Violet had spoken directly to her in weeks.

For an instant Ann found herself immobilized by the sound of her voice, unwillingly recalling those same sultry tones murmuring in her ear. Her insides tensed. If it had been any other member of the crew, Ann would have drawn her cutlass and relieved him of his tongue on the spot. "Stand down, Sister Violet," she warned, inwardly wincing at the strain she could hear in her own words. But Violet would not be intimidated.

"*Suffer the little children to come unto me, and forbid them not: for of such is the kingdom of God.* If you want to throw this child overboard, Captain, you're going to have to send me along with her."

"Well, that's easily done, ain't it?" Ann recognized Jenkins's thick Yorkshire accent. The heavily tattooed crewman made no secret of his hatred for Violet, ever since that first day on the ship when she'd insinuated rather explicitly that he preferred the intimate attentions of other men. He and the others who resented Violet's presence on board would happily take her up on her ultimatum if they could. Before anyone else had the opportunity to second Jenkins's opinion, Ann shoved Charlie roughly at Barclay.

"This is not a negotiation."

Barclay hauled Charlie to the starboard gunwale, ignoring the little teeth that sank into his forearm as she struggled to get away. At the edge of the deck he lifted the kicking girl into the air and flung her into the water below. Ann registered the girl's scream, wincing slightly at the splash when Charlie hit the water. She joined Barclay at the rail, but turned at the sound of feet pounding the deck. Violet was charging toward her.

Ann braced herself, but too late she realized that Violet had no intention of attacking her. Instead, Violet planted her hands on the rail and vaulted over it. Instinctively Ann reached out to stop her, but she had been caught off balance. Though she did catch Violet's wrist, Violet was already falling too fast. Her momentum pulled Ann over the gunwale as well.

Both women dropped into the ocean below. The cold salt spray rose up to meet them, and Ann's breath was knocked from her lungs as she hit the water. She tightened her grip on Violet's wrist. The water closed over their heads, then broke again as Ann kicked upward, and she heard Violet's sputtering cough. She could feel Violet struggling to remain afloat beside her, and quickly pinned her to her chest with one arm. Violet continued thrashing frantically.

"Bloody cork-brained chit, cease that floundering or you'll drown us both," Ann growled into her ear, desperately trying not to think about how sinfully good it felt to have those sweet curves pressed so close.

"Let go of me, then!" Violet gasped in retort. "I have to—" She choked a little as a wave doused them both. "I have to save her."

Ann looked up to see Charlie's tousled head bobbing a few yards away. "I think the kid swims better than you do," she noted dryly. "See for yourself."

Charlie was paddling steadily toward them. Apparently even being tossed into the ocean was not enough to dampen the girl's cheerful impudence. "Well, that was bangin' beautiful, weren't it? Serves you right for throwing me off like that."

Ann glared stonily as Violet asked, "Are you all right, little one?"

Charlie nodded proudly. "Ship-shape, Miss. I been swimming like a fish since I were a babe." To illustrate her point, she gleefully circled them in the water.

Ann looked up as Barclay called out overhead. "Taking a morning dip, are you, Captain?"

"Shut up and toss down a line," she called back irritably. Barclay obediently lowered a length of rope over the rail. Ann swam toward it, still holding Violet in one arm; luckily the winds were not strong this morning, and the *Ice Queen* was moving very slowly. When she caught the rope with her free hand, it tugged them gently through the water alongside the hull.

Ann hesitated. Every self-preservation instinct demanded she return to the ship alone and leave Violet and Charlie both to the mercy of the ocean before either could bring further trouble. It was the smart thing to do. It was even most likely the kind thing to do, as drowning was a far gentler death than what might otherwise happen to them in the pirates' hands. Yet even her usual careful pragmatism could not overpower the acute awareness of Violet's heartbeat pounding beneath her fingertips.

Ann started to thread the rope around Violet's waist, but Violet shook her head stubbornly. "I'm not going back without the girl, Captain."

"Aww, just leave them both, Captain Ann!" someone shouted

from above. Ann ground her teeth with annoyance. The crew had lined up along the ship's rail to see what she would do. She knew there would be hell to pay for her decision, but she would deal with it later. She called out to Charlie.

"Get over here, kid, and hold on!"

❖

When all three had safely returned to the ship's deck, water dripping from their clothes and hair, the pirates set up a clamor. They demanded to know why Ann had brought the two unlucky females back on board and insisted on a proper punishment. Amid the excitement Jenkins appeared with the quartermaster's cat-o'-nine-tails, a wicked leather whip used to discipline unruly sailors. He cracked it over his head several times to the cheers of his shipmates.

Barclay eyed Ann warily. "The Articles are pretty clear on stowaways and them what help them, Captain."

Ann knew that; she'd written the rules herself. Thirty strokes of the lash, at the very least. It would be a deadly penalty for most. The kid probably wouldn't make it past fifteen before she bled to death, and Violet...she was scarcely larger than a child herself. But her command over these men depended on their belief that she would invariably carry out the consequences set in the Articles. She could not afford to lose their respect, and she felt increasingly angered by the position she was now in. She had to think of something, and fast, before the crew decided to take matters into their own hands.

Jenkins thrust the whip beneath Ann's nose. "Go on, then, Captain," he said eagerly. "Show us the blue blood in those veins of hers."

Ann's temper exploded. "So, you want blood, do you, Jenkins?" She snatched the cat from his hands and snapped it cruelly. Scarlet lines appeared across his cheek and upper body as the nine knotted tails tore his skin. Jenkins fell back with an angry cry, and his hand went to the cutlass at his side.

"It ain't fair to spare the wench just because she fires up your nethers, Captain," he asserted defiantly. "I ain't the only one what thinks this bit of tits and arse is making you soft in the head."

Adrenaline shot through Ann's limbs. Faster than Jenkins could draw his blade she fell on him with the cat, striking his head, his chest, his shoulders until nearly every inch of the tattooed skin was raw and bleeding. Jenkins was driven to his knees in seconds as Ann finally let loose the rage that had built up over the past few weeks. Once he was lying motionless on the deck she reined in her fury with a solid kick to his gut, then scowled at the rest of the crew. "Anyone else care to tell their captain what they think she ought to do?"

The pirates were completely silent, all eyes pinned on the blood that pooled beneath Jenkins's prostrate body. Ann panted slightly as she turned, the whip gripped white-knuckled in her hand, to stare down at Violet and Charlie. "Tie them to the mainmast," she ordered, and the crew leapt to obey.

Ann stood back and watched as the two of them were bound to the mast with thick ropes that pinned their arms to their sides. When the job was finished, she moved to check that the knots were secure, and smiled humorlessly. "Three days." She held up three fingers to emphasize her words, then turned to address the crew. "No food. No water. If they survive, I will decide what is to be done with them upon their release. No one," she cast her gaze deliberately on Jenkins, "is to lay a hand on them, to help or harm them in any way. Am I clear?"

The pirates seemed to be collectively holding their breath. In many ways this was a far more terrible punishment than the cat. Three days in the sweltering sun without water? It would be torture of the worst kind, and it was very likely neither woman nor child would live through it. They would likely have been better off in the unforgiving arms of the sea. Ann looked around to be sure her command was understood. "Now back to work, all of you!"

Violet had never imagined the sun could be so hot. Surely this was what the prophets had meant when they wrote of Hell, this slow agonizing feeling of being roasted alive. The first day hadn't been so bad; she had been hot and thirsty and sunburned by nightfall, but it was the cool night air against her sweat-soaked clothing that had proven truly miserable. She grew so cold that her teeth chattered in her skull and it felt like her very bones were shivering. It was impossible to sleep, and so she and Charlie had done their best to entertain one another, singing folk songs and nursery rhymes through parched lips to pass the wretched hours.

When morning dawned, they had been glad of the sun's warmth. But the day quickly became just as sweltering as the one before, and now Violet's body did not even have enough water left to form sweat. Heat washed over her body in dizzying waves until her vision was nothing but a shimmering haze. The dark fabric of her trousers burned against her legs as painfully as the blistering sun on her exposed skin.

"Missus Watts?" Charlie's reedy voice broke hoarsely over each syllable.

"I'm here, little one." They were tied to opposite sides of the mast and could not see one another, but Violet knew the child's suffering had to be as great as her own.

"I'm sorry I got you into this. Really I am."

Violet's heart constricted. "Nonsense," she replied, the words gravelled and harsh in her throat. "This isn't your fault."

"Is, too. If I hadn't tried to snitch some extra salt pork from the galley, they never would have found me."

Violet was mildly amused to realize that the girl did not seem to regret stowing away, only being caught at it. "Charlie, why would you sneak on board in the first place? Won't your parents miss you?"

"Only got me papa, and he'll be at sea for two months yet. I have to stay with ol' Missus Cutterbuck when he's away, and I don't like her much. She's got wooden teeth and smells like cheese."

Violet would have laughed if she'd had the energy, but the sun was so hot and it was becoming a struggle just to hold her head up.

"You got kids, Missus Watts?"

The innocent question brought an unexpected stab of anguish. Violet had to close her eyes against the images that abruptly flooded her consciousness. Darkness. Pain. Loss. Charlie had no way of knowing how painful that subject was. Violet took several seconds to regain control before she replied, "No."

"But you do like them, don't you?" The raspy little voice almost sounded worried, and Violet smiled a little through parched lips.

"Very much."

Charlie seemed satisfied with that response. Perhaps she sensed that she should not pry any further, because all she said was "Good."

The two fell back into uncomfortable silence for a time as the heat continued to beat down mercilessly. The warm ocean breeze offered a little relief, but Violet was so thirsty now that she could scarcely think of anything else. She was almost grateful for the sharp physical suffering, as it kept her mind off the harrowing memories Charlie had inadvertently stirred up. She'd spent the past few years trying to forget about the darkest days of her life, and she had no desire to revisit them again.

The crew members passed by frequently as they went about their work, and more than once Violet considered calling out to one of them for a drink. Only the thought of Branded Ann stilled her tongue. If Ann had beaten Jenkins within an inch of his life for wanting to harm her, Violet could only imagine what the pirate captain would do to anyone who offered to help her. Ann seemed hell-bent on maintaining sole authority over Violet's fate, whatever that might be, and Violet would not ask one of her few friends among the crew to risk his life on her account. If she was to die out here, at least she would do so without cost to anyone else.

A soft, hoarse snore from the other side of the mast told Violet that Charlie had managed to fall asleep. She was glad of it, for the night's cold was sure to keep them awake again, and the child might as well get some rest while she could.

It was Charlie's treatment that angered Violet most. She posed no real threat to the crew and had done nothing to deserve this torture. If Violet could not protect the girl from Ann's wrath, at the very least she was determined to share in her suffering. *Father, this probably isn't very righteous of me, but on the day of judgment, I'm sincerely hoping you send that cold-hearted bitch straight to Hell.*

❖

Ann snapped upright in her bunk, sweat pouring down her face, strands of wild hair plastered to her forehead. She screwed her eyes shut and pressed her palms into them, trying to black out the remnants of her nightmare. Violet's screams. Ann's hands digging into that soft flesh, bruising, ravaging. Violet's terrified sobs, begging her to stop. Night after night, she dreamed the same evils.

Ann moaned and slid her legs from the bunk, leaning forward to rest her head in her hands. At a young age she had learned to accept that ruthless beast inside herself, the one that recognized the smell of fear, knew the taste of blood, understood the necessity of absolute power. It had kept her alive, brought her remarkable success in a world dominated by vicious men. She'd learned to do whatever it took to survive and bring herself closer to her goals, though in the process she found she'd become someone she really didn't want to be. But at least there had always been one personal moral that she refused to violate.

Now even that seemed to be crumbling. Ann had saved Violet from the brothels, but for what? Her own vile intentions? The very thought made her sick, and she was disgusted by the selfishness of her actions. She hadn't even been merciful enough to let Violet drown. She had condemned her to a slow, barbaric death, baked alive by the sun and wind, because she couldn't bring herself to get it over with.

The third day of the sentence had been almost unbearable, as all day long Ann had to endure the sight of the two sunburned figures lashed to the mast. Violet's cheeks and throat had blistered, her lips cracked from dehydration. Little Charlie couldn't even hold her head erect any longer. A somber mood had fallen over the crew as they worked that afternoon. It was one thing to see a throat slit or a body dismembered, but it was quite another to watch life draining away slowly before their very eyes—no bloodshed, no violence, just a constant, pitiless decline. As evening fell, it became clear that neither woman nor child was going to last the night.

Ann ran a hand through her hair. It was too late to take back her decision. Violet would be dead by morning, if she wasn't already, and then her torment would be over. Maybe then her nightmares would finally let her rest. Ann stood and went to the cabin door, and her hand trembled on the latch. She had to know. With a shaky breath she opened the door.

The two figures silhouetted against the mainmast were eerily still, save for the breeze that ruffled lightly at their hair and clothing. Ann's heart pounded as she strained to pick out any sign of movement. But from this distance, and in the dark, she could not see anything. Uneasily she took a few steps from the door, and then a few more. Finally she was standing right in front of Violet, who was slumped against the mast with her dark hair obscuring her face.

Then she could hear it—soft, ragged breathing, so shallow that it was barely audible. Ann's hand moved almost of its own accord, brushing the long hair out of Violet's sunburned face, tilting her chin up in the moonlight. The pretty, pouty lips were cracked and blistered, and Violet seemed unaware of anything, unable even to open her eyes. Deliriously, she mumbled something unintelligible.

Ann bent forward. "What was that?" she asked softly.

Violet mumbled again, just one word. "Water."

The plea burned in Ann's ears, and she straightened quickly. She didn't dare. If even one man on the crew caught her disobeying her own orders, she'd find herself keelhauled before the sun even rose. She'd come too far to lose it all now.

So why was she even considering it?

Determinedly Ann headed for her cabin. But as she lay hand on the latch she felt so sick to her stomach that she thought she might retch. What crime had Violet actually committed, to deserve such torture? If anything, the young woman had shown extraordinary courage. She'd defied an entire shipload of bloodthirsty pirates in order to save the life of one scrawny little girl. Ann was certain most of the men on her crew would not have taken such a risk to save their own mothers, let alone a complete stranger. Yet it was because of those same men that Violet was suffering now.

No, Ann corrected inwardly, *it's worse than that.* Violet was suffering because Ann herself wasn't even brave enough to stand up to these men the way Violet had. Cursing, Ann turned to look at the mainmast once more. And then she caught sight of Turtle at the helm. Before she could change her mind, she marched up the deck stairs and mustered her best glare.

"What the blazes are you doing?" she demanded.

Turtle looked genuinely confused. "N-nothing, Captain, I swear," he replied quickly. "Just taking my turn at night watch is all."

"That arm of yours is still healing! If we hit a storm you'd never have the strength to keep hold of the wheel. What idiot assigned you to night watch?"

"Mister Barclay, Captain, but he said that you said—"

Ann interrupted him by seizing the wheel impatiently. "I'll deal with Barclay tomorrow. As for you, get your ass back to crew quarters. I don't want to see you abovedecks until the sun's shining, savvy?"

Turtle nodded, though he still appeared extremely perplexed. Ann watched him cross the main deck and disappear beneath the forecastle, and when he was at last out of sight she let out a breath and scanned the rest of the *Ice Queen*'s decks carefully. When she was satisfied that she was alone, she tied off the wheel and made her way down to the water barrels.

Working as quietly as she could, she threw back the hinged cover and scooped out a dipperful of water, then carried it to Violet. Tilting Violet's chin up as she had before, Ann pressed the dipper to Violet's mouth.

"Drink," she said softly. "Quickly, now, before someone comes." She didn't know if Violet heard her, but the parched lips opened and accepted the water a little bit at a time.

When the dipper was drained, Ann heard her mumble, "Charlie..."

"I'll give some to the kid, too, I promise."

Ann made several more trips between the water barrels and the mainmast, keeping her eyes trained on the hatch and the door to the crew's quarters. But no one appeared to stop her. Finally, she dropped the dipper back into place, closed the barrel, and resumed her position at the wheel, her blood racing through her veins until she felt dizzy.

She'd done it—and she hadn't been caught. Of course, it might still be too late. Violet and Charlie were so weak, Ann didn't know if the risk she'd taken would even really do much good. But she didn't want Violet to die. As infuriating as she might be, as frustrating and dangerous and disruptive, Ann couldn't help being captivated by her remarkable strength. Violet was, in many ways, all the things that Ann most wanted to be, and it wasn't until she'd met this dauntless, compelling woman that Ann realized just how very far she still had to go. She stared intently at the mainmast.

Stay alive, Violet, she implored silently. *Just stay alive until morning, and I swear on my father's grave, I won't let anything else happen to you.* As an afterthought, she added, *Or to the kid, either.*

❖

When morning dawned, Violet and Charlie were still breathing, however weakly. When the crew had assembled around the mainmast, Ann gazed down at them silently for several minutes before speaking.

Worried that her relief might be audible, she was careful to use her sharpest sarcasm.

"It seems that both of you lack the common sense to die." The surrounding crew snickered. "Very well. If you enjoy our company so much, we will not deprive you of it."

She raised her voice. "The terms of this disciplinary action have been fulfilled, and we will not speak of it again. Our swabbie will return to her duties. We do not have sufficient stores to feed an extra mouth. If Sister Violet wishes, she may share her rations. However," she addressed Violet directly, "the girl is in your charge, my lovely. Keep her out of sight and find some way to make use of her, or next time I'll put a bullet between her eyes before I throw her off my ship, understood?"

Both Violet and Charlie appeared barely conscious, and it was not likely that either one of them had heard her. That wasn't important, anyway. The men were her real audience and her harshness was for their benefit. Ann stepped back and commanded, "Release them."

Mason and Maclairen moved to untie the ropes. Violet and Charlie slumped to the deck and were half dragged down the hatch, out of the sun. Ann caught O'Hare's arm as he prepared to follow them down to the infirmary.

"Captain?"

Ann bent to murmur in his ear, "You let them die, O'Hare, and it will be your hide."

He pulled back with a gap-toothed grin that Ann found rather discomfiting. "Aye, Lady Captain. Just you leave it to me."

From across the deck, Newbury watched the pirate woman thoughtfully. Ann was staring after the batty Irish cook as he disappeared down the open hatch. *Well, well. Everyone has a weakness*, he mused happily, *even the invincible Branded Ann*. Looking around at the disgruntled faces of the crew, he could hardly believe his good fortune.

Surreptitiously he elbowed the swarthy man next to him. "Is the captain always so...indulgent...of her bedmates?"

The man grunted. He, too, appeared to have noticed Ann's peculiar expression as Violet was taken away. "Never," he said in a faint Spanish accent.

Newbury shrugged nonchalantly. "Well, she sure took a shine to this one, didn't she? Even letting her keep that stowaway for a pet. Mighty strange."

The pirate grunted again without reply, but Newbury observed with satisfaction that he seemed to be mulling over his words. "The name's Patch," he said, sticking out a hand.

His companion shook it without looking down. "Ortega."

"Well, Master Ortega, you seem like a right smart sort of fellow. Don't suppose I could interest you in a few hands of cards this evening?" Newbury jingled his pockets suggestively. As he'd hoped, the Spaniard gave a half-nod, though his expression was noncommittal.

"I'll look forward to it, then," Newbury said, and as he walked away, he suppressed a grin. This was going to be far too easy.

CHAPTER ELEVEN

It took several days for Violet and Charlie to regain their strength. O'Hare prepared an unsalted chicken broth that he insisted on spoon-feeding to both of them several times an hour. While the bland, watery substance did not taste particularly pleasant, it was quite effective at curing severe dehydration. Their badly sunburned skin was treated with the same foul-smelling salve that O'Hare had applied to Violet's sore hands only a few short months ago, and gradually the blisters began to heal.

But the sleep! Oh, the blessed, glorious sleep was the greatest rejuvenator of all. Violet had never imagined she could be so glad of a thin canvas cot, of the simple luxury of being able to lie down and close her eyes in the pleasant coolness of the ship's infirmary. She knew she had to look absolutely dreadful. The skin peeled from her face and throat, and the itching was almost unbearable. But as her energy returned, Violet was quick to resume as many of her duties as she was able. She was not about to give Ann any further excuse to torment her—or to torment little Charlie, for that matter.

Charlie, for her part, seemed eager to help Violet however she could. After the trial they had endured together, the child seemed greatly enamored of her, and wherever Violet went, Charlie was right on her heels. Violet found it rather endearing and took pleasure in teaching the girl how to assist in the galley and care for the livestock on board. She didn't even mind sharing her rations. As a member of the crew, Violet was entitled to the same full portion that the men received, and she'd never been able to finish it all by herself anyway.

One evening, while Violet demonstrated how to properly scour the butcher's block after supper had been prepared, she heard voices from the other side of the bulkhead. The words "unlucky females" and "lunatic captain" reached her ears. After turning the task over to Charlie, Violet moved furtively to the edge of the bulkhead and peeked around it.

A few of the men had gathered in the infirmary, around Jenkins's cot. Jenkins had not yet fully recovered from Ann's beating, but it appeared that he was at least well enough to enjoy a few hands of cards with his shipmates. Violet recognized most of the men with him. Porter served as a deckhand. He was a thin, sour-faced young man only a few years older than Turtle. Next to him was the heavyset, thickly mustached Saunders, who was acknowledged as the worst bully among the crew. Violet was not surprised that these two were together. Porter and Saunders were inseparable friends and she scarcely saw one without the other. She was, however, rather astonished to see Ortega with them. The antisocial Spaniard generally kept to himself and rarely spoke in any fashion other than a few brief, unintelligible grunts. Violet also recognized one of the new recruits that had come on board with them in Port Royal—the navigator's apprentice, the one the others called Patch.

The entire assembly disturbed her, and she quickly shrank against the bulkhead, out of sight. Every last one of those men disliked her. They were the very ones she tried hardest to avoid, Jenkins in particular. She didn't know much about the new man yet, the apprentice, but she didn't like the way his eye raked over her every time they encountered one another. Violet had the sinking feeling that no good could come of such a meeting.

"Pass me that rum," she heard Jenkins say, and there was a clinking sound as someone handed him a bottle, then shuffling that meant someone was dealing the cards.

"As I was saying, Jenkins, me and Porter here sure do admire you standing up to her like that." Violet recognized Saunders by the slurping sound he made as he talked. The man had a revolting habit of sucking at his mustache while he spoke. "Ain't never seen the captain act this way, fawning over that chitty-faced tart like she ain't never seen a woman afore. Ain't right."

"You bet your sweet balls it ain't right," Jenkins growled. "I always knew it'd happen one day. Branded Ann's gone and lost her mind over a bloody trollop."

"The captain is a woman." That matter-of-fact grunt had to be from Ortega, who sounded as though he thought those five words explained everything perfectly.

"Well, I for one think there's a reason womenfolk should stay on shore where they belong." Violet assumed this was the one-eyed newcomer. "They can't separate sentiment from business. I've heard Branded Ann has more pluck than most, but in the end I wonder if she isn't just a female, with the same shortcomings as the rest of her sex."

"Women's bad luck," Porter chimed in. "I always said so. Bad enough we got one of them, then two, but now we got ourselves three unlucky females on board."

Saunders gave a dark chuckle. His words were slurring together now, the effect of too much drink. "Aw, now, Porter, the little one might not be that bad, you know. I like them small. Ain't nothing quite like a nice little…"

"Missus Watts?"

Violet jumped and almost hit her head on a low-hanging support beam. Her cheeks burned as fiercely as the rage that had consumed her at Saunders's words. She prayed fervently that the girl hadn't also been eavesdropping. "Charlie! What is it?"

"I'm done here." Charlie waved at the butcher's block, which had indeed been rendered spotless.

"Oh. Yes, of course." Raucous laughter burst from the infirmary, and Violet didn't even want to speculate how Saunders had finished his sentence. She had to get Charlie out of there before the child could overhear any other such despicable conversation. "I think that's enough for tonight, dear heart. It's late. We'll go to bed and tomorrow you may help me scrub the upper decks."

Charlie flashed a huge grin and wound her fingers into Violet's. "Sounds fun."

They made their way abovedecks to the crew's quarters. Violet did not want to spend another night in the infirmary, alone with Jenkins and his friends. She briefly considered going to Ann to request some measure of protection for Charlie, but dismissed the thought immediately. She and Ann hadn't laid eyes on one another in days, and Ann had made it quite clear that she didn't care what happened to the stowaway invading her ship. Charlie was Violet's responsibility, and she would just have to find a way to protect the child herself.

"We're sleeping in quarters tonight?" Charlie asked.

"That's right," Violet replied brightly. "We'll share my bunk, just like sisters."

Charlie's enthusiasm was evident. "This'll be great," she said, and gave a little skip at Violet's side. "I never had a sister."

Violet smiled down at her fondly, but her mind was still preoccupied by the ominous implication of Saunders's words. They entered the crew's quarters and wound between the rows of bunk beds until Violet found the one she'd been assigned. As she straightened the pallet and blanket and checked the position of her Bible carefully hidden beneath the thin mattress, she suddenly heard a familiar slurping, slurring voice behind them.

"Back to join the rest of us, Sister Violet?"

She gasped audibly and spun to see Saunders standing at the foot of the bunk. Had the card game really ended already? *Or did he see us leaving and follow us up here?*

Saunders's features twisted into a leer as he gazed down at Charlie. "Going to sleep in the good Sister's bunk, my pretty?"

Charlie nodded energetically. "Yup. Missus Watts says it'll be just like we're sisters!"

"Does she, now?"

Violet put a protective hand on the girl's shoulder. "That's enough, Charlie. Come, I'll boost you up."

Saunders reached out and took hold of Charlie's arm. "Aw, now, Sister, that bunk of yours is awful tiny, ain't it? Maybe this little one ought to share berth with me." The lecherous gleam in his eyes made Violet sick to her stomach. "What do you say, moppet, you want to come sleep next to your Uncle Saunders?"

"I don't think so," Violet snapped, and tried to tug the girl from his grasp.

He refused to let go. "You listen to me, woman, you ain't got no say over the brat—"

"Actually, she does," Barclay interrupted calmly, and Violet felt her knees weaken with relief as the burly quartermaster came up behind them. Barclay glared threateningly at Saunders. "The captain put the girl in Sister Violet's charge. If she says the kid stays with her, that's the end of it."

Glowering at all three of them, Saunders let go of Charlie and took an unsteady step backward. "Well, if the *captain* says..." he sneered.

"Up to bed, Charlie." Violet lifted the girl into the upper bunk, then moved to Barclay's side and watched Saunders stagger away. "Thank you," she said quietly.

But the look he gave her was no more friendly than the one he'd just given the drunken crewman. "I'll uphold the captain's orders," he grunted, "but that don't mean I like them any more than any other man on board. You've been nothing but trouble since the day you came aboard, and I'll thank you to keep both the brat and yourself out of the way, you hear?"

Violet nodded, though his sudden hostility was unexpected. She'd always thought Barclay was rather fond of her, and wondered at this peculiar change of attitude. Perhaps he blamed her for Ann's ill temper of late? She turned to climb into the bunk herself, but Barclay cleared his throat.

"You might as well take this," he said gruffly, and thrust the hilt of a short knife into her hand. "In case anybody bothers you again."

Violet accepted the knife and started to thank him, but he cut her off. "Just don't you go waving it about at anyone who looks at you crooked. Most of these men could take you down long before you'd ever get close enough to stick them with it. It's only for real trouble."

"I understand," Violet replied, and carefully tucked the blade beneath the mattress beside her Bible before climbing up to join Charlie. The girl seemed oblivious to the tension in the air and snuggled close to Violet.

"Sweet dreams, missus."

Violet wrapped her arms protectively around the little girl. "Sweet dreams, dear heart."

❖

Ann leaned over the map on the table intently as Carter tapped a spot with his finger.

"The Devil's Triangle lies between the coast of Florida and these islands here and here. Navigational instruments don't work real well for some reason once you cross into it, and it can be bloody tricksome to find what you're looking for once you get in. Right now we're here." He stabbed at another point on the map. "We'll be entering the Triangle here, where the seas are still pretty easy. But after that…" He sat back and rubbed his chin. "Well, if Black Dog's map is right, his island is near the heart of the Triangle, about five or six days' sail inside. We're sure to run into some nasty surprises before we get there, and even if we do, making it out's just as risky."

Ann touched the map. "We're here," she said slowly, "which means we should cross into the Triangle sometime tonight, if the winds hold."

"Aye, Captain."

Ann sternly quelled her rising excitement, but she did allow the hint of a smile to play at her lips as she sat back and looked around the table where Barclay, Carter, and Patch were gathered to go over the route once more before they entered the treacherous Devil's Seas. "Boys, we're about to make history."

"Provided we can get there and back in one piece," Barclay commented grimly.

Ann cocked an eyebrow at him. "Such pessimism, Barclay. You having second thoughts?" Apprehension flitted over his features, and Ann frowned. "Out with it, man, what's going on in that head of yours?"

"It's the crew, Captain," he said hesitantly.

"What about the crew?"

"Well, they're a bit…they're not…" The quartermaster chewed his lip. "They ain't happy."

Ann stiffened, suspecting he was about to start an argument, but all she said was, "Go on."

This seemed to bolster his courage. "Well, it's the girl, Captain," he said. "Both of them, really. The crew's starting to grumble. This is a ship of business-minded boys, and we're here for the gold. The women are getting in the way…" He trailed off, but she knew he wasn't finished.

"And?" she said quietly

He gulped. "And the men are thinking maybe you've lost your

head over Sister Violet…and perhaps you've lost heart for what we're doing as well."

"I see." From the corner of her eye Ann could see Patch snickering. "Tell me, then, Barclay, what do *you* think?"

He seemed to weigh his words carefully before replying, "I think they may be right."

"And what would you suggest?"

His reply was exactly what she expected, because it was the same answer she would have given in his place.

"Kill them."

When she remained silent, he seemed to grow desperate. "For God's sake, Captain, she's a bloody Cockney whore from the back alleys of London. Nothing but gutter trash! She ain't worth all this fuss 'n bother. I'll do it myself on your order, if you can't—"

Ann stood up so fast that if the table hadn't been bolted to the floor it would have toppled over. Her chair, however, was not so fortunate, and fell with a crash behind her. "Get out."

Barclay also stood. "Captain Ann, please—"

"Out!" she bellowed, and whipped a dirk from her sash that sang past his ear to embed itself in the wood of the cabin door behind him. Carter and Patch were on their feet and out of her quarters in a heartbeat, but Barclay still lingered, fear warring with concern across his gnarled features.

"She's going to cost you this venture, Captain, mark my words. You don't got no choice." He backed out of the open door slowly, as though he was trying to gauge how much further he could push without losing life or limb. "If you change your mind, you know where to find me."

Ann stalked purposefully to the door as he continued to back away, and she stopped in the doorway to watch him retreat to the aft deck. She glimpsed Violet, who was helping Charlie dump a bucket of water over the portside gunwale. Ann's limbs were still trembling furiously, and at the sight of Violet her stomach took a little dip at the same time, so that for a minute she completely lost her equilibrium. Slowly, however, she became aware that something else didn't feel right. The afternoon sun was bright, but there was a stillness to the air that prickled the hairs on the back of her neck. She turned to look at the eastern sky, where dark clouds were gathering on the horizon. The distinct scent of rain that drifted to her across the waves promised a storm. Ann closed her eyes wearily. "Perfect."

❖

The wind had picked up considerably by the time Violet and Charlie finished scrubbing the last of the foredeck. Violet was pleased to find that with her little helper's assistance, it didn't take nearly as long to complete the task, though she was careful to keep Charlie within arm's reach at all times. She could feel eyes on them as they worked, and the looks from the crew were anything but amiable.

As evening fell, the sky darkened, and the tension on board felt thick enough to strangle the breath right out of a person's body. Everyone seemed to sense it, and that only made matters worse. Maclairen produced his bagpipes and puffed at them halfheartedly, and then O'Hare appeared with a keg of rum from the *Ice Queen*'s stores.

"Are you sure this is a good idea?" Violet asked as the Irishman enlisted her help to roll the barrel of liquor beneath the mainmast.

"Couldn't hurt," O'Hare grumbled. "Right now feels like the whole ship's set to blow, like a spark to a powder keg. The lads could use a bit of loosening up."

And it seemed he was right, for after a drink or two Maclairen's playing was much improved, and the scowls darkening the faces of most of the crew seemed to relax into disgruntled lethargy. Turtle took Violet's hand.

"Give us a song, would you, Sister?" he pleaded.

Violet smiled, but shook her head. "I don't think that's a good idea."

Maclairen stopped playing in order to contradict her. "It's a fine idea. Just what we need to liven things a bit."

She wasn't so sure; the men already seemed to resent her presence so much that she did not want to do anything to further aggravate them. But O'Hare agreed with Turtle and Maclairen, and even the stoic Mason mentioned quietly from his seat nearby that "a song would be mighty nice." Maclairen piped up a cheerful sea shanty, and Turtle sang the first few bars.

Yonder stands a lovely maiden,
Who she is I do not know
I shall make attempt to court her,
She must answer: yes or no?

Turtle held his hands out to her expectantly, and gave her such a hopeful look that she could not refuse him. With a reluctant grin she chimed in with the line she knew he was waiting for: *Oh no, John, no John, no John, no!*

Mason took over for the second verse, in which the young admirer made several suggestive references to his lady's fine décolletage, and Violet could not help laughing at his exaggerated expression of disappointment as she gave him the same response. To her wonder, the crew seemed to warm to the song quickly, with a different man taking a turn at each stanza. The young lady continued to give the same protest, all the while letting her admirer take more and more liberties, until by the final verse she was refusing to let him out of her arms.

Maclairen transitioned smoothly into a rollicking rendition of "The Drunken Sailor," and Violet was delighted that the dismal mood that had pervaded the ship all day seemed to be dissolving under the influence of the music. Even Jenkins clapped along with the rest of the men as the songs picked up tempo. Violet began to whirl about the deck in the yellow light of the oil lamps, cheerfully playing along with the men as they sang and danced.

But as the rum continued to flow freely among the crew, the wind whistled over the decks with increasing agitation. After a particularly boisterous jaunt around the mainmast, Violet happened to catch sight of Carter's one-eyed apprentice whispering in Jenkins's ear. She couldn't hear what was said, but Jenkins's eyes slid thoughtfully over to her. Violet didn't have the chance to ponder what he might be thinking, because O'Hare took her hand and led her into a lively jig.

As she got caught up in the dancing once again, Turtle cut in and sent her for a spin across the deck. Violet found herself nearly on top of Jenkins's seat by the forward stairs. She felt hands at her waist, and suddenly she was pulled down into a man's lap and his hot breath was on her neck. Violet twisted to see Jenkins leering into her face. He reeked of spirits. She sprang up and backed away, and he stood, his face darkening.

"What's the matter, Sister, ain't I pretty enough for you?"

Violet's stomach turned as Jenkins's attention fell on Charlie, who was watching the fun from atop a crate nearby. Before Violet could stop him, Jenkins grabbed the girl by the arm and hauled her to her feet. "Maybe this little kitten'll be more friendly," he drawled, and ran a hand over Charlie's choppy hair.

All pretense of politeness forgotten, Violet yanked Charlie's arm away and pushed Jenkins back as hard as she could. "Get away from her," she snarled, putting herself between him and the girl. Maclairen stopped playing as the men turned to see what was going on.

Seething, Jenkins drew back and struck Violet squarely across the face. Pain exploded across her cheekbone as she stumbled backward, her hand flying up to cover her throbbing face. Charlie shrieked.

"Hey now!" Turtle leapt forward and pulled a knife from his belt, brandishing it at the heavily tattooed pirate. "Ain't nobody gonna treat Sister Violet like that!" He would have lunged recklessly at the bigger man had Mason not stepped up to hold him back.

Jenkins stared balefully at Violet, then turned to look at the rest of the crew and finally his attention focused on Turtle. "Your precious *Sister Violet*," he said spitefully, "ain't nothing more than a common wayside doxy, Master Turtle. Or didn't she tell you?"

Violet felt the blood drain from her face and she dropped her hand limply. *My God, how did he find out?* Had Ann truly grown to hate her so much that she would share Violet's secret with her most dangerous enemy on the ship?

"You're lying," Turtle bellowed and struggled against the beefy arms that held him.

"Ask her." Jenkins smirked.

Violet could feel every member of the crew staring, and all she could do was shake her head dazedly. Over Jenkins's shoulder she could see Patch grinning like a cat who'd just been offered a dish of cream. And he wasn't the only one who seemed inordinately pleased by this bit of news.

Jenkins's lip curled. "You ain't got nothing to say for yourself, Sister? Go on, tell the boys where you really come from. 'Twere a whole different kind of nunnery than what they think, weren't it?"

The vulgar term for a bawdy house was so blasphemous it made her cringe. Jenkins threw his hands in the air and addressed his shipmates. "Here we been suffering our lonesomeness in patience, men, and we've had a bona fide comfort under our noses all along." He turned to give Violet a malevolent smile. "I says we use her good and well!"

A streak of lightning punctuated those words, ripping through the sky, and for a split second the entire deck was bathed in cold, eerie light. That seemed to be the cue for chaos to erupt. Fat, cold drops of rain began to patter down onto the deck as Saunders, who was standing scarcely a foot away, lunged at Violet with a gleeful whoop. Someone else grabbed her from behind. Violet heard Charlie scream again.

Frantically Violet brought a knee up into Saunders's groin as he charged, and he reeled away. She drove her elbow into the ribs of her captor, who yowled but did not let go. It was Porter holding her, she realized, and watched in terror as Ortega and Jenkins moved to take Saunders's place.

As if by magic, Barclay appeared. He stepped between Violet and Jenkins and swept a cutlass at her attackers. "Enough," he roared. But Jenkins was well beyond taking orders now.

"Well, if it ain't the captain's obedient lapdog," he snarled, the rain running down his face and neck, making the tattoos and whip scars dance weirdly in the pale light of the oil lamps. His own blade leapt up to clash with Barclay's. "I'm through listening to that branded bitch, and if you know what's good for you, you won't get in me way!"

Horrified, Violet watched Barclay and Jenkins battle across the deck. The quartermaster was pushing Jenkins back and away from her, but that only left her open for Saunders to renew his advance.

Only it wasn't Violet that he attacked. Charlie screeched as the swarthy, mustached pirate barreled toward her, and desperately Violet struggled to free herself from Porter's arms as she realized Saunders's intention. She brought one booted foot down, hard, on Porter's toes and again slammed her elbow into his stomach. This produced the desired effect; he let go, and Violet launched herself at Charlie.

She reached the girl right before Saunders did and managed to push her out of the way before Saunders's weight collided with her and Violet was thrown to the deck.

"Run, Charlie!" she managed to cry out just before he landed a heavy fist across her jaw.

Piercing bells went off in her ears at the impact. Somewhere in the background she could still hear Charlie screaming. Saunders was on top of her, one hand wrapped around her throat in a chokehold. His eyes glazed over madly as he clawed at Violet's clothes with his free hand and grunted like a primitive animal.

Violet couldn't breathe. She fumbled at her belt for Barclay's knife, grateful the quartermaster had thought to give it to her the night before. Her fingers closed around the hilt and she yanked it out, but Saunders took his hand from her throat to catch her wrist. Violet gasped for air as he smashed her fist to the deck, forcing her to let go of the weapon.

Saunders drew back to hit her again, shouting, "Filthy whore!"

He gave an abrupt jerk. The point of a cutlass punched through the front of his chest, dripping crimson, and Saunders's eyes rolled back in his head. The blade retracted just as quickly as it had appeared, and he slumped to the deck.

Violet was shocked to see Ann standing behind him, her expression a terrible mask of rage. Rain soaked her shirt, plastering it to her body like a second skin, and Violet could make out the sharply defined muscles of the pirate's upper arms and the heaving of her rib cage.

Ann's gaze bored into Violet's for an instant, then slid pointedly downward. Violet realized Saunders had ripped the buttons from her shirt, nearly exposing her breasts. Flushing, she quickly covered herself. Ann spun to peel Barclay away from Jenkins, insinuating her sword between them.

"Missus, are you hurt?" Violet felt little hands at her shoulders and looked up to see Charlie tugging at her with tear-stained cheeks. She sat up, pushing Saunders's lifeless body off her, and gathered the child in her arms protectively as she watched Ann confront Jenkins.

"You should know better than to lay hands on what's mine," Ann said in a tone cold enough to raise goose bumps along Violet's arms.

"You should know better than to choose a poxy cockish slut over your own crew," Jenkins said belligerently. "We won't stand for it no more!"

And with that, it was as if some invisible hand had drawn a line down the center of the deck. The pirates divided, some moving to stand behind Jenkins, others behind Ann, until it seemed to Violet that every member of the crew had chosen a side. She was shaken to see Mason and Maclairen, men she had considered her friends, among those who were opposing the captain.

For what seemed like an eternity the two groups stared one another down, swords drawn, as the rain pelted them all with equal indifference. Violet was paralyzed with dismay. It looked as though the entire crew was about to become embroiled in a nasty civil war. Fought in such close quarters, the results would be devastating. She flinched as Jenkins lifted his cutlass in the air and howled.

At that moment, however, a blinding shaft of lightning fell from the sky and struck the mainmast with a deafening crack. The *Ice Queen* lurched, and Violet and Charlie skidded across the deck into the portside gunwale. Violet heard a terrible splintering sound and watched in horror as the mainmast snapped in two right before her eyes. The upper half went toppling to starboard, and pieces of rigging snapped from their cleats with reports like gunfire, unable to withstand the weight.

In a split second Ann was in command again. The orders she bellowed out went unchallenged even by those who had, only moments before, been threatening an all-out mutiny. The crew scrambled to cut the stays and rigging lines, for the broken mast was tilting the ship dangerously to starboard and would capsize them all if it wasn't freed first.

Violet clutched Charlie to her chest, protecting the child's head with her arms, as the last of the ropes were severed. The heavy mast fell into the sea, taking with it the crow's nest and topsail yardarm. The *Ice Queen* reeled with the sudden shift in balance, and a huge wave crashed over the rail as the ship was turned nearly on its side. The force with which the water doused them all yanked Charlie from Violet's lap and sucked her over the gunwale.

Violet shrieked the child's name and managed to catch hold of her shirt as the ship righted itself. She could feel the fabric tearing under Charlie's weight. "Your hands, Charlie, give me your hands!"

The little girl's eyes shone with fear, but she did as she was told and seized Violet's arms. "Don't let go, please," she cried, her legs dangling precariously above the raging ocean beneath them.

"I won't, dear heart, I promise. Hang on!"

The rail was slippery, and Violet fought to keep from being pulled over it herself. Another wave crashed over them both, and Charlie lost her grip with one hand as her body twisted from the impact. She screamed.

Oh Father, please, Violet begged silently, too overwhelmed to form the words aloud.

And then someone else also grabbed the child's wrists, and Violet felt a solid, welcome presence at her back. Ann dragged the sobbing girl back onto the deck and thrust her into Violet's arms. The rain streamed down the pirate's face in glistening rivulets, shining eerily with every flash of lightning overhead. Violet did not get the chance to thank her, because just as abruptly Ann shoved both of them at a waiting O'Hare.

"Get these two belowdecks and batten the hatches!" she roared over the howling rain.

Violet found herself almost pitched down the ladder onto the gun deck, and O'Hare leapt down after them as the hatch slammed closed above.

"Down again, lassies," he ordered, directing them to the hatch that led to the third level of the ship. "Too many portholes on this here deck, got to keep the water out of the lower levels or we'll sink like a stone. Down you go, now."

Violet and Charlie had no choice but to obey, and descended into the ship's hold. O'Hare closed the hatch above them, and Violet heard a scraping noise as he latched the cover firmly in place to seal it. Without even the dim light from the hatch, the cargo hold was pitch black, but the sounds of the raging storm outside were still all too keenly discernible.

"Missus Watts?" Charlie called out tearfully.

In the darkness Violet blindly stretched out a hand. "I'm here, Charlie." She felt the girl's fingers touch her own, tentatively.

"This is bad, isn't it?"

Violet saw no point in lying. Charlie was perceptive enough to know if Violet was telling her the truth. "Aye, Charlie, it's pretty bad." Little fingers tightened around hers, and then suddenly the deck dropped sharply beneath their feet and they both lost their balance.

As they fell, Violet heard a loud clang somewhere overhead. She had only an instant to realize the cargo was shifting with the tossing of the ship. Quickly she rolled herself on top of Charlie, trying to shield her from whatever was about to fall on them while at the same time taking the brunt of the fall with her elbows and forearms so she didn't completely crush the girl beneath her.

They hit the deck, and Charlie cried out. Violet felt jarring pain through her arms and shoulders. But then another much sharper pain shot through her head as something cracked over the back of her skull. She collapsed atop Charlie, and just before she lost consciousness, a passage from the book of Psalms whispered through her memory.

They that go down to the sea in ships, that do business in great waters; these see the works of the Lord, and his wonders in the deep. For he commandeth, and raiseth the stormy wind, which lifteth up the waves thereof. They mount up to the heaven, they go down again to the depths: their soul is melted because of trouble.

Her last, rather irreverent thought was that this Scripture summarized her entire disastrous life just about perfectly.

CHAPTER TWELVE

Her head was throbbing so painfully that it felt like someone was beating the base of her skull with a club. Violet moaned and struggled to open her eyes. Disoriented, she took several moments to recognize her surroundings; she was in Ann's cabin, nestled into the soft mattress and quilts of the captain's bunk. Pale daylight streamed through the portholes above the bed, and Violet lay very still as the memory of the storm and the fight that had preceded it came back to her.

She raised a hand to her cheek and flinched as her fingertips encountered swollen flesh. Jenkins and Saunders had both landed some painful blows before the lightning struck, distracting the crew from imminent mutiny. But as bad as the storm had been, the ship was still afloat, and Ann was still apparently in charge; she had to be, or Violet was certain she would not still be alive.

Turning over, Violet was startled to find Charlie lying next to her. At first she was relieved to see that the child was sleeping peacefully. One of her arms, however, was bound in a sling. Curious... Violet could not recall the girl being injured during the fight. Perhaps Charlie had also been wounded when the cargo fell on them? She could not remember anything after she'd lost consciousness in the hold.

Carefully, so as not to wake the child, Violet propped herself on one elbow and lifted the edge of Charlie's shirt to assess her injury. What she saw tore a gasp from her lips. The girl's shoulder was discolored by vivid hues of purple and blue, swollen to nearly twice the size of the other.

"My God, little one, what has she done to you?"

❖

Barclay joined Ann at the rail of the aft deck, watching the men below as they worked doggedly to repair the damage the storm had done to the ship. After the torrential rain and lightning, it was eerily still. The sky was completely hidden behind a thick blanket of clouds, the white mist hanging so low over the water that the ship was practically swimming in it.

"Report."

"We're patching the breaches in our lady's hull, Captain, and rigging the fore and aft sails to compensate as best we can for the loss of the mainsail." Barclay sighed and rubbed the back of his neck wearily. "We got lucky, only two casualties—Saunders, and that Chinese fellow, Yang Li, who was swept overboard. Five wounded, but O'Hare says nothing major save Scrappy, who lost a finger when it got tangled in a gaff line. Most of the cargo's accounted for, though it was tossed around something fierce. The loss of the mainmast's our greatest trouble. We're not quite dead in the water without it, but we sure won't be able to make much speed, and supplies are running low as it is."

Ann absorbed this information dispassionately, and nodded. "And Jenkins?"

Barclay gave an amused snort. "Sitting pretty in the brig, Captain, just like you ordered."

"I want you to keep an eye on Porter as well. He and Saunders were mates a long time, and I'm sure he holds me in no high esteem at the moment."

"Aye, Captain."

O'Hare appeared with a tray of food. "I brought what you asked, Lady Captain," he said brightly. "Vittles for Sister Violet and the little lass. Plenty of fresh meat, since we lost so many livestock in the storm…have to eat them up soon or they'll go to waste."

Ann took the tray from his hands. "Thank you, O'Hare." She did not fail to catch the disapproval on her quartermaster's face, and she gave him a long, cool stare before turning to descend the stairs to the main deck.

She knew Barclay would not be content to humor her whims much longer. Eventually he would turn against her, just as Jenkins and the others had. So long as Violet and Charlie did not interfere with their mission, most of the men could tolerate their presence on board with indifference. But for some of them, Charlie served as proof that Violet had exposed a weak spot in their otherwise fearsome captain. And if there was one thing that the leader of a band of opportunists could not afford, it was to be thought of as weak. Ann knew it was just a matter of time before every man on board was ready to overthrow her authority. Yet she could not think of any remedy for the problem that did not involve slitting Violet's throat—and that she could not do.

She balanced the food tray in one hand while feeling in her vest pocket for the key to her cabin. For their own protection she was keeping Violet and Charlie locked safely inside, where the crew would not have access to them. Right now there wasn't a man on board that she could trust not to pitch the girls overboard at the first opportunity, and she wasn't about to allow them the chance. Unlocking the door, she stuffed the key back into her pocket and stepped inside.

"Don't move."

Ann froze. Violet was sitting at the table, pointing one of Ann's own flintlock pistols squarely at Ann's chest. Her eyes were hard as jewels above the wicked bruises discoloring both sides of her face, and the hand that held the gun was trembling noticeably. Ann had never seen her look quite so angry, and her own blood immediately heated in response.

"What the hell is this?"

"How could you?" Violet spat, her finger tightening on the trigger. "She's just a child, you brute. Damn you, how could you do this?"

Ann looked over at Charlie's prostrate form in the bunk. "It was the only way."

"The only way to what? Torture a little girl?"

"Torture?" Ann snapped incredulously. "Is that what you think?" She kicked the door shut with one booted foot, then crossed the room in two steps and slammed the tray of food down on the table.

"Stay back or I'll kill you!" Violet shrieked.

Ann hissed with exasperation and stepped up to the barrel of the gun until it was pressed firmly between her breasts. With one hand she moved the muzzle directly over her heart and flung her arms wide. "Then do it," she said recklessly. "Go on, shoot." She felt the tip of the pistol shaking against her skin, and her muscles quivered with adrenaline as she stared Violet down. "I have done some terrible things in my life, Violet. But you have my word, I did not harm the girl."

"Her shoulder—"

"The bone was pulled out of place when she nearly went overboard. We didn't discover it until after we'd pulled the two of you from the hold." Ann had suffered the same injury several times in her years at sea. "I had to correct it. Considering everything else that might have happened to her last night, she was very lucky."

Violet's temper only seemed fueled by the reminder. "And just where were you, anyway, when your entire crew was trying to rape the both of us? So much for your precious Articles!"

Ann growled. "What did you expect, Violet, when you insisted on bringing her back aboard? These men are criminals! At best they're murderous thieves, and at worst..." She pinched her lips together grimly. "Pray that you never find out."

The cabin fell silent, and Violet glanced over at Charlie. The girl still slept soundly, seemingly undisturbed by the shouting. Violet jabbed the barrel of the gun into Ann's chest with renewed aggression.

"Why won't she wake up?"

Ann dropped her arms. "My guess would be the laudanum."

"Laudanum?"

"O'Hare keeps a supply in the infirmary for emergency amputations and the like. I had him dose the kid before I set her arm."

After a pause, Violet asked uncertainly, "So she didn't feel anything?"

Disconcerted by the sudden meekness in her tone, Ann could not reply, and she averted her gaze. The hand holding the gun went limp and fell to Violet's side, and Violet stared at Ann with such bewilderment that Ann cleared her throat awkwardly and moved away. She wasn't quite sure why she'd insisted that Charlie be put under first; she'd had to threaten O'Hare within an inch of his life to get him to part with the precious drug. Ann went to the washbasin against the wall and leaned over it, gazing into the small mirror bolted to the wall. Her cross-marred reflection looked back at her with troubled eyes. The laudanum hadn't eliminated the child's pain, only dulled it. Ann could still hear the girl's shriek as she'd yanked the bone back into its socket. But mercifully, Charlie had fallen almost immediately into a dead sleep, and Ann hoped fervently that when she awoke, she wouldn't remember.

"No matter how many years go by, I could never forget what it felt like," she murmured. "I wasn't much older than the kid when they did this to me, and I didn't want her to go through that kind of unnecessary pain." Absently she raised a hand to her face. "They were supposed to put it on my back, you know. But I was too hot-tempered even then...biting and kicking and trying to wriggle free. I must have twisted around at the wrong moment. At first I thought they'd blinded me, it hurt so much. I was too angry to black out, so I just screamed until I had no voice left."

"But why...who would do such a thing?"

Ann gave a humorless smirk. "Where I come from, when a man's convicted of piracy, his entire family—wife and children all—are branded as thieves and criminals right alongside him. The God-fearing citizens of Williamsburg thought if they could impress the Good Lord's mark onto us early enough, it might keep us from following in our father's footsteps." She caught Violet's horrified stare in the mirror and turned to face her. It was a story she hadn't told in more than a decade, but suddenly, inexplicably, Ann wanted Violet to know.

"My father was betrayed, you see, by his own shipmates. Me, my mother, my younger sisters, even my baby brother, who was just a few months old—we all got a share of his punishment before they hanged him." Ann closed her eyes. "I'll remember that day the rest of my life. My family's screams, the scent of their burning skin...watching my father dangling like a broken doll from the end of a rope...knowing that the ones who betrayed him were out there somewhere laughing at all of us. Before he died, Papa made me promise that one day I would avenge him by finishing what he'd started. And in all the years I've sailed these seas, chasing the phantoms of his past, nothing—no one—has ever gotten in the way of the vow I made to him that day." She gave Violet a wistful smile. "Until now."

❖

This was a rare lapse in the pirate's usual cocky façade. At last, here was a naked look at the vulnerability Violet had always sensed was there, buried deeply beneath the layers of violence and arrogance that Ann wore like a suit of protective armor. She had accused the pirate of torturing Charlie, when in fact Ann had gone to great lengths to lessen the child's suffering as much as possible. And it was clear that Ann was deeply troubled by the things she had done to ensure her survival in this world of depraved and violent men.

They were not so different from one another, Violet realized. Had she been in Ann's place she might have easily turned out the same, so focused on fulfilling her mission that she was willing to do anything, even kill, to bring herself closer to her goals. After all, was Violet herself not equally ruthless? Had she not used her body, the only weapon she had, to win the heart of a man she did not love in order to escape from her own personal hell?

Ann was not an evil creature, but had taken the form of one in order to survive. Violet's scars were not as visible, but still ran just as deep. Now, under that penetrating stare, Violet shivered for an entirely different reason. This was no longer a game.

She set the pistol down on the table and stepped forward, the hypnotic power of Ann's gaze impossible to refuse. With one hand she traced the cross-shaped scar, as if she could caress that irresistible vulnerability. Ann's sun-lined skin was soft to the touch, and warm. Ann's lips parted, just slightly, and Violet watched her pupils constrict in a way that made her toes curl. Impulsively she slid a hand behind Ann's neck and pulled the pirate's lips to hers.

In a split second Ann responded, wrapping Violet in powerful arms until her feet were almost lifted from the rug. She delved greedily into Violet's mouth, and Violet welcomed her inside, stroking the questing tongue eagerly with her own. An exquisite yearning welled up inside her, like nothing she'd ever experienced before, and Violet moaned. She grasped at the front of Ann's shirt and tangled her fingers in her hair, feeling suddenly feverish.

Ann was everywhere, surrounding her, covering her face and neck with kisses, brushing lips and tongue and teeth here at her earlobe, there at the delicate junction of neck and shoulder. Her hand slid beneath Violet's open collar and closed firmly over her breast, and then she bent and ran her tongue along the contours of Violet's shoulder. Violet let her head fall back, unfamiliar desire quivering through every inch of her body. Was this what it felt like to the men she attended—this delicious anticipation, this heat that stirred her blood and made her heart pound in her ears? She'd never craved anyone's touch like this before.

Violet deliberately pressed herself along Ann's hard, muscled length and used her own body weight to push Ann back against one of the chairs. "Sit," she ordered huskily.

The pirate sat, breathing hard through parted lips and clenched teeth. Unadulterated hunger radiated from every line of her lithe frame, and she stared at Violet with desire that looked very nearly like desperation. Violet swung herself easily into Ann's lap, straddling the narrow hips between her thighs, and pulled Ann's head back with one hand to expose her throat. She found the pulse point at the base of Ann's neck and covered it with her mouth. Ann groaned. Her heart was racing; Violet could feel it against her lips and tongue like the erratic beat of a drum.

She felt hands cupping her buttocks, and Ann's hips surging up between her legs to grind against her. Violet raked her fingernails down Ann's chest, just hard enough to leave four little pink lines trailing against the tanned skin, and skimmed the softest spot of Ann's throat with her teeth. She was rewarded with a savage, inarticulate growl.

Suddenly Ann bit down on her shoulder, sending tingles of pleasure dancing through Violet's body to center low in her belly. Her innermost muscles clenched sweetly, and she gave a gasping cry.

"My God, Ann…"

Abruptly she was pushed away. Ann held her at arm's length, looking wild and distraught. Violet looked down to see a ring of purplish teeth marks where Ann had bitten her. It had felt far too good to be painful, but before she could reassure her of this Ann shook her head almost frantically and shoved Violet off her lap.

"I won't do it, I won't." She stumbled out of the chair and ran a hand through her wavy hair.

Violet was confused, her breath coming in light pants as she reached out for her. "What's wrong?"

Ann slapped her hand away. "Don't touch me." She spun to face the mirror once again, leaning over the washbasin with heaving shoulders.

Violet came up behind her. "I don't understand."

"Of course you do, you said it yourself. I'm a monster." Her voice was hoarse, her breathing ragged. "Don't you see what you do to me? I know you have to feel it, it's all I can think about. Taking you. Possessing you. Ravishing you, whether or not you will it. Maybe the boys are right, maybe I really am losing my mind."

Violet's breath caught in her throat. "Ann, look at me." When she didn't respond, Violet took her shoulder, turning the pirate captain to face her. She had to duck slightly to catch her eyes. "Right now there's absolutely nothing you could take from me that I would not willingly give." Violet was surprised at how much she meant it; her heart was still hammering and she could think of nothing she desired more than the pirate's heated, silky skin beneath her fingertips.

But Ann shook her head again. "It's not enough." She cupped Violet's face with both palms, emotion darkening her irises nearly to sapphire. "I can't explain it, but it's not enough. I want so much more than just your body, Violet." She flushed and dropped her hands, and before Violet had time to process this strange declaration, Ann had turned and left the cabin.

Violet heard a click as the door was locked from the outside. She sank into a chair by the table, her mind reeling even as her core still throbbed in a tight knot of arousal. She was stunned as much by her own behavior as she was by Ann's curious rejection. Only minutes before she'd been ready to shoot the nefarious pirate through the heart, and now she found herself aching to be back within the circle of those powerful arms. Charlie was still sleeping just a few feet away. What was wrong with her? Wasn't this the woman responsible for her husband's death? Who'd tortured her and Charlie both almost to death?

She reached out and picked up the heavy flintlock pistol from the table, feeling the weight of the iron in her palm. For a few seconds, vengeance had been within her grasp. Ann had made it so easy, with that extravagant display of bravado. How casually she'd put her life into Violet's hands, as if it didn't matter whether Violet pulled the trigger or not. Had she somehow known that Violet wouldn't go through with it? Or did she really feel like she had nothing much to lose?

There was something about the pirate's occasional moments of fragility that captivated Violet, an almost childlike sensitivity that belied the militant self-control. She wondered if anyone else knew the real story behind Branded Ann's infamous scar—not a punishment from God or a battle trophy, but a cruel disfigurement inflicted on a child for the sins of her father. It was Ann's pain, not her temper, that made her dangerous.

Violet had never known anyone like her before, a woman who

commanded more respect than most men, strong and capable and full of breathtaking passion…but also deeply lonely. That loneliness called to Violet, though she didn't know how she was supposed to respond. *I want so much more than just your body,* Ann had said. But what did that mean? Violet had told her that she was willing…what else was there?

❖

It's like we've sailed into the land of the dead, Newbury thought fearfully as he watched the mists swirl over the *Ice Queen*'s decks, obscuring the faces of the crew as they worked. The ship had been becalmed for more than a week now, without so much as the faintest trace of breeze. The cold gray mist had grown so thick that when standing at the foredeck rail, one could scarcely see the aft deck stairs. And it was eerily quiet; the sea lay so still beneath the ship that it scarcely even lapped at the hull. There were no seagulls to cry out above them, no fish splashing in the water below. *Spooky.*

"Well, I'll be buggered…"

Newbury turned to see Carter staring with fascination at an instrument in his hands. "Something wrong, Master Carter?" he sneered.

"You could say that. Look." The sailing master thrust his compass in Newbury's direction. The needle was spinning in nonsensical circles, one way and then the other. "The Almighty Himself don't know which way is up in this infernal place," he declared. "In this fog we can't get our bearings by the stars, neither. We're floating aimless as a bit of soap in a washbasin."

The comparison was less than comforting, as Newbury was struck with a mental image of the whitewashed *Ice Queen* slowly dissolving into suds under his feet. It was all too easy to imagine that they might disappear out here, just vanish into the ghostly mists as if they'd never existed. For the hundredth time he cursed himself for ever thinking this was a good idea. He should have just nabbed the pirate woman when he'd had the chance, and skipped out of port with the reward jingling in his pockets. He raised a hand to scratch beneath the eye patch— another brilliant idea he wished he'd never had. It had seemed like an adventure at the time; the chance to wear a roguish disguise and adopt a nickname had a rather romantic appeal. But too late he'd discovered that his skin was sensitive to the rough leather, and in the past weeks he had developed an irritating rash beneath his eye.

Carter seemed to read his thoughts, and grinned. "Getting squeamish now, your officership? Things are just starting to get interesting."

Newbury glared at him. Their predicament was no laughing matter, and Carter seemed almost cheered by it, which was more than a little annoying. "Need I remind you that we're on a tight schedule? I was told this voyage would take no more than five months. It's already been more than three. If I do not return safely to Port Royal in precisely seven weeks, my associates in His Majesty's Navy will have no choice but to arrest your lovely wife." This was, of course, a bluff. In truth, Newbury had told no one of his plan to infiltrate the pirate ship and commandeer the treasure they were pursuing; he hadn't wanted to share the gold, or the glory, with anyone else. But Carter didn't know that, and right now it was the only bit of leverage Newbury had. He just hoped the lie didn't show on his face.

Carter's eyebrows knitted together. "I'm aware of the *shed-yule*," he replied, mimicking Newbury's careful pronunciation with more than a little sarcasm. "But bleeding Christ, man, I can't make the sun shine or the wind blow any more'n you."

"Then I think you'd better start praying for a change in the weather, Master Carter." Newbury turned his back but was arrested by the quartermaster's voice behind them.

"Carter, give me some good news."

"Afraid I don't got any," Carter replied as he held out the compass for Barclay to examine. "This place ain't called the Devil's Seas for no reason. There's strange forces at work here, says I."

Newbury picked up a navigational quadrant lying on the rail and made a show of putting it to his eye, though the sun was nowhere to be seen in the sky, which made the instrument quite useless. He trained his ears on the conversation. Barclay grunted as he bent over the malfunctioning compass. "And this confounded fog?"

"I've seen it afore, on other voyages. Seems to come and go as it pleases. Could lift tomorrow, might not lift for a month. No way to tell."

There was a scuffle below them and Newbury peered over the

rail to see Porter opening the barrel of drinking water, dipper in hand. Barclay called down to him, "Porter, you swab, what're you about?"

"Water for the prisoner, sir," came the reply.

Barclay shook his head. "Not this morning, Porter. Jenkins'll have to wait till afternoon. As of now we're halving the rations again. Supplies are running low, and until the wind returns we've little chance of seeking more."

The quadrant shook in Newbury's hands. Was it really that bad? The water supply was already rationed to the very edge of discomfort. Halving the shares again was certain misery. Porter seemed to share his apprehension because he slammed the dipper back into the water barrel with a splash.

"It's those damned females!" he exclaimed hotly. "The ship's bloody cursed!"

"Shut up, Porter, you know that ain't nothing but superstition," Barclay interjected firmly.

But Porter seemed not to hear him. "We should have killed them when we had the chance! They're drinking our water and eating our food, all the while bringing misfortune down on our heads. We're going to die out here." He turned to address anyone else on the deck within earshot. "This whole voyage is a fool's mission anyway, chasing after some hare-brained tale of Devil-cursed gold we don't even know really exists. We got a busted mast and barely any food, and no clue which way we're even pointing in this fog. I say we forget the entire bloody thing and sail back to Tortuga on the first wind."

Newbury was inclined to agree, and he wasn't the only one. Heads were nodding across the deck, punctuated by disgruntled mutters. But silence fell quickly as a set of familiar slender fingers took hold of Porter's shoulder.

"Don't you have duties to attend to, boy?" Ann asked quietly, her lips almost touching the scrawny crewman's ear.

Newbury watched the pirate woman's gaze flickering over the faces of the men, the cool challenge in her expression making his blood run cold. Female or no, he had to admit that Branded Ann was probably the most intimidating person he'd ever encountered. And she seemed to have the same effect on the rest of the crew as well; belligerent though they were, without someone to lead them no one seemed willing to engage her.

"That's enough," Barclay commanded from his position at the aft rail. "Get back to work, you bilge rats, unless you want a taste of the cat!"

The men eyed both Barclay and Ann balefully, but eventually they began to disburse. Ann moved to join Barclay on the aft deck, and Newbury remembered the quadrant in his hands. He pretended to fiddle with the instrument's settings as he heard Barclay say, "Captain, this ain't good, and you know it. You got to do something about those girls. Porter may be a superstitious blockhead, but he's right—the women are draining our resources. You don't got no choice."

"Sister Violet's a member of this crew, and she did a fine job for us until the boys decided to let their cocks do the work of their brains." Ann spat with evident contempt. "She's just as entitled to a fair ration as any other man on board, and she shares it with the kid, who doesn't eat more than a sparrow, anyway. They live, Barclay, and that's final. We will not discuss it again." Newbury caught a glitter in her eyes, like the sun glinting off a frozen lake. Barclay did not reply, but Newbury could see the displeasure on his face as he watched the pirate woman stride away.

Taking a risk, Newbury laid the navigational instrument down and approached the quartermaster. "Meaning no disrespect to the captain, sir, I have to say I agree with you. I've got nothing against the woman and the girl myself, but they sure are riling the crew."

Barclay turned and stared at him curiously. "You're a military man, aren't you, Patch?"

Newbury's breath seemed trapped in his chest. "I..." Barclay did not seem angry, so he wasn't sure he should deny it, though he was fairly certain the pirates would kill him if they discovered who he was working for.

The quartermaster chuckled and clapped him on the shoulder. "No need to look so nervous, man, there's plenty of us what have done a turn on a naval crew in our youth. I dare say it's where most learned their hand at sailing. Just that you ain't quite outgrown them stuffy formalities, have you?"

Relieved, Newbury shook his head. "I suppose not, sir."

Barclay chuckled again. "Best be careful or all this 'sir' rubbish might go to my head."

"If you don't mind my saying so, sir, perhaps it ought to." Barclay arched a brow, and Newbury licked his lips. "It's just that...well, as quartermaster you're essentially in charge of ship operations. The captain's here to lead fighting, but..." He gestured through the fog. "There isn't much need for her right now, is there?"

Barclay's eyes narrowed. "Be careful, man. Some might think you were talkin' mutiny."

"Not mutiny, sir," Newbury protested swiftly. "I regard Branded Ann as highly as the next man, truly I do, it's just that, in this one matter, her judgment seems a bit...impaired, doesn't it?"

"Sister Violet *is* a member of the crew," Barclay reminded him staunchly.

"But the child isn't. And anyway, does it matter? If Mistress Watts really were like any other crewman, wouldn't the captain have killed her long ago, without a second thought, for disrupting the order of the ship like this?" It was a point Newbury had overheard the men grumbling repeatedly, and he could see Barclay wrestling with the undeniable logic of it. "I'm not suggesting a revolt, sir. Just...well, if Captain Ann's blind to the most prudent course of action, and the fate of the crew lies in the balance, seems only right that we should take the matter—just this matter, mind you—into our own hands. Force the captain to do what's best for herself, and for all of us, whether she's keen on it or not."

Not wanting to press his luck too far, Newbury took a step backward. "Of course, it's up to you. The crew will certainly stand behind you, sir, whatever you decide."

He thought it best to leave without waiting to see the effect of his words. The important thing was that the seed had been planted in the quartermaster's mind. Newbury was now much more interested in survival than he was in the treasure—but he didn't want the pirates to kill Branded Ann, either, before he could bring her in for the reward. The best plan now was to unseat Ann's absolute control over the ship, so that when the wind returned the crew would insist on abandoning this foolhardy treasure hunt and sailing straight back to Tortuga. If Ann's authority was defied once, it would be all the easier to do it again when the time came.

❖

The flickering yellow light from the oil lamp was starting to make her vision swim, and Ann closed her eyes, rubbing her temples with her fingertips. The movement reminded her of the object in her hand, and she opened her palm to gaze at it again. Her father's golden skull ring, a thick metal band with a grinning face molded faintly into the soft metal. She couldn't remember a time when he wasn't wearing it.

Ann held the ring up and watched the light dance across the gold, catching in the tiny ruby eyes and sparkling faintly. This had been her nightly ritual for years, a few quiet moments spent in the presence of her father's spirit, but over the last few days it had occupied her even into the morning hours. She could not sleep, and so she sat with her father's ring and played the memory over and over again.

❖

"Listen, Annie, I don't have much time. Take this." He'd pressed the map over her heart, and her little hand had come up to cover his urgently. A wistful smile crossed his lips as he pulled his hand back.

"I want you to promise me that you'll always keep it with you. Don't let anyone take it from you, ever. This is my legacy to you, Annie, and to your mother and sisters and brother, and one day you must claim it for yourselves. It's up to you now. Promise me you'll care for them where I have failed."

Ann could still feel the unbearable sting of tears against her freshly branded cheek as she'd delivered the three little words that would determine the course of the rest of her life.

"I promise, Papa."

He'd removed his ring then, wetting the knuckle of his little finger with his mouth in order to get it off, and leaving a pale, indented ring of flesh where it had rested for so many years. The gold was still warm when he put it into her hand and closed her fist over it. "Don't forget me, Annie," he'd said earnestly, his voice catching over her name. "Don't ever forget that you have a papa who loves you always, even from the arms of Davy Jones."

❖

Ann laid the ring down on the map and pushed it with her finger until it perfectly encircled the red X that marked Black Dog's elusive treasure somewhere on the as-yet-unseen island. It grinned up at her sightlessly, like it was taunting her. Had she come this far only to break her promise now? She wanted to hate Violet for causing her to falter on the one path that had always been clearest to her. Every day that Violet still lived, Ann was losing ground with her men. And while she needed the crew and the ship to fulfill her mission, Violet had no such value.

But Ann couldn't hate her. There was no point in denying it any longer. She wanted Violet, needed her, craved her presence in a way she didn't understand. But even so, the depth and intensity of her desire scared her. Violet brought out the very best *and* the very worst in her nature. Ann knew she was going to have to make a choice, and soon. What troubled her was that she still had no idea what her decision would be.

"Captain?" Violet's voice, husky with sleep, sent a delicious chill down her spine, and Ann looked up. Violet propped herself up on one elbow in the bunk, her tousled hair cascading softly over her shoulders. "What are you doing up so late?"

Ann took up the ring again, concealing it in her hand. "Work," she replied shortly.

Violet held a hand out to her. "Come to bed, Captain," she said.

Though she probably did not mean to imply anything provocative, the invitation nearly stopped the breath in Ann's lungs. Every muscle in her body tensed as she became acutely aware of Violet's breasts straining against the fabric of her collared shirt, the shadows of her nipples just visible through the unbleached linen. Ann could still feel the soft weight of that flesh in her palm, could still hear Violet's moan of pleasure when she'd finally, just for a few seconds, allowed Ann's hands on her. An uncontrollable fire ignited her blood in seconds, and with it came a sharp bolt of fear. She clenched her teeth to keep from gasping out loud. Speechless, all she could do was shake her head.

"You've barely slept in days," Violet pointed out insistently. "You should see the circles under your eyes." She patted the mattress in front of her. "Come on, just for a few hours? I promise you can go right back to your brooding and sulking in the morning."

The teasing lilt in her tone drew a grudging smile to Ann's face in spite of her terror. "Very well," she conceded, her throat raspy. *I can do this*, she thought as she slid her father's ring onto her middle finger, then folded the map and tucked it inside her shirt. *I won't touch her. I just want...* Ann blew out the lamp on the table. *I want to be near her. That's all.* Violet held up the quilts so Ann could slide beneath them.

It was a tight squeeze with all three of them in the bunk; Charlie was sleeping soundly against the cabin wall, with Violet in the middle. Ann held her breath as Violet's soft curves melded warmly against her back, one arm wrapping about her waist. She lay stiffly, prepared to flee the cabin if that inner monster she so despised started to get the better of her. Yet to her very great relief, tonight she felt nothing of the insatiable greed that haunted her nightmares. Instead, the fire had subsided into a sweet, melancholic longing that throbbed gently in her chest. This was a feeling she could manage, and slowly she relaxed into the curve of Violet's body. Their intimate position should have made Ann too uncomfortable to sleep, yet she found it somehow comforting, even luxurious. She gave a sigh that was something akin to a purr, and closed her eyes.

❖

A crash at the cabin door awoke them all with a jolt. Ann sprang from the bunk just as a second crash splintered the lock, and the door burst open.

Before she could reach her weapons, several of the crew converged on her, pinning her arms behind her back. Ann started to fight them off, but stopped short when she glimpsed Violet in Mason's beefy arms, one of which was wrapped firmly around Violet's slender throat. Maclairen had Charlie by the hair. She was growling and kicking at him, but to no avail; the Scottish gunner only grunted and yanked more sharply at his fistful of wild curls until the girl shrieked and was still.

Barclay entered the cabin then and met Ann's gaze only briefly before commanding, "Take them outside."

"What's the meaning of this?" Ann snarled as she was escorted past, but he only followed them out of the cabin without reply. Ann didn't really need an answer, she knew what was happening. Her time was up.

The deck was still swathed in cool gray mist as Violet and Charlie were dragged beneath the broken mainmast. Ropes were tied around

Ann's wrists from behind, and she glowered at the quartermaster as he stepped forward, musket in hand.

"Mutiny doesn't become you, Barclay."

"It's not mutiny, Captain Ann," he was quick to correct her. "At least, it don't have to be. But we can't have them on board any longer." He jerked his thumb at Violet and Charlie. "It's time to do what should have been done a long time ago."

"Flea-bitten traitorous curs, the lot of you," Ann hissed, and punctuated the words by spitting on the deck.

"It's for your own good, Captain, as well as ours. You can give the order yourself, and we'll follow it and any others you want to give after it's done, or…" He didn't finish the sentence, but hefted the musket in his hand pointedly.

Ann knew what he was implying, but she wanted to make him say it aloud. A sick weight settled in her stomach as she asked grimly, "Or what, Barclay?"

After a tense silence, he looked her squarely in the eye. "Or I'm taking command of the ship."

CHAPTER THIRTEEN

If she didn't give the order, all three of them would die. Ann knew that, yet she didn't hesitate.

"Go to hell," she snapped, her eyes never wavering from Barclay's face.

He seemed surprised—or perhaps disappointed, Ann couldn't quite tell. His lips tightened into a thin line. "So that's it, then. In the end, you're really going to choose a couple of useless wenches over your crew?"

Ann curled her lip at him without reply, though her mind was racing. Even with her hands bound she was confident she could overpower the men holding her, but then what? If she killed Barclay, one of the others would take his place. She couldn't possibly hope to defeat them all, and even if she did, Violet and Charlie would surely be dead before the fight was over. They might be able to make it to the gunwale and jump overboard, but then what? Adrift in the ocean without so much as a stick of wood to cling to, they wouldn't last very long. One way or another, Violet was going to die today, and it was Ann's own fault. That knowledge made her furious, though she wasn't sure if she was angrier with the crew or with herself.

Barclay sighed. "All right, Captain, if that's the way you want it." He raised the musket to his shoulder and leveled the barrel at her.

"Sir," Patch interrupted from the starboard rail, "wouldn't it be wiser to put the captain in the brig for now? Perhaps after getting rid of the other two, she'll come around."

Ann snorted derisively. "He knows better," she sneered. "Don't you, Barclay? Best put a bullet in me now, because if you don't I'm going to rip your treacherous heart out with my own hands."

He lowered the gun, and for the first time since she'd known him, there was no fear in his expression. "You know what, shooting's too good for a captain who'd turn on their own crew for a bit of tits 'n ass." He turned and shouted, "Lamont, Edwards, Turtle, rig a dinghy!"

Ann didn't know whether to feel relief or dismay as the crewmen scurried off to obey. "You're going to strand me, then."

"Not just you." Barclay jerked his head at the other two captives. "You like the girl and her pet so much, you can all three bloody well die together."

Ann, Violet, and Charlie were herded to the aft deck. One of the small rowboats used for landing and boarding parties was rigged for launch. Ann gritted her teeth as Mason lowered Violet into the waiting boat. She noted an almost apologetic look on the ice ebony features and knew the gentle giant probably wasn't much happier with the situation than she was. She was grateful that he'd been the one to grab Violet first, as many of the other men might have done her harm or worse. Maclairen was not so kind to Charlie and practically threw the cursing, thrashing girl into Violet's arms.

Barclay stared hard at Ann. "Last chance, Captain. It's us or them."

Ann looked around at the crew—the weathered faces of unkempt stubble and missing teeth, all watching her with mingled defiance and apprehension. Then her gaze swept past them to the mangled mast of her ship, the familiar decks and sails and rigging and stairs, the hatch leading to the gun deck, the door of the crew's quarters that was just barely discernible through the thick mists. The *Ice Queen* was the only place she could call home. She'd fought long and hard to obtain her own ship, for the sole purpose of one day filling its belly with her father's blood money. This ship, and these men, were the key to achieving her life's goal.

Ann looked down at Violet and Charlie, huddled in the bottom of the dinghy. Little Charlie sat clinging to Violet's shoulders. Violet's hair was unbound, framing her face in tousled strands that emphasized her childlike features. She held the girl to her breast protectively, momentarily evoking the image of a beautiful guardian angel. Ann's breath caught.

She turned to meet the quartermaster's eyes once more. "Good-bye, Barclay." Without waiting for him to untie her hands, she swung her legs over the gunwale and dropped into the dinghy.

A stunned silence followed. Ann refused to look up, but she could feel Violet's gaze boring into her with disbelief—a sentiment that was mirrored on the faces of the crew above them.

Barclay was first to recover, setting his jaw angrily. "Very well, Captain." He yanked a pistol from his belt and tossed it into Ann's lap.

Ann eyed the gun. She knew without asking that it was loaded with a single shot; an old mariner tradition, both insulting and merciful. She snorted. "Do you believe me that much of a coward?"

He shrugged. "You're so eager to look after your little prizes, you can decide which one of you gets the easy way out. And may God have mercy on the other two." Barclay turned and snapped at the men holding the lines. "Drop them!"

The little rowboat was lowered into the waiting ocean, a little faster than was necessary, so there was a violent jolt when it came in contact with the water. The ropes hummed through the iron rings as they were withdrawn. And one by one, the men dispersed, returning to their work as though nothing out of the ordinary had just happened. Of course they had no other choice; there was still a ship to repair if they hoped to get home. The sea was so still that it took a long time for the dinghy to drift even a few feet from the *Ice Queen's* hull.

For several uncomfortable minutes, Ann tried to pretend she didn't feel Violet's eyes on her; tried not to dwell on the fact that the only home she'd ever known was floating away, inch by torturous inch, after her act of insanity. There was still time to call them back. One shout, that's all it would take to be back on board her ship again. But she also knew the *Ice Queen* would never really be hers again, even if she did call them back. The men would never fear her the same way now, and ultimately that loss would be a death sentence just as surely as the open sea.

These thoughts were unpleasant, and Ann preferred not to dwell on them. Awkwardly she shifted her weight and stuck out one booted foot. "Get my knife."

"What?" Violet said, sounding startled.

Ann sighed. "My knife. In the boot cuff. Get it out so I can cut these blasted ropes." She wriggled her bound arms for emphasis. When

Violet hesitated, Ann lifted an eyebrow. "Or would you prefer that I remain tied up while the three of us die of thirst out here?"

"I'll do it!" Charlie volunteered, and without waiting for a reply she stuck her little hand into Ann's boot and removed the small blade hidden there. Ann grimaced; the child's shrill voice was extremely annoying. But she twisted sideways and wriggled her fingers.

"Give it here."

Obediently Charlie dropped the knife into her hand, and with a flick of the wrist Ann freed herself from the complicated knots. She tossed the rope to the bottom of the boat in case it might be useful later. "That's better," she said, returning the knife to its hiding place and rubbing circulation back into her wrists.

"What're we gonna do now, Branded Ann?" Charlie asked exuberantly.

Ann rolled her eyes. The kid's face was glowing, as if this were all just another chapter in a great adventure tale, and Ann was tired of trying to convince her otherwise. The pistol in her lap was heavy, and Ann held it for a pensive moment before stuffing it in her belt and giving the child a sugary smile. "We're going to play a game."

"What kind of game?" Charlie asked excitedly.

"We're going to see who can take the longest nap." Ann slid down on her seat and leaned back into the prow, crossing her arms in front of her and dropping her chin to her chest. She closed her eyes, then opened one to squint at the girl. "Only one rule. No talking."

Violet furrowed her brow. How could Ann be so calm after what had just happened? *What did just happen, anyway?* She wasn't surprised that the crew had finally lost patience with her presence on board. But Ann's response to the revolt was completely unexpected. *Did she really just choose to die with us rather than take our lives?*

The thought was preposterous. Branded Ann was notoriously ruthless. Violet had always presumed that if Ann was forced to choose, she and Charlie would easily prove expendable. Yet here they were, stranded in the middle of the ocean, and the most feared pirate in the Caribbean had stepped into their floating coffin of her own volition. What could have possessed her to do such a thing? Violet could only

conclude that either Ann had some secret plan for their survival, or...
she really has lost her mind.

Maybe all it came down to was Ann's irrepressible pride. She
wondered if perhaps Ann had simply gotten in over her head and
preferred death to losing face with her men. But that, too, seemed
improbable. Violet had never known anyone so obsessed with controlling
her surroundings. Try as she might, she couldn't make sense of Ann's
behavior.

Charlie settled herself in the bottom of the dinghy, her worshipful
gaze never leaving the pirate, and leaned against Violet's knee. Not a
word did she utter, honoring Ann's command for silence.

Gradually the ghostly mists thickened around them until they'd
drifted far enough from the *Ice Queen* that Violet could no longer
distinguish the whitewashed hull of the ship from the thick fog that
surrounded them. The silence was nearly complete save for the
occasional soft splash of water beneath them, and Charlie's steadily
deepening breathing. Violet felt her own eyelids growing heavy, but her
brain was too occupied with confusion to allow her to sleep.

After everything the pirate had put her through—the death of her
husband, the back-breaking labor, the mockery and derision of the rest
of the crew, those three torturous days strapped to the mainmast—she
ought to hate Ann with every breath in her body. Instead, the more she
learned of this perplexing woman, the more she felt like she understood
her. Violet could only imagine how difficult it must have been for Ann
to survive in the deadly, male-dominated world of piracy. Like Violet,
Ann had done whatever needed to be done in order to stay alive.

The more Violet thought about it, in fact, the more she realized just
what a difficult position she'd put Ann in, simply by being on board her
ship. In a place where a careless spark could sink them all, or a single
spilled water barrel could mean painfully sparse rations for everyone,
Violet had seen men flogged for disobeying orders far less important
than the rules against stowaways. Ann hadn't wanted to see the girl die
any more than Violet had, she suddenly realized. But breaking one rule
would place all the rest in jeopardy. Ann very well might have saved
their lives by ordering them tied to the mast instead of allowing the men
to whip them to death.

The thought was unsettling, particularly as it was reinforced by
Ann's decision this morning to give up her ship, her crew, even her own

life, rather than kill Violet and Charlie. As futile as the gesture might ultimately prove, Violet could not help feeling grateful. For all Ann's insistence to the contrary, Violet knew she was not as monstrous as she would have everyone believe.

Violet had no idea how long they had been drifting; the sky was completely obscured by a veil of pale gray clouds and she could not judge the position of the sun. Gradually her mind quieted, but just as her chin touched her chest, movement from the prow caught her attention.

Ann was awake and had pulled a bit of paper from her shirt. Violet watched her unfold it. Lines formed across Ann's forehead, and Violet spoke quietly so as not to wake Charlie.

"What is that?"

Ann stroked it absently with her thumb. "It doesn't matter anymore."

Something about the document was vaguely familiar, and Violet found herself recalling that first day on the pirate ship. She suddenly felt queasy. "It's the map, isn't it? The one you…killed Isaac for."

Ann's eyes snapped up and held Violet's for a long moment. She sounded unusually subdued as she replied, "No, the one I took from your husband is still on board the ship. This one, my father gave to me."

A peculiar gentleness entered Ann's voice whenever she spoke of her father, and it touched Violet deeply. She felt a sudden, almost irresistible urge to reach out and take Ann's hand, and immediately laced her fingers together in her lap, grateful that Charlie's weight against her legs prevented her from moving. "That's what you meant, isn't it? When you promised to finish what he started. Your father was looking for Black Dog's gold, too, wasn't he?"

A smile toyed at the corner of Ann's mouth. "Not exactly." She looked out over the water, suddenly focused on some spot beyond the distant horizon. Yet again Violet noticed the faint freckles that peppered Ann's nose and cheeks beneath her Caribbean tan. She could sense that Ann had a story to tell, and stranded in a tiny rowboat in the middle of the ocean, there was very little to do but talk. Violet was content to simply admire Ann's sun-lined complexion while she waited for her to speak again.

"I'm sure you've heard that it took Black Dog and his crew more than twenty years to amass the treasure that's hidden away somewhere in this infernal Triangle."

Violet nodded, but Ann didn't seem to notice.

"Twenty years of violent, bloody raids amid volatile politics—the English and the Dutch constantly battling for supremacy in the West Indies, while the French and Spanish jealously guarded their own domains. With all the goods being imported and exported to the European colonies, piracy became both increasingly profitable and increasingly dangerous. For their own safety, more and more privateers sought out Letters of Marque."

Violet knew Ann had entered into such agreements herself from time to time. She'd heard the other members of the crew grumbling about the risk they were taking on this venture, sailing without any legal protection.

"But in spite of the danger," Ann continued, "Black Dog refused to sail under any colors but his own. He and his crew worked only for themselves, unallied with any greater power, and became outcasts even among their fellow pirates. Every last one of them had a bounty on his head the size of a small fortune. They were forced to set up their own private harbor on an obscure island, in the midst of treacherous waters that few of their enemies would dare enter. Somehow Black Dog's cunning made it possible for them to evade capture over and over again."

Ann paused, her grip tightening on the map. "Violet, my father served as gunner on Black Dog's ship for nearly twelve years. He was one of the men who helped collect the treasure and hide it away."

There it was again, the heart-wrenching note of longing in Ann's voice that made Violet's heart flutter. "And they betrayed him for his share of the wealth?"

"The treasure was more than enough to make every last man rich as a king. No, it wasn't the money." A muscle rippled along Ann's jaw as she ground her teeth. Violet had come to recognize the unconscious habit as a gesture of frustration.

"After so many years of battle and looting, the crew wanted to retire with their shares of the prize. But Black Dog wasn't ready for retirement just yet. 'One more run,' he'd insist, and they'd follow him, until one run turned into five, then ten, then twenty. The piles of gold on the hidden island grew bigger and bigger as the crew continued to suffer casualties. They watched men they'd sailed with for years die before their eyes, one by one, without getting the chance to enjoy the fruits of their labor. And finally they lost patience."

The memory of their own expulsion from the *Ice Queen* was still fresh in Violet's mind, and she could easily guess what had happened. "They turned against their captain?"

"Every last man, except one—my father. He and Black Dog had been friends since they were boys, and were close as brothers. My father refused to betray him."

Then Violet understood the full magnitude of what Ann was telling her. "And that's why..." She trailed off, her attention drawn to the cross branded on Ann's cheek.

"That's why the rest of the crew turned against him, too. It's also why Black Dog entrusted my father with this map. Without it, his mutinous men would never be able to find their precious gold. Black Dog was keelhauled, dragged beneath the boat for days until there was nothing left of him...a terrible way to die, and it grieved my father terribly. But they had something else in mind for him. When they reached port they turned him over to the Williamsburg authorities."

Violet reached for the paper in Ann's hand. "And they didn't know he had the other map." Her fingers brushed Ann's and Ann jerked a little; then slowly she allowed Violet to take it from her.

"No, they didn't. The second my father was off their hands, they hightailed it out of port after their gold."

Violet examined the map. The ink was fading on the yellowed paper, but she could still make out the outline of a pear-shaped landmass. The smaller half was dotted with trees, which Violet assumed represented a forest, but it was the larger half that drew her attention. A strange tangle covered nearly all of it, depicting tubes winding in and out of a rocky mass like a spider's web. Some led to small skull-shaped symbols, while other areas were just blank. A trail, marked in red, extended from the beach through the forest and into the maze, winding in an irregular spiral to the center. Where it ended, there was simply a large red X. Violet traced the scarlet line with a fingertip as Ann spoke again.

"Stories say the crew made it to the island, but once they arrived they couldn't find what they were looking for. They realized, too late, that without this second map the first is useless. The island is an ancient volcano, and the treasure is hidden at its very heart. Nearly all the crew died while wandering the tunnels, desperately trying to remember how to get back to their gold. When there were finally just a handful left, they gave up, returned to their ship, and went home. They claimed the treasure was cursed because of their treachery." A mischievous glint entered the pirate's eye. "Some even say it's protected by the spirit of old Black Dog himself."

Violet quirked an eyebrow. "I don't believe in ghosts, Captain."

Ann chuckled, leaned forward, and took her father's map from Violet's hands. "I don't suppose that matters, so long as *they* believe in *you*, eh?"

Violet watched as Ann carefully folded the map and tucked it back inside her shirt. Something about Ann's story bothered her, but she hesitated to ask the question that was burning on her mind. She wasn't certain she really wanted to know the answer. "Captain…"

Ann looked up, and Violet found herself unexpectedly tongue-tied. Heat flooded her cheeks as her attention drifted inadvertently to Ann's mouth. She suddenly recalled the breathtaking taste of those lips, Ann's thundering heartbeat against her tongue, the scent of rum, tobacco, and sea salt enveloping her senses. Violet's stomach knotted and she forgot how to breathe. For a moment she could not even remember what she'd wanted to ask.

Ann frowned at her quizzically, and then her eyebrows rose and a slow, disbelieving grin crossed her face. Embarrassed, Violet dropped her gaze. What on earth was she thinking?

"Isaac," she said quickly, tossing her murdered husband's name between them like a protective barrier. It worked; she could almost feel Ann recoiling. "He was one of Black Dog's crew, wasn't he?"

An awkward silence hung in the air, but Violet did not dare look at Ann again for fear she might lose her composure. After several moments, Ann replied simply, "Aye."

"And that's why your men killed him."

"Aye." Ann paused, as though uncertain she should say more. Finally she sighed. "Violet, Ironsides Isaac Watts was Black Dog's quartermaster. He led the mutiny."

Now it was Violet's turn to recoil. She sank back against the rowboat's hull. "I…He never told me." She remembered that last day on the merchant ship, the mad scramble for weapons as the Ice Queen approached. She could still hear her husband's words as he'd pulled the map from the trunk in their room and hidden it away in the cover of her Bible.

"What is it, Isaac?"

"An old regret..."

Was it really possible that her doting husband had been the man responsible for the terrible suffering inflicted on Ann and her family? Ann's mother, her sisters, her baby brother—mere children branded as criminals when they had done nothing to deserve it. Violet had known her husband was capable of the occasional underhanded business tactic, but such cruelty horrified her. And Ann would forever wear on her face the mark of Isaac Watts's treachery against one of his own men. Violet closed her eyes. "So all this time, you've been looking for him."

"Well, not right away." The faraway look returned to Ann's face. "In the years after Papa's death, my mother fell apart. Somehow she got it into her head that I was the source of every evil thing that happened to our family. I think it was because every time she looked at me she was reminded." Ann covered her scar with one hand. She looked so lost in the painful memory that Violet wondered if she was even aware of the gesture.

"I ran away from home when I was thirteen. Cut my hair, dressed as a boy, and took a job as swabbie on board the first ship that I could find—Mad Jack Raider's ship. Didn't take him long to find me out, of course. I was just a hare-brained kid, full of rage and vengeance, with no idea what I was doing. But I got lucky. When Raider heard my story, he offered to help."

"He took pity on you?"

Ann smirked. "Pity's not a common virtue among pirates. No, I think he was hoping for a chance at the treasure himself. But that didn't matter, because he taught me to sail, to fight, to make myself fearsome. He said fear would be the only thing to keep me alive long enough to find my father's betrayers. And he was right. I took his lessons to heart and in the end, even Raider was so afraid of what I'd become that he gave me my own ship and sent me on my way."

Charlie stirred in Violet's lap with a sleepy sigh. Violet gently stroked the girl's hair until she settled again. "And then you found Isaac."

"And you."

The statement was rather odd, and Violet looked up, startled. Ann was watching her intently, almost wistfully.

"All I've ever done is get in your way, Captain. You should have killed me from the beginning."

"I know."

"Or left me in Tortuga."

"I know." There was a glimmer of humor in her expression, and perhaps something else. Worry? Guilt? Violet couldn't tell. But there was a strange note in the pirate's voice when she asked, "Are you saying you wish I had?"

"Well, at least then I wouldn't be stranded and left to die in the middle of the ocean, now would I?" Violet retorted, and wound one of Charlie's shaggy curls around her finger. "And neither would she."

Silence followed that statement, and Violet was surprised to see Ann lower her head, wisps of hair falling forward to obscure her face. She couldn't help softening her tone. "But then, if it weren't for you, we'd both likely be dead at the bottom of the ocean somewhere already. *For the Lord of hosts hath purposed, and who shall disannul it?* Everything happens for a reason."

Ann dropped her hand over the side of the boat and trailed it in the water. "You're the only whore I've ever met who spouts more Scripture than a bloody virgin nun."

"Even a whore has to have faith in something, Captain," Violet pointed out dryly. "My entire life has been one long series of misfortune and miracles."

Ann met her eyes, this time without a hint of humor. "Then I'd suggest you start praying for one of those miracles right about now."

❖

Newbury was sulking in his bunk when Carter found him. He'd spent most of the previous day studiously avoiding the backbreaking work involved with repairing the ship and trying at the same time to look busy so Barclay wouldn't come looking for him with the cat.

Repairs were slow and difficult. They did not have enough spare wood to patch all the holes in the *Ice Queen*'s battered hull and had resorted to dismantling whatever crates and barrels were available in the hold. With the rigging shredded and the mainsail gone, the crew was hard at work weaving new ropes, mending the remaining sails, and salvaging anything they could find that might help them regain some sailing power.

Newbury cared little for such matters. He was preoccupied with the dismal failure of his plan. Now that both Branded Ann and the legendary treasure were out of reach forever, he was increasingly aware of how very stupid he'd been. He was trapped on a mutilated pirate ship in the middle of the Devil's Triangle, with little more than a phony eye patch and dumb luck standing between him and a crew of murderous criminals. He'd be lucky to make it back to Port Royal alive, let alone with any real profit. His only consolation lay in telling himself that when they made it back, he could at least capture the rest of the pirate crew. A few of them were bound to have some sort of bounty on their heads. It wouldn't nearly amount to the glory he'd have achieved by bringing in their captain, but at least it was something.

That was, of course, if he survived.

Carter poked his head around the corner of the bunk with a chuckle. "I've got good news, your officership. Seems the tides have turned a bit this morning."

"Meaning?"

"Meaning the sun's back. And so is the wind."

Newbury sprang from the bunk and followed Carter onto the main deck. It seemed the navigator was telling the truth. The morning had dawned bright and clear, with only a few scattered clouds remaining, and the thick mist that had enveloped the ship for days was fading, dissolving in the warm sunlight. Better still, when he looked up he could see the fore and aft sails billowing gently. It was not a strong wind, but it was there, and that meant...

"We're saved!" Porter crowed, emerging from the hatch with Jenkins on his heels. Apparently now that Ann was gone, the rest of the crew had decided to release her prisoner from the brig. "I knew them women was a curse on this ship! The minute we get rid of them, just look what's happened!"

"And about time, too," Jenkins grunted from behind him. Several other crewmen slapped his tattooed shoulders enthusiastically.

"Jenkins, you're a downright hero, says I," one of them asserted cheerfully. "The way you stood up to the captain…"

"We all should have done it long ago!" another man added amid a chorus of agreement.

Newbury was immensely relieved. With the return of the sun and wind, the pirates' spirits had been boosted. Now if they could only make it to Port Royal before the fresh water ran out, things might just turn out decently after all. He scanned the deck again, taking mental inventory of the crew and trying to calculate in his head what his total reward might be once they got back to port. Still a small fortune. Feeling much better, he moved to join the knot of cheering men at the rail.

From his position at the wheel, Barclay watched the crew celebrating on the main deck. He was as glad as any of them that the calm had lifted, but he couldn't help the sinking regret in his gut. Unlike the more superstitious among them, Barclay didn't credit this change in the weather to Ann's eviction from their midst. In fact, he was now wondering if he'd been too hasty after all.

True, he hadn't liked the way Ann had enslaved herself to a mere slip of a girl. Her weakness for the wench had been far too obvious for anyone's comfort, and her judgment was badly impaired. But in spite of it all, Ann was still one of the best captains he'd sailed with, with a reputation as far-reaching as the sea itself. No one could match her strategy in battle, and there was no one he'd rather have on his side in a fight. What a waste, that such power and skill should have been lost to the dulcet tones and cheeky temper of a common harlot. Though he had to admit, he'd rather liked Violet, too. Shame she'd shown up in the wrong place at the wrong time.

But no matter; it was done. Ann was gone, along with Violet and the stowaway kid, and the three were good as dead. There was no use brooding over it now.

A shout from the foredeck interrupted his thoughts. Turtle was waving excitedly from the prow. "Land!" he hooted. "I see land!"

The pirate crew surged up the deck stairs to have a look where he was pointing. Barclay stared hard at the portside horizon. At first it appeared to be a mirage, a misty shadow only a few shades darker than the blue of the sky. But the harder he stared, the more he could make out a definite solid shape.

"Carter!" Barclay bellowed, and in an instant the navigator was at his side, examining the object in the distance through a spyglass.

"Island," Carter affirmed. "I'd say she's about two hundred meters in elevation, maybe twelve leagues out."

They were in grave need of supplies, and land meant the possibility of fresh water, perhaps even materials to repair the mainmast and sails. Barclay spun the wheel. "Lamont, get your sorry arse up here 'n take the helm! Porter, Scrappy, mind the backstays! Patch, you make yourself useful or so help me, I'll hang your lousy carcass from the bowsprit! Carter"— he turned to address him—"see if you can figure out where the devil we are. I'm bloody sick of sailing blind."

"Aye."

Lamont stepped up behind him and Barclay handed over the wheel, calling more commands down to the men on the main deck. The ship exploded in a flurry of activity, and Barclay was mildly amused to note that even the shiftless one-eyed navigator's apprentice had busied himself with compass and quadrant at the stern, as far as he could get from the bowsprit he'd been threatened with. When Barclay was satisfied that their course had been properly adjusted and they were on their way, he went to the bow and gazed out again at the landmass they were headed for.

Inwardly he found himself praying. *Please, let there be water.* It was fortunate for him that most of the pirates were too poor with numbers to be able to calculate their remaining stores, but Barclay had known for more than a week that they didn't have enough to last the return trip. In fact, even on quarter rations they barely had enough to last another fortnight. He might have hoped for rain, but their ship was in no condition to weather another storm. *Please,* he repeated, staring so hard at the distant island that his head ached, *let there be water.*

"Captain."

It took Barclay a moment to realize that Carter was speaking to him. "What is it?" he snapped, irrationally annoyed by the title. The crew had elected him captain with very little controversy, but somehow it felt uncomfortable, like wearing another man's clothes.

Carter seemed unruffled by his brusqueness, a huge grin lighting his entire face. "I've done the calculations, and I'm pretty sure I know where we're at."

He paused as if for dramatic effect, and Barclay demanded impatiently, "Well? Let's hear it, man."

"Captain, I think we might have just found what we've been looking for!" He thrust a chart at Barclay. "Look here, you see? Sun's in the right spot. 'Course I'll know for certain when night comes and the stars are out…"

Barclay tuned him out, looking carefully at the yellowed map and doing some quick calculations of his own. "You're saying that's Black Dog's island?"

Carter nodded enthusiastically. "Aye, sir. Least I'm pretty sure of it."

"We found it?" Porter appeared at Barclay's elbow and snatched the map away, turning it one way and then the other in an attempt to make sense of the numbers and letters he could not read. Finally he settled for waving the paper over his head and yelling down to his comrades. "Hey, mates, guess what? We found old Black Dog's gold after all!"

Barclay tore the map from Porter's hands with a glare. "Shut up, you addlepated monkey," he growled, and held out his hands as the pirate crew, excited, clamored for confirmation of this news.

"Avast!" he commanded. "We still ain't sure what's what. And even if this *is* the spot we've been after, it don't matter. You boys forgotten what Captain Ann said at the start? Takes two maps to find the treasure, and we've only got this one!"

The jubilant whooping quickly faded into a dismayed murmur.

"The bitch didn't leave it in them posh private quarters of hers?" Jenkins demanded.

Barclay shook his head. "I went through every bit of paper in that cabin last night, looking for anything that might help get us home. No sign of the other map. She must've had it with her when we cast them off ship."

The muttering grew louder then.

"Perhaps we should go after the women, sir! Get it back." This unexpected suggestion came from Patch, and before Barclay could reply several others were nodding in assent, greed obscuring their common sense.

Barclay scoffed. "Impossible. They're like to be in the arms of Davy Jones already, and knowing the captain, she probably took the map with her the whole swim down. And even if they ain't dead yet, we're in too bad a shape to go traipsing 'round the Devil's Triangle looking for them." He wadded up the map in his fist, slowly and deliberately.

"No, boys, we're landing on this island, whatever it may be, but only for supplies and repairs. Then it's back to Port Royal for the lot of us."

He could see many of them shaking their heads with displeasure, and before the grumbling got out of hand he tugged the cat-o'-nine-tails from his belt and brought it down on the aft deck rail. Splinters flew off in multiple directions, and the resulting crack immediately impressed silence on the crew.

"That's the end of it," Barclay declared, trying to sound as menacing as possible. "I hear back talk from any man and it will be the cat and the brig for him, you hear?"

He watched, stony-faced, as the men reluctantly dispersed and went back to their various duties. But inwardly he felt like he was panting for breath. It was the right decision—the only decision, really, if they wanted to survive and get home. Men died on Black Dog's island. Even those who'd hidden the treasure there to begin with couldn't find it again without the second map. Not to mention all the stories of an evil power that guarded the treasure. Barclay was not a superstitious man, but in his experience even the wildest tales usually had some small basis in fact. However, greed had a way of stripping even the strongest men of their common sense, and Barclay knew he didn't command even half the respect and fear from the crew that Ann had. If they'd turned against her...how long would it be before they did the same to him?

CHAPTER FOURTEEN

Her mouth tasted like ashes, the back of her throat burned, and she couldn't feel one of her arms. Ann squinted against a too-bright sun to find Violet and Charlie using her right shoulder for a pillow. All three were curled together at the bottom of the rowboat, and as Ann gradually came to her senses she could feel the dampness of the seawater that had seeped into her clothing.

It had been a miserable night, she remembered, cold and wet, though fortunately the weather had remained calm. They were all hungry and thirsty. Ann had spent hours that afternoon trying to catch one of the slippery, silvery fish that darted beneath their boat, but to no avail; she had no net, no line, no hook or bait, and she was a sailor, not a fisherman. On occasion she'd seen other men catch fish with their bare hands, but she seemed to lack the aptitude for it. The failure only added to her dark mood, and even the kid had remained unusually quiet at the other end of the boat as Ann's frustration became more and more apparent.

As the sun went down and the air grew chilly, Violet and Charlie huddled together for warmth. Ann shivered herself and thought grimly of the pistol in her belt. She couldn't decide whether Violet or Charlie should get the bullet, when it finally came to that. If the weather stayed calm they might last two days, maybe three, before thirst and the sun killed them all. *And damned if this isn't the* second *time you've condemned them to the same torturous death.*

It was Violet's suffering she cared most about, but selfishly, she also had to admit that she didn't want to be left alone with the kid. Of course, it would be quick and painless enough to snap either of their necks if she had to. The idea felt like a cramp in her gut, but Ann would do it if there was no other way. It would be a far kinder fate than baking to death in the sun. Though if she took Violet's life, Ann didn't think she could live with herself. Best to save the single shot, then, just in case.

Such morbid thoughts had occupied her until finally she could no longer stand Charlie's soft, miserable whimpering. Ann lay down at the bottom of the boat and beckoned Violet to join her, and she wrapped both of them in her arms. The shared body warmth was more comfortable, and eventually they'd all fallen asleep.

But now, something didn't feel right, and it wasn't just that her arm had gone numb under the extra weight. Ann blinked up at the sky, trying to figure out what was missing. After a moment she realized they were too still. Their little rowboat hadn't stopped rocking all night, but now it was not moving. And as she stared up at the wispy white clouds marbling the Caribbean sky, they weren't swaying in her vision they way they should have been with the motion of the waves beneath them.

Ann sat up, not caring if she awakened the other two sleepers. She looked around and realized in an instant what had happened.

Violet sat up and stared in awe. "We've run aground," she croaked, her throat graveled with sleep and thirst.

The dinghy's prow was lodged in a bank of white sand that stretched about fifteen or twenty meters in front of them, disappearing into a line of thick trees. The tide had carried them up onto a beach, and now they were nearly completely out of the water. Charlie gave a gleeful whoop and leapt from the boat, running along the water line and turning cartwheels in the sand as she went.

Ann couldn't help a grin. "Well, Sister Violet, seems the Good Lord listens to those prayers of yours after all."

She stood and offered a hand, wincing when fiery needles shot up her arm as her circulation returned. She helped Violet up, and together they stepped onto the sand. Then Ann pulled the rowboat farther up the beach to keep the tide from sweeping it away. She brushed the sand from her hands and turned to look at the line of trees.

"Where are we?" Violet asked.

"No idea, my pet. Looks to be an island of some sort. But at least we're not adrift any longer, and look." Ann pointed at the tops of the trees, where green coconuts the size of a man's head were clustered around the trunks of the palms. "Breakfast awaits."

Without waiting for reply, she jogged toward the base of the trees, and after a little searching she found several ripened coconuts that had fallen from the branches above. Ann gathered these and deposited them on the beach. There were banana trees, too, she discovered, just a little deeper inland, and with a little experimentation she found that she could dislodge entire clusters of them with a few well-aimed stones.

In a few minutes she'd assembled a large pile of fruit on the sand. Violet picked up one of the hairy brown coconuts and eyed it doubtfully.

"What is this thing?"

"You've never seen a coconut before?"

Violet shook her head, and looked up at the trees. "The ones up there are so pretty and green...wouldn't they taste better?"

Chuckling, Ann took the fruit from her and shook it near Violet's ear so she could hear the sloshing sound inside. "We can eat those, too, but these are the ones that have what we need." She pulled the knife from her boot cuff and stabbed one end of the husk repeatedly until she'd broken a hole in the top. Tipping her head back, she poured a little of the cool, mildly sweet liquid into her mouth, then handed it back to Violet. "Here, drink."

She watched with amusement as Violet sipped gingerly at the opening. "It tastes strange."

"Coconut milk. Takes some getting used to, but it's the closest thing to fresh water we've got." Ann pulled another one from the pile and punctured it as well. "Hey, kid," she called to Charlie, who was cavorting happily by the water, "come here."

Charlie joined them, and several bananas and cracked coconuts later, Ann found that her temper was much improved. Which was a very good thing, since Charlie's energy seemed to triple as she ate, and so did her chattiness.

"Do you think we're gonna have to live here forever, Branded Ann?" Charlie asked cheerfully around a mouthful of banana.

Ann snorted. "I sure hope not."

"Why not? We could learn to fish and build a house to live in, you and me and Missus Watts, all together. My papa told me about these people he met once who live in houses way up in the trees—"

"But wouldn't you miss your papa if you couldn't go home?" Violet interrupted gently.

"But he'd come live with us *here*," Charlie said impatiently, as if this should have been obvious. "It's so much better than stinky old Port Royal." She tossed her banana peel onto the pile and scooted a little closer to Ann. "And you know, Branded Ann, my papa's real handsome." She waggled her eyebrows.

Ann wasn't sure what to make of this statement, but Violet burst into laughter. "I'm sure your papa's very handsome, dear heart. But somehow I doubt even the handsomest man alive could entice our incorrigible Branded Ann to settle down." She gave Ann a coquettish wink, and to her consternation Ann felt the tops of her ears burning. Violet's eyes widened innocently. "Why, Captain, if I didn't know better, I'd say you were blushing."

Undaunted, Charlie turned her attention to Violet. "What about you, missus? I bet you'd like Papa lots."

"Listen, kid," Ann said, "we're not staying here. As soon as I figure out where we are, it's back to Jamaica for you, savvy?" Without waiting for a reply, she rose and stalked across the beach to the rowboat.

Ann made a show of inspecting the little craft as if she had great plans for it. The truth was, until night fell and the stars came out she wouldn't have any way of determining their position, and even if she could pinpoint exactly where they were without navigational tools, she didn't have the first idea how they would survive a voyage back to Port Royal in such a tiny boat. But at least it gave her an excuse to leave the conversation before it grew any more awkward. She hadn't had her morning coffee and was feeling particularly irritable.

And, she had to admit, she hadn't really wanted to hear Violet's response to Charlie's question.

A low growl emanating from the trees made her look up, startled. She scanned the thick foliage but saw no sign of movement. She must have imagined it, Ann decided after a minute or two, and went back to her feigned examination of the rowboat's hull, only to snap up a second time when she heard it again: a deep, angry snarl that reverberated to the bone, and brought with it a strange chill that raised gooseflesh on her arms. Ann pulled the flintlock pistol from her belt and stared again into the line of trees.

Violet's voice sounded behind her. "Captain?"

Ann didn't turn around, just spoke quietly over her shoulder without taking her eyes from the forest. "Did you hear that?"

"Hear what?"

They both fell silent, listening. The waves lapped at the beach with soft liquid murmurs, and the breeze rustled in the palm leaves. Occasionally some tropical bird cried strange musical notes into the air, but the noise that had alarmed her did not come again. Ann's finger relaxed, just a bit, on the trigger.

"I don't hear anything," Violet said slowly.

Ann tucked the pistol back into her belt. "Never mind."

Violet peered at her. "Are you all right?"

"I'm fine. But the sooner we get out of here, the better. I don't know how much more of that kid's flapping tongue I can take."

"Charlie adores you," Violet replied with a laugh. "You ought to be flattered. You were her first pick for a new mama, even before me." She poked Ann's arm playfully. "I think perhaps my feelings should be hurt!"

"Perhaps they should," Ann replied wryly. "Any fool can see you were born for all that mothering rubbish."

She wasn't expecting the sudden raw agony that appeared on Violet's face. "I...thank you."

The look was gone as fast as it had come, leaving Ann stunned in its wake. Was Violet actually harboring a secret desire to become the girl's stepmother? She certainly seemed deeply attached to Charlie. *I wonder if she'd actually marry the kid's father, if we make it back.* It would probably be a good life for her. Ann had a brief vision of Violet in a demure calico Sunday dress and bonnet, off to church arm in arm with some tall, faceless man and little Charlie in tow. What man wouldn't love to have a woman like Violet for a wife? And hadn't that always been the plan, to make sure Violet never had to return to a whorehouse again? But irrationally, Ann felt angry.

No, not angry. Sad.

Then she realized Violet was still talking. "What was that?" Ann asked distractedly.

"I said," Violet repeated, eyeing her curiously, "that Charlie and I are going to go exploring. See if we can find anything useful, maybe fresh water. Who knows? There might even be other people here."

"No."

Violet blinked at her. "What do you mean, no?"

The thought of whatever had been growling in the woods made Ann grip the pistol in her belt. "Just no. Too dangerous."

"Come with us, if you like, then." Violet shrugged and walked away, calling for Charlie. She picked up the remaining bananas from their breakfast pile, took the girl's hand, and the two of them headed for the trees.

Ann was not accustomed to being so casually disobeyed. "Have it your way," she snapped at their retreating backs. "What do I care if you get yourselves roasted on some cannibal's skewer?"

She turned back to the rowboat, but there was no longer any point to pretending she had purpose with it; her audience was gone. She glowered down at the boat for a second before muttering "Bloody hell" under her breath. She had lost command of her ship and, she thought ruefully, she'd never really had command of Violet to begin with. The only thing she could claim authority over now was a flimsy, waterlogged dingy, and it certainly wasn't going to get her very far.

Maybe she could find some materials to repair the boat deeper in the trees. At least that would be a start to getting off the island. Besides, it wouldn't do for Violet and the kid to get themselves lost. She checked the knife in her boot and then reached down into the boat and retrieved the rope that had bound her hands the previous day. Patting the gun in her belt, she sighed and reluctantly followed them into the jungle.

❖

"Drop anchor!" Barclay called, and there was a series of loud, metallic clanks from the bowels of the ship as the crew obeyed. Barclay stared out at the island, still a good half league away, with wildly somersaulting emotions. Relief, mingled with a sense of guilt. A twinge of excitement that they'd found what they'd been searching for. Regret, for not giving Ann the benefit of the doubt for just one more day. And a sinking dread that almost amounted to terror. If Carter was right and this was Black Dog's island, then they could be facing just as certain a death here as they had on the becalmed sea.

He'd never expected to be here. At least, he'd never expected to arrive at this place as leader. Barclay had always taken it for granted that Ann would be the one to take charge of things once they arrived, guide them through the island's perils to the treasure. After all, this was her crazy quest to begin with, and the rest of them were really just along for the ride and a share of the fortune. But now Ann was gone, and the men were angry with him for refusing to continue her hunt for Black Dog's legendary gold.

But Barclay was no fool. If the very men who had hidden the treasure on this island could not find it without the second map, they had no hope of faring better.

He shouted commands without really thinking about them. They'd done this so many times before, harbored someplace to restock and repair, that the orders were automatic, and the crew were so habituated to the routine that verbal instructions were probably unnecessary. Men armed themselves, and rowboats were rigged, manned, and dropped over the rail methodically. A skeleton crew stayed behind to watch over the ship while the rest of the men went ashore for supplies.

Barclay was among the last to go ashore, but the men awaited his arrival before dispersing. Once he stepped on dry land he began barking orders again, dividing the crew into scouting parties to seek out water, food, and lumber for ship repairs. He remained on the beach to coordinate trips between the ship and the island.

In a few minutes the first supplies began stacking up on the sand, mostly tropical fruit that wasn't likely to last long on the ship but would still make a welcome supplement to their increasingly monotonous diet of hard tack and fish. Barclay started taking inventory; there was no point in loading up more than what the men could eat in a few days.

From within the jungle he could hear axes chopping and trees crashing to the ground. Soon they'd have a pile of palm trunks on the beach, ready to be shaved into planks. And if they were very lucky, they might just find a particularly tall tree that could be turned into a temporary replacement for the mainmast. Palm wood wasn't ideal for shipbuilding, but so long as it got them back to port, that was all that mattered.

"Captain!"

Barclay looked up as Turtle came running toward him. "What is it, boy?"

Turtle stopped in front of him, doubling over to pant for breath and resting his hook on one knee. "A boat, Captain Barclay. We found a boat on the beach, about two hundred yards east."

"What kind of boat?"

"Dinghy. One of ours. The women, they must have washed up here, too."

"Impossible," Barclay scoffed.

Maclairen approached from the same direction Turtle had come running, followed by Edwards and Mason, the other two members of their scouting party. "It's them, no doubt," he confirmed, rubbing his red beard agitatedly. "There's footprints all over the sand. Two grown women and the wee lass. Pile of fruit peels and coconut husks, too. From the look of things they ate and then headed off into the jungle."

"But that's just perfect, isn't it?" Patch spoke up from the supply boat he was loading, his words impeded a bit by the fact that he had a mouth full of papaya. He tossed aside the rest of the fruit and wiped the juice from his mouth with a sleeve.

Barclay was more than mildly annoyed. "Patch, you're stuffing your face when there's work to be done? So help me, I oughtta—"

"We're all eating as we work, Captain," he interrupted quickly. "Surely you don't begrudge us that?"

And he didn't, not really. It had been a long time since the crew had access to such treats as fresh fruit. But Barclay continued to glower at Patch anyway, fed up with his indolence. The one-eyed dandy wouldn't even be on board if Ann hadn't needed Ashford Carter's help. And now that the treasure hunt was over, Barclay saw less need for Carter, and even lesser need for his obnoxious tagalong.

Patch must have caught on to Barclay's hostility, because he continued in a much more respectful tone. "Captain, don't you think we should go after the map? It seems a shame to have come this far only to give up now, when we might still have a chance at the gold."

Not this again, Barclay moaned inwardly as several of the other men within earshot gathered around to hear his reply. "Look, boys, even if Captain Ann is somewhere on this island, who among you wants to be the one to try to take that map from her?"

"We beat her before, we can do it again," Jenkins called out defiantly. "I ain't feared of her."

"And maybe you're right, Jenkins," Barclay replied, fixing him with a glare, "but we've all heard the tales of this place. You really want to go wandering around looking for her?"

"They're just stories!" someone else shouted.

Fear gripped Barclay's chest as he looked around and saw only nodding faces. If the men were in agreement, they would go with or without his orders, and more than likely they'd run him through if he continued to deny them. How was it possible that among a crew of such superstitious men, he was the only one with the good sense to be afraid? Sweat broke out on his forehead.

Barclay opened his mouth, but before he could say anything further a terrible, snarling roar sounded from the trees, followed by a bloodcurdling scream.

Every man on the beach pulled his weapon and ran into the thick foliage, toward the source of the sound. It was not difficult to find, as several crewmen were already standing around in a knot of stunned silence. Barclay elbowed his way through them and stared down at a bloodied corpse lying in a twisted heap on the jungle floor.

"Who is it?" he asked. Four long, deep, jagged gashes ran across the man's face, and another set had opened across his chest as if he'd been mauled. The throat appeared to have been ripped out, and the disfiguration was so bad that Barclay couldn't even identify the body.

"Scrappy," O'Hare replied sadly. "I sent him to seek taller trees for the mast. Next thing I hear, he's screaming like a banshee."

"Did anyone see what did this?"

A chorus of negative grunts sounded in reply.

"Nay, Captain," O'Hare said, "I was first to find him, and by the time I got here, whatever killed him was gone."

Barclay took a step away from the steadily growing pool of blood surrounding the body and glared around at the crew. "Tell me again how they're just stories!" he snapped. Scrappy had been a good-tempered fellow, always telling jokes in funny voices to entertain the crew, and he was well liked. Most of the men seemed truly horrified by the sight of their shipmate's mangled body.

But not all of them. Jenkins grunted and crossed his tattooed arms. "So there's a critter out there what's got a bad temper," he said. "We've seen worse. We just make sure we're better armed than old Scrappy here." He put a hand on Patch's shoulder. "I still say we find that bloody map. I ain't about to turn tail and run home without getting what we came here for."

"Right you are, Master Jenkins," Patch agreed. "And what about the rest of you? Black Dog's gold is somewhere on this island. Do you really want to sail away without even looking for it?"

"Shut your trap," Carter yelled unexpectedly from the other side of the body where he was kneeling. "You want us all to end up like this?"

Patch glowered at Carter, and Barclay held up a hand.

"We got enough work to do just to have hope of getting home again. We don't got time to be running willy-nilly around the jungle, boys."

Jenkins spat on the ground. "If you're too yellow-livered to join us, then just stay here and keep on tinkering with the ship. But I'm gonna find me that map. Any man wants to come along, follow me!"

He strode off through the trees, cutlass clanging at his side. Patch and Porter were at his heels, followed by Ortega, Lamont, and a few others.

Barclay watched the rest of the crew as they looked uncertainly from the corpse on the ground to the retreating backs of Jenkins and his group. But no one else moved.

"Right then," Barclay said, "from now on, every man stays within sight of the others and keeps his guns at the ready. You see anything in those trees that ain't human, shoot it." He marched back toward the beach. It would serve Jenkins and the others right if he set sail for home without them once the ship was repaired.

But as he walked, he also found himself hoping fervently that Maclairen was wrong about the women—because if Ann really was still alive, Barclay was a dead man.

❖

Walking through jungle foliage, Violet discovered, was nothing like walking the cobblestones of London or even the swaying decks of a ship. Beneath her boots the earth felt spongy, sinking under her weight and in some spots even sucking at her heels as though it did not want to let her leave. Heavy green vines hung from the overhead branches and snaked around her arms, her waist, even occasionally her neck. She was constantly batting them aside only to be accosted by countless more. And even in the shade of the trees it was still hot enough that she was sweating. Her face and neck and even her clothes felt sticky, and she didn't even want to think about what tropical bugs were probably crawling around in her hair by now.

Charlie seemed to think the entire venture was some sort of grand nature walk. She kept darting ahead, only to return carrying some exotic flower she'd picked or a colorful beetle she'd managed to catch. She'd show her prize off to Violet proudly, and then she was off again.

"Violet, stop. We have to go back."

Violet ignored Ann's words as she pushed another curtain of vines aside and then nearly tripped over a huge mossy log right behind them. A firm hand took hold of her wrist, steadying her.

"I mean it, Violet. You don't even know where you're going."

"That's the whole point," she responded stubbornly, pulling away. "How are we supposed to know what might be on this island without taking a look around?"

"You're completely lost."

"I am not."

"Really? Then tell me, Mistress Watts, which way is the beach from here?"

Impatiently, Violet turned and pointed behind them. "Back the way we came, obviously. That way."

Ann sighed, then reached out and took Violet's shoulders. She turned her a good quarter-circle to the left, and abruptly Violet felt Ann's breath teasing warmly against her neck. "It's *that* way."

The quiet words, so close to her ear, made Violet's skin tingle all the way down her arms. Instinctively she leaned back, resting her weight against Ann ever so slightly. It was a subtle change of position, but she heard Ann inhale as her breasts pressed into Violet's back. "How do you know?" she asked breathily, enjoying the moment far more than she ought to. How Ann did this to her, how she could make Violet crave her touch, her nearness, like she'd never craved anyone in her life—she couldn't understand it.

Ann's lips caressed Violet's ear hotly with each word. "The sun."

The delicate contact made Violet shudder involuntarily against Ann's body, and she felt Ann's chest rising and falling sharply behind her. *She did that on purpose,* Violet realized, her heart quickening.

"The sun?" she repeated, turning to look up at Ann. Daintily she moistened her bottom lip with her tongue. *Two can play this game*, she thought smugly as Ann's gaze fastened uncontrollably to her mouth.

"I've been keeping track of its movement for the past hour." Their faces were only inches apart. "Which gets harder the deeper we go into these trees." Ann's pupils dilated until her pale irises were only a thin halo surrounding them. A thin sheen of sweat coated her forehead and glistened at her throat, and Violet couldn't tell if it was from arousal, fear, or just the tropical heat.

She gripped Ann's belt and yanked her hips closer, no longer caring if the desire she felt made any sense at all. Ann grunted hoarsely as Violet thrust against her. Her need was almost tangible, but so was the very great terror that was restraining it. *There's nothing to be afraid of,* Violet wanted to reassure her, as shimmering excitement swept every inch of her body. *For God's sake, Ann, kiss me!* But Violet couldn't speak, couldn't breathe, couldn't see anything but the wonderfully inviting lips hovering above hers.

"We need to...go back..." those lips said, and then finally, helplessly, they descended toward her. Violet closed her eyes.

"Branded Ann! Branded Aaaaaann!" Charlie's shriek echoed through the jungle to their right. Ann and Violet sprang away from each other.

"Charlie?" Adrenaline shot through Violet's limbs, accelerating her already hammering heart. She'd only taken a step forward before Charlie came barreling out of the trees, her cheeks flushed. She waved madly at them.

"Missus, Branded Ann, come quick!"

Violet stumbled to keep up with Charlie as she led them at breakneck speed through the trees. Her senses were in a complete jumble, but there was no time to ponder her reaction to Ann right now. Charlie didn't seem hurt, but Violet couldn't imagine what had upset the child so. After a few more steps she could hear the ocean. Had they reached the other side of the island already?

They broke out of the foliage and stepped onto a thick sheet of smooth black rock that swept down toward the beach, eventually disappearing beneath the sand. A craggy wall of rock held back the heavy jungle greenery, and only a few brave shoots of grass poked up between the cracks underfoot. Charlie stopped so abruptly that Violet nearly ran over her. She pointed at a tall outcropping near the edge of the clearing, where the sand met the stone, and hopped on one foot with nervous energy.

"Look, look, see what I found!"

Violet clapped a hand over her mouth. "God preserve us."

A skeleton lay propped at the base of the rock formation, its bones graying and brittle and covered with dirt, long ago picked clean of their flesh by the denizens of the jungle. The skull had fallen from the rest of the body and rolled a short distance away, grinning from its lopsided position on the craggy black rocks. Violet could see the glint of gold among its decaying teeth. A few shreds of fabric, all that was left of the dead man's clothing, remained stubbornly caught in the rib cage and joints. Lying across the thigh bones was a rusty cutlass, the sash that used to secure the weapon all but rotted away.

"I just came through the trees and there he was, lying on the rocks," Charlie declared excitedly.

Violet knelt beside the remains in wonder. "There were people on this island before us?"

"So it seems," Ann replied from behind her.

Violet reached out to the detached skull, but she didn't really want to touch it and withdrew her hand. "What happened to him, do you think?" She twisted around, but Ann didn't seem to be paying attention to the bones. Instead, she was staring at the rock formation they were leaning against. A strange, bewildered expression crossed her face, and Violet drew her brows together with concern. "Captain? What's wrong?"

"*La roche des amoureux malheureux,*" Ann whispered, seemingly more to herself than to Violet.

"What?" Violet looked up at the smooth black tower of rock, which stood a little taller than she was, and then back at Ann. "What are you talking about?"

Seeming greatly disconcerted, Ann replied, "My father used to tell us the most fantastical stories every time he came home from sea." She hadn't taken her attention from the rock. "My favorite was about a pair of lovers, shipwrecked in a terrible storm."

She was quiet for so long that Violet prodded, "Well, don't stop there. Tell me." She wasn't sure what this sudden reminiscing had to do with anything, but didn't really care. These rare glimpses of Ann's childhood were fascinating.

Ann's tone took on a singsong quality as she spoke again. Violet wondered how many times her father must have related this tale, as she seemed to have every word memorized. "Long ago, two ill-fated lovers from a faraway island nation boarded a ship bound for the other side of the great ocean. But on the seventh day of their journey, they were caught in a disastrous storm that destroyed the boat. They floated, clinging to bits of driftwood for days, and just as it seemed they would surely die, they washed up on the shore of a beautiful island. There they found water, and food, and in spite of the fact that they had lost everything, they could still rejoice, because they had each other.

"But their relief was short-lived. The following morning, the ground beneath their feet began to shake and crack, steam pouring up from under the earth. They realized that their island paradise was, in fact, a huge volcano, and it was about to erupt. Glowing, molten lava boiled from the volcano's summit and flowed down its sides in all directions to the sea. There was no place to run. And so the lovers embraced and waited for it to come, content to die so long as they could do so in one another's arms. But when the lava flow reached them, instead of sweeping them away, it encased them where they stood and locked them in an eternal embrace. They would be together forever."

A faint smile crossed Ann's face then. "My French mother was always teasing Papa for his sentimental stories. I remember her laughingly calling that one 'La roche des amoureux malheureux'—The Rock of Unlucky Lovers."

"It's a beautiful story," Violet said. She was tempted to add that Ann also looked incredibly beautiful as she was telling it, but held her tongue. Now didn't seem like the right time, as Ann seemed completely transfixed by the sight of the rock fixture. As Violet looked at the formation again she could understand why it had caught Ann's attention; the smooth black stone was curved and twisted around itself, and did look very much like two people with their arms around one another, the shorter one resting its head on the taller one's chest.

"I know where we are, Violet," Ann said, and Violet was stunned to hear Ann's voice trembling. Ann pulled her father's map from her shirt, gazing at it numbly before handing it down to Violet.

Violet unfolded it, and Ann touched a spot on the map with her finger. There, surrounded by trees on the diagram, was a tiny, unmistakable sketch of the very rock they stood beneath. She stood slowly and met Ann's eyes in utter astonishment.

"Are you telling me we're on Black Dog's island?"

Ann looked so uncharacteristically pale that Violet thought she might be ready to faint. She held up a fist, staring down at a large, gold, skull-shaped ring on her middle finger. Her hand shook. "I found it, Papa," she whispered. "After all these years, I actually found it." She swayed on her feet, and Violet caught her around the waist with one arm, placing the other hand against Ann's chest to steady her.

"Ah! Easy now."

Ann's hand, the one with the ring, covered Violet's. She pressed Violet's palm firmly against her breast, where Violet could feel Ann's heart pounding maniacally. The touch seemed to calm her, and Violet felt the wild pulse slowing gradually beneath her fingers.

"Your ring," Violet said, looking down at it. "What does it mean?"

Ann held up her hand, and Violet could see her fingers trembling slightly. "It belonged to my father. Black Dog gave it to him after my father saved his life during a battle. I never saw Papa take it off, until the day he passed it on to me." She tilted it in the sunlight. "Papa used to say—"

She was interrupted by a shriek that tore through the air overhead, and Violet stiffened as she recognized Charlie's voice. But Ann only rolled her eyes.

"Not again. What's that kid gotten herself into n—" She was cut off by a great crash and scuffle from the other side of the rock wall, followed by a strange squeal and another wail that sounded truly terrified.

"Charlie!" Violet cried out.

With lightning speed Ann whipped the pistol from her sash and, reaching down, snatched the rusty cutlass from the dead man's lap. "Stay put," she barked at Violet and then leapt up the rocky incline, her boots scraping against the black stone. She disappeared over the edge. Violet moved to follow her, but she was not as sure-footed and the jagged rocks scraped her hands. She'd have to go around the wall the way they'd come.

From the other side Violet heard more commotion, twigs snapping, leaves rustling violently and a heavy pounding against the ground that sounded like hoofbeats. There was loud grunting and another hideous squeal. Then a deafening shot rang out, echoing like a clap of thunder, and so loud that Violet's ears hurt. Charlie was screeching again.

Violet's heart stopped. "Ann!" There was no time to go around. She scrambled frantically up the rocks, heedless of the way they cut into her palms. "Oh God, Ann!"

CHAPTER FIFTEEN

B arclay mopped the sweat from his forehead with a sleeve. The afternoon was turning out to be quite productive, and he estimated that with the amount of wood they'd collected, the repairs to the ship could be completed in a week or two. After Scrappy's death that morning, the men were unusually somber; even the catch of two large sea turtles, which O'Hare was in the process of preparing for their supper, did not seem to lighten the mood.

And there was a more pressing issue on Barclay's mind. Water. In spite of all the scouting parties that had been sent out, none of them had yet located a freshwater supply on the island. He'd ordered that rain catchers be set up along the beach in the hopes that perhaps another tropical storm might come along, and for the time being the men seemed content with coconut milk. But without a water supply, the only option would be to spend several extra days filling the barrels with coconut milk to ensure they'd survive the trip home. Barclay didn't want to remain on the island any longer than was absolutely necessary.

His head snapped up when the faint report of a pistol shot sounded overhead, from somewhere to the west. Barclay searched the top of the trees as if he could somehow catch sight of the source, but of course the distance was too great. He turned to O'Hare. "Do we have any men out that far?"

The Irishman paused in the middle of scraping out a huge turtle shell and tilted his head as he eyed the trees. "Dunno, Captain."

At that same moment, members of the crew started pouring out of the trees, running toward Barclay.

"Did you hear that, Captain? What was it?"

"*Who* was it?"

"Maybe someone caught the thing what tore up poor Scrappy!"

"Pipe down," Barclay commanded, and cupped his hands around his mouth. "All hands, report to the beach!" he shouted, then turned and repeated the order in the other direction.

After a few minutes every member of the crew, save the ones who had left with Jenkins and the ones still left on board, had been accounted for. All of them denied that they'd fired their weapons.

"What do you think it means?" Turtle asked anxiously. "Maybe Jenkins and the others found Captain Ann after all!"

"If so, I'd wager she killed him where he stood," Mason grunted.

Barclay lifted an eyebrow. "Or perhaps," he interjected dryly, "Jenkins and his mates ran into Scrappy's mystery chum out there. Any of you seen signs of such a beast?"

The men shook their heads, and Barclay nodded. "Good. Then it don't affect us either way who fired off that shot, does it? Keep sharp, boys, and mind your weapons. Maybe if we're lucky the devil critter's tracking that fool Jenkins instead of us. O'Hare," he turned to the cook, "how long till mess?"

O'Hare gave a gap-toothed grin. "'Bout an hour," he answered.

"Hear that, me hearties? Back here in an hour for chow." Barclay dismissed the crew to their work once more, and as they dispersed, he turned and gazed uneasily to the west. What he'd told the others was true. It didn't really matter if it was Ann or Jenkins who had pulled the trigger out there. His objective hadn't changed. But as he stared at the tops of the trees, he found himself wondering which one of them he least wanted to face again. At this point, neither was a particularly appealing thought.

Newbury dawdled behind the rest of the group so he could lift his eyepatch and scratch at the rash under his eye without being seen. In this heat, the sweat stung so badly against his irritated skin that he was half tempted to rid himself of the thing altogether, consequences be damned. He was just grateful that the sun was going down now, and hoped it meant that the air would finally cool.

Eight men in total had defected from the main group to seek out

Ann and her treasure map, with Jenkins as their self-appointed leader. Newbury was beginning to doubt Jenkins's competency. They'd been tromping through the thick tropical trees for more than an hour, Jenkins insisting he was on the women's trail. Then a gunshot rang out from somewhere deep in the jungle to their left.

After what seemed like endless argument over whether the shot had been fired by their crewmates or the women they were pursuing, and whether the women even had a gun at all, Edwards reminded them that Ann had been given the traditional single-shot pistol when she was stranded. They'd only heard the one shot, and had it had originated too far out to be any of the men from the *Ice Queen*. When Dipper pointed out a peculiarly twisted tree trunk that they all remembered passing quite a while ago, and it became apparent that they were going in circles, Jenkins was finally convinced to turn around. By that time it was already starting to get dark.

Newbury was rather proud of himself, however, for doing this at all. There he'd been, ready to give up everything he'd risked his neck for, when Divine Providence had dropped a second opportunity into his lap. He couldn't think of a better sign that the Almighty Himself *wanted* him to have Black Dog's legendary treasure. And Newbury was certain that if it wasn't for his vocal support of Jenkins, they wouldn't have so many men with them now. Yes, he'd done well to be so courageous, and soon he'd be well rewarded for it.

As Newbury picked up his pace to catch up with the others, thoughts of Ashford Carter pricked at him with irritation. The navigator had contradicted him right in front of the rest of the crew, very nearly undermining Newbury's efforts at gaining cooperation. Up until then, Carter's behavior had been acceptable, if not ideal. But this most recent act of defiance was simply unacceptable. When they got back to Port Royal, Newbury decided, regardless of the success of this venture, he was going to have the man's wife arrested alongside the pirates. And if Carter made even one more half-witted joke at his expense in the meantime, he'd not only see the woman hanged after she birthed, he'd personally take the babe and drop it off the nearest dock as food for the sharks.

The thought filled him with smug satisfaction.

❖

"Mmm, that's good." Charlie licked her fingers and reached for another piece of the meat lying on several large banana leaves spread on the sand. The evening air was filled with the delicious scent of roasted pork. "I hope another one of these things chases me tomorrow, too."

Ann laughed and eyed the carcass of the wild boar. "Let's hope not," she said, "because that was my one and only shot. You're just lucky I have good aim."

"Got him good, too," Charlie mumbled with her mouth full. "Bam! Right in the eye!" She gesticulated with one hand and ended up smearing grease all over her own cheek. "You're the best hunter ever, Branded Ann."

"You're making a mess, dear heart," Violet admonished gently, though she was smiling too much for it to be a reprimand. She leaned forward and used the sleeve of her shirt to wipe the child's face.

"Ah, let the girl enjoy her meal," Ann responded cheerfully. "Plenty of time for washing up later, eh, kid?" Charlie beamed at her and she winked, then helped herself to another strip of meat as well. She winced a little as she sat back again.

"Your leg," Violet said with worry written on her pretty features. "It still hurts?"

Ann shrugged. "I imagine it's going to hurt for a while," she answered lightly, "since he did take a good swipe at me with those tusks of his." She bit off a chunk of pork and chewed, watching the frown lines deepen on Violet's forehead as she moved over to check the makeshift bandage on her left calf. Ann swallowed and waved her away. "No need to fret, my lovely, it's hardly the worst battle wound I've been dealt. And can't say I've ever had so fine a nurse."

Violet flushed, and Ann grinned. She wasn't sure why she was in such a good mood after the events of the afternoon. She'd made it over the rocks just in time to see a giant boar—two, maybe three hundred pounds—rushing at Charlie. It managed to slash at Ann's leg before she was able to divert it with a sharp swing from the dead man's cutlass. When it charged again, she put a bullet in its head. The leg wound wasn't deep, but it felt a little like someone had hit her shin with a sledgehammer.

She tugged Violet down next to her and handed her the piece of meat in her hand. "You haven't even touched the food yet. Stop fussing and eat."

Violet still looked anxious, but she did take a half-hearted nibble. Ann used her knife to cut more strips from the boar, offering some to Charlie before settling back with her own. Fresh meat was a welcome change after weeks of hard, flavorless biscuits, especially when the biscuits had started to mold. She chewed with relish.

Right after she'd killed the boar, Violet had come skidding over the top of the rocks, screaming Ann's name and nearly landing on top of her and Charlie both. Remembering the terror in Violet's voice made Ann feel almost giddy, which was ridiculous. *She was just afraid of being left alone. I'm the only protection she and the kid have got.* But she couldn't stop herself from replaying the sound of her name on Violet's lips, over and over again.

She could still feel the touch of Violet's hands as she'd ripped Ann's bloody pant leg all the way to the knee in order to inspect the damage. Ann had no memory of the pain, but she could recall in vivid detail the feel of Violet's gentle fingers on her skin. Between the two of them they'd managed to stop the bleeding and wrap the wound in Ann's scarlet sash, and they'd decided to make camp on the beach beneath the distinctive rock formation.

Out of the corner of her eye, Ann watched Violet eating and noted that the cuts on her palms had scabbed over, though her skin looked bruised. Ann hadn't asked her about the scratches, but when Violet was tending her injury Ann noticed that Violet's hands were also bleeding. The damage was probably caused by scrambling over the volcanic rock so fast, and that, too, gave her an odd little thrill in the pit of her stomach.

Stop that, Ann. Just stop it. She was letting her imagination get the better of her again. It was not a healthy habit, and besides, she felt rather foolish for letting such tiny things fill her with such illogical joy.

"So full," Charlie moaned, patting her stomach, and Violet put the piece of meat down to hold out her hands.

"Come on, then, let's clean you up." She stood and led Charlie down to the moonlit water. Barefoot, they waded in almost to their knees and Violet helped the girl rinse her hands and face.

Ann had to grin when Charlie splashed Violet in the face and Violet gave an exaggerated squawk of indignation. She watched the two of them chase one another across the sand, giggling, until finally Violet caught the girl from behind and spun around with her. Charlie squealed with delight. The kid wasn't really so bad, Ann decided. A huge bundle of trouble, to be sure, but when she wasn't being annoying she could be kind of fun. Ann found herself wishing she could join them, and the impulse amused her. She wasn't generally the playful type.

Instead, she busied herself in wrapping up the remainder of their meal in the banana leaves to protect it from the sand, and threw a few more sticks on the fire. When they'd made camp she'd used some green wood, the rope she'd brought with her, and a couple sticks of dry wood from the jungle to fashion a primitive bow and drill. It was a frustrating process, especially since she hadn't put that particular skill to use in quite some time. But after several tries she'd succeeded in getting a fire lit, and she was determined not to let it burn out and have to go through it all again.

Suddenly, from behind her, Ann heard a growl, the same sinister sound that had alarmed her that morning. Very slowly Ann turned to face the trees. In the darkness she couldn't see much more than slight movement in the undergrowth, and that was more likely due to the breeze than a wild creature lurking in the jungle. The noise came again, and this time it seemed farther off. She strained her ears, and after a few moments was satisfied that whatever it was, it was moving off in the other direction. She'd rather hoped that the boar she'd killed was the source of the threatening snarls, but it seemed that wasn't the case. Boars usually traveled in packs; perhaps it was just a family member?

"Captain?"

Violet lay a hand on her shoulder and Ann jerked. She turned to see Violet and Charlie, feet caked in sand, settling themselves back down at the fire.

"What is it? You look like you're brooding more than usual."

Ann smirked. "No, no more than usual," she replied flippantly, eyeing Charlie. When she was sure that the girl wasn't paying attention, she spoke again, softly. "There's something out there, Violet. In the jungle."

Violet's brows went up. "What kind of something?"

"Sounds like the dangerous kind, so we'd best be careful. Can you manage sleeping in shifts?" At Violet's nod, she said, "Good. I'll take first watch."

"Missus Watts?" Charlie spoke up sleepily. She had snuggled herself down into the sand, one hand tucked underneath her cheek. "Will you tell me a story?"

Violet smiled and moved to sit next to the girl. "Of course, dear heart. Close your eyes, now." Charlie took her hand and laced her fingers with Violet's, wiggling into a comfortable position.

Ann sat back as Violet began speaking of a man who, one day, to the bewilderment of his friends and neighbors, started building a huge boat in the middle of the desert. It was a tale Ann recalled vaguely from childhood, and as it went on she recognized it as one of the Bible stories her mother used to read on Sunday evenings. She listened, every bit as captivated by Violet's animated voice and gestures as Charlie was. Even without her Bible to read from, Violet obviously knew the legend by heart.

Thinking of Violet's beloved book, Ann felt a pang of regret that it had been left behind. She knew Violet had to miss it terribly. During all the nights they'd shared her cabin, Violet never failed to spend at least a few minutes reading before she fell asleep. In fact, Ann remembered with a grin, at first Violet had attempted to read the passages aloud, until Ann had threatened to toss the book overboard if she didn't keep her religious drivel to herself. *If we ever get off this island*, Ann decided, *I'm going to buy Violet the finest God-damned Bible she's ever seen.*

Charlie had fallen asleep by the time Violet finished her story, and she ruffled Charlie's curls fondly. "I wish I had a blanket for her to lie on, at least," she said quietly.

Ann hadn't even thought of that. "The boar hide will make a good sleep mat if I can cure it properly," she whispered back. "I'll work on it tomorrow."

Violet nodded without looking up and gently disentangled her fingers from the sleeping girl's. Ann felt a lump rise in her throat. Watching Violet with Charlie was indescribably touching. There was such tenderness in Violet's face, such warmth in her voice when she interacted with the child, that it made Ann long for…well, she wasn't sure exactly what it was she longed for, only that it was most likely something she had no business wanting at all.

"Did you and Watts ever think of having children?" The words were out of her mouth before Ann realized she'd said them, and when the agonized look crossed Violet's face as it had that morning, she wished she could take them back. "I'm sorry. I shouldn't have asked."

Violet met her gaze incredulously, the pained expression suddenly replaced with one of shock. "Captain...did you actually just *apologize* to me?"

Ann snorted. "I never apol—" But she trailed off in disbelief. "I did, didn't I?"

"I think you did, yes." Violet smiled, her cheeks dimpling, and Ann caught her breath. "Well, I suppose there's a first time for everything, hmm?"

Ann was too overcome to answer, and dropped her eyes. She'd experienced a lot of firsts with Violet around. Emotions she'd never felt before, desires she'd never felt before, and now this...

Violet rose and moved to her side, settling next to Ann on the sand. "To answer your question, Captain...children were never a possibility for Isaac and me."

Ann had never heard such profound sadness in Violet's tone. She lay a hand gently on Violet's knee. "Don't. You don't have to tell me."

"No, I don't." Violet turned to face her then, her enormous eyes turned nearly black in the darkness. Ann could see the orange-red flames of the campfire reflected in them. "I've never told anyone, in fact, except my husband. But as I said, there's a first time for everything. Just keep in mind," she drew a breath, "that it's a long story." Ann knew she should withdraw her hand, but was reluctant to break the contact. She left it where it was and traced slow circles on the fabric of Violet's trousers as Violet spoke again.

"The London bawdy-house where I was born and raised wasn't the biggest or the most fashionable brothel in the city, but we were popular." She paused before amending softly, "*I* was popular."

Ann could easily believe that. In Tortuga, even behind a huge feathered mask Violet's remarkable beauty set her apart.

"We attracted a wide variety of patrons, from wealthy businessmen bored with their wives, to hot-blooded boys just discovering the wonders of the female sex, to unruly pirates fresh off the boat and looking to squander their newly acquired plunder. That's how I met Isaac Watts.

"Isaac was one of my regulars for years. Every time he came into port he'd pay the house mistress an exorbitant sum to keep me the entire night. I liked him. He always brought me pretty presents from his travels, and he was...*good* to me. Gentle, unlike the rest of his kind."

Ann chuckled, and Violet's cheeks reddened. "I didn't mean—"

"I know perfectly well how most pirates treat a woman, my lovely," Ann interrupted quietly. She could not stop herself from reaching up to stroke Violet's face, the flushed skin warm and silken beneath her fingertips. To her surprise, Violet's hand came up and captured hers, and then somehow Violet had curled into a ball at her side, her head pillowed in Ann's lap. The movement was so smooth Ann wasn't even sure how Violet had pulled it off.

"Well, as I said, Isaac was different."

Ann was reeling from the sudden change in their positions, the soft, precious weight now resting on her thighs and Violet's fingers playing lightly with hers. She had to will herself to concentrate on what Violet was saying.

"But about two years ago...almost three now...my life changed completely. I discovered I was with child." Violet's voice broke over the last few words, and Ann immediately forgot any awkwardness she might have been feeling. Not knowing what to say, all she could do was fold Violet's hand in hers.

"I hid it for as long as I could, because I was scared. I thought, if the baby was a boy the mistress would make me give him away, but if it was a girl, she'd grow up in the whorehouse like I had. Either would break my heart. I didn't know what to do, so I just kept working. Eventually, one of the other girls started whispering to the mistress that I hadn't cycled in several months. And that was when..." A tear escaped down one side of her face. "That was when I found myself in hell.

"The mistress screamed that she couldn't afford to lose me for the time it would take to carry the child to term. She started hitting me. Beat me with a cane until I could no longer stand, and then started kicking me in the belly until I lost consciousness. When I woke up, I was lying on my pallet in the back room, and a doctor was there...he was a frequent customer. I will never forget the astonishment on his face when he told the mistress that, miraculously, my baby had survived. She started screaming again, and I fell back asleep.

"The next time I woke up, I was in a strange place. Dark. Cold. Cramped. There was a strange old woman, bent and twisted, who spoke to me in a language I didn't understand. Isaac told me later that she was probably a Gypsy. She forced me to drink the foulest thing I've ever tasted. It smelled like...like rotted flesh." Violet made a gagging noise. "I slept again for a while, but awoke in terrible pain. It felt like my body was turning itself inside out. I'd never experienced anything like it. There was so much blood, everywhere underneath me. I thought I was dying. Hours it went on, and so did the bleeding, until finally the baby was stillborn...nearly five months too soon. The old woman appeared and took it away." Ann could see Violet's entire body trembling. "In the end I never even found out if I'd had a boy or a girl."

"My God," Ann breathed.

"But the house mistress hadn't counted on what the Gypsy's poison, and the beating, would do to me. I couldn't go right back to work like she'd expected. For days the bleeding didn't stop, and I got weaker and weaker. In frustration she finally gave up and closed me in the back room to die. That was when Isaac came back to London. He wouldn't accept the mistress's excuses, insisted that he be allowed to see me. And when he did, he took me away. Paid the brothel more money than I'd probably made in all my years of work put together, took me to his own home, and called for one of the finest doctors in London."

"And you healed," Ann said in wonder, running strands of Violet's hair through her fingers.

"Yes, and Isaac and I were married. But..." And here Violet turned her face away. "I am no longer able to have children."

Ann sensed Violet's pain like it was a knife in her own gut, thinking of how tenderly Violet cared for Charlie. What a damned cruelty, that someone who took so much joy in a child should forever be denied one of her own. "I'm so sorry, Violet."

Unexpectedly, Violet gave a short laugh and rolled back to look up into Ann's face. "That's your second apology of the evening, Captain," she pointed out, "and now you're saying you're sorry for things you didn't even do. Are you feeling all right?" She made as if to press her hand to Ann's forehead.

Ann batted her away with a chuckle, relieved that the humor seemed to dissolve some of Violet's sadness. "I'm fine."

"Really? You could come down with all sorts of things if that leg of yours gets infected. Maybe I should look—"

Ann grinned and grappled with Violet as she reached for the bandage on Ann's leg. She held Violet's wrists, but somehow Violet managed to wriggle one of them free and reach for her leg again. Laughing, Ann grabbed the wayward arm and wrapped Violet tightly against her, rolling so her body weight would pin the other woman down. They ended up lying in a pile on the sand, Ann on top, straddling Violet's hips to keep her still. Violet was giggling, all traces of melancholy apparently forgotten. Ann propped her elbows on either side of Violet's head so she wouldn't crush her. Suddenly she was acutely aware of every inch of their touching bodies—hips, thighs, stomachs, and she could feel Violet's breasts crushing softly against hers with every breath.

Oh God. The hunger tore through her with brutal force, taking command of every muscle in her body. Raw heat kindled in her belly and spread until she could feel it in her face, the back of her neck, her thighs, the soles of her feet. Violet was beneath her, panting, and Ann could still see the flames of the campfire reflected in her eyes. That was how she felt, like her very soul was on fire.

It hurt.

Ann got up quickly, needing to separate herself from Violet while she still could, and planted herself a safe distance away. "Fire's getting low," she said stiffly, and poked the embers with a stick as she added a few more pieces of wood.

Violet sat up. A minute of awkward silence passed before she said tensely, "I suppose that I should get some sleep if we're going to go after that treasure tomorrow."

Surprised, Ann looked over at her. "What?"

"Black Dog's treasure. Isn't that what we came here for?"

"We got here by accident," Ann reminded her.

"There are no accidents, Captain." Violet's tone was insistent. "We're meant to be here." Her tone almost seemed to imply another meaning to that statement, but Ann knew it was only her heated imagination playing tricks on her yet again.

She went back to poking at the fire, more because it gave her something to do than because the flames needed encouragement. "I'm not so sure."

"How can you say that?"

Ann didn't know quite how to explain. But it seemed like this entire expedition had somehow, all on its own, developed a completely different purpose than the one she'd thought. All her life she'd been seeking her father's long-lost gold, but since the day she'd met Violet that goal had been diminished, even hindered, by Violet's presence. The discovery that they'd finally made it to the elusive island had been more a staggering shock than a triumph. And if she was going to be perfectly honest with herself, the gold really wasn't that important anymore.

"Captain Ann." Violet scooted closer. "Listen to me. I'm well aware of just how much I've cost you. You gave up your ship and your chance at fulfilling a promise to your father...and I don't really understand why, but I know it was because of me. Yet even in spite of that, somehow we made it to this island. As far as I'm concerned, the Good Lord Himself might just as well have plucked us from the sea and dropped us here." She curled up at Ann's side then, laying her head down on one arm and tucking a hand beneath her cheek. "You're going to keep that promise you made to your father, Captain. And Charlie and I are going with you to help however we can. So don't forget to wake me up when it's my turn for the watch."

And with that she yawned and closed her eyes, and in a matter of seconds her breathing deepened as she fell asleep.

Ann stared down at Violet in the flickering firelight, watching it transform her creamy skin into a wash of gold. She was achingly beautiful, with her sweet, heart-shaped face, rosebud lips, and thick, dark lashes. Ann's throat felt tight.

The horrors that Violet had managed to survive were astounding, and the more Ann learned of them, the more her admiration for Violet deepened. That strength, that courage, that dazzling vivacity...her dusky, sultry voice and brilliant dimpled smile...if they ever made it off the island, Ann didn't know how she'd go on living without them. How could she just let Violet walk away, possibly into someone else's arms, when Violet was everything, *everything* that made life worth living? From the first day those enormous jeweled eyes met hers, Ann was lost. She found herself doing, saying, and feeling things she'd never imagined. She wanted Violet so fiercely that it frightened her. Not even her lifelong quest for her father's treasure meant as much as this one perfect woman who had somehow stolen her heart.

And looking down at her now, Ann knew that nothing would ever mean as much again. "God, Violet," she whispered, reaching out to stroke her temple lightly. Even that light contact burned against her fingertips. "I think…I love you."

Ann couldn't even remember the last time she'd said those words. Had she ever said them? But as they passed her lips Ann felt a surge of uncontainable emotion. She was stunned by the sudden wetness that spilled down her cheeks. Tears. Another thing she hadn't experienced in a very long time. This was a night of firsts, indeed.

Like most of the men Ann was acquainted with, Ironsides Isaac Watts had been a criminal. He was the traitor responsible for her father's death, her family's disgrace, the misery of her childhood. But the man Violet described was so different from Ann's perception: gentle, compassionate, generous. And capable of giving Violet far more than Ann could ever hope to offer. As she ran a hand through her hair, the towering rock formation caught her eye. In the darkness, it could be even more easily mistaken for the silhouette of two lovers wrapped in one another's arms. Ann gazed at it sadly. *What have I done?*

She withdrew the map from her shirt and unfolded it. In the end, Watts's death had been for nothing, really, aside from revenge. The map she'd taken from him had led them to the Devil's Triangle, but Ann had ended up on the right island purely by chance. She was sitting on the shore of the fragment of land she'd sought all her life, and what had it cost her? What had it cost Violet? No amount of gold was worth all of this. No amount of gold could bring Violet's husband back, or restore Ann's innocence. She'd turned herself into a monster, destroyed countless lives, all for the sake of a promise she'd made to a dead man.

Papa would be ashamed of me. Ann didn't know why this hadn't occurred to her before. She held up her hand and stared into the ruby eyes of her father's skull ring. If he truly had been watching over her all these years, how her descent into darkness must have grieved him. Dan Goddard had been a pirate himself, it was true, and wasn't the gentlest of men, but she knew he wouldn't have wanted this. He would never have asked this of her.

As more tears streaked her face, Ann did the unimaginable: she threw her father's map on the fire.

CHAPTER SIXTEEN

The map burned slowly. The edges curled and blackened and small holes formed in the diagram, expanding outward. Ann watched the flames eagerly consuming the yellowed paper, stunned into numbness by her own actions. Yet she also felt a strange sense of satisfaction. *There are no accidents*, Violet had said. Perhaps this was the point all along. Perhaps if she could somehow redeem herself, she could also redeem her father's memory. There was still time.

Something jabbed her in the back.

"Good evening, Captain Ann."

"Jenkins?" Ann exclaimed, and twisted to see the barrel of a flintlock pistol just inches from her left eye. Other men were surrounding them now, though in the darkness Ann couldn't identify any but the one holding her at gunpoint.

"Aye. Seems us sorry souls washed up together in the same spot after all."

Ann heard Charlie squeak from behind her and turned to see Ortega hauling the girl to her feet. Patch grabbed Violet. Ann had never liked the shifty way he stared at Violet, and she bristled. After glaring at Patch pointedly, she turned back to Jenkins. "Where's Barclay?" she demanded. Ann couldn't imagine Barclay handing command over to someone like Jenkins without a fight, and she wondered if Jenkins had killed him.

"Probably still down on the beach, playing with his broken ship." Jenkins spat into the sand. "I ain't here on no rescue mission, woman. You got something I want."

Ann met his gaze coolly, in spite of the gun blocking half her vision. "And what's that?" she asked, though she could venture a fairly good guess. It probably hadn't taken Carter long to figure out where they'd landed.

"Hand over the map."

"You mean that one?" Ann pointed at the fire, where the bottom corner of the map, marked with Black Dog's distinctive, jagged signature, was just disappearing into the flames. She crossed her arms smugly. "I'm afraid you're a little too late."

A string of gasps and curses followed her statement as the pirates realized what she'd done. Somewhere mingled in the exclamations she heard a distinct *"Mon dieu!"* and knew that Lamont, the only other French speaker on the crew, must be among them.

"You *burned* it?"

At Violet's astounded inquiry Ann turned back around. Patch was holding Violet with one arm, his gun pressed beneath her chin, but Violet seemed far more concerned at the loss of the map than the imminent danger to her life. She gaped at Ann in disbelief.

Patch, too, was staring at her open-mouthed. "What the bloody hell did you do that for?" he choked out incredulously.

Ann shrugged. "Call it a shift in priorities."

"I call it madness, more like!" someone shouted from the darkness.

On the other side of the fire, Charlie thrashed in Ortega's arms. "Let me go, let me go!" She bit down on the Spaniard's wrist and beat him wildly in the shins with her heels until he lost his grip. Grunting, Ortega pointed his pistol at the girl, and Violet screamed.

Suddenly looking panicked, Charlie scooped up a fistful of sand and flung it into Ortega's face. He reeled backward, scrubbing at his eyes. The girl turned to Ann uncertainly, as if she didn't know what to do next.

She was too far away for Ann to get to her before the shot did. There was only one other choice. "Run, kid!" Ann barked as Ortega took aim again, and she heard a few of the other men cock their weapons. Charlie hesitated, and Ann roared, "Run! Now!"

That seemed to jolt the child into action. She took off barefoot toward the trees behind them. Ortega fired in a puff of smoke and Violet screamed again, but Charlie was still running. She disappeared into the thick undergrowth as a few more shots went off. The jungle was probably just as dangerous for the girl as the pirates were, and Ann didn't feel particularly relieved. She hoped Charlie would have the good sense to stay close to the beach where she wouldn't get lost. And she fervently hoped the kid didn't run into whatever mysterious creature was lurking in the trees.

"Never mind the brat. We got no use for her," Jenkins commanded, waving his gun at Ann to get her attention. "You're a bloody fuckwit, burning that map. But I ain't giving up, savvy?"

"That's fine by me," Ann snapped. "Wander the island all you like. Perhaps you'll get lucky and stumble over the gold. Of course, then you'll also have to remember how to get out of the maze again."

"Maze?" Jenkins repeated.

"That's right." Ann pointed off to the north, where a cone-shaped hill of black stone appeared to rise right out of the jungle trees. "Lava tunnels, formed hundreds of years ago. Infinite tangled passages with death at the end of every wrong turn. You're standing on a sleeping volcano, boys. And the gold you're after…well, Black Dog hid it in the safest spot on the island." She smirked. "Enjoy your treasure hunting, Master Jenkins."

Jenkins gave a howl of frustration, and the pistol shook in his hand. "I'll see you die first!"

"Sir," Patch spoke up as Jenkins's finger tightened on the trigger, "it seems to me the captain has spent a great many years studying that map."

"So?" Jenkins snapped.

"Well, sir, if a person spends that much time staring at the same piece of paper day in and day out, I'd say they ought to have a good part of it impressed onto their brains, so to speak. And my money says Branded Ann can still lead us to the gold."

Jenkins's eyes narrowed thoughtfully, but Ann scoffed. "Impossible. The route's far too complicated—"

"Perhaps you simply lack proper motivation," Patch interrupted. Ann heard Violet yelp with surprise, and she spun around to see his hand inside the collar of Violet's shirt, groping at her breast.

In half a second Ann was seeing red. "Take your hands off her." She lunged forward.

Patch cocked the flintlock that he was holding beneath Violet's chin, and it made a distinct click. "Another step and I'll blow her pretty little head off," he warned, though the defiant words spilled out a little too quickly and with a slight squeak.

Ann stopped dead in her tracks. Rage seared through every muscle of her body as she glowered at him. Patch might be afraid of her, but right now that only made him more dangerous to Violet. So without moving, she continued to give him her most murderous glare, willing him to read in her face the promise of what she would to do to him if he dared go any further. The look seemed to work. Patch licked his lips nervously and slowly removed his hand from Violet's shirt.

Jenkins moved to Patch's side and eyed Violet appreciatively, keeping his own gun trained on Ann. "Well, now, Patch, I'd say you have the right idea." He didn't touch Violet himself, but he looked up and met Ann's eyes with a grin. "If you don't want to help us out, maybe we'll all just help ourselves to your precious Cockney whore."

Ann found herself gazing desperately at Violet, and the situation struck her as fittingly ironic as she recalled how Watts had looked when Violet was first dragged from the hold of his merchant ship. She felt new sympathy for the man; who could ever have thought that one day the same woman would be her own greatest weakness? And just as she had on the first day they met, Violet appeared entirely unruffled by the threat. She seemed far too busy scanning the jungle undergrowth anxiously, and Ann knew she was looking for signs of Charlie.

Digging her nails into her palms, Ann grated out, "Any one of you touches her again and I'll strangle you with your own entrails."

"Say you'll take us to the gold," Jenkins replied, "and you have my word no man will lay hand on your little doxy."

Quickly Ann took a quick count of the men. Seven or eight of them, and it was safe to assume they were all armed. If Patch or any of the others decided to follow through with the threat, she wouldn't be able to stop them without getting herself killed. As a corpse she'd have a rather hard time protecting anyone.

"Very well. I'll do it." Ann wasn't even sure she *could*, but she wasn't about to say so. At least this might buy more time to come up with a better plan.

The grin that spread across Jenkins's face revealed several missing teeth.

❖

"She's been out there for so long," Violet whispered.

"Try not to worry, pet," Ann replied, also whispering. She turned over her shoulder so Violet could hear her a little more clearly. The pirates had tied them, back to back, on opposite sides of the lovers' monument. "The kid's smart, and tougher than she looks. I'm sure she'll be all right."

"Can you really find the way to the treasure from here? The path took so many turns, I don't know how you could possibly remember them all."

"I don't. But I'm hoping I can remember enough to keep them busy until I can figure out another way to get you out of this."

"I still don't understand why you burned the map."

Ann didn't answer. She didn't want to have to explain how ashamed she was of all the things that single piece of paper had compelled her to do. Instead, she watched the men, who were seated at the campfire a short distance down the beach. They were happily gorging on the boar meat. Patch jerked his head in Violet's direction and made an obscene gesture, and the others laughed. When he caught Ann scowling at him, he paled a little and quickly looked away.

Violet sighed. "I don't think you should help them. It's not as if my virtue's worthy of protection." She gave a bitter laugh. "I gave that up long ago."

"I won't let you get hurt, not again." Unpleasant memories rose to the surface of her thoughts—Violet's despondent expression when Watts's throat had been slit, the wretched bruises on her face and thighs at the bordello in Tortuga. *You dumped me on this God-forsaken island to be raped half to death...* What had happened to Violet had been her fault, and Ann ground her teeth. "Not ever again."

"Captain—"

"The one good thing about being a prisoner," Ann interrupted firmly to curb further argument, "is that one of those jackanapes will have to keep watch all night. I'm going to get some sleep." She leaned back and closed her eyes. "I suggest you do the same."

From the other side of the rock she heard Violet muttering with annoyance, and couldn't help a little grin even as she pretended not to notice. The slab of volcanic rock beneath her was hard and uncomfortable, to say nothing of the hunk of stone they were tied to. As

Ann was drifting uneasily into sleep, an eerie, inhuman howl resounded from somewhere deep in the jungle. She found herself thinking of Charlie. The girl was clever and resourceful, but she was still very small, and right now she was out there alone with countless unknown predators lurking in the dark. Ann was exceedingly uncomfortable with the thought. *Be careful out there, kid.*

❖

Barclay was awakened by an ungodly shrieking coming from the water's edge, and he threw back the blanket and rubbed his eyes irritably. "What in hell—" The other members of the crew were also yanked from their sleep by the noise, sitting up to stretch and stare at the source of the sound.

Up the beach, Mason was wrestling with an object scarcely half his size, which he proceeded to lift over one shoulder and carry, still squirming and screaming, toward them. He plopped his burden down in the sand in front of Barclay.

"Found her watching us from the trees, Captain."

Barclay recognized the stowaway they'd sent off the ship with Ann and Violet. The girl was covered in dirt and scratches from head to toe. "What're you doing here?" he asked, genuinely surprised. Nervously he eyed the line of trees behind them. "Where's Captain Ann?"

"The others got her and Missus Watts all tied up on the other side of the jungle," the girl replied, her words coming out in such a squeaky rush that Barclay could barely make sense of them. "Branded Ann burned the map and they're making her take them to the gold without it, and I got away but I can't save her by myself so you got to come quick and stop them."

"Slow down, now," Barclay commanded, rubbing his temples. "You say Jenkins's group has captured the captain?"

At the child's frantic nod, O'Hare snorted. "The lassie lies. You knows the Lady Captain would never be bested by the likes of Jenkins."

"I ain't lying!" Charlie screeched in such a high pitch that it actually hurt Barclay's ears. "He said he'd hurt the missus if she didn't help him!"

"And just how did you get away?" Maclairen asked suspiciously, "and manage to get all the way to the other side of the jungle by yourself? 'Tain't likely, says I."

"I'm betting it's a trap, Captain!"

"Nah, Fletcher, the kid's telling the truth," Turtle said. "Just look at her feet! All tore up like she's been walking on splinters all night."

The men gathered around, bending over to inspect Charlie's feet. Mason even picked the girl up out of the sand so they could get a better look. Turtle was right; the soles of her feet were thickly caked in sand and blood, and dark bruises spread all the way up her ankles. It was a wonder the girl was standing at all, Barclay marveled.

It could be a trap, certainly, but he doubted Ann would have sent the kid to do her dirty work when it would have been easier and far less complicated to simply attack while the crew was sleeping.

But even if Charlie's story was true, it wasn't really their concern anymore. Why not let Jenkins and Ann fight it out amongst themselves?

Charlie was wriggling again in Mason's arms and demanding to be let go at the top of her lungs. Barclay winced and plugged one ear. "God's balls, Mason, put the girl down." He turned to O'Hare. "Get something to clean up her feet." When O'Hare picked up a nearby bucket, heading for the ocean, Barclay shook his head and called him back. "Not salt water, Master O'Hare, unless you want the kid's screaming to deafen us all. Find something else. Now," he focused his attention on Charlie, "did you say Jenkins is making Ann lead him to Black Dog's gold?"

"You heard me," Charlie snapped impatiently. "She's going to take them through the mountain, over there." She pointed north.

Barclay followed her finger. The northern end of the island was hardly a mountain, but it did rise, dark and craggy, above their current elevation. "The treasure's there?"

"I don't know." Charlie shrugged impatiently. "I ain't never been there."

Barclay rolled his eyes with exasperation, but his mind was working fast. There was only one possible reason why Ann would agree to help Jenkins: Violet. Either Violet had asked her to, or Jenkins had threatened Violet's life if she didn't cooperate. Given Jenkins's animosity toward Violet, Barclay was willing to bet on the latter.

It was only a matter of time before the rest of the men threw off his authority, and it was unlikely he'd even survive the return voyage home at this rate. He needed Ann. They all needed her. But he'd led the crew against her to begin with, which was just another type of death sentence. Unless…

"Captain, sir…" Carter approached. "There's something I ought to tell you."

"Can it wait?"

"I think I've waited too long already, sir." Carter shifted from one foot to the other. "It's about me apprentice. Patch."

"What about him?" Barclay asked, only half paying attention, still absorbed in his train of thought. If Ann was being held against her will, then this might prove to be a life-saving opportunity. Ann never forgot a debt. If he helped her get away, saved Violet's life, maybe Ann wouldn't kill him after all.

"Sir, Patch ain't…well, he ain't who everybody thinks he is."

Barclay snorted. "He's not a useless, foppish popinjay?"

This seemed to give Carter pause, and then he guffawed. "Well, that he is, Captain, but it's more than that. He ain't no sailor, and," the smile disappeared from his face, "he ain't exactly my apprentice, neither. He's…well, sir, he's a bloody pup of the Royal Navy."

Now *that* got Barclay's attention, and he turned to face the navigator with deadly seriousness. "Master Carter, I suggest you start talking fast."

❖

The sharp reports of gunfire jolted Violet out of her already uncomfortable sleep. Her head ached from a night spent dozing upright with a volcanic rock formation for a pillow, but the screams and snarling from the jungle quickly brought her to her senses. She watched as the pirates took off for the trees in search of the source of the sound. A few moments later, Patch came running back onto the beach, doubled over and with a strange greenish tint to his complexion.

"What is it, man?" demanded Dipper nervously. Assigned to prisoner watch, he was the only one who hadn't gone tearing off into the jungle.

Without answering, Patch turned and vomited into the undergrowth with disgusting noises that made Violet feel like she might be ill herself. Wiping his mouth, he turned to Dipper.

"Porter and Roberts. We found them out there. Or at least, we found what's left of them." He went into another spasm of heaving.

Dipper went visibly ashen. "What's left of them?" he echoed tremulously.

"Something killed them."

"Ripped them apart, you mean," said Edwards, who came stumbling out of the trees after Patch. "Like they was made a' paper! They go off to take a piss and next thing I hear, they're shooting and hollering. We get there and they're already in as many pieces as a busted parish window. It's that creature, says I, what killed poor Scrappy. It's after us now!"

"Scrappy's dead?" Ann questioned from the other side of the monument.

"Aye. Some jungle devil ripped his throat out," Dipper answered.

Violet gasped. "Oh, that's awful." While she wasn't terribly concerned with the deaths of Porter or Roberts, both of whom had been vulgar bullies, she'd liked Scrappy. He always knew how to make her laugh, even in her darkest moods. Last night Ann had said there was something dangerous in the jungle, and now it had killed three fully grown men. *Oh Father, please,* please *look after Charlie.*

Jenkins emerged from the trees then, looking just as shaken as the others. He didn't say a word about the dead men, just moved to untie the ropes that bound Ann and Violet to the monument. Keeping his pistol pressed uncomfortably to Violet's throat, he grated, "Time to go, Captain."

❖

Barclay leveled his cutlass at Carter's neck. "You scurvy coward, I ought to cut you down where you stand. You're telling me you brought a naval officer on board our ship so he could steal our gold and turn us all in for villains?"

Carter winced, but he didn't budge. "I didn't have no choice, Captain. Me wife and babe—"

"If you're so concerned about them, why tell me all of this now?" Barclay growled, and pressed his blade just a little harder against the skin of Carter's throat.

"Because, Captain," the navigator's expression was sad, "I don't think that Newbury fellow—Patch—is going to let them live either way. The only way I see out of this is if we somehow make it back to Port Royal in the next six weeks. And even then, I'd need help to escape the place with me family so's none of Newbury's mates can find us. That takes more money than I got, sir."

Barclay chewed the inside of his cheek thoughtfully. "And you're hoping I'll order us to chase down Black Dog's treasure after all?" Out of the corner of his eye he could see the other crew members perking up at this.

The more he thought about it, the more it seemed this really could be the most advantageous course of action. If he could rescue Violet from Jenkins's hands, and simultaneously bring down a malicious intruder in their midst, he might be able to gain Ann's favor again; the men would have their gold, and the responsibility of leading them would be lifted from his shoulders.

While he was still pondering it over, gunshots again rang out faintly from the northwest, four of them, in sharp succession. "Well, I suppose that tells us which way to go, don't it?"

"We're going to go save them?" Charlie exclaimed happily. Her injured feet were immersed in a bucket of coconut milk, and O'Hare tsked as she nearly toppled over trying to stand up.

Barclay lifted an eyebrow. "The men and I will be going after them. You," he said pointedly, "will be staying right here."

"Will not."

"Oh yes, you will." The last thing he wanted was to have the kid on his hands while they were trudging through the jungle. He turned to the pirate standing nearest to him. "Harris, take the girl back to the *Ice Queen*. Tell Kent and the others to lock her in the brig if she makes trouble."

The man scratched his grizzled chin and nodded, then moved toward Charlie.

"Oh, and Harris," Barclay added as an afterthought, and Harris turned back around, "you'd best be telling them that like as not, Captain Ann may just be coming back on board. They'd do well to be mindful of her claim on the girl, lest they get a belly full a' steel on her return." He watched Harris's face closely to be sure he'd understood the warning. The kid was an annoyance, but most of the trouble she caused wasn't truly her fault. Barclay didn't want a repeat of the crew's previous brawl, and the last thing they needed was to set Ann off by laying hands on her property.

"Aye," Harris grunted, and took hold of Charlie's arm, ignoring her shrieking protests as he hauled her down the beach to one of the rowboats.

Barclay turned back to the men, who appeared rather excited at the prospect of pursuing the treasure after all. "All right, boys, it looks like you're getting your wish. But just to be clear, we ain't just going after the gold. That little one-eyed bastard's tried to cheat us all, and far as I'm concerned, that makes him a far greater monster than anything that might be hiding in these trees." A murmur of agreement followed that statement. "So see to your arms, my hearties, and prepare yourselves. We leave within the hour."

Barclay turned and began rolling up his own blanket as a sign that the others should get to work. While they could probably track Jenkins's group through the jungle, Barclay had no idea what to expect once they reached the black hill that covered the northern end of the island. All he knew was that if they were to catch up, they didn't have a moment to lose.

❖

If Violet thought it was difficult traveling through the jungle undergrowth before, it was twice as bad now that she had a hand gripping her shoulder and a gun pressed into her neck. Every time she tripped over a stone or low vine, she was certain her captor's finger would slip and the pistol would go off. But by now, danger was nothing new. It seemed her life had been in constant jeopardy since the day the pirates had taken her prisoner, and it was becoming far more tiresome than frightening. Violet was beginning to understand Ann's cavalier attitude toward death; where Violet had always had her faith and even her apathy to give her courage, she could now add a strange sort of boredom, or perhaps curiosity, to the mix. It almost felt like a game, to see how things would end this time.

The deaths of two of their comrades did not make for a good start to the day, and the remaining six men—Jenkins, Patch, Ortega, Lamont, Edwards and Dipper—were tense and jumpy. Jenkins dragged Violet along behind Ann, who was steadily leading them northward through the trees. Violet's stomach was rumbling already, only about a half hour into the trek, but she didn't dare ask for food. It was all she could do to keep up with Jenkins and try to avoid falling every time something caught at her feet.

At last they broke out of the trees and found themselves facing a steep wall of black volcanic rock. Ann paused, looking both directions before leading them east along its base. They only had to go a few hundred meters before they saw it: a huge opening in the rock, rounded at the top and pitch black just a few short meters in. To Violet it rather had the appearance of a giant, gaping mouth, just waiting to swallow them up, and she didn't find the impression a welcoming one.

"This is it, then?" Jenkins demanded.

"This is where we go in," Ann replied without looking back. She was focused intently on the inky blackness as if she could somehow pierce it by sheer force of will. Violet could only imagine what Ann had to be thinking. Somewhere, inside this mountain, was the gold that had cost Ann's father his life, that had placed the scar on Ann's face, that had cost Violet her husband. Violet was surprised to experience a thrill of anticipation, praying fervently that whatever lay beyond the cavern mouth might put Ann's demons to rest at last. Ann had been carrying them for far too long already.

Jenkins showed no such signs of sentiment as he reached out and snatched from Ortega's hands a torch he had found near the cave entrance. "Edwards, Dipper, Patch, get wood so's we can make more of these damned things. We're going to need more light. Lamont, use your flint to light this thing." As the men moved to obey, he turned back to survey the mouth of the tunnel. "Well, Captain, so far so good."

He still had one arm wrapped around Violet, pressing the barrel of his flintlock into her neck. With the other hand he waved the newly lit torch, and Violet winced as embers landed on her sleeve, scorching quickly through the fabric and burning her skin. She clenched her teeth but didn't allow herself to make a sound. Ann was shaking her head.

"I got us here, but this was the easy part. You don't know what it's like in there."

Violet did. Or at least, she remembered the impossibly tangled web of tunnels on the map, so many of them ending in that ominous little skull symbol.

"I don't know if I can remember the way," Ann said grimly. "If we get lost…"

Jenkins gave a short laugh and suddenly shoved the torch into Violet's hand, closing her fingers around it as more embers fell onto her wrist and sleeve. Violet gripped it in surprise as Jenkins's gun moved from her neck to her back, between her shoulder blades.

"Well, you'd just better think real hard, then. 'Cause your little strumpet's going to be leading the way. Anything bad happens, it happens to her first."

Ann opened her mouth to protest, but Violet shook her head and spoke softly. *"Though I speak, my pain is not assuaged, and though I forbear, what am I eased?"* It was the same verse she'd quoted long ago, upon their first meeting, and Ann's expression went from startled recognition to understanding as she grasped Violet's meaning. Arguing with Jenkins would be useless, and at this point would only give him more power over both of them. For a while Ann stared at her, amazement and admiration playing on her face, and Violet felt suddenly self-conscious, as if she was being paid a great compliment. She offered a shy smile but could not say anything else because Dipper and the others returned.

Jenkins held her wrist so the others could light their newly fashioned torches from hers, and then poked her forcefully with the end of his pistol. "In you go, then, me pretty," he ordered, and Violet had no choice but to step into the cool darkness of the tunnel. The blackness swallowed them up in seconds as the tunnel abruptly curved away from the opening.

Violet held the torch out as far ahead of her as she could, both to light the way and to prevent any more of the embers from burning her wrist and hand as they fell. Beneath their feet the tunnel floor was smooth and flat, where the lava flow had ebbed and cooled long ago. After only a few paces, they reached a division where the tunnel branched off in two different directions. One was a much larger opening than the other, and Violet paused uncertainly.

"Which way?" Jenkins asked, turning to Ann.

After a pause, she answered, "Left. The smaller one."

Violet nodded and started in that direction, but Jenkins seized her shoulder. "Not so fast." He pulled a knife from his belt. "Just in case anything happens in there," he eyed Ann pointedly, "we're going to mark our way back. Give me your hand, missy."

Violet wasn't quite sure what he had in mind, but before she could comply Ann had already thrust her own hand in front of Jenkins's nose. "I'll do it."

"Well, ain't that noble," he sneered. "All right, then, Captain, have it your way."

Violet gasped when, in one quick motion, he slashed Ann's palm with the blade. A thick crimson line opened along her skin, and Ann opened and closed her fist repeatedly until it was coated in blood. She moved to the tunnel wall and found a flat spot where she could press her palm against the stone, fingers pointing to the left. When she pulled away, Violet could see a distinct handprint glistening against the dark rock. She was stunned by what Ann was willing to sacrifice in order to protect her, even offering her own blood in place of Violet's. She couldn't think of words adequate to thank her for such selflessness.

Jenkins grunted. "Won't be easy to see when it dries, but it'll have to do." He nudged Violet with the gun. "Right then, on we go."

They continued down through the tunnels in this way. Every time they came to a junction, Ann would think carefully, pick a direction, and then mark the way with a bloody handprint. When the cut on her hand started to close, Jenkins would helpfully reopen it with another slash of his knife. After about the third or fourth repeat of this process Violet found herself cringing uncontrollably. By the time they reached the treasure—if they did in fact find it—it seemed doubtful Ann would have a drop of blood left in her body.

She found herself keenly aware of Ann's presence behind her; she could hear the tension in Ann's tone as she sent Violet down each new path. And as they moved slowly deeper and deeper into the maze of tunnels, Violet could not stop her thoughts from wandering back to their encounter the previous night.

As always, she'd sensed the hunger, that same wild desire that took over Ann's entire being whenever they shared a moment of intimacy. And as always, she'd sensed the terror that held it in check. Violet had come to understand that Ann believed there was only one personal, sacred ethic that separated her from absolute depravity; and she knew that somehow Ann had it in her head that if she let herself go, allowed Violet to satisfy that hunger, she would lose even that last remaining vestige of her humanity.

It didn't make any sense to Violet, because she knew there was so much more to Ann than that. She could see it in her face, hear it in her voice even now. Tenderness. Adoration. Worry. Perhaps even—

Violet gripped the torch tighter in her hand. Last night she'd been so frustrated by how swiftly and decisively Ann had pulled away. Trying to cover up her own embarrassment and yes, her disappointment, she'd wanted Ann to think she'd fallen asleep. Maybe it had only been a dream, or some fanciful imagining, but she could still remember it so vividly…the soft touch on her brow, the words so full of sincerity and longing. *God, Violet, I think I love you.*

Had she really heard it? And even if she had, why did the idea make her feel so fluttery and tight in the pit of her stomach? She couldn't even count the number of men who'd said those same words to her without effect. Her husband had said them every day, often nearly every minute they were together, and while she'd appreciated his ardor, it never made her feel anything more than a general warm affection in response. Yet those same words on Ann's tongue made her shiver, filled her with happiness and exhilaration. It wasn't even the triumph she'd have expected to feel. No, this was different: a blissful, hopeful sense of elation that had nothing whatsoever to do with her usual power games.

Lust was an entirely new experience for Violet. She'd never wanted anyone the way she wanted Ann. She'd even told Ann she'd give herself freely, and there weren't many she'd made that offer to. But Ann had turned her down, saying she wanted more than just Violet's body, and now Violet was starting to realize what Ann had meant. Even more perplexing, she felt like she might just be capable of giving it to her. But if she did, would Ann be able to overcome her fear enough to accept it?

They reached yet another divergence, where this time the tunnel split off into three different directions, and Violet stopped, waiting for Ann's instructions. When Ann remained quiet a little longer than usual, Violet turned to look at her expectantly. Ann's eyes were closed, her brows furrowed in an expression that was almost akin to pain.

"Captain?" Violet asked quietly, and Ann's frown deepened.

"I need a minute."

Behind them the pirates shuffled their feet impatiently. "Hurry it up," Jenkins commanded impatiently.

Ann opened one eye to squint at him. "Do you want to get through these tunnels alive, or not?"

"*Ridicule!*" Lamont muttered from behind them, and brushed past Violet, torch in hand. "We waste time. It is not that difficult. I show you, see?" Without waiting for reply he marched down the nearest tunnel, the one to their right.

"*Non, Lamont!*" Ann called out, but he had already disappeared into the darkness. She turned to Jenkins. "I remember now, it's the one in the middle. He went the wrong way."

Even as the words left her lips, a cacophony broke out to their right; shouting, snarling, and a gunshot. The pirates pulled their weapons as something came lurching out of the right-hand passage.

"Hold your fire!" Jenkins yelled as Lamont collapsed on the floor of the tunnel, screaming frantically in French.

Dipper and Edwards ran over to him, holding out their torches, and the firelight glinted darkly across a steadily growing pool of blood beneath their shipmate's body.

Violet's torch fell limply from her hand. "God in Heaven," she gasped, and turned away from the man's mangled face. Ann was right behind her, and Violet grasped the front of her shirt, buried her face against Ann's shoulder and screwed her eyes shut, trying to get the image out of her mind. She felt Ann's arms surround her, and found the steady thudding of her heartbeat immensely comforting.

"*Chien noir! Chien noir! Chien—*" A gurgling sound interrupted Lamont's panicked cries, and he coughed.

"Damn your eyes, man, speak bloody English!" Jenkins snapped, but it was too late. Violet heard a deep, shuddering breath, and then all was silent.

"He's dead," Edwards said solemnly.

Jenkins cursed, and picked up the torch Violet had dropped. Keeping his pistol trained on her, Jenkins still managed to deliver a kick to the dead man's corpse. "What was all that gibberish about, then?"

"*Chien noir,*" Ann said hollowly, and everyone turned to her. Violet looked up, her face so close that she could see the tiny beads of sweat along Ann's cheekbones. "*Chien noir.* It means 'black dog.'"

Gently she released Violet and stepped back. The sudden loss of Ann's body warmth made Violet feel strangely lonely.

Jenkins kicked the body again. "Damn fool couldn't even tell us nothing useful."

"You think the critter, whatever it is, followed us in here?" Dipper asked.

"It is more likely that this is the Devil's nest," Ortega responded grimly, and the rest of them cringed. The very thought made Violet wish fervently that she could step back into the safety of Ann's embrace. She wondered if Ann would hold her again, if she asked her to.

"Maybe…" Edwards began uncertainly, "the gold really is cursed, after all."

"Nonsense. You don't really believe that rubbish, do you?" Patch scoffed.

It was evident from the looks on the others' faces that they were certainly open to the possibility. But evidently Jenkins would not even allow the prospect of an encounter with malevolent spirits to hinder his determination. He shoved the torch at Violet. "I'm going to find this treasure," he proclaimed stubbornly, "and ain't no jungle critter, ghost, or dead man's curse going to get in my way. So, woman," he waved his flintlock at Violet and indicated the middle tunnel, "start moving."

Violet met Ann's gaze questioningly, and Ann nodded. With a deep breath, Violet took the torch from Jenkins once again and lifted it over her head. From behind her she heard Ann's hiss as Jenkins reopened the wound in her palm, and the wet slap as yet another handprint was left on the tunnel wall. Without looking back, Violet stepped into the waiting darkness of the next passage.

Chapter Seventeen

Mingled apprehension and relief swept over Ann as they stepped into an immense cavern, and she recognized it immediately. Jenkins sent the others around the perimeter in order to get a better look. In the flickering torchlight, they could see that the chamber was circular, and easily large enough to fit the entire *Ice Queen* inside. Five tunnels branched off in all directions, nearly perfectly spaced like the arms of a starfish. Ann remembered this spot on the map well because it had been so distinctive, and this meant they were still on the right path.

So far, so good. She had yet to come up with a plan for their escape; though there were only five men remaining, Jenkins was careful to keep his gun on Violet at all times, and unless she could distract him, he'd kill Violet before she could get her away. Ann had considered deliberately taking the men down the wrong path, but the problem was, the map hadn't been specific about the dangers that awaited at the ends of each wrong turn; the skulls warned of death, but that wasn't much information to go on.

Still, she thought wryly, recalling Lamont's dying cries, *there's always the chance that if we stay in here long enough, this place will kill the rest of them off all on its own.*

"So?' Jenkins said impatiently, and Ann realized he was waiting for her to give the next set of directions.

"That way." Ann pointed toward the opening directly across from them.

Jenkins shoved Violet toward it. "Let's not just stand 'round gaping, then, boys."

The pirates reassembled behind Violet, jostling one another as she led them into a narrow tunnel. She moved slowly, holding the light out as far ahead of her as she could and seeming to test each step she took before putting her weight down. While outwardly Violet's expression showed no trace of fear or even concern, her movements were cautious and even timid, and Ann was certain that she had to be frightened.

This passage was much tighter than the others they'd passed through, and noticeably hotter. Ann felt her shirt sticking clammily to her ribs, and sweat stung her eyes. Her leg, where the boar had gored her the day before, was throbbing painfully with every step, and she was glad for Violet's slow pace.

The others, however, were not so patient. "Come on, come on," Edwards finally burst out, and he reached around Jenkins to give Violet an impatient shove in the back. She gave a surprised exclamation and stumbled, which caused both Jenkins and Edwards to trip into her unexpectedly.

And with that, Violet disappeared from sight. Ann couldn't believe how fast it happened; one moment Violet was standing there and the next, she wasn't. Neither was Edwards. But Jenkins managed to recover his balance just in time, waving his arms frantically to keep from going over the edge of the cliff that had suddenly materialized beneath their feet.

"Violet!" Ann bellowed, and shoved Jenkins aside, collapsing to her knees on the rocky ledge.

Violet called up frantically from below. "Help! Please help us!"

"Someone bring a light!" Ann commanded, and a torch appeared over her shoulder. She snatched it away and held it out over the cliff.

She saw Violet's hands first, wrapped white-knuckled around a small projection of stone just an arm's length beneath where Ann was kneeling. "Oh God."

Violet was clinging desperately to the rock, and as Ann lowered the light to get a better look she realized that Edwards was hanging on to one of Violet's legs. Or rather, she corrected herself as she heard fabric tearing, he was hanging on to the leg of her trousers.

"Whatever you do, Violet, don't let go." Ann threw herself flat against the ledge. "Ortega, Patch, Dipper, hold my ankles." There was a pause, and she twisted around to see the men looking uncertainly at Jenkins for authorization. "If she dies, you die, savvy?"

They quickly knelt and braced Ann's feet.

"That's better," she grunted, shifting forward until most of her torso was hanging over the edge. "Now when I give the word, pull." Ann bent down toward Violet and extended her arms.

"Okay, pet, carefully now. One hand at a time, I want you to move fast and grab my arms, right here." Ann tapped her forearm. "First the right, then the left. Ready?"

"You're crazy!" Edwards shouted from below them, and then he squawked as Violet's trouser leg tore a little further and he found himself flailing for a better grip.

Violet looked up at her, and for the first time Ann saw true fear reflected in her face. A chill clenched her chest as Violet's fingers slipped just a little against the stone, and she heard Violet gasp. Ann stretched her arms even farther downward. "You can do it, love. I won't let you fall."

At last Violet gave a nod. She took a deep breath and snapped one hand toward Ann's arm. Ann closed her fingers firmly around Violet's wrist just as Violet lost her remaining grip on the rock. For one heart-stopping second both Violet and Edwards dropped and dangled, swinging, from Ann's grasp. The sudden force nearly wrenched Ann's arm from its socket, but she held on. She felt the men behind her tighten their hold on her ankles as she was pulled over the edge. Then Violet brought her other hand up, and Ann seized that one, too, ignoring the stinging cut on her palm.

"Pull, boys!"

The pirates yanked her back, and her injured leg smarted sharply with the force. Violet didn't weigh much, but Edwards was a big man, and his considerable bulk proved too much for Violet's tattered trousers. With a sickening rip the fabric tore completely. Edwards fell, screaming, and the darkness swallowed him whole.

Every one of them froze in shock. Ann listened, but there was no thud, no splash, nothing but silence that stretched on far longer than it should have taken for Edwards to reach the bottom. If there was indeed a bottom at all... She took a deep breath and hauled Violet up onto the ledge beside her. Immediately she took Violet's face in her hands. She could feel her own pulse in the back of her throat, as though her heart had jumped right up her chest and into her mouth.

"Are you all right?"

Violet was breathing hard, but she nodded and then abruptly threw her arms around Ann's neck. "Thank you."

Ann's muscles quivered with the aftereffects of the adrenaline rush. She clutched Violet tightly to her with one arm. Now that the immediate danger had passed, her body could finally allow itself to experience the full terror of what had almost happened, and she couldn't seem to stop shaking. That had been far too close.

But Jenkins wasted no time in pressing his gun to Violet's back yet again. "You best pay more attention, if you don't want the sweet Sister to die next time. On your feet."

Violet was snatched from her arms, and it was all Ann could do to keep from protesting aloud. She vehemently wished to claw Jenkins's eyes out with her own fingers, or at the very least to shove him off the cliff and finally be done with the man once and for all. But he'd just end up taking Violet along with him, and Ann had only barely managed to keep from losing her. She stood up, slowly and with far more dignity than she felt, and clenched her teeth to contain her temper. Stiffly she followed Jenkins and the others back into the huge cavern with its five exits.

Jenkins led them directly to the middle of the room. "Dipper, give the wench your light, she's lost hers." Dipper complied, and Jenkins sent Violet around the periphery of the chamber, looking for the handprint that would indicate which tunnel they'd originally emerged from.

"Found it," Violet finally announced, and waved the torch from where she stood.

Jenkins, who had followed Violet's every move with the barrel of his gun, now turned to Ann. "Pick better this time."

Ann walked slowly over to where Violet stood and turned to face the main cavern. She stared at the four other tunnel openings. "Damn him, I don't remember," she muttered softly.

"Well, we already know that way," Violet pointed to the passage directly across from them, "isn't right, so it has to be one of the other three."

"I know, but I don't *remember*," Ann repeated in frustration, and balled her fists.

"It's all right, Captain. Just take your time…"

"It's not all right," she snapped, and when Violet's brows rose in surprise she rubbed her forehead. "You could have died! If I'm wrong again…"

"It doesn't matter."

"What the hell do you mean, it doesn't matter?"

Violet laid her hand on Ann's arm, and Ann noticed a smear of her own blood on the shirt cuff where she'd gripped Violet's wrist with her bloodied palm. *"But He knoweth the way that I take: when He hath tried me, I shall come forth as gold."* Violet's eyes twinkled in the torchlight. "Or in this case, God willing, you shall come forth *with* gold, and lots of it."

"Violet, you and everyone else seem to think I'm some kind of invincible hero. But I make mistakes, and they're going to get you killed."

Violet squeezed her arm gently. "This isn't about heroism, it's about destiny. You've tried to walk away from this over and over again. You gave up your ship, even burned your father's map…yet still, somehow, here we are." She swept the torch toward the cavern. "Even if you're wrong again, it doesn't matter. You're meant to be here, Captain, I'm certain of it, and I know you're going to find what you're looking for."

But no amount of gold could ever be worth what you *are to me.* Ann had just enough self-control left to prevent those words from actually spilling out, but she couldn't keep the emotion from her question. "And what about you?"

Violet smiled, just enough for the hint of a dimple to form at one corner of her mouth. "Maybe I'm meant to be here, too. I can't think of any other reason why the merciless Branded Ann hasn't slit my throat a hundred times over for all the trouble I've caused her. Such a wonder is far too Providential to be mere luck."

As usual, Violet's gentle humor proved extraordinarily calming. "Maybe you're the one with the remarkable powers. A few bats of those bloody amazing eyes," Ann fluttered her own lashes for dramatic effect, "and blast it all, I can't seem to keep my wits about me." A pretty tinge of pink swept Violet's complexion as she laughed.

"Quit the chitchat over there," Jenkins demanded testily. "Figure out where we're going next, or so help me I'm putting a bullet in the holy harlot's brain."

Ann bristled, but Violet merely handed her the torch. "Hold this."

When Ann took it, Violet stepped behind her and covered Ann's eyes with her hands. "Now," she said over Ann's shoulder, "I want you to concentrate. Imagine you're back in your cabin on the ship. You're in one of those dark brooding moods of yours, and you've been staring at that map for hours."

Concentrating on anything was going to be a challenge with that delicious, teasing voice in her ear, but Ann did her best to focus. "All right, I'll try."

Picturing the map was easy, with its familiar yellowed paper and blotchy pear-shaped sketch of the island. She could even envision the soft glow of the lamplight flickering over its creased surface. Ann tried to remember what the chamber where they were standing had looked like on the diagram: a distinctive large space with five branches surrounding it like the spokes of a ship's wheel. The red path they were to follow had entered the chamber through one of the upper branches, and exited... She wrinkled her brow. The exit was the second to the right of the entrance. Second to the right, not second to the left. She'd gotten her directions switched.

Ann raised a finger and pointed blindly. "It's that way."

"You're sure?" Violet asked as she lowered her hands.

"I thought it didn't matter?"

Violet grinned back and shrugged. "I trust you." Reaching out, she took the torch from Ann's hand. "Let's go."

❖

"Hotter than Hell in here," Turtle complained behind Barclay as they wound through yet another dark passageway. So far, they'd managed to trail Jenkins and the captive women without much difficulty thanks to the still-damp, bloody handprints marking each new junction. Barclay was thankful for that, as the tunnels were a complete maze and without the markers they would have been lost immediately.

He led at a quick pace because the prints were hard to see against the smooth dark rock of the lava tunnels once they'd dried. The farther they went, though, the fresher the marks appeared, and so he knew they had to be catching up. More light would have been helpful, and Barclay wished they'd thought to bring a lamp or two from the ship, especially after two of his men had accidentally gone down the wrong corridor and unwittingly carried their lit torches into a pocket of flammable volcanic gas. The result had not been pleasant. After that incident, the dubious privilege of carrying the remaining torches had to be decided by lot, and none of the winners were terribly pleased with their newfound responsibility.

"It's a volcano, kid, what do you expect?" Fletcher replied irritably. As one of the reluctant torch-bearers, he was in a foul temper.

"I don't, I didn't think it'd be so...alive, still." Turtle paused uncomfortably. "You don't think it might blow while we're down here, do you?"

"Might," Carter said in an unhelpfully flippant tone. He, too, was carrying one of the torches and seemed far less concerned about it than the others. In fact, the more dangerous their situation became, the more cheerful he appeared, and even Barclay was beginning to find his high spirits somewhat aggravating.

"That's why we're in a hurry," Barclay called over his shoulder as he stepped out of the tunnel and into a dark, open space. "Fletcher, Willy-boy, Andrews, Carter, get your sorry arses up here with those lights, will you?"

The four men came forward with the group's torches and spread out to take a look at where they'd ended up. They kept going until it became clear that they were in an enormous chamber of some sort, with a ceiling so high above them that Barclay couldn't even see it and openings to new tunnels seemingly on every side. "Okay, my hearties, take a look at those holes in the wall 'n tell me which of you sees the next waymarker."

Fletcher gave a shout to their left. "Found it, Captain!"

Barclay had started toward him when Andrews also called out from the tunnel entrance just to the right of Fletcher's. "I got one over here, too!"

Barclay paused, confused. "Well, that can't be right." He marched to Fletcher's side and took the torch from his hand, holding it carefully to the wall where the crewman had indicated. The print was faint, just a dry brownish smear against the rock, and he scratched at it with the tip of a fingernail. A rust colored substance flaked onto his fingers, and after eyeing it carefully, he gingerly sniffed it and then touched it with his tongue. "Blood, for sure," he said firmly, striding over to where Andrews was standing. "You've got to be mistaken—"

But the print Andrews was pointing at was still slightly wet, glistening darkly against the stone. Barclay broke off in midsentence and scratched the back of his neck in puzzlement. "Well, I'll be buggered."

"What now, Captain?" Turtle asked.

Barclay scowled. "Shut up and let me think."

❖

"You dumb bitch, this is a bloody dead end!" Jenkins shouted. Violet flinched as the end of his gun poked her rather painfully in the ribs. "You're wrong again."

"I'm not wrong," Ann said firmly, and went to the rock wall, running her uninjured hand along the stone. "I know we're in the right place. There should be another opening right here."

"But there ain't," Dipper said impatiently.

Ann's fingers found a hanging root, and Violet watched as it pulled away from the rock in a long, uniform line. It wasn't a root at all, she realized as she watched Ann give it an experimental tug. It was a rope. She followed it upward and pointed. "She's right, there is another tunnel. Look!"

The end of the cord disappeared about ten meters above their heads, into a small passageway. Ann yanked at one sleeve of her shirt until it tore off, then wrapped the fabric around the cut on her hand. She looped the rope around her waist and under one thigh, and bounced her weight against it a couple of times.

"What do you think you're doing?" Jenkins demanded.

Ann fixed him with a cool stare. "Unless one of you ape-wits would like to be the first to test out the ancient and probably half-rotted rope, I'm going up."

Jenkins pursed his lips and then squeezed Violet's arm and positioned the barrel of his pistol just beneath her throat. "Just you remember, I got your little missus down here. You try anything funny-like…"

"And you'll blow her head off. I heard you the first few hundred times."

Violet swallowed, which was difficult with the gun against her windpipe. "Be careful," she managed to say. Ann was strong, but her leg and hand were injured, and a fall from that height could easily break her neck. The cocky wink Ann gave in response made her heart skip. Apparently, while Ann distressed herself to the point of anguish over Violet's safety, her own bothered her very little.

Ann started climbing, and Violet followed her every move anxiously. How Ann managed to find all those hand- and toeholds in the slick black rock was a mystery, and yet she ascended steadily, taking up the slack in the rope as she went. The lean muscles of Ann's arms bunched and flexed as she moved, her slender dirt-shadowed fingers gripped each new spot with unwavering confidence, and those long, powerful legs propelled her up. It was a magnificent thing to watch, and Violet was startled by the shimmering excitement that blossomed suddenly in her belly, pooling hotly between her thighs.

By the time Ann reached the top and lifted herself into the passageway opening, Violet felt like her knees might just give way. She heard a scuffle and then Ann's pleased exclamation, and a ladder of knotted rope and wooden planks dropped down. Ann's familiar cloud of wild hair appeared over their heads.

"Seems someone decided to make it easy for the rest of you," she quipped.

Entirely forgetting about Jenkins, Violet tried to take a step forward. He yanked her back with a laugh. "Oh no you don't, not yet." He gestured at Patch. "Take that torch up there."

Patch eyed the ladder doubtfully, but under Jenkins's glare he didn't seem inclined to argue. He started climbing awkwardly, hooking his elbows behind the wooden rungs and transferring the torch gingerly from hand to hand as he went, careful not to scorch the ladder's ropes in the process. Jenkins tapped his foot impatiently as he waited; it took Patch nearly twice as long as it had taken Ann to reach the top. Eventually he made it, though, handing the torch up to Ann in order to clamber into the passageway next to her.

"Good," Jenkins grunted. "Now get your weapon out." Patch pulled his flintlock from his sash and pointed it at Ann, and Jenkins sighed. "No, you numbskull, you think she's scared of your bullets? The girl, man. Keep it on the girl when I send her up so's they don't take off together. And get that torch back so's she don't sting you with it when you're not looking." He shoved Violet toward the ladder. "Now it's your turn."

Just as Violet took hold of the first rung, a terrible snarl echoed through the chamber. Violet looked around, but Jenkins shouted nervously, "Go, woman, go!"

She started up awkwardly, the ladder shaking and swaying as she went. When she was about halfway up, another thundering growl resounded around them, and she twisted to see a huge black shadow burst from the cavern entrance and launch itself at Ortega. She felt something warm spray her face, and lifted a hand to her cheek. When she drew her fingers away they were coated in blood. She shrieked.

"Violet, climb!" Ann ordered from above her, and Violet pulled herself up the remaining rungs with a vigor that impressed even herself. Ann lifted her into the safety of the upper tunnel as gunfire boomed out beneath them.

Violet turned to see Ortega's torch sputtering on the rocky floor, illuminating the dark puddle surrounding his inanimate body. Dipper's torch, too, was on the ground, and Violet could hear him howling, with fear or pain she couldn't tell. She could only just make out the immense silhouette of the creature, whatever it was, as it delivered a mighty blow that silenced Dipper in mid-cry.

Jenkins raised an arm and shot, but he missed. There was no time to reload, and he yanked the cutlass from his belt, clenched the blade between his teeth, and started climbing the ladder. The beast roared again and surged forward, and Jenkins yelled. Both torches below had gone out, so Violet couldn't tell what had happened, but she heard the metallic clank as the cutlass fell from Jenkins's mouth. In the light of Patch's remaining torch, Jenkins's face appeared as he neared the top, sweat shining on the tattoos swirling his forehead and cheeks. He was gasping in obvious pain, and straining with his arms on the wooden rungs as if he'd lost the use of one—or maybe both—of his legs. Still, he was climbing.

Then, to Violet's shock, Patch pushed her out of the way and lowered his torch to the ladder. The ropes lit quickly and burned right through, and Violet heard a bloodcurdling scream as Jenkins fell back down into the cavern. Another roar vibrated the rock around them, and then all was silent.

❖

"Both ways can't be right, Captain," Andrews pointed out as they all stood scratching their heads over the second mark.

"Well of course they can't both be right," Barclay responded curtly. "They must've made a wrong turn, then come back and gone a new way. I'm guessing," he jabbed at the moist print with his finger, "this is the right one, since it's freshest."

"You sure?" Turtle asked nervously, coming up behind him. "It could be awful bad, Captain Barclay, if we're wrong…"

Several loud gunshots suddenly cracked through the air, emanating from the tunnel in question and reverberating so thunderously in the giant chamber that bits of rock tumbled down from the unseen ceiling. Barclay lifted an eyebrow.

"I'm damn sure now." Without bothering to hand the torch back to Maclairen, he took off down the tunnel, toward the noise, with the rest of the men close on his heels.

❖

Violet stared at Patch in bewilderment. "You killed Jenkins!"

"Don't tell me you're complaining." His own gun was now pointed steadily at her face, and there was a mad gleam in his eye.

"Well, no, but—"

Patch thrust the torch into Ann's hands, tore the eyepatch from his face and stuffed it into his belt. "At last. That is so much better."

The skin of his upper cheek and brow was red and swollen, but in the flickering torchlight Violet could see that the left eye was just as clear and sharp as the right. Now she was even more confused. "Why were you wearing that thing if you didn't need it?"

"I can't tell you how often I've asked myself the same question, sweetness. Now," he turned to Ann with a dangerous smile, "I hope you'll think twice before getting any wise ideas. There may only be one of me now, but I'm not like Jenkins." Violet cringed as Patch leaned close and ran his tongue slowly, almost sensuously, up her cheek, licking off the blood that was spattered there. Ann made a growling noise deep in her throat, and Patch drew back with an even wider grin. "I won't just shoot your pretty pigeon, you understand. 'Twould be a waste of a fine commodity. So if you please, ma'am," he jerked the barrel of his gun toward the waiting tunnel, "we have a treasure to find."

❖

Newbury rather liked the feel of Violet's body pressed against him, his gun jammed against her rib cage, and he held her a little tighter than was necessary to prolong the sensation. Finally, everything was falling into place. The others were gone, and there would be no one to challenge his claim to the treasure. Once they'd found it, he'd kill the pirate woman and perhaps even enjoy her luscious little consort a bit before returning to the other men on the beach to report his great discovery. Together they'd load up the *Ice Queen* and sail back to Port Royal, where he could turn them in; he'd just have to make certain the Navy never found out about the gold so they couldn't confiscate it for themselves.

Or perhaps... Newbury hadn't considered the possibility before, but he felt like he might be developing a knack for the piracy trade after all. What if there was a way to depose Barclay as captain? *Just think of it!* He, Malcolm Newbury, who in one fell swoop had discovered Black Dog's lost treasure and vanquished the notorious Branded Ann, as captain of the *Ice Queen* and most feared scourge of the Spanish Main. Perhaps he could create a much more impressive nickname this time, too—Malcolm the Marauder. Bloody Newbury. Captain Dread...

He was so lost in his own daydreams that he nearly tripped over Ann when she stopped walking. "Fool woman, watch where you're—"

He was stunned into silence as Ann touched the tip of her torch to the ground. Or rather, she dipped the torch in a small trench by her feet, and a streak of flames shot along the edge of the chamber they'd just entered. An unmistakable glitter in the center of the cavern caught his eye. And as the fire surged around the full circumference of the room, Newbury felt his heart stop.

"We found it," Violet gasped as the flames came full circle, lighting the entire chamber bright as day.

Piled in the center was a collection of wooden crates, boxes, chests, even canvas sacks, that were stacked six and seven high and packed tightly from one end of the enormous cavern to the other. Several had split open, and coins spilled across the black volcanic stone like a glorious golden river. Scattered here and there Newbury could see the twinkle of gemstones; heavy, gaudy, priceless jewelry that had probably been lifted from the necks and fingers of Black Dog's most affluent victims. To the right sat a huge golden statue of a fat-bellied man with emerald eyes that looked like it came from some exotic Eastern land and was far too big to fit into a crate. At the base of one broken trunk, plates, cups, and jewel-encrusted tableware had tumbled out to join the stream of gold and silver coins dripping from a sack that had burst its seams.

Newbury couldn't even begin to estimate the total value of this literal mountain of gold. He'd never seen so much wealth before in his life, had never even imagined that such riches existed. There was far too much here to even be brought back in one shipload. To collect it all, they'd have to make quite a few trips.

Forgetting about Violet, forgetting about Ann, Newbury ran forward and slammed the butt of his pistol into a crate, watching with delight as Spanish pieces of eight rained from the broken wood to fill his hands and collect on the ground with warm, clattering sounds.

He laughed maniacally, clutching the slivered coins in his fists, the flintlock pistol dangling awkwardly from one finger. "I'm rich!"

"*We're* rich," a deep voice corrected, and Ann was startled to see Barclay enter the chamber behind them, followed by a good dozen men. He was carrying a musket, which he leveled evenly at Patch. "And you're going to die, you squirrely son of a poxy whore."

Patch stuffed his handfuls of gold into his trouser pockets and scooped more out of the crate. "Come, Captain Barclay, you know I didn't mean it that way. There's plenty here for all of us!"

"Where's your eyepatch, your officership?" Carter called from over Barclay's shoulder. Patch stiffened and clapped a hand over his eye, apparently only just remembering that he wasn't wearing it. Slowly he turned to face the pirates, for the first time looking truly alarmed.

Ann looked over at Carter. "What's going on?"

"Turns out Patch here," Barclay jerked the end of his musket, "ain't no navigating apprentice at all. He's an officer of His Majesty's Royal Navy, here to steal our gold and see us all hang as villains. Ain't that right?"

Patch went pale and licked his lips. "I don't know what that fool Carter's been telling you, sir, but let me assure you—"

"Shut up." Barclay took a step forward. "You know what we do to liars like you?"

Before he could elaborate, Patch lunged forward. Ann didn't comprehend his intention until it was too late; he threw an arm around Violet's throat and dragged her backward with his gun pressed to her temple. "I won't let any of you take this away from me!" he screeched.

"Let her go!" Ann snarled, but as Barclay lifted his gun she pushed the barrel down. "Don't, you'll hit her!" He snorted and started to raise the weapon again, but this time Ann took hold of it firmly and waited until he met her gaze. "Please, Barclay," she pleaded.

He hesitated.

A ferocious roar reverberated through the chamber, and suddenly a huge black shape burst through the wall of flames on the opposite side of the cavern.

In the light, Ann could finally see the creature clearly. "*Chien noir*," she gasped.

An enormous wild dog crouched, growling, just a short distance from where Patch and Violet stood. It was a dog, unquestionably, though Ann had never seen one like this before; nearly the height of a man, with thick black fur that bristled around its head and down the center of its back like a mane, and tall, narrow ears that were flattened dangerously against its head. Its sharply pointed muzzle was drawn back to reveal gruesome teeth, some of which had to be as long and thick as Ann's fingers.

The dog leapt, and Patch let go of Violet to shoot at it with a trembling hand. At that range, he couldn't possibly have missed, and yet the animal seemed entirely unaffected. Ann dove toward Violet and knocked her out of the way as the massive dog tackled Patch. The man's scream was cut short when his throat was crushed between two enormous jaws.

Its head came up, muzzle stained crimson, and Barclay shouted, "Shoot, boys, shoot the damn thing!" He fired his own musket, which was followed by a dozen more, until the air by the entrance hung thick and blue with gunsmoke.

Several of the crates behind the creature burst as the bullets struck them, yet the dog itself didn't appear wounded in the slightest. It was as if the dark animal was made of shadows, and the shots had somehow passed right through their intended target. With another growl it surveyed the chamber until it fixed its eyes on another victim.

"No!"

Ann threw herself between the dog and Violet as it charged. She punched the animal in the face with her left fist, which was still wrapped in her shirt sleeve. She felt the dog's teeth slam against her knuckles. It weighed far more than she did, so rather than try to knock it backward she twisted so it would skid off to their right. With a furious yelp the dog slid into a stack of crates, which tumbled down on top of it and shattered, but even that didn't seem to slow it down for more than a few seconds.

The animal rose from under the heavy pile of gold, slipping on the loose coins as it regained its footing. Ann reached behind her, her hand closing around the narrow stem of a vase made of silver. It was heavy and solid, though hardly a sufficient weapon against an adversary of this size. But it would have to do. Ann drew her arm back and braced herself for another charge.

To her surprise, however, the dog didn't attack again. It snorted and shook its head almost as if it were confused. It seemed to be staring at her—or rather, it seemed to be staring at the vase in her hand. Slowly, it approached her in a near crouch, keeping its ears back and its head down in a strangely submissive position.

When it got close enough, it whined, long and sharp. Ann lowered her arm uncertainly. She felt rather silly as she offered the vase to the creature...surely an animal such as this would have no use for such a thing? But it wasn't the vase the dog was interested in. It seized the thing between its teeth and flung it aside, returning its gaze to Ann's hand. Ann looked down at her own fist, trying to understand what the dog found so fascinating.

It's the ring, she realized suddenly. The black dog's attention was entirely captivated by the small golden skull grinning from the middle finger of her left hand. With another whine, the creature sniffed her hand and licked at the ring with a warm, gummy tongue. And then, to Ann's utter astonishment, it looked up at her. For a long moment she found herself gazing directly into a pair of glittering black eyes.

The dog backed away several steps. Without another sound it turned and walked to the edge of the chamber, leaping once again through the barrier of fire and disappearing into the darkness behind it.

Ann held up her fist in disbelief, looking from Patch's dead body, to Violet's bewildered expression, to Barclay and the other pirates who were all gaping at her as if she had just performed some kind of divine miracle. That was just about the strangest thing she'd ever seen in her life. A murderous beast that had killed every last one of Jenkins's men, and God knew how many others besides, suddenly tamed by the mere sight of her father's ring?

Yet as it had looked at her, Ann could have sworn she'd seen recognition in the animal's gaze. *As if it knew me, somehow. But that's impossible.*

Violet's hands suddenly encased her fist, and Violet, too, stared down at the golden skull on Ann's finger. "It seems Black Dog's ghost really does guard the treasure after all, doesn't it?"

"I thought you didn't believe in ghosts," Ann pointed out with a raised eyebrow.

Violet winked up at her. "Someone once told me that doesn't matter...so long as *they* believe in *you.*" She turned to Barclay and the others, who were still standing slack-jawed by the entrance. "Looks like Black Dog's decided to give Captain Ann his fortune, boys," she called out, and Ann noted the careful emphasis Violet placed on her rank. "Don't just stand there. You know it's going to take ages to haul it back to the ship."

At her words the men surged forward, burying their hands in the piles of gold with delighted cheers. Ann nearly laughed aloud when Turtle lifted a ruby and diamond necklace and wound it gaily around the hook affixed to his arm, waving it in the air with an incongruously dainty flourish. At Violet's giggle, she turned to see Andrews draping a rope of huge pearls around Mason's gigantic ebony shoulders. But when Violet looked up at her again, her beautiful eyes outshone every other jewel in the room.

"You did it, Captain," Violet said excitedly, and rose on tiptoe to plant a triumphant kiss on Ann's cheek. "After all this time, you've finally found your treasure."

All Ann could think was that Violet had no idea just how true those words were.

Chapter Eighteen

Violet lifted the cutlass over her head and brought it down in an arc, slicing neatly at the spot where Mason's arm had been just seconds before. He blocked the attack with his own blade and she stumbled back, just a little, from the sheer force of his body mass.

"Good," the giant grunted, "but remember most folks you'd be swinging at are bigger than you. Got to use their weight against them or they'll mow you down. Again."

Obediently she lifted her sword and tried the swing again, just a little faster, and as he met the strike with his cutlass she deliberately sidestepped. This time it was Mason who stumbled forward, thrown off balance. Violet moved in behind him and pointed the tip of her blade at his throat.

Mason laughed. "Fast learner, you are."

"Can I try?" Charlie asked eagerly, brandishing a sword of her own. It wasn't so much a sword as it was a large knife, but it was the heaviest weapon the girl could handle at her size. Her bare feet kicked up showers of sand as she attempted an attack.

From her vantage point on a small hill overlooking the beach, Ann watched Turtle take the knife from Charlie and hold it out, demonstrating the proper grip and a few quick thrusts upward, while Mason continued to spar with Violet. Ann could not seem to stop smiling.

"Captain?"

Ann turned as Barclay approached. "Report."

Barclay grinned. "Our lady's full near to bursting, Captain. I think we've loaded her up with as much gold as she'll carry, this time out. The crew's already talking about a return trip."

With a chuckle Ann resumed her observation of the beach. "We scarcely survived this one, and they want to come back?"

"You know the boys. No matter how much loot we bring back, it'll never be enough for some of them."

"That's because they'll have spent it all in a fortnight on booze and brothels," Ann replied with amusement.

"They've been asking," Barclay huffed slightly as he sat down beside her, "whether you might be inclined to lead us back, when the time comes."

"You were all so quick to be rid of me," Ann reminded him wryly, "and Violet and the kid, too, for that matter. And now look. Electing me captain again, teaching the two of them to handle themselves in a fight…"

Barclay also gazed down the beach at the lessons taking place near the water's edge. "Well, they've earned it. This past week they've pulled their weight as well as any other man, even the girl. And…well, the boys're pretty much ready to forgive you anything, seeing as how you're something of our savior, Captain. If it weren't for you that beast might have killed us all."

"Barclay," Ann looked over at him with a slight frown, "you don't really believe…"

"That the big critter what killed near half our crew is Black Dog's ghost, set to guard the treasure till you came back for it?" The quartermaster grinned.

Ann took a stick from the ground, scratching nonsensical designs into the sand by her feet. "I know that's what they're all saying."

"You know I don't put much stock in all them ghost stories and tall tales." Barclay rubbed his stubbled chin. "Though I'd be hard-pressed to come up with a better explanation for what happened. We haven't seen naught of the animal since he walked off that day in the caves. And in any case, I'm just glad to hand over the captain's hat again."

"Authority didn't sit well, eh?"

"I never wanted it to begin with, you know that."

"I know." Ann smiled at him. "You're a good quartermaster, Barclay, the best I've sailed with. You've always preferred sailing to leading, and that suits me just fine." She punched his shoulder gently. "So, sailor, when are we casting off this island?"

"I'd say another day or two. Thanks to Violet, who found that fresh spring on the other side of the jungle, we've just about finished stocking up our water supplies along with everything else."

"Will we get back to Port Royal in time?" A few months ago Ann would have had Carter hanged from the yardarm without a second thought, but now she found herself more sympathetic to his plight than she would have imagined.

Barclay knew what she was referring to; they'd discussed the matter of Carter's family several times in the past few days. He nodded. "Aye, I believe we will, though he'll need help smuggling that family of his out of port once we arrive."

"You two just make sure we get there in time. I'll take care of the rest."

Peals of laughter drifted up from the beach, and Ann turned to see Charlie whooping as she rode on Turtle's shoulders and brandished her miniature sword at Mason. Mason dodged out of the way easily, but Violet put out a hand as they went by and tickled the child in the ribs, making her shriek with delight. A strand of her dark hair had escaped its braid, and Violet tucked it behind her ear as Turtle turned for another pass.

"What about the girl?" Barclay asked as he watched them continue the game.

"I suppose when we get to Port Royal I'll have to track down her father."

Barclay elbowed her good-naturedly. "I meant the *other* girl. The one you ain't able to take your eyes from."

"Violet?" Ann was doing her best not to think about that. "I don't know what her plans are."

He sat back a little. "Don't tell me you're just going to let her walk off."

"Why shouldn't I?" Ann said defensively. "You said yourself she's earned it. She isn't my prisoner, Barclay, I set her free a long time ago."

"And I wasn't suggesting that you take it back, Captain. It's just that a blind man could see you've pretty much fallen arse over tit for the wench, and it ain't getting any better."

Ann stiffened. "All the more reason for her to get away," she replied glumly. "As far and as fast as she can."

"Now why would you say something like that?" Barclay sounded genuinely surprised. Ann couldn't reply, the weight in her chest had suddenly grown so heavy. After a moment he asked hesitantly, "Is it 'cause you ain't a man?"

That particular thought actually hadn't occurred to her. Ann could remember in excruciating detail every last tiny flirtation that had passed between them, every half-lidded glance, every coy smile. "That's not it." Lately Violet had been responding to her touch with unmistakable desire. In fact, that was part of the problem.

"Then what?"

How could she explain her deepest fears without sounding as if she'd gone mad? Ann struggled to find the words, and finally just managed to mumble, "She's not safe with me."

"Bugger that!" Barclay exclaimed incredulously. "There's no one on God's green earth the girl is safer with, not with you looking out for her like she's made of bloody glass."

"You don't understand." Ann rubbed her forehead with both hands and wished that such a simple action could somehow blot out the darkness in her mind. "I want too much from her. More than I can even name. The fact is, she'd be much better off if she'd never met me."

"You don't know that," he said. "For all you know she feels the same as you. I, for one, think it's high time you ask the lady what *she* wants."

"And just how am I supposed to do that?"

"You could try wooing her properly, for one." He rose to his feet, dusting the sand from his pants. "And don't you look at me crooked like that, you know what I'm talking about. I seen you charm your way into the heart of many a girl."

"This is different," Ann said despondently, but he only grinned.

"'Course it is. This time you actually got something to lose." He started down the hill.

"Why does it matter to you, anyway?" she called after him.

He turned around and lifted a shaggy brow. "Way I see it, we got at least five, maybe six more weeks before we get back to Port Royal. I'd rather not spend them with you sulking and stalking about the decks like you was the whole first half of this voyage." With a cheeky whistle he headed down toward the beach.

Ann mulled his words over as she returned her attention to Violet. The sky was starting to get dark, and Violet, in her dark boys' trousers, white cambric shirt, and neatly laced bodice, had resumed her fighting practice with Mason. She was barefoot, her hair braided at the base of her neck, and as Ann watched her circling Mason in the sand, carefully imitating the strikes and thrusts he demonstrated, her heart ached. Lately Violet appeared so at home among the crew. A part of Ann was elated to see her finally becoming more to the men than just a galley maid, more than just the captain's plaything. But she also felt guilty. With her remarkable survival skills, Violet was making the best of a bad situation, but it was a situation she would never have been in if Ann hadn't interrupted her life to begin with.

Woo her. Ann wasn't even sure where to start. She'd kidnapped Violet, mocked her, abandoned her, manipulated her, tortured her, lusted after her. Directly or indirectly, she'd widowed her, too. And everything she'd done to save Violet's life had only served to prolong the harm she'd caused later. Now, with her share of the treasure Violet could easily make a fresh start for herself anywhere in the world she wanted to go. So what could Ann possibly say? She had no right to ask to remain in Violet's life, not after everything she'd put her through.

Ann had never given much thought to what she would do with herself once she'd succeeded in her quest. Now, still a few years shy of thirty, she was suddenly staring at the end of that journey, and realizing she had no idea how she wanted to spend the rest of her life. The only thing she knew for sure was that she desperately wanted Violet to be a part of it. The thought of saying good-bye was misery.

Violet paused to wipe the sweat from her brow and looked up at Ann sitting on the hill above them. The brilliant, dimpling smile that Ann so loved spread across her features, and she waved. Ann lifted a hand in response, and watched Violet take up the sword again.

If I don't at least try, I'm going to regret it the rest of my life. Rising from her seat, she made her way down the hill and went in search of O'Hare.

"Why won't you tell me where we're going?" Violet puffed, batting away the undergrowth as she followed Ann through the thick trees.

"Because it's a surprise," Ann answered, sounding just as patient as she had the first hundred times Violet asked. Violet gave a small growl, but she wasn't really annoyed. A mischievous light had been in Ann's eye all day, and Violet was fairly certain that whatever Ann wanted to show her, it was something exciting.

"It's starting to get dark, you know," Violet pointed out breathlessly.

"We're almost there. Just a few more—here we are." Ann held some of the low-hanging foliage back so Violet could step through, and to her surprise, Violet found herself standing on the same slab of black volcanic rock that she remembered from their first day on the island. Directly in front of her stood the unlucky lovers' monument, their dark forms curving sensuously around one another. Curious, Violet moved toward it, wondering why Ann would have brought her back here again.

After she'd taken two or three steps from the trees, however, she stopped. Her mouth dropped open. Just a few meters down the beach, a fire pit had been built, almost exactly where their original campfire had been that first night. A quilt was spread neatly on the sand, and it was covered in gold dishes and bejeweled tableware that had to have come from Black Dog's hoard. A giant silver bowl of fruit rested in the middle, and a wine bottle, probably from Ann's private supply, stood next to it. O'Hare was busy stirring something in a big kettle that hung over the fire, and a delicious scent drifted to her nose on the breeze. The sun was setting on the horizon and the entire sky was awash in stunning hues of gold, pink, and orange that reflected, shimmering, across the ocean's surface.

She turned questioningly to Ann, only to find her grinning ear to ear as she handed her a bright pink hibiscus.

"Join me for dinner?"

Violet accepted the flower with a laugh. "What is all this?"

"It's our last night on the island. I thought we should do something special."

"But…" Violet turned to look at the dishes on the quilt. "It's only set for two."

"It's a proper Captain's dinner," O'Hare answered from his position at the fire. "But 'twould be a shame for her to dine alone." With a final stir to whatever was simmering over the fire pit, he wiped his hands on his apron and came up to them. "Everything's ship-shape,

Lady Captain," he said happily. "You lassies have a good evening, now." With a tip of his tri-cornered hat, he shuffled off into the trees.

Ann offered her elbow. "Shall we?"

Violet tucked the pink hibiscus behind her ear and took her arm. "You've been planning this all day, haven't you?"

"Something like that." Ann escorted her down to the quilt and indicated that she should sit. Violet lowered herself, cross-legged, to the sand. Ann removed her boots and socks, setting them aside, and Violet followed her example. She watched with interest as Ann picked up two heavy, solid gold bowls and carried them over to the kettle.

"It seems a great deal of trouble for just a meal," Violet commented, suddenly feeling rather self-conscious as she realized Ann would never have gone to such lengths merely for her own benefit. She found herself recalling the silver scrollwork box of hairpins Ann had given her when she had joined the crew. Every now and then, the pirate captain proved herself capable of some truly lovely gestures. "Did you...surely you didn't do all this just for me?"

Ann smiled faintly as she ladled something brown and steaming into each of the bowls. "I owe you a great deal, Violet. You've been through terrible things these past months, most of them at my hand. Yet you've continued to work alongside me all this time." She carried the bowls back and set them down, taking a seat next to Violet in the sand. "If it weren't for you, I would have given up searching for my father's lost gold."

"So is this a thank-you, or an apology?" Violet teased.

Laughing, Ann said, "Both." She picked up her spoon, and then set it down again and took a deep breath. "And it's more than that."

Violet eyed her quizzically. "Oh?"

"You're...I wanted you to know..." She faltered, and finally looked away. "I like having you around," she finished quietly.

Violet exhaled. "I like being here." She wasn't sure why her heart was suddenly beating so hard. The way Ann had been gazing at her, Violet had almost thought she was going to say something else. To distract herself, she picked up her own spoon and poked at the stuff in her bowl. "So what is this, exactly?"

"Salmagundi. O'Hare may not be much good in a fight anymore, but he still makes the best salmagundi you'll ever taste."

Violet tasted it and was pleasantly impressed. It had the texture of

MERRY SHANNON

a rich stew, with meat and fish and even a hint of pineapple. "You're right, it's wonderful."

Ann poured wine into heavy gold goblets with rubies inlaid around their rims. She held hers up. "To Black Dog, who has just made us all very, very rich."

Violet lifted hers as well. "And to Branded Ann, terror of the Spanish Main, who finally succeeded in reclaiming the gold he died for." She clinked her cup to Ann's and drank.

"So," Violet said as they resumed eating, "what are you going to do with all your newfound wealth?"

"I'm giving it to my family in Virginia."

"All of it?" Violet asked, surprised.

Ann shrugged. "I'm keeping the promise I made to my father. I don't really have need of it, anyway. So long as I have the *Ice Queen*, I have everything I could want."

"So it's back to your old ways, then, after this?"

"Heh. Not exactly. I'll never feel quite at home on land, I don't think, but I'm thinking perhaps I'll contract out to a shipping company. Transport goods and the like between Europe and the Americas, keep them safe from pirates." Ann winked.

"Sounds like fun," Violet said without thinking, then blushed when she realized that could easily sound like she was inviting herself along. "I'm sure you'll do a fine job of it," she added quickly. She'd already caused Ann so much trouble, and she was sure the last thing Ann wanted was a tagalong.

"What about you? What are you going to do with your share?" Ann put another spoonful of food in her mouth and watched Violet out of the corner of her eye.

She sighed. "You know, I really have no idea. Settle down somewhere, I suppose."

"I'd have thought you'd be more excited."

"So would I. But…" Violet gestured at the shoreline. "Out here, a person feels so alive, you know? I mean, when they're not busy trying to keep from becoming dead." Ann chuckled, and she smiled back. "I feel rather like I've been living in a storybook the past few months. It's hard to figure out how to go back to a normal sort of life."

Ann opened her mouth, then closed it again and nodded. "Makes sense," was all she said. Violet felt disappointed, almost childishly so, and she discovered that a part of her was hoping perhaps Ann would invite her to stay on board after all. It was an utterly impractical, not to mention selfish, thought. Ann must have noticed, too, because she was looking increasingly uncomfortable.

"I could go to the Colonies," Violet said optimistically, hoping to ease Ann's discomfort. "Or even stay in Port Royal for a time with Charlie." She was hoping for some sort of positive reaction, but the uneasy look never left the captain's face. In the deepening twilight, the firelight flickered warmly over the angled planes of her cheeks, and her eyes were shadowed.

Violet caught a note of melancholy as Ann replied, "I'll be glad to take you wherever you want to go."

Damn it, Ann, I want to go with you! Violet nearly burst out. She held her tongue only because she had no right to make any such request. Setting her empty bowl back on the quilt, Violet turned her gaze out to the water. The sun had drifted below the horizon now, and the moon was hanging high and full over their heads. No stars were visible yet, though, as the sky was still blue-gray near the horizon, deepening gradually to purple and then to black directly above them.

As much as Violet didn't want to leave this adventure behind just yet, there was more to it than that. Branded Ann…the notoriously wicked, impossibly infuriating, devilishly charming woman had made her life a living hell, and somehow at the same time made her feel more alive than she'd ever thought possible. She was such a fascinating mix of contradiction, cold and hard as ice, yet capable of searing passion, even tenderness. Thanks to her, Violet had enough money to start a new life, completely on her own, without need of either whorehouse or husband for survival. It was the greatest gift she'd ever been given.

But Violet found that, even after everything, all she really wanted was Ann herself. Maybe Ann's confession of love those many nights ago, on this very beach, really had all been just in her imagination. But what if it wasn't? What if Ann was just too shy, too ashamed, too afraid to say it again? Knowing Ann's damnable pride and penchant for brooding, it was quite likely that she'd allow Violet to walk away without ever bringing it up, and then spend God knew how long sulking moodily over it afterward. And Violet knew she wouldn't soon be able to forget her feelings for Ann, either, no matter how much time or distance was between them.

She pulled her braid over her shoulder and untied the end, slowly working out the plaits with her fingers. There was only one way she could think of to get Ann's guard down enough to find out the truth.

❖

Violet's attention appeared focused on the beach, where the waves were rolling slowly up onto the sand. Ann watched her pretty face in the glow of the fire as she absently unbraided her long, dark tresses, and she gradually steeled her nerve. She was captain of a pirate ship, for God's sake…she could do this.

Clearing her throat slightly, she began, "Violet, I—"

"Let's go swimming," Violet interrupted brightly.

"What?"

But Violet was already up and running barefoot for the water. She paused at the edge of the wet sand and turned, the moonlight shining in her unbound hair. "Come on!" she laughed, yanking the crisscrossed leather thongs from the front of her outer bodice and shrugging out of it. She dropped the stiff garment carelessly at her feet, then lifted the linen shirt over her head.

Ann gasped.

In all the nights they'd slept next to one another, even in the most intensely heated moments they'd shared, she had never seen Violet naked. Yet suddenly there she stood, pale and glorious in the light of the Caribbean moon like some ageless, mythic sea siren. The perfect globes of her breasts were crowned with large, exquisite nipples. Her rib cage tapered into a slender waist, which blossomed into full, luscious hips—a natural hourglass figure that most women had to corset the air out of their lungs to achieve. Ann's eyes hungrily traced the softly rounded belly as it curved between prominent hipbones and disappeared into a pair of low-slung boy's trousers, held on the hips with a drawstring. Now Violet was tugging on those ties as well.

Ann's ears started ringing.

In seconds Violet had wriggled out of her trousers. She stretched her hands out to Ann with a smile. "Are you coming or not?"

Ann could barely hear Violet's words, the blood was pounding so loudly in her ears, and she felt dazed, hot and cold at the same time, as though someone had just dumped a bucket of ice water over her head without warning. Yet somehow her body responded; she felt her legs moving, carrying her across the sand.

Violet turned and jogged into the water, and Ann watched the waves come up to cover her ankles, her slim calves, her thighs, and finally her buttocks as well. When the water was waist-high and the ends of her hair were just starting to get wet, she turned to face Ann again. "Ah, this feels marvelous," she called, and ducked under.

When she came up again, her back arched, the water streamed in glistening rivulets from her face and hair and skin, trickling down her throat and breasts. She smoothed her wet hair back with one hand. Ann stood, paralyzed, at the water's edge. She couldn't move, could barely remember to breathe. *Bloody hell.* Violet couldn't possibly know the effect she was having, but Ann felt like her entire body was wound tight as a watch spring. She couldn't remember ever wanting a woman more.

Violet moved toward her with a smile. "Well, come on, then, Captain. Let's get you out of those clothes."

Ann swallowed, hard, as Violet stepped onto the sand and reached for the ties of her shirt, untying it with one hand while using the other to tug the hem free from her belted trousers. She knew she ought to put a stop to this right now, to move Violet's hands away and make some excuse, but just as she was gathering her self-control, she felt Violet's fingers skimming her bare skin beneath the linen. It was all she could do to keep from moaning aloud.

"Arms up," Violet ordered, and Ann complied helplessly, as though her body had a will of its own. With torturous delicacy Violet lifted the shirt away, her palms sliding up Ann's sides and down her arms. Ann shook her head to get her wild hair out of her face as the shirt came off and joined Violet's pile of clothes nearby. Violet's fingers lingered on the pewter cross pendant that hung around Ann's neck.

"Matches your cheek," she said in an appreciative tone, returning the bit of metal to its resting place between her breasts. For the first time, Ann found herself glad to be wearing the brand that she'd always otherwise considered a hideous blemish. Violet's hands drifted to her belt then, undoing the buckle and smoothly pulling the strap of leather from around her hips. She felt the buttons of her trousers releasing, one at a time, and Violet knelt, drawing her pants down with the same light touch. Ann was shaking as she stepped out of them, and she knew that by now Violet had to have noticed, but Violet tossed the garment aside without comment and rose again.

"That's better." She took Ann's hand and led her into the water, and Ann followed, feeling like she might explode at any second, yet utterly unable to resist. At that point she would have willingly followed Violet to the very end of the earth if she asked her to. The cool water closed around her legs, a welcome relief from the sweltering heat that persisted here even after dark, and she waded in after Violet until Violet stopped and turned.

"There, you see? Isn't it lovely?" She cupped her hands under the water and splashed Ann's torso playfully.

Ann couldn't take it anymore. She caught Violet's wrists gently. In the moonlight, Violet's eyes looked more purple than she'd ever seen them. Her breath was coming hard, and she didn't trust herself to speak. It was happening again, that raging desire that commandeered her body whenever Violet got close, a primal instinct that was so frenzied, so uncontrollable that she was terrified of what she might do if she got swept up in it. She wanted Violet too much. Had always wanted her too much. And Ann knew she had to get away, now, before she—

Violet stepped forward, somehow getting one hand free and tangling it in Ann's hair. Her intent was suddenly perfectly clear, and Ann had only a brief, stunning instant to realize that this had been Violet's purpose all along—and then Violet was kissing her, bringing their bare skin together, the lush softness of her breasts crushing into Ann's. Her mouth was sweet, commanding, and this time Ann could not contain the groan that escaped as Violet's tongue brushed past her lips and melted softly against her own.

"Oh God."

"Touch me, Ann, please," Violet pleaded breathlessly against her lips, and Ann couldn't have denied her the request if she'd wanted to. Splaying one palm against Violet's lower back, Ann drew her closer, and with her other hand cupped Violet's breast and squeezed. The nipple was already erect and hard against her palm, and Violet's back arched as she pressed into Ann's hand even more forcefully. Ann's muscles quivered with the effort it took to keep her touch gentle. "I'm so afraid I'm going to hurt you, Violet."

Beneath the water, she felt Violet's hand stroke her hip, then her thigh, drawing it forward just a little. Then Violet's thighs enfolded her leg, the sudden heat of her sex contrasting sharply with the coolness of the water and setting Ann's blood on fire. Violet rolled her hips brazenly, rubbing herself against Ann until Ann could feel a slickness coating her skin that had nothing to do with the ocean they were standing in. "Does it feel like you're hurting me?" She brought her hand back up to Ann's face. "You aren't going to break me, you know."

Leaning forward, Violet licked a trail up the side of Ann's neck and closed her lips around one earlobe. She sucked gently before withdrawing just enough to whisper into Ann's ear, "I want you inside me."

The dam burst, flooding every inch of Ann's body with the craving she'd kept caged for so long. She pulled back, and Violet smiled just a little. "That's the first time I've ever said that to someone and meant it."

With a growl Ann kissed her again, deeper this time, thrusting her tongue into the inner recesses of her mouth. She let her fingers play with one hardened nipple, pinching and rolling the puckered flesh firmly between her fingertips. She'd wanted this for so long. Even if Violet never felt the same way she did, Ann could no longer deny herself the chance to touch her, to accept what she was offering. But this time she wasn't going to let Violet turn this into one of her power games.

"Is this what you want?" Ann asked hoarsely, driving her thigh up and kneading the breast beneath her hand.

"Yes," Violet gasped out, clenching her fist in Ann's hair as her hips bucked against Ann's thigh. Ann lowered her lips to Violet's breast, tracing the turgid nipple with just the tip of her tongue before drawing it fully into her mouth. She sucked hard before biting down on the small bud. Violet cried out, but it was not a sound of pain. "You feel so good. More." She took Ann's hand and insinuated it between her body and Ann's thigh.

Ann touched the hard, swollen prominence of Violet's sex for the first time, and Violet inhaled sharply, clutching at her shoulders, grinding insistently against her hand. Ann was dizzy, her vision swimming in a wash of red as Violet shuddered against her. But once again Violet had managed to usurp control of the situation.

"Come here," Ann commanded, sinking a little deeper into the water and lifting Violet up until her legs wrapped around Ann's waist. Ann positioned her fingers, and as Violet's weight came down, she entered her smoothly.

Violet gave a gasping cry of surprise, and her nails dug into Ann's bare shoulders. With lips slightly parted and her breath coming in short pants, Violet rocked against Ann's hand, driving herself harder and deeper onto Ann's fingers. Ann's body throbbed with arousal as she watched Violet's eyelids fluttering with pleasure, and she forgot all about keeping track of who was in charge of the situation. Violet surrounded her completely, and the sensation of being inside her, of their skin sliding against each other, the warmth and softness of those secret inner places, kept Ann from being able to concentrate on anything else. She matched Violet's pulses with her own, wanting Violet to feel the same intoxicating release she'd bewitched Ann with so long ago. As Violet's speed increased, Ann kept up with her, until their movement thrashed the water around them into foam. Violet's excitement was making her crazy, and Ann thought she might come herself without Violet ever even touching her.

Ann felt Violet's innermost muscles contracting, and Violet cried out hoarsely as she came down, hard, one last time. That sound had to be the most beautiful thing Ann had ever heard, and she clutched Violet tightly as her body went stiff and she raked her nails across Ann's back, leaving stinging trails in their wake. Ann stilled her hand, delighted by the way Violet continued to spasm around her fingers for several minutes. She closed her eyes and buried her face in Violet's neck, pressing little kisses all the way up to her jaw.

"I love you, Violet," she whispered. "I love you so much." Violet pulled back, her expression unreadable. She was quiet for so long that Ann grew nervous. Gently she withdrew her hand from Violet's body. "Look, I know bloody well I don't deserve you, and you're probably going to be much happier when I'm finally out of your life for good. I just…"

Violet stopped her with a finger against her lips, unwrapping her legs from Ann's waist and standing on her own again. Taking Ann's hand, she tugged her toward the beach and up to the fire pit, where she moved the wine bottle and glasses, then swept everything else carelessly off to the side. The sight of her naked, wet skin in the firelight just made the ache in Ann's abdomen that much worse. Violet sat down on the quilt and stretched an arm out to her, beckoning seductively.

"Violet, I...I can't."

"Can't what?" Violet asked, reaching out and taking her hand, pulling her forward.

Ann resisted, pulling away from Violet's grasp. "I thought I could do this, but it's too hard."

"Shut up and get your arse down here," Violet ordered petulantly, but there was a twinkle in her eye. Ann sighed, knowing she didn't have any other choice. It was either spend the night here with Violet, or find her clothes and traipse back through the jungle in the dark to rejoin the men. She was going to be in agony either way, she realized, because the heart of the matter was that while Violet might desire her, she didn't share Ann's feelings and probably never would. But maybe Ann could pretend, just for tonight, that it didn't matter.

Ann sat slowly, and as soon as she was settled Violet gave her a little push so she would lie down. Violet rolled on top of her, her soft weight pinning Ann to the quilt. Every inch of Ann's wet skin tingled lecherously. Violet bent and kissed her neck, nipping gently. "Do you want to know the truth?" she asked, her voice a low purr. Her kisses moved downward until the liquid heat of her mouth enclosed Ann's nipple, and Ann groaned.

"What truth?" she finally managed to ask.

Violet tugged the taut nub with her teeth before releasing it, her fingers already teasing the other into attention. "The truth is, I think you've spoiled me with all this freedom and fresh air. Now the thought of settling down someplace is just, frankly, rather dull in comparison." She slid a hand down Ann's belly, ever so slowly, and Ann felt her abdomen contracting eagerly. But she stopped, just short of the thick curls that covered the apex of Ann's legs, and instead rocked back on her heels, spreading Ann's thighs. While Ann was not particularly shy, the unabashed desire with which Violet was staring down at her almost made her feel like blushing.

"The truth is," Violet repeated as she trailed one hand lightly down Ann's inner thigh, "that if I could have anything in the world, I'd want to stay at your side." She again stopped just short of Ann's heated center, and drew a matching line with her fingertips down the other leg. "Even though I know it's not fair, because I've always caused you nothing but trouble, the truth is that wherever in the world you go, what I really want is to go with you."

Ann's legs were quivering, her nerves alight with excitement, but now her mind was playing tricks on her yet again, because surely Violet hadn't just said what she thought she'd heard. She gave a moan that came out halfway as a whimper.

And then Violet was touching her, lightly, right where Ann most needed her, gently stroking up one side of the aching flesh and down the other, pinching it gently with her fingertips. "The truth is that I don't know how you did it," she bent to plant a kiss on Ann's inner thigh, "but I've fallen in love with you, Branded Ann."

A sob escaped Ann's lips as suddenly Violet's tongue flicked teasingly against her pulsing sex, and her hips jerked as heat sizzled through her veins. Violet seemed to know exactly when she was going to reach climax, because just as the first surge broke she drew Ann fully into her mouth and at the same time sank two fingers deep inside.

Ann cried out, pleasure racking her body in waves so intense they were almost painful. Violet filled her so completely that she couldn't contain it, and she was shattering. Flying off in a million different directions, never to be whole again. At least, not without Violet to fill the empty places.

Violet, her body coated in sweat, drew up alongside her. "Are you all right?" she asked with concern, and Ann opened her eyes to see Violet's face hovering just inches from hers. A hot tear rolled down her temple, and Violet wiped it away with wonder. "Are you *crying*?" she asked incredulously, and Ann gave a half laugh.

"So it would seem," she grunted, and propped herself up on one elbow. "Violet, tell me that…tell me I really did hear you say that you love me."

Violet reached out and traced the scar on Ann's cheek tenderly. "I love you," she said firmly.

Ann inhaled, and the air felt so sweet, so light in her lungs. "Say it again."

Laughing, Violet leaned forward and punctuated each word with a kiss. "I. Love. You." She pulled back. "And I meant what I said, about going with you. I know it's not fair to ask—"

With a grin, Ann flipped her onto her back and straddled her hips.

"I've changed my mind," she said, sliding one hand up and closing it over Violet's breast. "I'm not letting you go after all. I'm afraid, Mistress Watts, that you're stuck with me. At least," she lowered her lips to Violet's throat, "for as long as you'll have me."

"How does forever sound to you?"

The happiness that flooded Ann's system was almost too much to bear. "I'd say that sounds just about perfect."

Violet's hands came up to rub her back, in long, sensual strokes. "So…can I have you right now?" she asked softly.

Ann waggled an eyebrow at her. "Ah, my lovely, you can have me all night long if that's your wish."

And with that, she took Violet's mouth with her own once again.

EPILOGUE

From the aft rail of the pirate ship, Ann gazed out at the slowly retreating shore of the island, her right arm resting securely at Violet's waist. She couldn't remember the last time she'd felt so happy. Never mind the hundreds of pounds of gold in the *Ice Queen*'s hold; never mind the promise that she'd finally fulfilled, or the fact that they'd managed to survive what was likely the most dangerous voyage any of them would ever undertake. She had just spent an entire night making love to the woman who had stolen her heart, and once they reached Port Royal, she wasn't going to have to leave her behind. That alone was enough to make her feel like she was on top of the world.

And she was already trying to figure out if they could sneak away from Barclay's watchful eye, as soon as the launch was complete. Violet's sexual appetite, when properly stimulated, was just as voracious as her own, and Ann couldn't stop thinking about those soft curves, that husky voice calling her name.

Violet seemed to be of a similar mind, and she was pressed as tightly to Ann's side as she could get without completely violating the rules of decency. "I want you so much right now," Ann murmured, enjoying the way Violet's eyelids grew suddenly heavy.

"Same here," Violet responded, and Ann couldn't resist letting her hand drift down to cup the well-formed buttocks. "Hey," Violet protested, looking up at her, "someone's going to see."

"It's all right, everyone already knows I'm an insufferable rake," Ann said flippantly as she squeezed. But her hand snapped away quickly and she flushed as Charlie piped up behind them.

"Hey, look at that!" she called out, pointing.

Ann squinted at the beach, where a familiar black shape stood just at the water's edge. The enormous wild dog had emerged from the jungle and stood in the sand watching them sail away.

"You think he wants to say good-bye, Branded Ann?" Charlie giggled as she started waving.

"I doubt it. It's just a dog, Charlie." But as the animal continued to stare at them from the shoreline, Ann looked down at her father's skull ring, still on her left middle finger.

And then, somewhat hesitantly, she also held up her hand in farewell.

About the Author

Merry Shannon has been writing stories for as long as she can remember. Fantasy, adventure and romance are her favorite themes, and most of her work incorporates all three! In addition to writing, Merry is a full-time social worker, and spends much of her free time with friends, sewing, dancing, and traveling. She currently lives in the Denver area with her girlfriend, Shasta, their two small dogs and three large cats. Her first novel, *Sword of the Guardian*, earned 2007 Golden Crown Literary Awards in both the Speculative Fiction and Debut Author categories. *Branded Ann* is her second book.

Books Available From Bold Strokes Books

Branded Ann by Merry Shannon. Pirate Branded Ann raids a merchant vessel to obtain a treasure map and gets more than she bargained for with the widow Violet. (978-1-60282-003-6)

American Goth by JD Glass. Trapped by an unsuspected inheritance and guided only by the guardian who holds the secret to her future, Samantha Cray fights to fulfill her destiny. (978-1-60282-002-9)

Learning Curve by Rachel Spangler. Ashton Clarke is perfectly content with her life until she meets the intriguing Professor Carrie Fletcher, who isn't looking for a relationship with anyone. (978-1-60282-001-2)

Place of Exile by Rose Beecham. Sheriff's detective Jude Devine struggles with ghosts of her past and an ex-lover who still haunts her dreams. (978-1-933110-98-1)

Fully Involved by Erin Dutton. A love that has smoldered for years ignites when two women and one little boy come together in the aftermath of tragedy. (978-1-933110-99-8)

Heart 2 Heart by Julie Cannon. Suffering from a devastating personal loss, Kyle Bain meets Lane Connor, and the chance for happiness suddenly seems possible. (978-1-60282-000-5)

Queens of Tristaine by Cate Culpepper. When a deadly plague stalks the Amazons of Tristaine, two warrior lovers must return to the place of their nightmares to find a cure. (978-1-933110-97-4)

The Crown of Valencia by Catherine Friend. Ex-lovers can really mess up your life...even, as Kate discovers, if they've traveled back to the eleventh century! (978-1-933110-96-7)

Mine by Georgia Beers. What happens when you've already given your heart and love finds you again? Courtney McAllister is about to find out. (978-1-933110-95-0)

House of Clouds by KI Thompson. A sweeping saga of an impassioned romance between a Northern spy and a Southern sympathizer, set amidst the upheaval of a nation under siege. (978-1-933110-94-3)

Winds of Fortune by Radclyffe. Provincetown local Deo Camara agrees to rehab Dr. Bonita Burgoyne's historic home, but she never said anything about mending her heart. (978-1-933110-93-6)

Focus of Desire by Kim Baldwin. Isabel Sterling is surprised when she wins a photography contest, but no more than photographer Natasha Kashnikova. Their promo tour becomes a ticket to romance. (978-1-933110-92-9)

Blind Leap by Diane and Jacob Anderson-Minshall. A Golden Gate Bridge suicide becomes suspect when a filmmaker's camera shows a different story. Yoshi Yakamota and the Blind Eye Detective Agency uncover evidence that could be worth killing for. (978-1-933110-91-2)

Wall of Silence, 2nd ed. by Gabrielle Goldsby. Life takes a dangerous turn when jaded police detective Foster Everett meets Riley Medeiros, a woman who isn't afraid to discover the truth no matter the cost. (978-1-933110-90-5)

Mistress of the Runes by Andrews & Austin. Passion ignites between two women with ties to ancient secrets, contemporary mysteries, and a shared quest for the meaning of life. (978-1-933110-89-9)

Sheridan's Fate by Gun Brooke. A dynamic, erotic romance between physiotherapist Lark Mitchell and businesswoman Sheridan Ward set in the scorching hot days and humid, steamy nights of San Antonio. (978-1-933110-88-2)

Vulture's Kiss by Justine Saracen. Archeologist Valerie Foret, heir to a terrifying task, returns in a powerful desert adventure set in Egypt and Jerusalem. (978-1-933110-87-5)

Rising Storm by JLee Meyer. The sequel to *First Instinct* takes our heroines on a dangerous journey instead of the honeymoon they'd planned. (978-1-933110-86-8)

Not Single Enough by Grace Lennox. A funny, sexy modern romance about two lonely women who bond over the unexpected and fall in love along the way. (978-1-933110-85-1)

Such a Pretty Face by Gabrielle Goldsby. A sexy, sometimes humorous, sometimes biting contemporary romance that gently exposes the damage to heart and soul when we fail to look beneath the surface for what truly matters. (978-1-933110-84-4)

Second Season by Ali Vali. A romance set in New Orleans amidst betrayal, Hurricane Katrina, and the new beginnings hardship and heartbreak sometimes make possible. (978-1-933110-83-7)

Hearts Aflame by Ronica Black. A poignant, erotic romance between a hard-driving businesswoman and a solitary vet. Packed with adventure and set in the harsh beauty of the Arizona countryside. (978-1-933110-82-0)

Red Light by JD Glass. Tori forges her path as an EMT in the New York City 911 system while discovering what matters most to herself and the woman she loves. (978-1-933110-81-3)

Honor Under Siege by Radclyffe. Secret Service agent Cameron Roberts struggles to protect her lover while searching for a traitor who just may be another woman with a claim on her heart. (978-1-933110-80-6)

Dark Valentine by Jennifer Fulton. Danger and desire fuel a high-stakes cat-and-mouse game when an attorney and an endangered witness team up to thwart a killer. (978-1-933110-79-0)

Sequestered Hearts by Erin Dutton. A popular artist suddenly goes into seclusion, a reluctant reporter wants to know why, and a heart locked away yearns to be set free. (978-1-933110-78-3)

Erotic Interludes 5: Road Games, ed. by Radclyffe and Stacia Seaman. Adventure, "sport," and sex on the road—hot stories of travel adventures and games of seduction. (978-1-933110-77-6)

The Spanish Pearl by Catherine Friend. On a trip to Spain, Kate Vincent is accidentally transported back in time—an epic saga spiced with humor, lust, and danger. (978-1-933110-76-9)

Lady Knight by L-J Baker. Loyalty and honor clash with love and ambition in a medieval world of magic when female knight Riannon meets Lady Eleanor. (978-1-933110-75-2)

Dark Dreamer by Jennifer Fulton. Best-selling horror author Rowe Devlin falls under the spell of psychic Phoebe Temple. A Dark Vista romance. (978-1-933110-74-5)

Come and Get Me by Julie Cannon. Elliott Foster isn't used to pursuing women, but alluring attorney Lauren Collier makes her change her mind. (978-1-933110-73-8)

Blind Curves by Diane and Jacob Anderson-Minshall. Private eye Yoshi Yakamota comes to the aid of her ex-lover Velvet Erickson in the first Blind Eye mystery. (978-1-933110-72-1)

Dynasty of Rogues by Jane Fletcher. It's hate at first sight for Ranger Riki Sadiq and her new patrol corporal, Tanya Coppelli—except for their undeniable attraction. (978-1-933110-71-4)

Running With the Wind by Nell Stark. Sailing instructor Corrie Marsten has signed off on love until she meets Quinn Davies—one woman she can't ignore. (978-1-933110-70-7)